# ASSIGNMENT TO

# NUREMBERG

# ASSIGNMENT TO

# NUREMBERG

# RAYMOND M. WEINSTEIN

**Jordan & Simon Publishers**
**White Plains, New York**

United States Copyright Office # 1-749236781

ISBN – 13: 978-1523993413
ISBN – 10: 1523993413   (paper)
ASIN – BO1DUTFOV2  (e-book)

Published in the United States

Jordan & Simon Publishers
c/o R.M. Weinstein
2 Old Mamaroneck Road
Apartment 4C
White Plains, NY, 10605
914-258-8094
e-mail: rayw@usca.edu

COVER DESIGN by Andria Mikkola

PHOTOGRAPH OF MERRELL BARRACKS
    by permission of Thomas Spahr

Dedicated to my two sons

**RODNEY J. WEINSTEIN**

and

**MARSHALL S. WEINSTEIN**

# TABLE OF CONTENTS

PAGE

# PROLOGUE: REMEMBRANCE OF LIFE PAST

*In January 1959 I left Fort Ord, California with orders in hand that simply read "Seventh Army, USAREUR," but I knew it meant I would be stationed somewhere in West Germany. I had been a soldier for just over eighteen months, since I graduated from high school, and the new assignment was to be my final tour of duty.*

*I was sent to Ord after completing the 33-week radar repair course at Fort Monmouth, New Jersey that I enlisted for. After only five months, the Army decided I was needed overseas. They granted me travel and leave time and told me to report to Fort Dix, New Jersey for processing no later than the thirtieth of the month. I was no stranger to Dix, my induction center and basic training camp, only seventy-four miles from my hometown. There I would learn the identity of my new Signal Corps outfit and the city and Staat in the Federal Republic I was to be dispatched to.*

*After the war U.S. troops remained on German soil to maintain law and order over a vanquished enemy and to counteract the new Soviet threat to the peace in Europe. For the next seventeen months, I would be part of this American occupation force, marching in the boot steps of the men that guaranteed the security and independence of the people we spilled so much of our blood to defeat not fourteen years earlier. I might have to bear arms in a town Allied armies and air forces pounded mercilessly and reduced to rubble and ash. I could be ordered to hurl my body in front of Germans who resented the American conquerors for crushing their redoubt-able Wehrmacht, for leaving a wearied people bereft of life's basic necessities.*

*Elvis A. Presley was already in Germany and I would join him and the quarter million other G.I.s shouldering M1 rifles in the defunct Fatherland. It was not comforting to think that the generous financial aid for reconstruction we Marshalled to a rogue nation may be out of mind or count for naught among the bitter and broken. There was a Cold War being fought in the Neue Deutschland I was headed to and the German was no longer the object of our fear and hatred. My C.O. back at Ord said I would be an ambassador of good will, sent to engage in chummy relations with our wartime opponent. There was a different enemy now and the once despised combatants were on our side.*

*At the port of Bremerhaven I would step into a Germany that was roundly different from that at war's end. The toppled people had rebuilt their economy and cities impressively, forged a thriving democratic political structure, and rearmed under a watchful American eye. Would I be stationed near Elvis and his tank unit? I wondered. Both of us might engage in war games or field maneuvers with a Bundeswehr that was the centerpiece of the NATO alliance's military strategy against the Eastern-bloc states. We could be shaking hands with Soldaten whose fathers or uncles had aimed rifles, tossed grenades, and lobbed mortar shells at our fathers or uncles. What could be said to men who a short while back may have bulged their Tiger Panzers through George Patton's Third Army lines, to women who may have lost a Mann or a child to a U.S. bomb?*

*I looked forward to serving in the postwar Germany I had read about. I welcomed the opportunities my impending tour presented, to travel throughout Europe, experience foreign lands and peoples firsthand, visit places seen only in the movies or imagined. Racing through this young man's mind too were piquant thoughts of fraternization with those Fräuleins he heard so much loose talk about in stateside barracks—the blond, blue-eyed, fair-skinned maidens eager to lay down for the American occupiers.*

*My transfer across the Atlantic was also greeted by passions of a more ominous nature. The peacetime soldier knew he was en route to a Germany that in recent memory had started a war of aggression and caused incalculable death and destruction in the world, had systematically exterminated six million Jews and untold numbers of Gypsies, Slavs, political dissidents, and mental defectives, a nation whose moral character was still in doubt. This was the same Germany the victorious Allies decided had to be punished for its crimes against humanity, whose former generals and Nazi Party members were tried in Nuremberg and then executed or imprisoned. I would be a sentinel in a land whose citizens were regarded with suspicion and contempt for claiming ignorance of and denying responsibility for the Third Reich's dastardly deeds. My next stop was a post-Nazi society whose culture had to be cleansed of swastikas and SS runes, tributes to Hitler and Himmler, Sieg Heils and Brown Shirts, Aryan doctrines and anti-Semitism.*

*The night before the deadline for reporting to Fort Dix for overseas duty, I was with my family in New York. I could not know then that the coming morn would inaugurate a challenging phase in my being, a bittersweet engagement with a foe-turned-friend that pierced cultural and sexual boundaries. I had no inkling the alien ground on which I was about to tread would seep so sweepingly and lastingly into my sensibilities both sacred and profane. What I did know was that the morrow was my nineteenth birthday, I was glad my enlistment was more than half over, I cared little for martial duties, and had decided on going to college after my discharge.*

*Today, tunneling back to that time, a former soldier's remembrance of bloom in a recreated Germany unlatched the portal to a seasoned young life sealed for more than fifty years.*

# PART I

# GERMANY BOUND

# CHAPTER 1: THE SEVENTH ARMY LIST

On December 27, 1958 my life as a soldier at Fort Ord changed on two fronts. On base in the morning I learned I would be going overseas within two weeks. Later in town I spent the entire evening with a girl for the first time, a WAC whom I had met at the EM club the month before.

It was a cold Saturday morning in central California, too cold to jump quickly out of my bunk. I was in Company D of the 41st Signal Battalion. I thought about my transfer to this post five months earlier. A number of my classmates at Monmouth, as well as those in classes a week or two or three after mine, likewise came to Ord and were assigned to the 41st. We had a radarman's squad of sorts, troopers with the same MOS who knew each other for much of the past year, who went together in small groups to chow, the movies, the snack bar, and the EM club.

Events of the previous evening were on my mind, notably the young female soldier I hardly knew who readily consented, after some mutual kissing and squeezing, to accompany me to a local hotel. We both were Army privates, the first class kind, with overnight passes to facilitate our private affair. Would she in fact show up at the bus station at five p.m. as we had arranged? I kept asking myself. I knew what was going through my mind, but what was going through *hers*? The light-skinned girl knew I was white. She knew, I was sure, I knew she was not.

It was the Christmas holiday and things were slow around the barracks and Orderly Room. Many of the troops, NCOs and EMs and even some officers, were off post at home since there were no scheduled company activities or were on leave with their families out of state. This was my second Christmas in the Army and I rather enjoyed the time off from regular duties for a religious holiday that I did not celebrate. After breakfast I was planning to attend services held in a chapel on the other side of the base.

This December 27th marked my being in the Army exactly a year and a half, the midpoint of my three-year obligation. I was still apprehensive about a transfer to Korea though, an assignment that carried a 13-month tour of duty, well within the time I had left. Back at Monmouth, when I completed the radar course, I narrowly missed going to the Army's "Hell Hole," as almost everyone in uniform called it. For two months in classes ahead of me, most of the graduates headed across the Pacific after being handed their certificates. It was possible I could be ordered to Korea at this time and I did not relish the thought. I had no desire for the duration of my stint to sleep in metal Quonset huts next to dozens of young men, patrol the 38th Parallel with a rifle on my shoulder, take cold showers in the field, and gawk at gook girls.

As much as I liked being in California, I had the feeling that I was wasting my time. I was not working my MOS, was not learning the trade I had joined the Army for, and was not "seeing the world" as was advertised in Army recruitment posters. My Monmouth buddies felt the same way as I did and we used to talk about the probability of foreign tours frequently. We all had signed up for radar school, and we all wanted to work our MOS and gain practical experience for jobs in civilian life. It was only in Korea and Germany, the two most com-mon overseas assignments, with troops in battle gear on the front lines in two Cold War hotspots, where we would ever get our hands on electronic equipment to repair. Germany seemed out of the question as a two-year tour of duty was usual, and with Korea out of my favor this was cause for some disconcerting

I finally got out of bed and went to breakfast that Saturday morning thinking more about my planned overnight stay with the WAC than a potential deployment out of the country. The latter thought was always in the back of my mind but the former was front and center and held my undivided attention. What was about to transpire, therefore, a sudden change for the better, was a complete surprise to me. Looking back on it now, after more than fifty years, only serves to reinforce the notion that this event was a major turning point in my life.

Out of the mess hall I came. No sooner had I started walking briskly back to my barracks building when suddenly I heard my first name called from behind. I recognized the voice as that of Nunzio, or Nunz as he was known to most of us, the battalion mail clerk and fellow classmate from Monmouth.

"Wait . . . wait," he continued crying out from a distance. "You're going to Germany."

I stopped dead in my tracks and turned around. I faced the bearer of this momentous news. Nunz's jet-black hair and eyes, swarthy complexion, and wide smile that lit up his whole face always stood out to me. In our few months at Ord, while the rest of us, all PFCs, were every day doing inconsequential tasks and shitty details because our battalion had no electronic equipment, he had been given a regular job in the mail room and soon was promoted to Specialist 4. Nunz apparently saw me ahead of him and could not wait to tell me what he had just learned. I was stunned by this revelation.

"What?" I said, as my friend approached me. "How do you know?"

"Orders came down late last night," the Italian-American from Philadelphia added with a faint, but sufficiently shrewd smile. "I saw them at battalion headquarters a few minutes ago. All the guys from Monmouth are going overseas in a couple of weeks."

At about the same time I was kissing the WAC and running my hand underneath her blouse in a dark corner near her barracks building, and proposing the all-important date with her the next day, the all-important orders were clicking over the teletype from Sixth Army HQ. "You sure I'm going to Germany?"

"Positive," Nunz all but guaranteed me. "Your name is on the Seventh Army list."

Every soldier was aware that the Seventh Army is only in West Germany. "What about the other guys?" I wanted to know.

"Half of them are going with you."

"And the other half?"

"They're going to Korea," Nunz said without emotion. "They're on the sheet marked 'Eighth Army'."

My good fortune was hard to believe. Here it was, just a simple statement about names and lists, seemingly based on chance, and my whole life changes. My fate was probably determined by some dull lieutenant or hick sergeant at the Presidio of San Francisco picking names out of a helmet liner or by random numbers while looking out over the bay or to the Golden Gate Bridge from a barracks office window. The highest numbered Army was the lowest in desirability, but who knows how my name happened to turn up on the wanted list. Standing there looking at Nunz I felt a tremendous sense of relief, pleased beyond belief to be bound for Germany rather than the other way across the Pacific but unable and unwilling to express the joy in words. In military lingo, I was truly at ease.

"Where are *you* going?" I said after a moment's pause just to make conversation, almost afraid to ask that question. His name could be on the *unwanted* list.

"I'm not," Nunz indicated smugly.

"I thought you said everyone from Monmouth is going?"

"Everyone except me."

"How come?" I was puzzled and really wanted to know.

"The sergeant major pulled to keep me here."

"Oh," I exclaimed weakly.

I understood the situation but did not wish to criticize the buddy who did me a good deed for accepting a special privilege. Nunz being well-liked by someone in authority determined his future. I was happy for my South Philly friend, but at the same time I resented the fact that one soldier's destiny was not decided simply by lot or luck like everyone else's. At my tender age, a month shy of nineteen, I had my first taste of how personality and power, one's own and someone else's, can affect life-altering events. It was apparent from the look on Nunz's unshaven face that he was glad to be staying in the States. Since he got bumped up, he shared a private room with another spec four in the barracks. And he knew he would probably be getting an umbrella over his bird before long. I was content to be leaving, as my transfer to Germany meant the peril of being shipped to Korea was removed permanently, and I might still get to work my MOS.

My plan to go to religious services after chow was set aside temporarily. I thanked Nunz for the unofficial information and waved goodbye to my now better, and in his eyes lucky, buddy. I was so excited about going to Germany I telephoned New York to tell my parents and then sat around the day room for a couple of hours just thinking about it. The next time I go to chapel to pray, I vowed, I would thank God that I was not going to Korea.

My whole life turned on a dime that Saturday morning in late December of '58. In two seconds, on a gravel side street near my sleeping quarters at Fort Ord, I realized my remaining time in the Army would be radically different. The news about the great transition was delivered to me so casually and routinely by a person I happened to share a classroom and barracks with for limited periods of time.  What this foreign duty-bound soldier was unaware of then was that the brief street bump with a comrade he was not real close to would be the initial force gliding him through a door that opened to an opposing culture and human experiences destined to remain a prominent part of his consciousness for decades to come.  Too bad the E-4 comrade I left behind at Ord would not be a beneficiary of the good news he imparted to me.

Later that day, when I hopped to the bus station to meet the WAC, I knew that I had much to celebrate and an additional reason to party with her.

# CHAPTER 2: GOODBYE, G.I.

On Thursday evening, January 29, 1959, I was in my bedroom lying crossways on the bed, flipping through the pages of a current magazine but unable to focus much attention on either the words or the pictures. There was a lengthy article on the takeover of Cuba by Fidel Castro and a news item about a young senator from Massachusetts who might run for president the following year. Fort Dix and the West Germany to which I would soon be sailing to were in my thoughts. On the floor was a long duffel bag with my Army clothes, an AWOL bag with toiletries, and an overseas bag with civilian clothes.

Suddenly I heard footsteps. Someone was in the building coming up the stairs to our apartment, the only one, two flights above the ground floor. There was a knock at the front door at the other end of the hallway near the staircase. Less than half a minute later the door to my bedroom opened.

"Richie is here," my sister said. "He wants to see you."

Richie D'Agostino was my best childhood friend. He lived with his parents directly across from us on Mermaid Avenue between West 22nd and 23rd Streets, in the four-room front apartment on the top floor of a four-story building. Richie was a year and three months older than I, born on that Halloween Eve in 1938 when Orson Welles did his famous *War of the Worlds* radio broadcast. With chestnut brown hair and hazel eyes, Richie looked more Irish than Italian, favoring his mother over his father. He had a few freckles and his fair skin caused him to sunburn easily.

Before I could say anything Ritchie came into my room. "Let's go out," he urged me.

"It's after ten. I'm leaving tomorrow morning."

"I know," said Richie, as he glanced around the room and noticed my stuffed duffel bag standing upright against the dresser. "That's why I came tonight."

My friend pestered me to go out with him for a little while. I knew full well his little while usually turned into several hours. But, it was my last night at home and I thought he might have something special planned. "All right," I agreed, and got up from the bed. "Let me get my jacket."

As kids Richie and I were almost always around each other. Until the third grade, he went to parochial school at Our Lady of Solace Church on 17th Street and Mermaid. When I was with him and his Catholic friends they often did not know I was Jewish until he told them. With dark brown, almost black, hair and eyes and a good tan in summer months, I was taken for Italian more than he. For a time we moved in the same adolescent circles, especially during the summer at nearby Washington Baths and the beach. We often went to Steeplechase Park together. Our paths began to separate some-what when we went to different high schools, he to a vocational and I an academic.

Richie himself was back from Germany just three months. He joined the Army Reserves at age seventeen after he quit high school. He did what a lot of other young men did, those who did not want to wait four or five years to be drafted but yet only wanted to serve the required two years: he pushed up his draft when he turned eighteen. After basic Richie was sent to AIT and then straight to an Infantry unit in Germany. This was the typical pattern the Army drew for its draftees, even Private Presley, its most famous one. I enlisted because I had no desire to be an infantryman and wanted to choose an Army school. Richie came home, coincidentally, on the U.S.S. *General Randall*, right after that troop transport ship carried Elvis to Germany.

My mother entered the hallway and saw me with my jacket on. "So where you boys going so late?" she asked.

"We're just going out for little while, Mama."

My mother, more than twice our age, moved more quickly than we did and positioned herself in front of us. She pointed and shook her finger at my childhood friend in a gesture of playful admonition. Then she said a few words in Yiddish, telling him not to keep me out so late. After Richie came home, my mother said simple things to him in her native tongue just to see if he had learned some German and could comprehend her. He gave an understanding smile once again.

"Don't worry. I'll take care of your son," he promised in English as we left. Had my mother suspected what Richie really meant, I'm sure she would have protested vociferously and put a broom to his backside.

It was not too cold outside and the air was dry, good for walking this time of year. We went down 22nd Street the one block to Surf Avenue, then turned and walked to Stillwell Avenue. We stopped at Nathan's for some hot dogs, French fries, and an orange drink. I noticed that *Kings Go Forth* with Frank Sinatra, Tony Curtis, and Natalie Wood was playing in the Loew's Theater across the street. It was an interesting war movie that I had seen two weeks earlier with a free ticket from the USO club on Times Square.

After we finished eating, Richie wanted to go to the Clam Bar on 17th Street where his uncle hung out. It was about the only eating and drinking establishment on Surf open during the winter months. Neither of us was twenty-one and of legal age but my friend always managed to get served alcohol.

The Clam Bar was fairly crowded this time of evening for a week-day. All sorts of characters from the neighborhood frequented the place—prizefighters, fences, bookies, loan sharks, gamblers. They usually sat at certain tables they called their own. We took a small table in the back.

Richie's uncle saw us and before long came over with two bottles of beer. The stocky-built man in his late forties had dark thinning hair and bushy eyebrows. I heard him speak Italian on and off to others in the restaurant. The uncle was reputed to be in the Mafia but everyone saw him simply as a bookmaker and small-time fence. I was sure Richie was influenced by his uncle since at times he was involved in questionable or illegal deals.

Richie filled his glass with what was left in the bottle and ordered another. I was still tickling my beer. "I'm sorry I joined the Army for three years," I confided to my friend who just got out.

He looked at me but offered no immediate response. I continued my lamentation. "I didn't like the radar school I signed up for. I spent over eight months learning a trade I'm not planning on using when I get out."

"What do you want to do when you get out?"

"I want to go to college."

Richie finished his second beer. I was still drinking my first. After a pause, he spoke. "You want to work with your head and not your hands."

I nodded. We then started talking about the Army. A third bottle was put down on the table in front of him. "What kind of duty could I expect in Germany?"

My Germany-wise friend revealed that overseas duty is not as bad as stateside, not as much chicken shit, less attention paid to silly rules and regulations. He assuaged my concerns by telling me I should have it easy over there because I was in Signal. Most of the time I'll be on post and not in the field, fixing the equipment the Infantry and other units messed up on maneuvers. Richie chatted about the shady activities some soldiers get into, buying cigarettes in the PX with their ration cards for a buck a carton and then selling them on the black market for five or six times that amount.

Cigarettes were just one way soldiers made a little extra Gelt, Richie went on to tell me. They also sell American food—coffee, tea, canned meats and fish, honey, sugar—anything in short supply in Germany. The foodstuffs can be bought in the Commissary but only married G.I.s living off post are issued ration cards and a pass to get in.

"Some soldiers go crazy in Germany. They sell army blankets, boots, overcoats, jackets, hats, gloves, anything they can steal from the company supply room or the Quartermaster or just pick up what's left around in the barracks."

"No shit," I noted naïvely.

"Yeah, it's fucking kalt in the winter."

Richie pointed out that Germans pay dollars or Marks for what they want, money they probably made selling other stuff on the black market.

My friend looked at me, smiled, and told me to watch out for the Fräuleins. He described how local women do the dirty work on our camps, what the men will not even do, and for peanuts too. They work in the PX and the mess hall. They scrub floors in the barracks, wash laundry, cook and clean in the snack bar.

"Every young German girl wants to marry a G.I. and come to the States," he stressed.

I glanced at my watch and saw it was almost midnight. "I should be getting home soon. I've got to get some sleep tonight."

Richie's third beer was all gone. Unexpectedly, the conversation turned personal. "How's your rifle doing?" I was asked. "Been shooting it off lately?"

"I balled a WAC before I left California."

"Was she white?" Richie wanted to know, as if it mattered.

"No, mulatto . . . real light."

"When was that, a month ago?"

I nodded.

"Nothing in New York since?"

This time I shook my head.

"Maybe I could get you some action tonight? A going-away present. A birthday present."

"That would be nice," I agreed unhesitatingly. I was glad he remembered my birthday. Suddenly my need for sleep seemed unimportant.

"I know a PR on Twenty-first Street. We could walk over there now."

"Don't you have to call first?"

"Nah," my considerate friend assured me. "She always lets me in." He laughed at the unintended pun.

The puertorriqueña lived in a basement apartment on West 21st Street, just before Neptune Avenue, two houses down from the poultry slaughterhouse on the corner near the bay side of the island. Walking along Surf to her place I could smell the salt air from the ocean, but now a stench of blood and raw chicken pervaded this part of the block, even though by this time of night all cutting and disembowelment had ceased hours earlier.

Richie rapped on the door. To the right of the door, on a sort of raised landing in front of the windows, stood six garbage cans, some with their lids off and overstuffed. A light flashed in the window furthest from us and then a few seconds later in the window next to where we were standing. The door opened slowly. A Puerto Rican girl who could not have been more than eighteen or nineteen appeared in a bathrobe, tugging at it with her left hand to cover the nightgown underneath.

"It late, Reechee," she  pleaded in her thick Spanish accent. "I already in . . . ."

Richie pushed the door back and stepped into the apartment, cutting the girl off and ignoring her appeal. Somewhat dazed, she pulled back, reluctantly accepting the unwarranted intrusion. I positioned myself slowly into the apartment. Richie simply said I was a friend. I did not hear him give my name. I doubted whether she fully understood, or cared for that matter, exactly who I was.

I stood near the door, not knowing what to do, looking around in what appeared to be the living room. The furniture was old and ragged, with sheets or other coverings on the sofa and chairs. On one of the walls were a picture of Jesus and a crucifix. Other religious objects rested on two tables on both ends of a sofa. A small kitchen was straight ahead and another room off to the right. There was a musty odor in the apartment redolent of frequent floods.

Richie and the girl were standing together on the far end of the room, by the doorway to that other room. He was saying something to her in a low voice that I could not quite make out, cocking his head every few seconds in my direction. The girl was obviously discomposed but at the same time seemed acquiescent. Her hand no longer clutching at her bathrobe, I could see the outline of her full breasts beneath the nightgown. Richie then came over to me.

"Have a seat . . . relax," he said. Without waiting for an answer and giving me no further instructions, he took the girl by the elbow, led her into the other room, and closed the door.

Richie knew I would just wait for him, that no explanation of what he was doing or how long it would take was necessary. I sat down on the sofa, or rather *sank* down into the sofa. As I looked around this strange apartment, I felt uncomfortable just sitting there, not knowing if anyone else lived here or if someone might barge in at any moment. There was stillness in the air but I could hear nothing of the two of them in the other room. This certainly was an interesting and exciting turn of events that began just two hours earlier. Now past midnight, it seemed the day of my departure from New York would be a memorable one.

It was after one when the door opened. Richie came out. The girl stayed in the other room. "Now it's your turn," he told me. I stood up and started walking toward the bedroom door. As I passed him, Ritchie whispered. "You don't have to pay her. I took care of it. She owed me some money."

The other room was a small bedroom with high windows on two sides that exposed the backyard and the alley. The girl was making up the bed when I came in. She was in her bathrobe and it was tied around her waist so I could not tell if she had anything on underneath. When she saw me she excused herself and said she would be right back. The room was cluttered with cardboard boxes in the corner against the back wall. The dresser looked like it needed to be put out in the street. Since there were no chairs in the room, I sat down on the edge of the bed. I faced away from the crucifix on the wall just above the headboard. I unbuttoned my shirt but did not remove it. I heard the front door close and then the sound of water running.

When the girl came back to the room, her bathrobe was untied. She was wearing red panties but nothing on top. Her breasts were now partially visible and I watched them flop around as she moved about the room picking up articles of clothing and putting them in drawers or the wooden closet. She then closed the bedroom door even though Richie must have left and there was no one with us in the apartment. I wondered if he told her anything about me.

The girl Richie procured for me was not real pretty but was not bad looking either. She had broad cheeks, a low hairline, and a sprinkling of acne on her face and neck. What appealed to me most was her figure. She had good tits and a petite body frame with curves that accented erotic femininity. She was enough of a looker, though, for the purpose to which I was in her bedroom at one o'clock in the morning. With a week or two of processing at Dix and another week to ten days of an ocean voyage standing between me and the next time I could be in line for some female companionship, I was in no mood to turn down what was readily available because of a less-than-perfect appearance.

The girl came over to where I was sitting on the bed and started to undress me. I stood up and helped her, then placed my clothes and underwear on top of the boxes. She slipped out of her bathrobe and got on the bed next to me. She was upright on her knees and tried to guide me to lie down on my back but I sat up next to her. I reached over and positioned my hand in her crotch. I rubbed her up and down several times with my thumb and index and middle fingers. Then I worked my way under the skimpy red garment, opened her a little, and felt her softness and wetness.

She seemed uncomfortable with her knees in the mattress so I maneuvered her on her back. She lifted up, allowing me to remove her panties. I moved closer to the object of my desire and continued toying with it. I opened her again with my touch and with my other hand groped at various sites on her body. The girl reached over and cupped me in her hands. My plane of passion was now quite stirred and hoisted. When she saw I was very chubby, she raised herself a little and rolled me onto my back. She caressed my face and stroked my hair.

"You handsome americano," she said. "I happy make amor with you." She leaned over and kissed my face several times, deliberately avoiding my lips I thought.

"Gracias," I answered, rolling the *r* to pronounce it right and appreciative of the compliment. She then crouched down toward my middle. Richie's gift to me, it seemed, was going to be head *and* tail. The girl patently fancied oral endearments. She absorbed my growing hardness in incremental measures, moving her head and neck up and down slowly like a timing device. I could feel she was trying to just ferment and unsettle my carnal sensuality but not unleash it. In her mind, perhaps she transposed my face to another part of my body.

I lifted her up by the chin and then took her by the elbows and slid her on top of me. She effortlessly straddled my hips to fit me in. I was surprised she did not pull out a rubber or ask me to provide protection. She was nice and tight and it felt good, perhaps better than with any other girl I had known. I stayed in this position for a few minutes, working with her, holding myself back. Before long I changed positions and climbed on top of her. I grasped the sides of her face with every thrusting motion, as if to steady her for the approaching quake. Her knees jerked up and down alongside my body producing movable ridges in the sheet. She tried to look straight at me but I glanced away. The point of culmination was soon upon me, twittering us in unison, merging mind and body like no other human activity. We separated on the bed, remained on our backs for a few moments, and caught our breaths.

It was almost two when I left the girl's apartment. She stood in the doorway to see me off, much to my surprise still in a pleasant mood despite the late night encroachment on her privacy and person by two young men. Without thinking, I turned and kissed her on the lips, as if we were longtime lovers or I expected to see her again soon. For a moment I lost sight of the fact that I was still a soldier and in a few hours would be going away for some time.

The girl smiled. "Goodbye, G.I.," she said in accented speech that sounded cute. "Happy birthday." Richie *had* told her all about me.

It was a short walk back to my parents' apartment and I went straight home. At this hour of night I was sure no one on 21st Street who knew me would be looking out of his or her window and wondering why I came out of a Puerto Rican girl's basement apartment. Had I thought discovery was a problem, I would have gone home the opposite and somewhat longer way, via Neptune and 22nd or 23rd Street. The air was cold, the streets deserted, and I felt alone, almost abandoned, the whole way. In the calm of the evening, I could hear waves in the ocean breaking hard against the rocks and the clang of bells from the life buoys.

Back in my bedroom, I thought of what it would be like if I were out of the Army, able to pay the busty puertorriqueña a late-night visit anytime I wanted. She was a terrific shtup. I was sure I would be reliving it in my head often on the boat to Germany.

If my mother asked, I would tell her Richie took care of me like he promised.

## CHAPTER 3: A FORMER ENEMY

The sound of a young girl's voice calling my name woke me up. Her words at first seemed part of my dream but then I realized I was being jolted from the bed

"David . . . David," I heard again. "Mama said to wake you."

My sister was still standing over me when I opened my eyes, shaking me with all the force a nine-year-old could muster. A beautiful round face, eyes glistening in the partial darkness, was smiling at me. I could see the center part in her blackish-brown hair and the long braids banging against her shoulders as she swayed.

"You'd better get up," she added. "You have to leave today."

My sister's admonition brought to mind the importance of the day just as I was coming into full consciousness. Yes, it was time to go. Whether I wanted to or not, I had to leave not only my family and my home but my country as well. I would be traveling thousands of miles to a foreign land, to live and work for almost a year and a half with a former enemy of the United States.

"Okay, okay," I muttered in return, groggy from my short night's rest. "I'll be up in a minute."

"Mama's making you breakfast," she said, and then turned around.

My sister left my bedroom quickly, her gait resembling someone bouncing from a mission just accomplished. I sat up in bed for a few minutes, looking at the fixtures in the room and thinking about the journey on which I was to embark. The shade on the window facing the street was not quite drawn all the way down and thin rays of early morning light forced their way in. I could see my Class A green uniform hanging on the outside of the closet door. The single yellow stripe on the sleeves almost glowed in the darkened room. Barely visible were the white letters spelling STREIBER on the black nametag pinned to the jacket just above the right breast pocket. My eyes turned to the round dress hat on top of the old varnished-covered bureau. The hat's reflection in the attached mirror was noticeable from where I was sitting.

It was colder this morning than what I felt not six hours earlier walking back from 21st Street near Neptune. Through the space between the windowsill and shade, I could see snow flurries swirling

26

about. It occurred to me that if sheets of ice already formed on the sidewalk in front of our building, I would be better off wearing my boots than my dress shoes.

I enjoyed my stay in New York, particularly the unanticipated late-night encounter with the neighborhood girl Richie arranged for me. All that was left for me was to take the subway to Port Authority in Manhattan and catch the bus to Fort Dix.

A feeling of strangeness came over me as I looked around the bedroom. My being home on leave was the first time I had actually lived in this apartment. We had seven rooms on the top floor of a three-family brick storefront building. We were in the middle of the block and the attached houses were virtually the same save the two large apartment buildings on either corner.

My parents moved to these more spacious living quarters only six months earlier after renting the small three-room apartment in back of the store on the ground floor of the adjacent building for sixteen years. I had just left Fort Monmouth and I helped with the moving. It was quite comforting to now wake up in my very own bedroom in a much roomier apartment. Comfort aside, the bedroom underscored my conviction that it was a mistake to have committed myself to Uncle Sam for three years. If the new apartment had been secured *two years* earlier, I might have gone to college first.

I got out of bed, showered, dressed except for my jacket and tie, and went into the kitchen at the other end of the apartment from my bedroom. My mother was wearing dark slacks and a light pullover sweater, looking modern it seemed to me like most of my friends' mothers, those who were born here and adopted more youthful styles of dress. This surprised me as I could not recall ever seeing her in the house in anything but a plain housedress. I always thought of my mother as old fashioned, sticking to tradition. Perhaps the new apartment and no longer having to deal with the landlady next door made the difference. She had an apron on and was standing in front of the stove, cooking something in a frying pan that made a crackling sound. Next to the stove was an open box of Manischewitz Matzoh Meal.

"Here Dovidl," my mother voiced delight as she served me. "Have some potato latkes. Your cook sergeant won't be making you this."

I rolled the sleeves of my dress shirt halfway up my fore arms and sat down at the table. Full morning light was coming in now through the window facing the back of the building. From where I was sitting I could see clotheslines hooked to telephone poles in the yard below.

"Take some sour cream or apple sauce," she added, pushing two small glass bowls toward my full plate. My mother buzzed back-and-forth from the stove, table, and refrigerator like a bumblebee between flowers. It pleased me to see her work in this larger kitchen after watching her for so many years prepare food in cramped conditions.

"Thanks, Mama, but I can't eat all these latkes. I've got to get going."

"Since when you can't finish?

"I'm just not hungry this morning. I had something at Nathan's last night," I said, leaving Richie out of it.

"So what time you got home?"

"After midnight," I noted simply, not wanting to be too specific about my late arrival.

"I'll fix that italiener," she said as an empty threat. "He promised to get you home early."

"That's not what Richie promised, Mama."

"No? So what he promised?"

"He said he would take care of me." I hoped she would not pursue this matter further.

"Well, he took care of you all right, keeping you out late eating goyische food."

My mother kept a kosher home and my parents never ate treife outside the house but they knew the children were not that religious and did not insist we be as observant as they. "I'll get something to eat later at the bus station," I said, trying to divert attention away from Richie.

"Why waste money on more chazerai?" she added. "Ess."

I gulped the rest of my breakfast. It was futile to argue with my mother about not eating. I peered out the back window to get a last look at the famous part of my neighborhood. I could see in the distance the beach and the ocean and a small piece of the deserted Boardwalk. Our building stood just two blocks from the water and five blocks from Steeplechase at the western end of the amusement section. I got up from the table and went over to the window. Off to my left and visible from where I was standing was the 250-foot Parachute Jump, the tallest structure on the island, now closed for the winter.

"Is Zeyde awake yet?" I asked my mother. "I want to say good-bye to him?"

"I'll go look. You get together your things." She patted me on the back and pushed me away. "Go already."

I went back to my room. I put the T-shirts, socks, and shorts lying on the dresser into a packed but open duffel bag, forcing the clothing down. I folded the eyelets over a hook, fastened the shoulder-strap clasp to the hook, and then secured it with a combination lock. My toiletries and a shaving kit I placed into a black-and-green AWOL bag and zipped it up. On the floor also was a large brown overseas bag that I had purchased before I went to Fort Ord, packed solid with my civilian clothes. I put my tie on, then my jacket without buttoning it.

My mother and sister came into the room. "Did you take on the dresser the clean laundry I left you?"

"Yes, Mama. Thank you."

My mother handed me a little jewelry box. "Papa told me before he went to work to give you this."

I opened the box and saw it was a Jewish star with a gold chain. "Mama, you know I don't like to wear anything around my neck. It cuts me when I sleep."

"Since when a mogen dovid cuts anyone? Wear it. God will protect you. Besides, the goyim should know who you are."

"Thank you, Mama. I'll put it on later. And thank Papa for me." I closed the box and put it in my jacket pocket.

My grandfather entered the bedroom. He was wearing a robe over his pajamas. He dragged his feet in his old pair of slippers as usual. His thinning gray hair was uncombed, sticking out clumsily as if he just jumped out of bed.

"Hello, Zeyde," I said. "Did Mama wake you?"

"No, I vas up already," he responded in his ever-noticeable Yiddish accent. "I vanted to see you before you vent avay."

My grandfather used to live in a bungalow on Canal Avenue about

29

a half mile away, on the western end of the island near Gravesend Bay. Eight years earlier he sold the bakery he owned on Mermaid near 32nd Street and retired. When my grandmother passed away three years later, he stayed with us to sit shiva and then moved in for good.

My mother walked up to me and started buttoning my jacket. "Dovidl, where do you think they'll send you, the Army?" There was more trepidation than curiosity in the tone of her voice.

"I told you already, Mama. Some place in Germany. My orders just say Seventh Army, USAREUR." I sounded *yoosareur* out for her.

"Yoosa . . . what?"

I laughed. "It means United States Army Europe. I'll be in Germany but I won't know the city until I get processed at Fort Dix."

My mother worried about me going to Germany. How fortunate it was for her family to have left Europe when they did, I thought. My grandfather came over first, then the wife and children in 1927. They immigrated to America just in time so as not to be among the countless victims of the Nazis. My father too was lucky as he was born here, but most of his family came from the other side in the early 1900s. Talking about the war was not as difficult for my parents as it was perhaps for those who had experienced it firsthand. I often heard them speak in anger about what had happened in Europe with Hitler and the Jews. And I often heard them speak both lovingly and sadly about relatives lost—grandparents, aunts, uncles, cousins—flesh-and-blood beings once but now just fading memories of former selves.

I thought how fortunate it was for me too. Had I been born in a shtetl in Eastern Europe like my mother and some of my father's family, I could have spent the first five years of my life in a ghetto or concentration camp and who knows if I would have survived the war. Not a pleasant musing for someone about to spend almost a year and a half in the land of those who were once committed to his destruction.

"Dovidl," my mother added cautiously, and then finished buttoning my jacket. "You be careful in Germany. Don't get friendly with the Germans. They're no good, all of them."

"Don't worry, I won't get friendly," I assured her, not wanting to disagree.

"Don't even talk to them."

Now she was getting ridiculous. "How can I not talk to Germans, Mama. I'll be there almost a year and a half."

"They're all Nazis," she asserted, raising her voice somewhat. "They killed six million of our people."

I tried to put on an air of objectivity to counter my mother's injection of raw emotion into an otherwise casual conversation. "All Germans can't be Nazis. The war's been over a long . . . ."

"Fourteen years not such a long time," she cut in, her voice now louder still. "People don't forget so fast. And people don't change."

"But they're not our enemies any longer. The Army told us the Russians are now . . . ."

"Never mind the Russians," she cut in again. "*I* know the Russians. You just keep away from the Germans."

"Not all Germans are bad, I'm sure," I continued, advancing a positive stance much to my surprise given my own apprehensions. I really had no idea how a once military foe quickly became a valued ally after the war, or whether anti-Semitism was still rampant in Germany. "What's the harm in talking to them?"

"Plenty harm. The Germans all went along with Hitler. They built the camps, with the ovens and the gas."

"There are no more concentration camps, Mama," I reassured her naïvely. "And," I added, without realizing how trite it would sound, "people should be judged as individuals, not as members of a group."

"Individuals, shmindividuals . . . what do you know?"

"I know today's young Germans are not responsible for what their parents or grandparents did . . . or didn't do." I tried to be philosophical as well as detached.

"You think you're such a smarty pants," my mother shot back. "Remember little Anna . . . and her mother?"

I nodded. I did not forget the refugee girl who came from Germany after the war and was in my sixth-grade class.

"Well, who do you think put those numbers on their arms," my mother went on, "the immigration department at Ellis Island?"

"Mama, I know they were in a concentration camp. You were the one who told me what the Nazis did to them."

"Yes . . . and young Germans, old Germans, makes no difference. A Nazi is a Nazi."

"Leave him alone," my grandfather said in Yiddish, jumping in against my mother and sparing my knowledge further testing. "Let your son go in peace. He is too young to know everything that happened. He will find out for himself in good time."

"I just wanted to warn him," she responded in Yiddish. "Who knows what is going on in Germany now."

"He is a smart boy. He won't get involved with the German people."

"He is a *young* boy," she said. "He won't see how two-faced the Germans are."

"When I brought you from Poland over thirty years ago, you thought all Americans liked the Jews. You had to learn too in your own way and in your own time. Don't worry about Dovid." My grandfather always called me by my Hebrew name.

"You ask me not to worry. How can a mother not worry about her children?"

"Enough already," I said in English. "You both don't have to worry about me. I know what happened to Jews during the war. I won't talk to Germans unless I have to, okay?"

"You promise, Dovidl?"

"He promises," my grandfather assured my mother. "Now leave him alone."

"Believe me," I said to both of them with the hope of finally ending this kind of talk. "I'm not going to get involved with anything or anyone while I'm overseas. I just want to finish my time, come home, start college, and . . . ."

Just then the telephone rang. "I'll get it," screamed my sister as she turned and ran toward the door. I could hear her running all the way to the other end of the apartment. I started to put on my hat and overcoat.

"Okay, no more talking," my mother said. "You have to go now."

"Can I help you? Such a big bag you got." My grandfather reached to grab hold of my more than three-foot long duffel bag.

"I can manage, Zeyde. Thanks."

I carried my duffel and AWOL bags through my bedroom door to the hallway running outside the apartment. My mother and grand-father followed me. My sister entered the hallway from the foyer on the other side.

"David, it's Richie. He wants to talk to you and . . . ."

"Not now," my mother interrupted. "He has to leave." If it was my father calling I'm sure she would have said I had time to talk.

"I told Richie you were leaving now. He said he'll meet you downstairs."

"He probably wants to say goodbye," I said. "I came home by myself last night."

"You came home by yourself?" my mother asked. "For what? Didn't he stay with you?"

"Yes, for a while, but then he went to see his uncle at the Clam Bar." I did not think I was telling a lie to my mother as this is probably what Richie did after he left the girl's house.

"Where was he in Germany?" my mother asked, apparently still preoccupied with these issues. "Did he get into trouble like he used to?" She turned toward my grandfather. "A neighbor told me if they didn't take that italiener in the army in jail he'd be now."

"Daughter, why must you repeat gossip?" my grandfather retorted in Yiddish. "Don't be a yenta?"

"It's all right, Zeyde. Everybody knows Richie was a wild kid. That's why I stopped hanging around with him and his friends years ago."

"So where was he?"

"Mama, Richie was stationed in a small town near the Czech border." I did not tell her that he was almost put in the stockade over there, or that he got a German girl pregnant. But I did add, "He hated the Army because he was in the Infantry and in the field a lot. He was always talking back to the sergeants and he got busted to private, lost his stripe." I pointed to the single stripe on my sleeve.

"Don't you get in trouble, Dovidl."

"Don't worry, Mama. I'll be okay. I know how to soldier in the Army."

She looked at me inquisitively but did not say anything.

"I know how to stick within the rules."

"He is a smart boy," my grandfather said for the second time. He often said that about me to someone either in English or Yiddish.

I lifted my sister and kissed her. "See you in June nineteen-sixty, doll face. You'll be a big girl by then." I put her down, hugged and kissed my mother, then hugged and kissed my grandfather. I put my duffel bag over my right shoulder and held my AWOL bag in my left hand. I started walking down the stairs. "I'll call you from Fort Dix and tell you where to send the other bag," I said, talking over my left shoulder.

I heard a whisper in Yiddish. "Be well, my son."

I did not look back but I knew there were tears in my mother's eyes.

"Don't forget to write," my grandfather added in English.

"Bye, David," my sister said. "I love you."

# CHAPTER 4: FRAU HITLER

Leaving the new apartment, I could not help thinking about the terribly small one we used to live in next door, about how hard my parents, my mother especially, had striven for years to move. I remembered how much we all wanted to escape from the building's landlady or, I should say, more to the point in light of my impending journey, the *German* landlady.

It was a dinky three-room flat on the ground floor in back of a notions and yarn store. The kitchen was small, at the end of a foyer leading from the front door. The table against the wall was always so cluttered with food and packages that only two people could sit down to eat. The main room was multi-functioned—a living room, a bedroom for my parents and sister, and a dining area for holidays and special occasions.

I shared the third room with my grandfather. A window in it opened to an airshaft in common with the adjoining building, the one we moved to in 1958. Sound traveled easily and loudly through it. We were often kept awake, especially on hot summer nights, by the neighbors' frequent yelling and cursing, grist for the block's gossip mill.

The kitchen had a windowed back door that opened to what we called "The Yard." A tall wooden pole stood at its southern perimeter, with clotheslines running to the building's three levels. The Yard was a large open space paved with concrete, ideal for family gatherings. Only a wire fence separated us from the clumps of grass and dirt beyond our pale. Since there was no general entrance to the backyard that the two families above us might use, we alone had unrestricted access. The Yard was our only consolation for living in a tiny abode.

All my friends had larger apartments than we did. It was embarrassing for me to invite friends in. I disliked our quarters intensely. Not only were we very cramped, it symbolized how wanting our economic situation was. My parents had taken the apartment a week before Pearl Harbor, after a fire devastated our four rooms in a building on 24th Street between Mermaid and Neptune Avenues. I often tried to imagine what my life might have been like were it not for that fateful fire. The apartment at 2216 Mermaid was smaller than the one we had on 24th Street, but it was available when we were desperate for housing and affordable at twenty-five dollars a month.

"It was supposed to be only temporary," my mother said in confidence to me, "but rents went up after the war and Papa never got a better job."

Saying that Papa never got a better job was an understatement. Ppa was always worried about *losing* the low-paying job he did have and not finding another one. My father did not have a high school diploma, a not uncommon situation for men of his generation. He worked in a factory in lower Manhattan, as a textile printer in an industry that was undergoing fundamental changes. Many shops in New York's garment district were either closing or relocating to non-union states in the South or to cheap-labor countries in the Far East. My father's uncertain job situation was always a dark cloud hanging over us.

On the top floor of our building there was an elderly couple whose children had long moved out. I had never been inside that apartment so I never knew what two people had to fill seven rooms with. The man was a house painter, an occupation heavy with Jews at that time, always coming and going in paint-stained overalls and cap. I thought half the rooms must have had wall-to-wall gallon buckets of paint.

The store in our building was owned and operated by the landlord. He was a pleasant, easy-to-talk-to man, an American-born small businessman who took over the property from his elderly father. The old man oftentimes just sat around all day as if in a daze. My mother called him der Alte and always spoke to him in Yiddish. She told me he escaped from Russia during the Revolution of 1905 and had known Trotsky. The landlord lived with his wife and two children miles away in a comfortable single-family home in Flatbush, unaware and apparently unconcerned about the goings-on at the building after he closed his store. The other families in the building used to leave shopping carts, vegetable boxes, and bags with garbage near their stairwells. We always left the baby carriage and my two-wheel bicycle in the hallway outside our door. We all knew these practices were against the city's building codes but the landlord was too polite or too oblivious to say anything against the liberties we took.

We were on very good terms with the landlord. In the storage room in back of the store there was a small sink but no toilet. He greatly appreciated my parents allowing him to use our bathroom just across our foyer from the store's back door. I had no key to our apartment. My mother was afraid I would lose it and then someone would rob us, but what valuables we had I was not aware of. The landlord always let me walk through his store and enter our apartment through its back door if there was no one at home

My mother usually knew when the landlord had something on his mind. He would use the bathroom more frequently than usual and took more time walking across our three-foot foyer. One day in late summer 1951, a great change was about to unfold. I was eating in the kitchen and saw and heard it all. My mother's intuition was correct. After three visits to the bathroom in less than an hour, the landlord finally walked meekly into the kitchen where my mother was standing at the sink peeling potatoes. I knew she could see him through the corner of her eye.

"I have to sell the building," the man said, straining to get the words out. "There is a prospective buyer."

My mother turned and looked at him but said nothing. I sat there appearing to read my comic book but rolled my eyes up without lifting my head.

The landlord told my mother about the necessity for him to dispose of the property. He said the couple on the top floor was retiring and moving out soon and, imploringly it seemed to me, proposed that we buy the building instead. He stressed that we could then move into the much larger apartment. If we did not buy the building, he could not give us the apartment. The seven-room vacant apartment was the primary selling feature.

"Mrs. Streiber," the landlord pleaded, taking a folded handkerchief from his back pocket and wiping his brow, "all you need is two thousand dollars and the bank will note you the rest."

Even as an eleven-year old, I knew the answer my mother would give before she said a word. My parents did not have much more than two *hundred* dollars in their savings account. My father, who still talked about the Depression and never took a loan in his life, was adamant in his conviction not to get involved with banks. His shop in the city was on the verge of closing and there were few employment possibilities in his trade. The landlord wanted to sell the building to us, and not a stranger, because he trusted us to let him keep the store. All we could do was to assure him we would continue to let him use our facilities.

About a week later I was home again when the landlord came in, this time through the front door, with an austere looking elderly woman. My mother escorted them into the kitchen and closed the door to the main room. The old bag was short and noticeably plump in the sleeveless summer dress she wore that did not become her, for it exposed the large amount of flab on her upper arms. From behind her rimless glasses, she squinted at us and glanced around our living quarters. She dragged her feet as she walked, drawing attention to the heavier-than-normal lower portion of her legs.

"This is Mrs. Mittler," the landlord said, introducing her to my mother. "She just bought the building and will be moving into the apartment on the second floor."

My mother waited for our new landlady to speak first. When she did it sounded more like an interrogation than a conversation.

"How many peoples in zis apartment?" I heard her say in an unmistakable German accent. She sounded like Sid Caesar on television in his parody of Germans speaking English. The woman moved in a little closer and then I noticed the small silver Jewish star around her neck. "Und how much rent do you pay," she added in a guttural voice with a strongly rolled *r* before my mother had a chance to respond.

My mother began to speak in Yiddish. I could tell she was visibly nervous. The gruffness of this woman's tone and the autocratic quality of her demeanor surprised and even frightened me. My mother instinctively wished to relate to the building's new baleboste on common ground or perhaps she was simply more at ease in her native tongue.

Mrs. Mittler continued in her broken English. She completely ignored my mother's Yiddish whether she understood it or not. After a few unresponsive exchanges my mother reverted to English. It was in my mother's nature to put on a pleasant face and to make every effort to be courteous to people and I could tell she was trying her best here. This strange lady, however, with her cold, formal way of dealing with people was enough to make anyone uncomfortable.

"I'm ze owner here, I make ze rules," I kept hearing her say.

I remember they argued about a key. The budding building boss wanted a key to our flat so that she could gain access anytime she wanted to the backyard and boiler in the cellar. My mother flatly refused. The former landlord just stood there grim-faced, unable to offer any suggestions to settle the dispute. All this seemed alien to him. He never needed a key to our apartment, since he could get inside from his store's back door, but he also never came through with a repairman to fix the boiler without first asking my mother's permission. The stern vixen stormed out, vowing to take the issue to court. Thanks to her, my first impression of German people was less than favorable.

Not long after she occupied the recently vacated apartment on the top floor, the word was out on Mrs. Mittler. We stopped wondering why a single woman would want to live in, and have to take care of, a seven-room apartment. Our new landlady began renting furnished rooms to elderly, unmarried men and women.

Mrs. Mittler had come to this country after the war, a widow, a refugee from the Nazis, but apparently not a penniless one. She reputedly purchased our building with the reparations she had received from the West German government, with the kind of money unavailable to my family and any of the others in the neighborhood, Jews who had emigrated from Eastern Europe before the war. There was at the outset a great deal of resentment toward this stumpy Jewish woman who refused to speak Yiddish and who did not hesitate to flaunt her superior economic status. I often heard the older people say to each other, "To survive how many Jews did she tell on or turn in?"

Mrs. Mittler was different from the other elderly Jewish ladies I knew. She always acted with an air of haughtiness around people on the block, speaking German, criticizing neighbors, not really associating with anyone. She was very friendly with her boarders, people she had control over, but not with us or the neighbors. We all saw her for what she was, a niggling, autocratic, and contemptuous woman. My mother attributed the dissimilarity to the fact that Mrs. Mittler was *German*, that the German Jews thought they were more German than Jewish.

Life in the building was never quite the same after our new owner moved in. The change was both sudden and shocking. Mrs. Mittler acted dictatorially with everyone, Jew and Gentile, and made no pretense of amicability. She installed a front door with a lock but no buzzer or intercom system to each apartment. We were given one key and were instructed, or rather *ordered*, not to make copies. With visitors, we were expected to know in advance who was coming to see us and then be there to unlock the door at the appropriate moment.

To everyone's utter amazement, Mrs. Mittler posted a list of rules on the wall in the hallway—no children are to loiter in the building, no pets are to be brought in, no visitors after midnight, no bicycles or baby carriages anywhere, no this, no that. She frequently waved her stubby-fingered hands at people threateningly, children especially, who deviated from her arbitrary prescripts.

Those of us who lived in the building had to tolerate the land-lady's mishegas, but others did not. With or without my blessing, friends of mine, Richie chiefly, would do things that greatly upset Mrs. Mittler, such as knock on her door and then run away, spit on her mailbox, or leave empty boxes by her stairwell. She always came to my mother first to blame me for any devilish act, never to the lady on the second floor to accuse the son or daughter. When Richie could not get in one day he forced the locked door open, the symbol of our—and by extension, his—confinement. Mrs. Mittler called the police, whom she swiftly and personally led to our door.

"I vant zis boy arrested," she shouted, pointing a shaking hand at me standing in the doorway with my mother. "He broke ze lock und ze door." She grabbed me by the arm and tried to pull me into the hallway but one of the two policemen stopped her.

My mother quickly came to my defense. She told the officers I had been home with her, that I did not need to break into my own house, and that Mrs. Mittler lives on the third floor and could not possibly have seen me or anyone else fool with the front door. The cops questioned others in the building but since no one was willing or able to identify the guilty party the complaint was promptly dismissed. I gathered my mother was secretly pleased someone had finally broken the hated lock. And it was apparent to me that my mother had guessed Richie must have done it but was not sure whether I put him up to it or not. She never said another word about the incident. I think that was the point I began to really hate Mrs. Mittler, when I could have been taken into custody for something I took no part in.

What invariably rubbed people the wrong way about our landlady, what did not endear her to anyone she came into contact, was her blatant authoritarian manner. Not only did she boss around and try to control the tenants in her building, she acted the same way toward visitors and next-door neighbors. She herself thus provided people with a ready source of mockery that became a cruel form of self-punishment. The older Jews on the block who knew some German derisively called Mrs. Mittler "Frau Hitler." Others then picked up on it and no matter what else she did, she could never escape that ignominious label. Mrs. Mittler turned red in the face when the twisted term was used within her earshot

My mother would not utter Hitler's name, even to ridicule someone she disliked intensely. She always referred to Mrs. Mittler as "The Witch." I suppose my mother's appellation was apropos since it seemed as though some evil spell was cast over us. The landlady was indeed bewitching, always looking to harass us one way or another.

Mrs. Mittler's mean spiritedness was apparent one day. At eight o'clock on a Saturday morning, there was a loud knock at the door. My mother was warming my sister's bottle, I was finishing my breakfast, and my father was still sleeping. I went to open the door, ignoring my mother's plea to wait. Mrs. Mittler was standing in her slippers, the leather cutting into her swollen bare feet, wearing an unbuttoned heavy coat over a robe and nightgown. She was dwarfed by the two tall men standing next to her, one very Italian looking with thick black hair and menacing eyes, tool box in hand, the other a stout and balding Schwarzer in a one-piece grease-stained uniform, the name "Willie" embroidered above the right pocket.

"Ve vant to see ze boiler," the landlady said, and before anyone could stop them or straighten things in the apartment, she led the charge down the foyer, through the kitchen, the men brushing perilously close to uncovered food and baby nipples on the table, and out the back door. I could see my mother was enraged at this unannounced and, as we knew of no malfunction with the boiler, unnecessary intrusion into our privacy so early in the day and on the Sabbath too.

That was merely the first of many such incidents obviously meant to both annoy and humiliate us. Mrs. Mittler then tried to restrict us from using the backyard, especially when we had family gatherings there, claiming it was her property. It bothered her to look out her window and see us enjoying ourselves below. But all she could do was talk and we simply ignored her. Within a year she took us to court in downtown Brooklyn. My mother had to travel the long distance on public transportation carrying my little sister and tugging me along as a possible witness.

"I vant a key to ze apartment," Mrs. Mittler demanded of the judge in her characteristically shrill voice, "und I vant a restraining order to keep zem out of my backyard."

"I am always home," my mother countered matter-of-factly, "and she can come in to fix the boiler anytime." My mother explained that the ground floor of our building was different from the others on the block. In the other buildings, the stores were smaller, the apartments in back had their kitchens as the first room of three behind the store, and the wider spaces between the foyer and the backyard were storage and not living areas. People or repairmen going to these other backyards did not have to trudge through the kitchen of the family on the ground floor.

"I can't stop my son from playing in the yard," my mother continued, "and I go back there to hang out the wash." I could see the judge was visibly moved when my mother testified that Mrs. Mittler on the third floor deliberately hung out soaking wet bed sheets to drip down on our drying clothes.

The judge sided with us on both counts, ruling that our apartment was personal living space and the backyard common property. We thus retained our privacy in the apartment and the continued use of The Yard, the only luxury we as tenants enjoyed, a sort of free recreational locale for the downtrodden.

My junior high and high school years were marked by continual battles with the landlady. We were paying so little for our rent-controlled apartment that she was motivated to do everything she could, be it legal or extra-legal, to force us out. The couple on the second floor acceded to Mrs. Mittler. One could not help noticing how affable they became with her, flashing smiles and mouthing pleasantries every time their paths crossed. My parents steadfastly refused to ingratiate themselves to this domineering woman who tried to do us in at every turn, someone that had all the earmarks of a transsexual Hitler sans mustache. They both averted their eyes from The Witch every time they happened to pass in the hallway or on the street and spoke to her only in response to something related to the building.

In the years before I joined the Army, Mrs. Mittler took us to court several times, trumping up one charge after another. She blamed me for vandalism, claimed my parents were undesirable tenants, or invoked some law or legal privilege that gave an owner the right to evict renters at will. My parents fought back, answering tit-for-tat, inconveniencing themselves with court appearances and once suffering the loss of my father's pay for a day. We won every legal action brought against us.

Mrs. Mittler did not stop with us, however. She tried to force the former landlord out of the store. She thought he too was paying too little rent or perhaps she wanted to remodel the whole ground floor for some other business purpose. Not the contentious type, he took it personally.

"What am I to do?" I overheard him say to my mother more than once. "I never should have sold Mrs. Mittler the building. She promised me I could keep the store."

My mother had no advice for the poor man. The store was his only livelihood and she had no knowledge of the law in these matters. Sadly, our former landlord died of a heart attack at age forty-four a month before I left home to go into the Army. He predeceased his septuagenarian father who now milled about in the store like a puppy dog without its master.

During high school it was a struggle for me to live in that apartment. I shared a room with my grandfather, had no desk or private place to study, and using the kitchen table for doing my homework was always uncomfortable for me. In my last year I planned to go to college and I hoped my parents would soon move to a larger apartment. Even though we were winning the court battles, my mother was desperately trying to find something for us. But we had nowhere else to go.

I felt I had to get away from home and the Army seemed the way out for me since I had to serve at some point anyway. My parents signed for me as I was not yet eighteen. To their credit, they never encouraged me to enlist or to move out of the household just to ease the burden on the family.

Halfway through basic training at Fort Dix, I got my first weekend pass. For someone who joined the Army to escape, I was now homesick and tripping all over myself to return. It felt strange coming to the neighborhood in uniform, a seventeen-year-old boy turned soldier for all to see. It was a Saturday afternoon and, much to my surprise, no one answered my knock at the door. I then went around to the store so I could get into the apartment. The widow of the former landlord was now working there. She was noticeably thinner and I'll never forget the forlorn look on her face. I wanted to say something to her other than ask if I could go through, to tell her how sorry I was that her husband died, that I knew Mrs. Mittler had contributed to his premature death, but I said nothing about such matters.

The apartment seemed even smaller upon seeing it for the first time since I left home. What did we win in court? I wondered. Was it the right to live in a hole-in-the-wall and be tormented by the owner? Later that day, Frau Hitler saw me in the hallway and looked angrily at me.

The opportunity to move finally came a year after I went into the Army. The elderly couple living in the apartment on the top floor of the adjacent building was planning to retire to Florida. My mother engaged the assistance of this next-door neighbor, a Landsmann of hers, and he pleaded our case to the landlord. He needed to return to New York a few times for a day or two in the coming year, and my mother promised to put him up. The landlord let us have the apartment for the same rent, sixty-five dollars a month, as we did not ask for any improvements. My mother was ecstatic. We also promised the neighbor, as a favor, to keep the boarder who had been living there for years. We certainly could spare one room out of seven, the man always took his meals out, and his twenty-two dollars made the higher housing cost more affordable. Overnight my mother was transformed from a struggling housewife into a landlady of sorts herself.

We moved next door in July when I was home on leave. I had just graduated from radar school and received my orders for Fort Ord. It took a whole day to carry all the furniture and packed grocery boxes from one building to the next and up two flights of stairs. When everything was in the new apartment, including the larger and more modern refrigerator we bought, I looked around but my mother was nowhere to be seen.

"Where's Mama?" I asked my father.

"Probably in the other building," he said.

I went back to the old apartment and found my mother standing in the middle of the darkened main room. She would not respond to anything I said. I just stood alone with her in the empty space for a few minutes. I practically had to force her from her home of almost seventeen years. This was the last time I would ever be in the surroundings I joined the Army to get away from.

My mother cried as I led her out of the old apartment. No one in my family would ever again have to deal with the likes of a Frau Hitler.

# CHAPTER 5: PARTING WORDS

Richie was waiting for me in the hallway at the bottom of the stairs. He was shivering and was noticeably out of breath, apparently from running down the three flights of stairs in his building and then across the street. He was wearing nothing over his T-shirt save his Eisenhower jacket, unbuttoned all the way to his waist. I could see the impression on his sleeves where the single stripe had been removed. Small pieces of white thread revealed a tri angular pattern on his left shoulder, the place where the Seventh Army patch was once sewn.

"Hey, Davey. Let me help you." Richie reached for the AWOL bag and then took it from my hand. He walked to the door first, opened it, and held it for me. The numbers 2214 in black painted on the glass above the doorway, appearing backwards from inside the building, stood out amid the bright white light coming through.

Once on the sidewalk I instinctively looked to my left, toward the building next door where I had lived for most of my life. There was no one on that side of the block on this cold morning. I half expected to see Mrs. Mittler either looking out from an open window on the second floor or standing in the doorway gleefully shouting auf Wiedersehen to me.

Richie and I turned and walked toward 22nd Street, where the bus stop was. "Why did you leave me at the girl's place?" I asked. "I thought you'd wait for me."

"You didn't need me anymore. Besides," he said indifferently, shrugging his shoulders slightly, "I had to see somebody."

"Who was that girl?"

"Some spic chic just come from PR."

"I mean, how do you know her?"

"I know her."

"Is she a hooker?" I asked innocently, as if it made a difference.

"Don't worry about it. I took care of it."

"She was very good."

"She give you a trip around the world?"

"Yeah. I really needed it. But I'll be horny as hell again by the time I get to Germany."

"Don't worry about it," my friend repeated. "The frauleins will be

46

looking for you."

We passed a barbershop, a fruit and vegetable store, a hardware store, a luncheonette with a newspaper stand in front, and a corner grocery store. We crossed 22nd Street and waited near the corner. To avoid the cold and wind, we stood in the doorway of the still closed shoe store and waited for the Mermaid Avenue bus. Richie had a gleam of anticipation in his eyes I had never seen before.

"I got something to tell you before you take off," my friend said at last.

Richie stared at me eerily. He was the type of person who seldom was serious about anything. The determined look on his face caused me to take notice.

We must have looked odd next to each other that morning on the street, representatives of the old and the new Army, Richie in his olive drab waist-length jacket and brown boots and I in my green uniform with its longer jacket and black boots. Right after I enlisted the Army began issuing the new greens instead of the old OD's. Dressed to current regulations and with a packed duffel bag at my feet, I was looking like a soldier for the first time in weeks. Richie was disheveled and wearing the footwear color and top piece of the Army's uniform that were both slated for discontinuance in the near future.

Richie and I were two different types of soldiers in what was called, euphemistically it seemed, the peacetime Army. Richie was "US," a draftee in the U.S. Army, while I was "RA," an enlistee in the Regular Army. These two-letter designations were used as prefixes for serial numbers and served, immediately and unquestionably, to differentiate soldiers in terms of both their mode of entry into the Army and the time they had to serve.

"What's that?" I put to Richie, surprised by his sudden and uncharacteristic seriousness. I turned to face him and did not take my eyes off of him.

"It's important," he said. Richie still had that somber look about him and he seemed uncomfortable standing in the cold not fully dressed.

I peered at my friend in the old Army uniform and colors. He was still in the Reserves and had to play soldier one weekend a month and go to a training camp with his unit for one month a year during the summer. I knew he did not like to do this but he had no choice in the matter. His total commitment, and mine, was for six years.

"Is it about that girl last night?" I wanted to tell him how I felt about her, that she pleased me greatly, that I really liked her, but he responded too quickly for me.

"Forget that Spanish slut," Richie countered in a forceful and urgent tone, perhaps aware that the bus should be coming soon.

My longtime friend was normally crude, but now the crudeness was more than necessary and I began to pay more attention to him. Evidently he wanted to tell me something he believed was signif-Icant to my departure. "Is it about Germany?" I asked.

"About the girls you'll meet in Germany."

"What about them?" I had no idea what he was working up to tell me.

"I got some advice for you," he said.

"What kind of advice?" I braced myself for some kind of earth-shaking news or morsel of criticism about my life or ways.

"Advice you should take."

I had never seen Richie so serious. He was the most cavalier person I knew.

"Don't get married," Richie blurted out after a short pause. The icy, unflinching look I was given signaled it was unnecessary for him to repeat himself.

I looked straight at my friend. I did not miss the meaning of what he just said but I did not comment on it. A blank expression on my face I must have had.

"Don't come back with a Nazi schatzie," he added, driving his point home.

Richie voiced a term I had not heard before. From the intonation and symbolism, I had no doubt it was one that was appropriated by American soldiers to characterize German women in an uncompli-mentary manner. The directness and simplicity of his advice, or warning I should say, stunned me. He might just as well have prefaced his remarks by saying "Achtung." The way Schatzie, a word I was unfamiliar with, rhymed with Nazi, both having the harsh *tz* sound, rendered my friend's utterance all the more forebod-ing.

Why did Richie think I might get married in Germany? He got up early that morning, telephoned me, dressed hurriedly, ran out into the street, met me in the hallway of my building, and waited for a bus in the cold with me for more than ten minutes. What possessed my boyhood pal to go to such lengths just to tell me something he should have realized I already know? Richie knew I wanted to go to college when I got out. How could he believe I would jeopardize my future by coming home at age twenty with a wife to support?

It should have occurred to me that Richie, having just returned from Germany, was trying to tell me something about intimate encounters over there. It should have occurred to me that he knew more about a soldier's weaknesses and proclivities toward women than I did at this time in my life.

I had no thoughts whatsoever about marriage to a German girl, or any girl for that matter. I had no desire to go down the path taken by many boys from the neighborhood. Not going to college, marrying a girl from the next block, taking an apartment near her parents, having children at an early age, and ending up in an uninteresting or low-paying job were all behavior patterns and life choices that were anathema to me. To think about bringing home a Gentile, let alone German, wife was nothing short of preposterous to me.

The Mermaid Avenue bus pulled up and I got on. There was no time to respond to Richie's surprise comment about marriage. I was sure he knew I understood what he said. My friend and now overseas counselor took my duffel bag and lifted it to the second step. I turned around to get my bag and faced him once more. He waved to me, still with a serious tinge in his eyes. I put a dime and nickel in the coin box and looked for a seat.

Richie's parting words were the last I heard before I left home.

## CHAPTER 6: LAST EXIT FROM BROOKLYN

There were few passengers on the bus this time of morning. I could have sat almost anywhere but I took a seat in the last row, with its continuous seat cushion the full width of the bus, in order to keep my two bags stretched out next to me. I looked out the rear window and waved goodbye to Richie again. His six-foot frame, normally quite impressive, became dwarfed as we pulled away.

It was difficult for me to relax for I would be getting off in just four stops. As the bus neared 21st Street I instinctively looked to my left, toward the house where I had been earlier that morning in bed with the puertorriqueña. In alternating shifts I looked out through windows on both sides of the bus, to shops and stores and apartment buildings on the street that was the life-blood of my neighborhood. Mermaid Avenue was the main artery of the residential area adjacent to the amusement area, running parallel to and between Neptune Avenue to the north and Surf Avenue to the south.

The bus came to 19th Street. I again turned to my left to see halfway down the block the public school I had attended until the sixth grade, and on the corner the Catholic Church I went into once when Richie had his Confirmation. For a Jewish boy not quite eleven it was a strange and unnerving experience to look at stained-glass windows of people with wings and halos, statues of a woman with a baby, people dipping their hands in a water receptacle and then crossing themselves, and a large cross with a man hanging from it in outstretched arms and crossed feet.

In passing 19th, an unmarked boundary of sorts was crossed, the edge of the Italian district. Like the fabled marine creature, Mermaid had two different parts to its body, two largely segregated ethnic groups.

The complexion of the neighborhood was changing at that time. Schwarzers were moving into the West 30s, especially between Mermaid and Surf, to streets that contained many summer bungalows and substandard housing units, closer, ironically, to hoity-toity Sea Gate. Puerto Ricans were taking the basements of two- and three-family brick houses, often hastily converted into apartments, on streets all through the West 20s from Neptune to Surf. Mermaid Avenue was conspicuously still white. The Italians preserved the character of their part of the neighborhood east of 19th Street by steadfastly refusing to rent to the darker newcomers. Many longtime residents, Jewish more so than Italian, were moving out of the neighborhood, to Flatbush and other nicer sections of Brooklyn. Some of our neighbors were waiting to move into apartments in the new Luna Park Houses under construction around West 10th and 12th.

The bus stopped at 16th Street, in front of the haberdashery on the corner where I bought shirts when there was a sale. As we approached 15th Street I could see the Carolina Restaurant on my left, just before Stillwell Avenue. I had never eaten there but I heard people say it was famous for serving some of the best Italian food in New York.

Before reaching the subway station, the bus stopped on the corner of Stillwell. It was only to let passengers off. No one paid a fare just to cross the street. The bus stop was in front of the Terminal Hotel, a large three-story white-and-green building known to all who were not blind as a home and hangout for derelicts, alcoholics, drug addicts, and prostitutes. The block that extended from the entrance of the hotel all the way to Surf was known as the Skid Row of the neighborhood.

I did not have to see the Terminal Hotel and accompanying Skid Row on the morning I was leaving for Germany to remind me that one of the reasons I joined the Army was to get away from all this. I planned to move out of the neighborhood as soon as I graduated from college.

The Mermaid Avenue bus jerked into the Stillwell Avenue subway station and I got off. With duffel bag on one shoulder and AWOL bag in other hand, I walked up a few steps and then a long incline leading to the trains. At the top of the incline I turned and walked under the hanging sign for the IND Line. I went up the full set of stairs to the D train. Once on the platform I dropped my two bags and stood in front of the free standing, two-sided white sign that identified both the subway stop and my neighborhood. I looked at the words **CONEY ISLAND** in bold black letters.

From the platform I could see the Terminal Hotel, the rundown portion of Stillwell Avenue, the Loew's Theater on the corner of Surf, and Nathan's across the street from it. Even this early in the morning, a crowd of hungry people blocked passage on the sidewalk in front of the famous hot dog establishment. Easily visible in the distance were the Wonder Wheel and the Parachute, giant attractions now stilled and muted. During the winter months, almost every amusement or ride or food or game concession in Coney Island was closed. Along Surf Avenue and the numbered side streets, West 8th to 19th from Surf to the Boardwalk, every small business stand was boarded up tight. The whole area had an eerie quality to it. It became a winter ghost town, an urban core abandoned by its people in cold weather.

I could also see the small wooden shack, open all year round, on Stillwell Avenue between Surf and the Boardwalk, a section of street that had been widened considerably. The red, white, and blue sign in front read "U.S. Army Recruiting Station." During my senior year in high school, I often got off the Surf Avenue bus at Stillwell, to stop in and talk to the sergeant on duty. He was a tall, thin E-6 with a southern drawl and fake smile who only spoke of the Army and its enlistment programs in positive terms. It was there that I fell prey to a veteran noncom's pitch, not unlike the ballyhoo of every sidewalk barker in the amusement section.

The D train noisily rolled in to the platform on which I was standing. It stopped and made a loud hissing sound like an emission of gas or smoke. The doors opened and several people got out. I entered the train toward the front and sat down on the right side by a window facing the Parachute and Nathan's. No one else boarded the car I was in. About five minutes later the train pulled out. In silence I said goodbye to Coney Island.

The elevated track ran along Surf Avenue to West 8th Street, the first stop. The train moved slowly. Directly beneath me, West 10th to 12th from Surf to Neptune, once was the location of Luna Park, the most innovative of Coney's amusement parks. I thought about that day in 1949 when I and two friends left P.S. 80 at lunchtime, ran to the subway terminal, and witnessed the last of a series of fires that swept through Luna and destroyed it  "The Heart of Coney Island," as the park was called and spelled out within a large heart-shaped red sign above the entrance, was broken.

At the 8th Street stop, I could see the Cyclone roller coaster diagonally across the street. It cost a quarter to ride, compared to ten cents for the bumping cars or the carousel, and I had been on it many times. The station had a sign with an arrow pointing to the New York Aquarium that opened the same month I graduated from high school and went in the Army. The Aquarium was on a patch of land that embraced the most ambitious and esthetically appealing of the amusement parks fifty years earlier. Between 5th and 8th Streets, from Surf Avenue to the Atlantic Ocean, stood Dreamland, the "Gibraltar of the Amusement World" as it was dubbed. The Dreamland fire on Memorial Day in 1911 was a turning point, the beginning of a long period of decline for the world's most famous resort and amusement center.

After 8th Street the elevated train curved around to the left, heading north to Manhattan. I could see the old Luna Park site being cleared for new high-rise buildings. A little farther up on my right was a vast expanse of ramshackle bungalows and dilapidated small houses. The area contained mainly nonwhite welfare families and extended from 8th Street to Ocean Parkway, north of Neptune Avenue to just before the Belt Parkway. I used to pass through this transient district each morning riding the Surf Avenue bus on my way to Lincoln High. There was talk that the city planned to relocate these poor people, bulldoze the whole area, and erect more and taller middle-income cooperative apartment buildings. Once completed, both developments could signal another turnaround for my neighborhood, a better Coney Island in the future.

The elevated train continued on its way to Manhattan. When we passed over the Belt we officially departed Coney Island. A number of stops later the elevation declined and we traveled at ground level. In mid-Brooklyn, the train finally bored underground. The lights occasionally went off for five or ten seconds at a time. I turned my head to look through the window and saw a perfect likeness of myself in the glass. The darkness of the tunnel outside the train caused the ghostly reflection.

I thought of this special moment, my last exit from Brooklyn, and how I must have appeared to the people sitting next to me. Was I not more than a young soldier with all his gear in two bags marching off to serve his country in some unknown Army installation? one could have asked. Who is this teen G.I.? Where is he going? How long will he stay there? Who will he meet? These were all mysteries to the strangers around me. Present environs aside, I was as much in the dark as they were.

The train pulled into the West 4th Street/Washington Square underground station. The D line I was on ran along Sixth Avenue in Manhattan, two avenues away from where I was headed. I carried my bags and walked up two flights of stairs to transfer to the A train, which geared over and ran along Eighth Avenue. I stepped into the crowded A train, an express, and stood by the door, bags touching my feet. I looked down at my bags continually and never released physical contact with them. The 42nd Street station was soon upon me. I forced my way through the incoming passengers to get out the doors.

I carried my bags with both hands while in the crowded station. A shoulder mount for the duffel would have given me less visibility to find my way and could have knocked into people's heads. I walked in the direction of the signs for Port Authority Bus Terminal.

# CHAPTER 7: ANNA'S SIDE OF THE WORLD

Mrs. Mittler was not the first German or first victim of the Nazis I came into contact with when I was growing up. That distinction belongs to the little refugee girl I knew in elementary school. I thought of her the day I left home en route to the country she came from.

Many Jewish families settled in Coney Island after the war, a number of them within a block or two from where I lived. They came primarily from Eastern Europe—Poland, Hungary, Romania, Czechoslovakia, Lithuania—but some were of German or Austrian stock. What these people all had in common was that they were in concentration camps during the war and DP camps after the war. They lived in Germany for a few years until their cases were heard and then received reparations from the new German government for the loss of loved ones and suffering they endured. Some refugees used the reparation money to purchase businesses and buildings along Mermaid Avenue. Others did not own any property, were less conspicuous to neighbors, and lived quietly on one of the side streets in a furnished room or small apartment.

In habits and behavior this group of Jews seemed different from my parents and grandparents and others like they who emigrated one, two, and even three decades before the war. It was said that refugees were tight with money and less-than-sympathetic to fellow Jews. From the talk I overheard, people assumed that during the war they betrayed friends and neighbors in order to save themselves or loved ones.

I first heard the word "mocky" used in reference to these postwar foreigners, in a derogatory way by Jews who had been American citizens for some time and also by Gentiles. I was sure the ethnic slur attached to them was due to a mixture of envy and resentment, as most were or were thought to be financially better off than the rest of us in the neighborhood. On warm days, when short-sleeve shirts or sleeveless dresses were commonly worn, I could visibly set mockies apart from other Jews, not to mention Gentiles, by the numbers tattooed on their forearms.

I became aware of the war and its victims and survivors at about age eight or nine. Until that time I knew only that I was from an immigrant family and that being Jewish meant some people did not like me. My mother was always talking about Poland after the first war, the persecutions against the Jews in her shtetl, the voyage on the ship to America, and her going to night school to learn English. She spoke of Hitler and the Nazis in one breath, and in another of her maternal grandmother the family left behind in 1927 when they emigrated and never heard from again after Poland was invaded by Germany in 1939. Little by little I began to understand that some-thing terrible happened to the Jews on the other side of the world although I could not quite put my finger on it.

The film *The Search* with Montgomery Clift put it all together for me. Seeing all those orphaned children from various countries speaking different languages, left alive in Germany after hostilities ended with no place to go and no one to care for them, helped me grasp the consequences of the war. I was the same age as many of the boys and girls shown living in the DP camps. Had my mother's family not emigrated before Hitler came to power, I could have been one of them.

One day in September 1950, my sixth-grade teacher left the classroom for a couple of minutes. Through the half-glass door, I saw the principal in the hall motion her to come out. The teacher returned holding the hand of a rosy-cheeked little girl dressed in a beige sweater and dark plaid skirt. She had brown hair parted on the side but in an angle, a somewhat different style than the other girls in the class. There was both an innocence and sweetness about her. The girl had a dazed look in her eyes and she stood partially behind the teacher, tugging at the long pleated dress.

"This is Anna," the teacher said, facing all the children and then looking down for a moment at the card she brought back into the classroom with her. "Anna just came over from Germany. She'll be in this class for the rest of the school year. She doesn't speak any English so help her along and make her feel welcome."

My classmates and I all looked at the girl and the teacher standing up front but said nothing. Then the teacher looked my way.

"David," she called out with her strong voice and eyes piercing at me. "Anna lives on your block." I suddenly remembered seeing, when I left my house earlier that day, some pieces of furniture on the sidewalk across the street next to a parked moving van. "Would you walk her home after school? She doesn't know the way."

I took the teacher's request as a directive and did not ask to be released from it. But I was not sure I looked forward to my new role as neighborhood guide for lost children. Later some of the boys in the class kidded me about being chosen to walk a girl home, a greenhorn no less.

That afternoon I walked with Anna the four blocks to our homes. I did most of the talking. How much she understood, I could not tell. When we came to Mermaid Avenue, I pointed to Steeplechase a block away on Surf and told her what a wonderful amusement park it was. She noticed the tall Parachute ride and looked up in amazement. On 20th and Mermaid there was a candy store with freezers out in front on the street. I bought Anna an Italian ice with the nickel my mother gave me for milk that I did not buy that day.

"Danke," she said, when I handed her the little white paper cup.

When we reached 21st Street I pointed to the synagogue around the corner and referred to it as a shul, the Yiddish word. She turned to me and smiled at my utterance, no doubt interpreting it as Schul in German. Finally, we came to 2215 Mermaid Avenue, the building next to Richie's. The moving van was gone and there was no furniture on the sidewalk.

"Komm ins Haus?" Anna asked me, motioning to me with one hand and opening the outside door with the other. I understood she was asking me to come into her house.

I walked into the hallway with the little girl, up three steps to the ground floor and then up a full flight of steps to the first floor. Her apartment was in the rear of the building. The door was unlocked and she led me inside. A woman came out from the kitchen, wiping her hands in an apron. Anna ran over to her, hugged her, and started talking in German, looking back and forth to me several times. Anna seemed excited about my presence in her new home. The woman then came over to me. She spoke in English, much to my surprise.

"I am Anna's mother. Thank you for showing her the way home from school."

"I live across the street . . . in twenty-two sixteen."

"What is your name?" I was asked.

"David."

"David what?"

"David Streiber."

"Streiber is a German name."

"Yes, I know," I said.

"It could mean a striver, someone who strives."

I just looked at her. I did not comprehend what she was saying.

"Do you know German?" she then asked.

"No. Only some Yiddish."

"Yiddish is similar to German."

"Yes, I know," I said again.

"Then I am sure you will understand Anna and I want her to learn English from you . . . and from the other children."

Anna came over to me with a plate full of cookies she picked up from the kitchen counter and held it out. "Hier, nimm, bitte," she said.

I took a cookie and said "Thank you."

"Would you like a glass of milk?" Anna's mother asked me.

"No, thank you. I have to go home now. I have to watch my little sister while my mother goes shopping."

"Can you come again tomorrow morning, to show Anna the way to school?"

"Yes, I will come." With that commitment established, I said goodbye to my new friend and her nice mother.

I lost no time telling my mother about my walking a German girl home from school, meeting her English-speaking mother, and eating a cookie at her house across the street. My mother already knew about the new family from a neighbor.

As it turned out, I only had to walk Anna to school a few times. Before long, she was walking the four blocks each day with two girls who also lived on the block but were in different sixth-grade classes. Anna made few friends among the girls. It was I, her first contact at school, gender difference notwithstanding, whom she took to. I sensed Anna needed someone her own age to help her adjust to the New World. I learned later I may have reminded her of someone she knew in the Old. I felt sorry for her. With her accent and sweet appearance, I projected onto Anna an image of what my mother might have been like as a young girl in Europe.

Anna's apartment was small, only three rooms, but big enough for two people. It was sparsely furnished, nothing fancy. If her mother had received reparation money, she apparently was saving it for a later day. Anna slept on a convertible couch in the living room, her mother in the only bedroom. The apartment was always dark. Its windows faced the backyard and the airshaft that connected with the adjacent building prevented much sunlight from entering. Anna and I were often alone together in her apartment after school.

Anna's mother was thirty-five, two years younger than my mother, but had a more youthful appearance despite having been in a concentration camp. She dressed in more modern styles of clothing than my mother, but like my mother never wore jewelry. From what I observed and from what my mother told me, Anna's mother was very well liked in the neighborhood. She always spoke Yiddish to my mother and the older Eastern European Jews, and slowly began speaking English to Anna in public. I never heard her speak German in the street to anyone other than her daughter and only when it was necessary. There were some German-speaking Jews on the block but she spoke to them in English, refusing, I once heard her say, to speak the language of the murderers. Anna's mother worked for a lawyer in Manhattan who did war-related international cases. She did not get home until dinnertime.

Anna's mother also came from Poland. However, unlike my mother, she did not grow up in a shtetl in the Pale of Jewish Settlement. Her family lived in Cracow, a big city in Galicia, the region formerly held by Austria before the first war. She went to a secular school and, besides Yiddish, spoke Polish and German. In 1932, at age seventeen, she moved to Berlin to study at the university. There she met a young law student and fell in love, a German Jew with a Gentile grandparent. They married in 1935, unaffected by the law passed that year prohibiting marriage and extramarital relations between Jews and Germans.

In 1938 Jews were not allowed to practice law in Germany and Anna's father then had to work in his family's clothing business. Anna and her twin brother were born in February of the following year, the same day that an ordinance was issued calling for the confiscation of gold and valuables owned by Jews. When Anna was about a year old, by order of the German government, her parents' food ration cards had to be stamped with the letter *J*, which meant, of course, less food could be purchased. Anna's father tried to secure four exit visas but was unsuccessful. No country, the United States especially, wanted to get involved with Hitler and the looming war and refused take in Jewish refugees from German-occupied lands. By mid-1941 Jewish emigration from Germany was strictly verboten, against the law. Later that year, Jews in Germany and Austria were required to wear armbands with the Star of David. Mass deportations of Deutschen Juden soon followed.

The end of 1942 brought disaster to Anna's family. Her father and brother were deported to Auschwitz in Poland while she and her mother were sent by boxcar to Ravensbrück north of Berlin, the only all women's concentration camp. The little girl not yet four shared a straw bunk with her mother in Block 12 near the barbed wire fence and the cremation ovens. Anna's mother was forced to work in the Siemens factory located just south of the campsite alongside the railroad line.

In early 1945 gas chambers were constructed at Ravensbrück. The story around the neighborhood was that Anna and her mother survived because the gas chambers were not functioning on the two days prior to the liberation of their camp by the Red Army. The father and brother did not survive.

After V-E Day, Anna and her mother were sent to the Düppel Center, a DP camp in the U.S. zone of occupation in divided Berlin. About half the inmates were Gentiles—Poles, Lithuanians, Latvians, Estonians, Ukrainians, and Yugoslavs—some of whom had collaborated with the Nazis and were afraid to go back to their home country and others who just did not wish to live under the new Communist rule. Conflicts soon erupted between both groups of DPs living side-by-side in the camp.

In early 1946, separate DP camps were established for Jewish refugees. Anna and her mother were transferred to the Bergen-Belsen DP camp in the British zone. The former concentration camp was now being used to house and repatriate Jewish survivors of Nazi atrocities. Inmates were not allowed to leave the camp for fear that they would attack the local German population. They had no method of contacting relatives. They stayed in the barracks, had no work to do, and wore their former concentration camp uniforms, the striped pajamas, or the Wehrmacht and SS uniforms given to them.

The DP camp had a barbed wire fence around it and was patrolled by armed guards, some of whom were ex-Nazis. Jewish DPs often said "We were liberated, but we are not free."

Anna's mother did not wish to return to Poland because of the outbreak of anti-Semitism and violence against Jews there right after the war. She claimed German citizenship under her husband's status and the fact that she had lived for years in Germany before the war. With the fall of the Third Reich, Anna was no longer a legal pariah in the land of her birth. Eventually, they were allowed to leave the DP camp and take up residency in a German town. Anna's mother chose not to remain in Germany and help rebuild the society that killed her husband and son and from which she and her daughter narrowly escaped death. As soon as permission was granted, they immigrated to the United States.

It took about six months for Anna to learn English to the point where she could carry on a decent conversation with someone. She was not the loquacious type, however, even when her language skills improved a great deal. The foreign girl was quiet and reserved, not at all boisterous like some other girls in the class. There was a pleasant quality about her, something that could not always be said about her American counterparts. At school, she usually sat at her desk with hands clasped and paid close attention to the teacher, behavior I myself did not have a reputation for. In class discussions Anna participated little. I could not help noticing that she often kept her right hand over her left forearm, covering up the blue five-digit number. Her fingers fidgeted with pencils or erasers or anything else she happened to be holding.

In school or out, Anna never talked about her brother or father. She never talked about anything at all related to Germany, the war, concentration camps, or DP camps. Every time I looked at her, I could see sadness in her eyes and I thought how different she was from her American-born peers. I also sensed Anna fashioned a kind of protective veil around herself to mask the unspeakable human suffering she undoubtedly witnessed and experienced. Once, inadvertently, I said something about where she used to live and she immediately became frightened and pulled away from me. I thought she was going to cry, but she did not shed a tear. I never broached the subject of her past again. What I heard about Anna and her family came from the idle talk of my mother and neighbors that I was privy to.

Anna was almost a year older than I but, since she was on the short side, seemed the same age as the other girls in the class. The principal purposely left her back a year to give her time to learn English.

Anna turned twelve that year in sixth grade. I was not, of course, unaware of her developing body. She often wore a small-sized sweater that drew attention to her budding breasts. I very much wanted to touch them. It was with this German girl that I had my first puerile sexual encounters.

Anna and I had normal curiosities about each other's body parts and functions, curiosities that seemed to surface as soon as we found ourselves alone together in her apartment. Once, when I had to go to the bathroom, the door was left ajar accidentally. I could see over my shoulder that she was standing in the doorway watching me unzip, pee, and zip up. What I was doing no doubt was a great mystery to a young girl.

Another time, when I just finished peeing, Anna stood behind me and asked, "I can see what you have?"

I thought she was making a statement but then I realized she could not see my front and was actually asking a question. "If you show me what you have," I said. I did not know where this strange conversation was going, but obviously I was not displeased that Anna and I were now involved in an intimate verbal exchange, opening up I presumed the possibility for me to explore, if not satisfy, the sexual instincts I felt at that age.

"First you."

I hesitated a moment, then responded, "Okay," believing that what she was proposing was fair. Boys should take the lead in these matters, I thought. I then turned around toward her slowly, my zipper still down. I was hanging out but I did not look at myself. Instead, I looked straight at Anna and saw her lower her head and eyes, gazing expressionless upon me.

"Now it's your turn," I said, trying not to sound threatening to my demure and shy female friend, but nevertheless asking for what I thought she just consented to.

This time it was Anna who hesitated, and for a little longer, all the while looking at me in the eye, even when I zipped up. Then she took a step backward and pulled up her dress. She just stood there, hands up in the air, clutching the hem in two places, like I was a robber taking something valuable from her.

"Don't I get to see more?" I inquired.

"No."

"Why not?" I said, now feeling cheated, but not wishing to upset her.

"Because I not want to."

I let it go at that. I did not insist on the reciprocity I believed we agreed to. But, I felt it was not fair for me to have to show her more than she showed me in return. At age eleven I had an early lesson in female modesty and control. I wondered what allure lay beneath that little pink garment.

Anna became my prepubescent erotic consort. I would think about her when I was not with her and anticipated being alone with her again in her apartment. I was willing to pay the higher price she exacted from me for her participation in our secret liaisons. After a few months of just show and half-show, there came a time when our childish sexual experimentation, undeniably bad and verboten in any country, progressed to a higher level.

"I can touch you?" Anna asked one day.

By now I was used to her grammatical inversions and understood she was asking me a question. I looked at her for a moment, not knowing if I was interpreting her meaning correctly. "Where?" I questioned.

"Where you know."

"Down here?" I lowered my hand to my crotch.

"Yes."

I moved over to where she was standing and pulled my trousers and underwear down to just above my knees. I acted quickly, eager to set myself up for her foray into my private part, willing to accommodate whatever action she had in mind, not waiting to gain any commitment from her for reciprocity.

Anna reached with her right hand and touched me timidly, using only the tips of her fingers. I felt an initial sting, almost an electric shock, an exciting moment that roiled my emotions too. It seemed unreal, this first physical intimacy with a girl.

"Now I want to touch you," I said, pulling away from her slightly.

The German girl thought for a moment, then stepped back and sat down on the couch. She leaned her head on the pillow against the armrest, pulled up her skirt, and lifted her left leg up onto the couch, keeping the other foot on the floor. I sat down in the space between her legs, my trousers still down, feeling nervous as well as embarrassed.

I placed my hand near her crotch slowly, fearful that she might suddenly cry or scream or push me away. Anna did not move or say anything. She just looked at me. I then ran my fingers up and down her center, more excited by the thought of what I was doing than by actually touching female flesh. At that age, I knew what a girl looked like down below but not what it felt like. I dared not ask her to take off her underpants, so I began to work my fingers underneath instead.

"Nein," she gasped suddenly as she forced my hand away. I understood her in any language. For the little refugee girl who thought in German, I had gone too far.

Anna got up from the couch and pulled her skirt down. She looked away from me but I could see her face was flushed. I knew Anna was insecure and I suppose I should not have taken advantage of her, but it was *she* who initiated the encounter. And of her own accord she spread out on the couch and picked up her skirt. My conscience may not have been completely clear, but I had no overwhelming sense of guilt for having done anything wrong. I was only sorry I had not touched her on top first.

After the couch affair, Anna and I ceased playing our juvenile game of doctor-and-patient in alternating roles. Somehow we just stopped without our ever discussing it. I wanted to continue, of course, as I never got to touch in the flesh what girls had down there. For that realization to come my way, I would have to wait another four years.

Anna and her mother moved out of the neighborhood at the end of the school term, less than a year after they came. No one on the block knew for sure where they went to. I never saw or spoke to Anna again, although I did think of her often. I always retained a certain fondness for the girl who introduced me to her side of the world.

Two months later, another postwar refugee from Germany entered my life, this time someone who would be feared and hated.

It was probably a good thing Anna and her mother no longer were on the block when Mrs. Mittler bought and moved into my building. I shudder at the thought of little Anna coming into my hallway to knock on my door and Frau Hitler suddenly frightening the shy twelve-year-old with remonstrations and commands in German.

There surely would have been fireworks on the street if Mrs. Mittler and Anna's mother ever happened to meet. One can only wonder what open exchange of insults might have transpired between the obdurate old German Jewess who exuded a quasi-Nazi demeanor and the enlightened Polish Jewess half her age who turned her back on the German people she knew and language she spoke.

## CHAPTER 8: TERMINAL ENCOUNTER

The Port Authority Bus Terminal was exceedingly crowded this hour of the morning. I stood for a moment in the center of the first floor, trying to locate the ticket counter. In the immense space I watched people around me hurriedly walking in every direction, crisscrossing the promenade, brushing up against each other as they passed. Boys and girls in their late teens or early twenties were out of breath and slightly hunched from the school bags and knapsacks weighing on their backs. A troupe of nuns in black habits struggled with their small suitcases in a slow and steady march. Young men in military uniforms breezed by me, sometimes two or three abreast, talking loudly, oblivious to anyone near them. A salt-and-pepper Mutt and Jeff janitorial team wielding broom and basket effortlessly swooshed along the floor's middle corridor picking up butts and bits.

A heavily rouged white woman around thirty, wearing a short pleated skirt with wide belt buckle, a jacket swung over her shoulder, nonchalantly walked up to me. "Want a date, soldier?"

"No," I said simply, without giving it any thought.

It looked as though she was going to say something else, perhaps name a price or describe services, but she just turned around and sauntered through the Terminal. I watched her as she approached a marine and then two sailors, one of whom walked off with her.

I saw the Greyhound booth off to the side and walked toward it with my two bags in tow. "One way to Fort Dix," I said to the ticket clerk.

"That'll be three-twenty."

I handed the clerk a five dollar bill. Through an opening in the glass barrier he slid a ticket in a small envelope towards me, then a single dollar and change. "What time's the next bus?"

"Eleven thirty."

"Where do I get it?" I asked.

"Gate thirty-nine. Downstairs . . . to the right."

I had more than an hour's wait. There was a glass-enclosed waiting room at the other end of the floor. Lifting my bags again, I went to it. I took a seat near a corner, away from the other travelers. It was warm inside and I removed my round dress hat, the new dark green color of my Class A's, and olive drab overcoat. I kept the

66

duffel bag on the floor between my feet and put the AWOL bag on the bench beside me. A discarded folded *Daily Mirror* lay on the seat in front of me. I claimed it and read for a while. My mind, however, was not on the news of the day.

Had Port Authority been my point of destination, instead of departure, I might have taken the young woman up on her proposition. With more time on my hands and blowing into town for the first time in months, I probably would have been more receptive to a five- or ten-buck casual encounter. I envisioned being led to a grimy room in a flea bag hotel on some side street off Eighth Avenue, handily kept no doubt for quickies with the volume of servicemen who pass through the Terminal every day. On this particular morning, even if there were hours before my bus's scheduled departure, I had no desire or compulsion to get into bed with a station-walker at least a decade my senior or anyone else for that matter. Fresh in my flesh and consciousness was the late-night rifle shooting that Richie targeted me for.

"Cigarette, buddy?" a deep voice called out on my left, interrupting my lack of concentration on the people around me.

I put the newspaper down I had only been glancing at. I turned and saw a fortyish white man sitting less than two feet from me. He was holding his hand out with a pack of Lucky Strikes, the tips of two cigarettes above the others. The stranger was ruddy complexioned and balding and had a small brown birthmark on his right cheek that was facing me. I noticed he had no bags or suitcases with him.

"I don't smoke," I answered.

"Take one or two anyway," he insisted. "For your buddies in the barracks."

"No thanks," I said warily.

I was unaccustomed to such friendliness in New York City. It must have been the uniform that invited conversation. I looked away but could still see him in my peripheral vision.

He retracted his hand and leaned back on the bench. I heard him exhale slightly as if he were annoyed that I did not play into his lame attempt to engage me in some kind of personal contact. He tried again a few minutes later.

"You in the Sixth Army?" He apparently saw the shoulder patch on my left sleeve with the six-pointed star.

"Not anymore."

"Oh, you shipped out?"

"Yes."

"Where were you in the Sixth?"

"Fort Ord."

"California?"

I nodded.

"Gee, that must've been nice," he commented childishly, turning away from me for a moment. "Never been to California myself."

I said nothing, hoping he would not ask me any more questions. I was in no mood for small talk with a total unknown.

"Where you headed?" he asked, ignoring my signal.

"Fort Dix," I said, not to be rude. I gave in to my better instincts.

"You gonna be parked there for a while?" he shot back, looking at the duffel bag on the floor. His Boston accent now came through.

"No. I'm going overseas. I'll be at Dix only a week or so."

"Where overseas?" he jumped in again, not giving me a chance to tell him of my own accord.

"Germany," I answered, after some hesitation.

"Oh," he said, this time sounding relieved, as though he finally hooked onto something. "I was there in forty-five and forty-six with the Third Division . . . in the south, near Ansbach. Our bombers destroyed half the city. Damn Gerries wouldn't surrender. Hitler ordered everyone to fight to the death."

"Sure, while he killed himself to avoid capture by the Russians," I commented sarcastically.

"The Nazi commanding general was taken prisoner by Ansbach's mayor and the resistance to stop the . . . ."

"Resistance?" I said, cutting him off. "In Germany?"

Something clicked as not right in my mind. I thought only countries *occupied* by the Germans had resistance movements. I turned to look at the stranger.

"Oh, yeah," he explained, now smiling assuredly at me. "Every Kraut city had a small group against the Nazis. In Ansbach they came out to assist the mayor with the surrender after we threatened another bombing attack."

Here I was learning interesting tidbits about the end of the war and

I had not yet set foot in Germany. To this last comment I did not respond.

"Where you going in Deutschland?" he soon added. Was he trying to impress me with his German or test me on mine?

"I don't know yet."

"What a time that was," he rattled on, clasping his hands behind his head and looking up. "German women were crawling all over us. First it was against regulations for G.I.s to fraternize with them but we did it anyway. If we got caught, to avoid punishment all we had to do was say they were DPs. Shoot, you could get a whole night of love for a Hershey bar and a can of soup."

I was not impressed with this stranger's characterization of the women I looked forward to meeting soon, perhaps even annoyed by his denigration of the seemingly not unreasonable things defeated people had to do to survive after a war.

"I suppose times were hard."

"The damn Gerries deserved hard times," he injected in a remonstrance manner, repeating a pet term of his. He took his hands down and looked at me.

"We're not fighting the Germans anymore. Now they're our allies. We need them to fight the Russians."

"Is that what the Army told you?" he said in a way that I might have thought insulted my intelligence.

I looked at him but did not say anything.

"Fifteen, twenty years ago the Germans were animals," he asserted, "worse than the Russians today. Look what they did in the war. They killed millions of soldiers and civilians and committed barbaric acts. And for what?"

He positioned his body closer to mine and then extended his head outward to read my nametag on the other side from where he was sitting. Now I was starting to feel uncomfortable both by his movements and language.

"You're German, aren't you?" he said.

I did not answer him.

"I'm sorry. I shouldn't have said those things. The war was a long time ago. It's water under the bridge now."

I still said nothing, hoping he would go away or leave me alone.

He held out his hand for me to shake. "I'm Irish myself. Name's

Mike O'Brien."

I reluctantly shook his hand.

"Hey, can I buy you a drink? There's a bar across the street."

"I don't drink," I said.

"Have a coke then."

"I have to catch my bus soon."

"How soon?" he asked cautiously.

I looked at my watch, now annoyed by this stranger's familiarity and determination for some kind of encounter. "In thirty minutes."

The Terminal man leaned back against the bench. He wiped his mouth with one hand. He seemed to be thinking about what to say next. What's with this ass hole? I asked myself.

He reached over as if to touch my arm or leg but then rested his hand on his own leg. "You know, you're a good-looking guy," he said. "Has anyone ever told you that?"

I just sat there, turned away from him. What could I say?

"You could be an actor?"

I still did not answer him.

"No . . . really. You could be in the movies."

"First I need to get out of the Army," I said, glancing in his direction. He seemed pleased I was facing him now.

The man I knew nothing of stared at me and started to say something but then held back. His behavior was now quite annoying. Just as I was going to break eye contact and turn away from him, he stuck his tongue out and slowly moved it sideways across his upper lip. He just looked at me with those piercing green eyes, trying to penetrate the psychological barrier I erected for just this sort of advance.

"Excuse me," I said and turned away. I got up and collected my things. "I've got to get on line. I can't miss my bus." Part of me wanted to simply leave without saying anything at all. I walked out of the waiting room sans another word, no goodbye and certainly no good luck. I should have felt insulted by this aging queer who hangs around the bus station and approaches young men but I did not. I caught a fleeting look of the chagrin on my admirer's face.

It was just past twelve when I reached Gate 39. There were a dozen or more persons ahead of me on the line that formed against the wall, soldiers for the most part. It was not difficult to pick out the recruits and trainees among them, the only ones in the green uniform with no stripes on their sleeve and heads all shaved with barely a quarter inch on top.

The bus driver called out that there would be a fifteen-minute delay in time of departure. He announced he would begin checking luggage and then stepped out of the doorway and into the street beside the Terminal. He struggled to lift and secure the long panel on the side of the vehicle. I did not push myself to the head of the line. When the driver got to my two bags, he slung them on top of all the others in the cavity between the double sets of wheels. I saw I had time to relieve myself before we were to leave.

The men's room down the corridor from Gate 39 was closed for repairs. I took the escalator up to the main floor and looked around for another restroom but saw none. Instinctively I walked toward the waiting room I was in before.

I saw a sign for the subway with pointed arrow and headed in that direction. I took an unmarked turn and before long found myself near the end of a long hallway that fed into a restricted area of electrical utility rooms and maintenance closets. Several workers with handfuls of equipment were walking toward me. One directed me to a toilet up ahead on the left. As I approached it, the unmistakable odor of urine hit me. I would have turned back were it not for the fact that I had to go badly.

The toilet was no barracks latrine ready for inspection. There were several small yellow puddles on the floor. Both sinks had blackened areas where the porcelain enamel had worn away. Not much white could be seen on the revolving cloth towel that hung lifelessly from the broken box on the wall. All three urinals had dirty water with cigarette butts in their base pockets. One stall had no door and in the other the door was partially unhinged. There was someone in the open stall, the second one from the back wall. I could see some part of bare legs and trousers bunched up around black shoes. I moved to the urinal closest to me, the one farthest from the back wall.

I stood close to the fixture and gazed downward. Someone came in behind me and through the corner of my eye I saw he went straight to the urinal next to the back wall. I heard funny clucking

71

sounds on my left, one after the other. I ignored the sounds and continued peeing. When the clucking did not stop I lifted my eyes and turned to see what was going on. Standing comfortably back from the fixture was a Puerto Rican six or seven years older than I, hanging out and almost fully erect, stroking himself and playing with the fat head. He looked at me but I said nothing and expressed no emotion.

I could not believe what I was seeing, such a brazen and vulgar approach to a complete stranger in a public place. I knew some men preferred other men but I had no idea a men's toilet in a bus station would be the locus for genital positionings and pantomime signalings. Needless to say I did not respond or copy his behavior in any way.

As I zipped up I saw a white hand extend from the open stall and make a beckoning motion to the PR, still exposed, who had just swiveled around. He took a few steps to the stall and stood upright past the doorway. I could see two sets of legs and feet facing each other. Just then another man, much older, came in. He passed the stall with the two men and went directly into the other stall. His head suddenly popped over the partition and he looked down at what must have been an unfolding impersonal intimate encounter. No doubt perched on the seat, the old man kept only one hand on the partition to hold his balance.

I started to leave but I first inched sideways toward the center urinal situated directly in front of the stall with the two men. The man standing had his hands clasped around the back of the other's head while the one sitting clutched the back of his partner's thighs. Both men were locked in some kind of payoff action, huddled together in an unholy union better suited for a dark and distant corner. The PR on his feet began to tremble and moved a little to his right, giving me an almost full view of the one on his ass receiving him. It was Mike O'Brien, the ex-G.I. fag who tried to enlist me for such a sordid encounter not thirty minutes earlier. I watched as the Irishman disengaged, bowed his head to one side, and spat on the floor. When he resumed his preferred and procured love activity, this time with just his tongue, he caught a glimpse of me staring at him and his face reddened.

A pang of terror or disgust, I did not know which, seized my body and mind. I fled the toilet and almost double-timed it back to Gate 39. I boarded the bus still breathing heavily less than two minutes before we pulled out. It was a while before I cooled down. My handkerchief was wet with perspiration from my forehead and neck. We were halfway to Fort Dix before I finally *calmed* down and started thinking about something other than my initial and unanticipated observation of the seamier side of a man's world.

The action I saw on the home front before going overseas was locked and loaded into my sensibilities. A soldier's recollection of his short time with a neighborhood girl in a basement apartment and his visual brush with a middle-age veteran in a public shit house was a mixed send-off for fighting a different kind of war in Germany.

## CHAPTER 9: FORT DIX BUDDIES

Someone in the barracks was running up and down the center aisle shouting about an airplane that crashed in a corn field in Iowa and the noise woke me up. The soldier unknown to me was in his underwear and socks, holding a portable radio to his ear, excited about telling everyone the tragic news.

It was Tuesday, the third of February. I had been at Fort Dix four days. Late on Friday I arrived at the Reception Center, the same place I came to my first day in the Army. Most of the post activities were shut down for the weekend and there was little to do. I went to the movies three times in nearby Theater No. 3 and frequented the Service Club off Florida Avenue. On Monday I was sent to the Overseas Replacement Company of the Special Training Regiment on the other side of the base to begin processing. The printed notice on the bulletin board indicated I was to report to Classification and Assignment any day after 1800 hours.

The commotion in the barracks at 0600 annoyed me. Not being in a regular company, there was no reveille and the troops could sleep later on weekdays than was usually the case. Breakfast was served until 0730 so for this first morning in Overseas Replacement I had set my alarm for seven o'clock. The ruckus was an unwelcome intrusion into my temporary reprieve from the Army's rise and shine.

I felt estranged from everyone around me. I had a bunk, one of two dozen or more, on the first floor in one of the barracks and I knew no one. All of us were simply soldiers in transit, bored barracks-bound boys who came from different forts and camps across the country and now were awaiting transportation to their new European posts aboard a U.S. naval ship. In the next building there were a number of guys I knew from Monmouth and Ord. Some were scheduled to ship out in a few days while others, who arrived at Dix before I did, were not yet given orders and a departure date. We had little to do during duty hours save hang around our bunks or go to the post snack bar.

"Buddy Holly died in a plane crash," the soldier on my floor kept repeating. "One o'clock this morning."

"You mean the singer?" a someone in the upper bunk next to me

74

said.

I looked around and everyone seemed dazed from what we were hearing. Most of the guys were now awake and sitting up or leaning on an elbow in their bunks.

"Yeah, the singer," the one with the radio added. "He did *That'll Be the Day* and *Peggy Sue.*"

"He sang good," a trooper on the opposite side of the floor remarked.

"Three other people also died in the crash," we were told. "The pilot, J.P. Richardson, and Ritchie Valens."

"J.P. Richardson, who's he?" another one asked.

"The Big Bopper," I answered, not hesitating to jump into this conversation.

"He sang good too," I heard again in ungrammatical English typical of barracks talk.

"They got bopped all right," a dim-wit with a shaved head three bunks away from me added unnecessarily. A few rotten teeth were visible when he flashed a silly smile. Every company of soldiers, I mused, had its insensitive types.

"What in hell happened?" I heard someone remark.

The one with the radio sat down on a footlocker near me and ran his naked forearm across his brow. "They just finished their gig at the Surf Ballroom in Clear Lake, Iowa," he continued, obviously uncomfortable with his assumed role as bearer of bad news. "The plane took off in lousy weather. Snow and ice all over. They went down eight miles from the airport."

"Jesus, how old was he?" the same one asked again.

"Twenty-two," I said, remembering I had read that somewhere.

With that statistic out a general silence hovered over the barracks this hour of the morning as if we were still sleeping. Some guys slumbered in their bunks. Others got up, dressed, and went to chow.

The passing of Buddy Holly weighed on me all day. I could not get the famous singer who was not much older than I out of my mind. I very much admired Buddy Holly. Unlike most other singers, he composed his own songs and wrote the lyrics too. He was creative and his music had a unique sound. His records were No. 1 on the charts. How tragic it was for so bright a star to dim so prematurely and so suddenly. How wretched it was to be the victim of so fatal an accident that could so easily have been avoided by just waiting for better weather.

What fate awaited me overseas and then after the Army? I wondered. Life and death, I sensed then and there at my tender age, were merely a corporeal differentiation seconds apart in the vast continuum of time, two divergent worlds for all eternity.

After dinner I reported to C. and A. The building conveniently was right next to the mess hall. There was a short line extending into the compound. Soldiers in front of me were standing in the doorway and on the steps. When I got inside, I gave my name and rank without saluting to the man sitting on a stool behind the high desk separating us. He was in his Class A shirt, which had no rank on the sleeves, but a green jacket with three stripes and two rockers hung on a clothes rack just behind him. The SFC apparent did not lift his eyes from the papers in his hands.

"Serial number?"

"R-A, one-two, five-three-five, nine-one-nine."

"Date of birth?" I was asked, as a few pages were thumbed through.

"Thirty . . . January . . . forty."

"Oh, turned nineteen a few days ago," the sergeant remarked casually, now looking up at me. "You'll love it where you're going. Did two tours myself."

I took the mimeographed paper he handed me and stepped to one side. I almost went cross-eyed trying to read quickly all the light-printed detailed information amid the many columns and rows. I found my name with the *S*'s in the middle of the page. My classification read "Radar Repairman" with an MOS of "282.10". My new assignment was listed as the "176th Signal Company (Repair), 379th Signal Battalion (Support), APO 29, Boeblingen, West Germany. "

"Where's Boblingen?" I asked, interrupting the veteran soldier who was busy with someone else.

He glanced at me for a moment and then pointed to the large map on the w all labeled "Seventh Army" with little blue and red pins stuck in it. I thought he was going to chew me out because I uttered no deference to his NCO rank. Had he done so I would have feigned ignorance and explained that the jacket hanging behind him could have been someone else's. "Near Stuttgart," he replied, disregarding my gaffe. He pronounced the city as an American would, with the *S* sound rather than the *Sh*. I knew better than to call his mistake to his attention. He dropped his arm saying, "Look to the bottom left of Deutschland." No young soldier, he apparently assumed, knew what Germany was in German.

I found Böblingen on the map. It was in a Staat called Baden-Württemberg. From the legend and scale, I could tell I was going to a small town about twenty kilometers southwest of Stuttgart, one of the larger cities in Germany. France and Switzerland were not far away. A pleasant sense of apprehension ran through my body.

My orders stated that on 11 Feb 59 I was to board the U.S.N.S. *General Rose* docked at the Brooklyn Army Terminal. How lucky I was compared to the other soldiers around me. I would be going to my hometown again before shipping out to a strange land.

In the next few days I completed the necessary processing steps for a European tour of duty. I was subjected to another physical examination, the first since enlisting, and I received four vaccinations, including a booster polio shot. I attended classes on security procedures.

We were warned not to go with prostitutes, not to talk to foreign nationals about what kind of work we did or to divulge any military information no matter how insignificant it may seem. We were not to wander into off-limits zones, not to buy or sell dollars or goods on the black market, not to father any out-of-wedlock children, not to get drunk and disorderly in public. We were advised what to do if we contracted VD or woke up one morning in bed with a strange woman and had no memory of how we got there.

Instructions were given for situations where we were approached by a suspicious-looking foreign male or female, were kidnapped by enemies of the United States, or were accused by local police of committing a crime or fathering a child. We were told what would happen to us if we went AWOL, broke Army regulations or local laws, gave out military secrets, admitted paternity of a foreign child, or married a local without permission from a commanding officer. Finally we were handed our 201 File, unsealed in a Manila folder with metal clasps at the top of each side, and directed to give it to the company clerk in our new outfits. Despite cautions to the contrary, I opened my personnel file when no one was around and perused its contents. I learned I had an IQ of 126 and had passed the written test for OCS. I was judged by superiors as having a problem accepting authority. On various personality profiles my scores were similar to males who enjoyed reading books more than playing or viewing sports, and had difficulty establishing relationships with the opposite sex.

Saturday afternoon, with nothing much to do, I returned to my basic training unit. I looked at the large map of Dix that hung on the Orderly Room wall and saw it was not far from where I was. I walked to the area that was the cantonment of the 2nd Training Regiment. Soon I located the 1st Battalion and its Company B that I was in.

My former barracks, billeting the 3rd and 4th Platoons, was situated between Manhattan and Queens Avenues, an appropriate coincidence for a Brooklynite. I stood outside and looked at Building 6816, my home for eight weeks two summers earlier. Inside the walls of this unimpressive and standard clapboard matchbox structure, a seventeen-year-old Jewish boy from Coney Island was on his own for the first time.

Those first months in the Army came back to mind. I thought of the forty young souls in my platoon spending half of each day indoors domesticating in spatial confinement and the other half outdoors training in physical proximity. What a rude awakening it was to witness so soon in life the breakdown of all privacy and pretense in personal relations with peers. Few facts of one's life, foibles of character or emotion, past misdeeds, or present deviations escaped exposure, scrutiny, or criticism.

My barracks mates were a mixed bag of races, religions, and nationalities. Only one other trainee was a Landsmann, Joel Waxman from the Bronx. He was upstairs in the 4th Platoon, I downstairs in the 3rd. Together we comprised less than three percent of the building's population, the same proportion roughly as Jews generally in the United States. He was almost three years older than I and had gone to college for two years before submitting to the draft. At first I thought I would be buddies with him but we were seldom together in training, bunked far apart from each other, and the age difference underscored dissimilar interests.

There were more than a half dozen Schwarzers in my platoon. Most were from New York, either the Harlem or Bedford-Stuyvesant neighborhoods, the rest from Newark or Jersey City. One of them, Rufus Straight, tall and thin like a Knicks player, slept in the bunk above me, both feet sticking out over the railing all the time. I remember late one weekend evening he came back from the Service Club and hopped onto his bunk forcefully as if high jumping over a six-foot bar, shaking the double-bed unit with me in it, and then faced two of his black buddies on the other side of the floor.

"Man," he said enthusiastically. "You see that colored boy in the band at the Club? He played those drums like a motherfucker."

That was the first I heard the MF word used as a descriptor for a positive attribute. Some white soldiers mouthed the word too but only negatively and not as often and certainly not as rapaciously.

There were two Spanish speakers in the barracks who seemed almost joined at the hip. One was a Puerto Rican from the island that came to do his time like every other U.S. citizen, the other had an Anglo name and never identified himself with any group. The latter often had to translate for the former.

The few Italians were typical of those I had known in New York, guys who walked with a swagger, had hot tempers, and were quick with their fists. Oversized silver metal crosses attached to dog-tag chains hung conspicuously around their necks. The paisani in both platoons palled around together like members of some secret society. When they talked about their rifle oil, one of the non-Italians would invariably say "Rifle Earl, who's he?"

We also had a German not yet naturalized who spoke little English. He elected to take the Army's battery of written tests in his own language. Once he happened to sneeze and when I said "Gesundheit" he quickly responded with "Dankeschön." It seemed we were the only ones in the platoon who understood that.

Another barracks mate, Tommy Quinn, made a big to do about his Emerald Isle background. He often said "There are two kinds of people in the world, those who are Irish and those who wish they were Irish." One day I commented to him "Where does that leave me, I'm neither?" but he did not reply. No other Paddy in either platoon reflected such national consciousness. Tommy was also the pugilistic type, pushing, poking, and prodding anyone that uttered a cross word to him. I called him "John L. Sullivan the zweiter" but it turned out to be my private joke. The German boy understood my Yiddish pronunciation of zweiter but did not know who John L. Sullivan was, while the others knew who John L. Sullivan was but did not know what zweiter meant.

Most of the fellows in basic were not similar to those I had encountered in New York or grew up with in my neighborhood. They were from the small towns and rural areas of upstate New York, New Jersey, and Pennsylvania, young men of Protestant and Anglo-Saxon background who knew very few Jews and seldom came into contact with them.

One such WASP, Whitey Stone, I got along with very well in spite of our dissimilarities. The nickname Whitey dogged him for years because of his pallid complexion, high forehead with light blond hair, colorless eyebrows, and immature beard. He was a farm boy from southern New Jersey who, like I, had enlisted after high school but nevertheless was an unlikely buddy for a big city denizen. We were in the same squad and he occupied the lower bunk next to mine. We pulled KP together several times and shot live rounds with our rifles on the firing ranges alongside each one another. We simulated against each other hand-to-hand combat exercises. At times we went to the snack bar and movies after duty hours. Going to chapel and sharing a bed were about the only activities Whitey and I did not do together.

I went into the two-story building. The latrine on the first floor to the left of the doorway was the same, clean but unruly this Saturday afternoon of free time. I walked halfway to the rear to what used to be my bunk on the side facing the company training area, an open field used for reveille, formation, and marching. It seemed the soldier occupying it now was away or on overnight pass. The blankets fit tautly around the mattress and you could bounce a quarter off the bottom one, a platoon sergeant's favorite test for regulation bed making. I was a stranger to the young troopers in T-shirts and fatigue trousers sitting on their bunks or footlockers polishing their boots, belt buckles, and brass. Much to my surprise, no one reacted to me or questioned who I was.

On the second floor there were two small rooms above, and covering the same dimensions as, the latrine. One was occupied by two NCOs, the other was a day room with tables and chairs and a small couch for trainees to sit or talk or write letters. The lights stayed on in the day room after 2200, the time for lights out in the two large barracks rooms. I used to go there late at night when I was not tired or when I wanted to read.

One evening in the day room, halfway through basic, I was talking to three WASPs. Two were from my platoon but in different squads, one from the other platoon. I had almost no contact with them during training and hardly knew them. They all hailed from a little township in western New York and had been drafted together. The country buddies were about six years older than I and two were married with young children. Every night they were up late writing letters home and bullshitting to each other. I gathered I caught their attention because of the age and cultural differences between us. They called me "Kid" and thought of me as such. They did not call me "Jew boy," at least not to my face. A personal interest they seemed to take in me.

"What business does your father own?" one of them asked me. He had his feet propped up on the leg support bar of another chair and was in a relaxed position. The bluntness and precipitance of his question startled me.

"My father doesn't own a business."

They all looked at me with a blank face. A moment later another remarked "Every Jew where we live owns a business."

"Well, where I live most Jews don't," I said.

"What does he do then?" They still seemed dumbfounded.

"He works in a garment factory. My father prints ladies' scarves and colors fabrics."

"You mean you're not rich?"

"No," I said, shaking my head. "Would I have joined the Army to learn a trade if I were?"

"Every Jew we know owns a business and lives in a big house," the third one from the sticks said. I was not sure if he envied the Jews he knew back home or was simply making a general comment about his sense of social reality.

"We don't own a house either. We rent an apartment, and a very small one at that."

They seemed even more stunned by these answers. "What kind of car does your father drive?" Some small assurance was being sought for their preconceived notions.

"He doesn't own a car . . . he doesn't even drive."

"How does he get to work?" They were obviously ignorant of what type of family I came from and how we lived.

"He rides the subway . . . like everyone else in New York," I said in what must have been a final blow to their distorted image of Jews in America.

A look of incredulity remained on their faces. What I said contradicted everything they came to know about Jews from their personal experiences. The stereotype they formed in their minds just did not square with me. It must have been a revelation for these hometown hick buddies to learn of big-city Jews in America who were not part of the capitalist class. They found it hard to accept the fact that many Jews have moderate or below-average incomes and own no business and possess few, if any, material signs of wealth.

The Fort Dix buddies might just as well have espoused the Nazi propaganda of twenty years earlier about a Jewish financial conspiracy in the world. These had difficulty believing my father was merely a poor working stiff like theirs, a proletarian who printed colors through a silk screen in lieu of lifting hay with a pitchfork.

A week later the upstate New Yorkers questioned me again in a personal way. "Kid, you ever been laid?"

I hesitated a moment, then said, "Yeah, why?"

"How many times?"

"Once."

"Shit," another one said, drawing out the *i* like an *e*. "You ain't never had any pussy."

"I'm only seventeen," I explained.

"Shit," he said again in the same way. "When I was seventeen I was in the haystack pulling up a dress twice a week . . . a different dress."

"You're a regular Li'l Abner with many a Daisy Mae." He did not seem to appreciate my facetious characterization of him with a teenage consort.

"Who was your one-timer?" he shot back somewhat conde-scendingly.

"A girl from my neighborhood."

I had broken my cherry with a girl on 24th Street when I was fifteen. Richie had her too.

"White?"

I nodded.

"A Jew?"

"Jew*ess*," I said, not hesitating to correct him.

"Huh," he uttered in total bewilderment, like the dumb detective at the end of *The Maltese Falcon* who asked what the black bird was and Humphrey Bogart said it was the stuff dreams are made of. The English teachers in rural New York apparently did not give adequate attention to gender forms of various nouns in their classes.

"Why do you ask that?"

The third inquisitor looked around the room and to the open doorway. Then he looked at me sternly, his eyes swelling. "We thought you liked chocolate-coated babes?"

"What makes you say that?" I queried after a moment's pause.

"We've seen you with your chum, that double-dipped tall mother."

"You mean Rufus?" I was beginning to resent this line of questioning and their vacuous analogies to skin color that I had not heard before.

"We don't mean Whitey." They all laughed.

It bothered me that they were spewing racial slurs about a friendship I had made in the Army. I liked Rufus. We were the same age. He played basketball in high school and would have gone to college on a scholarship if his father had not died in his senior year. He lived in Harlem in the projects near 125th Street and Lenox Avenue.

Rufus had to support his mother and younger brother. Fifty dollars a month was taken out of his pay. He only received twenty-five dollars on payday, not much spending money for a whole month. More than once I loaned him a few dollars. I sympathized with the heavy burden he had to carry. I had often wondered what

I would do if something happened to my father. Rufus mentioned that he went to Coney Island frequently in the summer and loved the Steeplechase rides. He asked me what it was like living there all year round and I told him. We had common interests and I felt comfortable around my upper-bunk mate, albeit admittedly not when he was with his blood-buddies.

"Rufus sleeps near me," I told the three WASPs indignantly. "He's often next to me in formation and on the chow line. So I talk to him a lot. So what?"

"Maybe you like coons more than your own kind?" one said in a low voice.

So now I'm *their* kind because I'm white, not different because I'm a Jew. "I like all kinds of people," I told them, as if I were defending my constitutional right to associate with whomever I choose. "What's the big deal?"

"We don't want you hanging around us if you hang around one of them."

With that statement of intentions clearly demarcated, I left the day room and went back to my bunk without saying another word.
In bed, unable to sleep, like a mute psychotic wandering about, I kept talking to myself. Was I one of them? Was I a white Negro as they thought? So, in the Army, you're either with the whites or in the enemy camp. You can't hang your helmet on both sides of the barracks aisle, you can't march in two different parades. No one is going to tell me with whom I could be friends. Fuck those guys. From Gentile jerks, I don't need social acceptance. In a couple of weeks basic will be over and I'll be leaving Dix for Monmouth. I'll probably never see those hick pricks again. Rufus I might run into in New York someday.

I returned to my building in Overseas Replacement after supper. It seemed deserted and desolate. Only two other guys were there, lying in their bunks, passing the time. "Where is everybody?" I asked.

"They all went to Wrightstown," one of them said.

Wrightstown, what little there was of it, I remembered well. Located just outside the perimeter of Fort Dix on its northwest corner, the tiny town had evolved over the years into a crass commercial islet catering to the needs and pleasures of soldiers and civilians assigned there. Every evening and weekend trainees and cadre would pick up their passes, walk or share taxi-cab rides, and head for Wrightstown's bars, diners, pawn shops, souvenir stores, movie theaters, and tattoo parlors. Prostitutes of both races worked their trade on the young men, often transmitting a VD to them that had to be treated by military doctors and strained Dix's medical facilities. When I was in basic, I went into the border town only once for an afternoon to experience being a soldier in uniform away from home, to parody what I had seen in films by the likes of a Montgomery Clift, Aldo Ray, and Audie Murphy.

That last Saturday evening in overseas processing, I could have signed out and gone into Wrightstown for some female company but I decided against it. I much preferred to recall the dark-haired puertorriqueña who a week earlier took me in by mouth and pouch. And I liked dreaming of an attractive blond, blue-eyed Fräulein who in three-weeks-time might likewise be doubly open with me.

In four days, I would be waving goodbye to Fort Dix, but I was on a two-way street to Germany. I fully expected to return in 1960 more than sixteen months later. Dix became the largest Separation Center on the East Coast at the end of the war, and all G.I.s coming back from the European Theater of Operations had to pass through here. Dix was also, toward the end of the war, a POW camp mostly for Germans. In 1945, the soon-to-be repatriated Soldaten were on a one-way path to Germany.

# CHAPTER 10: THE *ROSE*

"Get rid of that damn suitcase, soldier," the crusty sergeant barked at the top of his lungs. He looked straight at the nervous private standing a little to my right in the line in front of me.

It was 0845 on Wednesday the eleventh of February, almost time to board one of the long military transport buses parked in a row with doors open in the street in front of Overseas Replacement. I was one of hundreds of troopers standing at ease in Class A uniform, duffel bag and AWOL bag at our feet, lined up almost shoulder-to-shoulder in four columns on the sidewalk next to the barracks and the buses. Three buddies from Monmouth and Ord were in formation with me. It was cold but the skies were clear and the sun was partially shining this early in the morning, by every indication a good day to travel.

All eyes were on the hapless E-2 being reproached by the sergeant. He was the only one with something other than an AWOL bag, a piece of luggage conspicuously different from what we were permitted to carry on the ship. Resting by his left foot was a bright orange-colored fancy leather suitcase that looked brand new. It was almost twice the size of the bag he should have had at his side.

"My parents gave me this as a going-away present," the private said meekly in an obvious attempt to justify his transgression from Army regulations.

"I don't care if the Pope gave it to you," the NCO with three stripes and one rocker squawked again. "Get rid of it fast."

"No one told me I couldn't take a suitcase," the boyish-looking trooper added, now trying to excuse his behavior by blaming others. His voice quavered and panic seemed to grip him. He unbuttoned the lower part of his overcoat, pulled a handkerchief from his trouser pocket, and ran it across his forehead, tilting his dress hat upward in a silly position.

The staff sergeant could have been an E-5 sporting the old chevron or, if he was promoted during the past seven months, the new E-6 rank. In either case, he was acting like every other noncom I had come into contact with in the Army, unconcerned with the feelings or hardships of subordinates. Any effort to get him to back off would be to no avail. Even if a legitimate or compelling reason for the violation was proffered, and thus far I heard none, challenging or arguing with a direct order, especially in public, would only harden the stance of those in authority and spell doom for an underling.

I wanted to intercede on the private's behalf, to perhaps suggest to the sergeant that he take hold of the suitcase and parcel post it back to the young man's parents C.O.D., but I held my tongue. The sergeant could have been coming with us on the buses, he did not seem to be the magnanimous type, and had I spoken out of turn I surely would have been asking for trouble myself.

"I won't tell you again, soldier," the staffer shouted. "We're moving out right now and you ain't taking that big ball-buster."

The craven young man was ashen and stony-faced. He bent down and opened his precious suitcase, removed articles and stuffed what he could into his duffel bag and pockets. He then broke ranks and walked forty or fifty feet to where two garbage cans stood by the back door of a barracks building. He deposited the near empty suitcase into one can that apparently was quite full as everyone could see most of the orange leather protruding above the rim, and started to walk away.

Two troopers in fatigues standing near the building saw and heard what transpired and sauntered toward the cans. The private who was just berated by the sergeant noticed them and immediately turned back. Some primordial instinct seemed to take hold of him, as if he was still under fire. He retrieved his forsaken gift, dropped it on the ground, jumped on it twice with both feet puncturing the walls, and then tossed the wrecked luggage into the garbage.

I had never seen anything like this before, a person out of spite or anger or humiliation destroying a perfectly functional and attractive artifact he could not use or own any longer in order to ensure that no one else would benefit from his prized possession. Taking his place in line, the private was flushed and looked heartbroken, practically in tears. He could not save himself from the pity of his peers but he did avert being mocked by those around him had total strangers in full view picked up his pristine suitcase and gratuitously walked off with it. He would sooner ruin something he loved than see others enjoy it at his expense. It was not pleasant to watch a fellow soldier cast into an impossible situation, or witness firsthand fear of ridicule consume a person's passions.so violently.

The bus ride to New York took over two hours. I had a seat near a window and, for most of the trip, looked out at the rolling hills, animal pastures, and oil refineries of New Jersey. I thought about the sergeant and the private, a veteran superior acting unnecessarily cruel to a lowly recruit and an unworldly eighteen- or nineteen-year-old letting his emotions get the better of him in front of others.

The repugnant incident between two soldiers of unequal rank occurred just as I was leaving Fort Dix, not an auspicious beginning to a much-anticipated overseas stint. Was there a lesson in this? I wondered. Would it augur well for me the rest of my time in the Army? The private boarded a different bus than I did and, with him out of sight, I tried to forget the balky facets of human nature I observed.

We entered the city via the Holland Tunnel. I always felt a sense of excitement coming into Manhattan through one of the tunnels, either the Lincoln or the Holland, upon seeing the slowly expanding outline of tall buildings through a widening circle of light that I was moving toward. The bus turned onto Canal Street, passed through the western tip of Chinatown, traveled south on West Street, and rolled into Brooklyn from the Battery Tunnel. We took the Brooklyn-Queens Expressway westbound, fed into the Gowanus Expressway, and exited at 39th Street. The driver cut over to First Avenue, jockeying around the many long trucks double-parked on the streets and sidewalks, then went along the water's edge for about a mile.

The Brooklyn Army Terminal stood between Upper New York Bay and 2nd Avenue, from 58th to 64th Streets. It was the largest military supply and storage base on the Atlantic Seaboard. The site had very large warehouses and piers, and the Terminal was immediately adjacent to the Long Island and Pennsylvania Railroads and had direct connections to the New Haven Railroad. The bus stopped at Pier 3 where the U.S.N.S. *General Rose* was docked. I was impressed by the imposing nine-story concrete structure called Building A that all four piers connected to.

The *Rose* was a naval transport ship, named in honor of Major General Maurice B. Rose, Commander of the 3rd Armored Division, killed in action in Germany near the end of the war. General Rose was the first and only division commander to perish in Europe during the war. In the last days of fighting, he was leading an attack against a Panzer training center outside Paderborn. Rose, in his jeep with the driver and an aide, was at the head of the column and ran into a Tiger Tank. A young German opened the turret hatch and fired his submachine gun. The firing was due to a misunderstanding about an order to surrender, but the general was killed just the same.

The two-propeller ship that would carry me to Germany had staterooms for 510 officers and dependents, but I would sleep in one of the 1,685 racks for enlisted men. I was not so lucky as Elvis, who was given a stateroom, along with two buddies of his choosing, so that the King of Rock 'n' Roll would not bother, or be bothered by, the packed troops down below. My vessel steamed mainly between New York and the Port of Bremerhaven carrying military dependents, European refugees, and combat-ready troops.

On the port side of the ship, the Fort Dix contingent of troops boarded alphabetically. From the fourth floor of Building A, we walked through an encased pier shed that bridged the quarterdeck of the *Rose* to the dock. I got separated from my buddies, the only people I knew. Also embarking were soldiers who arrived at the Bay Ridge branch of the LIRR on troop trains en masse from particular units around the country who did the necessary processing at their previous camp. Also getting on the ship were airmen from McGuire Air Force Base in New Jersey and Manhattan Beach Air Force Station in Brooklyn. We were instructed to take the first unoccupied rack we came to. There were so many men on board in such a confined space you could not move anywhere except at a snail's pace pushing and shoving and bumping into others all the time.

It took me more than an hour to navigate passage to a sleeping bunk. I carried my AWOL bag and dragged a heavy and bulky duffel bag down the stairs to the first deck, the one with the staterooms. Then I got to the second deck by negotiating narrow spiral stairways, long gangways, and thick bulkheads, only to find no empty racks to grab. I continued down to the third deck, finally coming to a compartment with available places. The third deck was the end of the line for the troops being transported. The ship's mechanical and electrical systems were housed on the bottom level.

The racks were stacked in threes from deck to overhead. I picked one in the middle, a plain cloth hammock about the height of my chest. I was not keen on having two guys sleep over me or having no one above but at risk of hitting my head on metal pipes and protruding handles or wheels every time I maneuvered in and out of bed. There was almost no room to walk around the compartments. Duffel bags were upright in the constricted aisles between the racks or lying sideways on the floor, coats and jackets hung from hooks or hangars in common spaces, AWOL bags sat alone on hammocks to signal occupancy, articles of underwear and toiletries were strewn about.

I changed into my fatigues, folded my Class A uniform, put it in my duffel bag, and secured the lock on it. This seemed to be the only way to avoid theft on a transport boat as there were no lockers for our gear. Any shipmate could easily take something from an open duffel bag or pick up loose items, but his trying to disembark with two duffel bags, assuming his spine held up, would not go unnoticed. Having settled in, I looked for the guys I knew from radar school and California, found one of them, and went to chow.

After lunch I searched for and located on the second deck the Orderly Room for the troops. It was a small office and there was only one person inside, a totally gray, older sergeant major in highly starched fatigues that looked more like a costume than a work dress. He was a new E-9, the highest enlisted rank in the Army. The three shiny yellow stripes and three rockers with a star in the center on both sleeves, dominating the uniform because of their size and significance, caught my attention. He was not short but he had a slight physique with tapered shoulders. At first glance he lacked the commanding presence that might be expected of someone in his position.

"What can I do for you, soldier?" he said softly but somberly. His voice likewise lacked the verve and strength of the NCOs I knew.

"Can I make a ship-to-shore phone call, Sarge?" I was used to addressing lower-grade sergeants informally but this was the first time I did so with a sergeant major.

The senior soldier in both rank and age peered at me. He gazed down at my nametag and then to my face, studying it I thought. "Why?" he asked.

"I need to call home."

"Why?" he asked again.

"My parents want to see me off tomorrow. I have to tell them the place to come to . . . and what time."

"Where are they coming from?"

"Brooklyn," I said, "not far from here." I thought I would surely clinch the sergeant's approval when I added, "It's a local call."

"There is no ship-to-shore phone service."

"No ship-to-shore phone service?" I repeated, puzzled by what he said. I knew that could not be true. "What if there's an emergency?" I asked, not openly doubting the sergeant's veracity.

"No ship-to-shore phone service for personal calls," he clarified.

"I'll make it quick," I pleaded. I was not willing to give up just yet. "Two minutes."

"No personal calls," the sergeant major told me simply, but he did not jump all over me for challenging his decision.

"Then can I go to the Terminal and make my call there?"

"You can't leave the ship," he said.

"For a few minutes only?"

"It'll take you longer than that just to climb ashore. Besides, if I let you go, I have to let everyone go."

"Everyone is not asking to go," I continued to argue, even though I was losing confidence in a resolution in my favor.

The sergeant major looked at my nametag again. "Is it *Stree*ber or *Stria*ber?"

"*Stria*ber," I pronounced for him.

"Streiber, I want you to forget about calling your parents."

"What if they call me here on the ship?"

"Then I want you to tell them not to come tomorrow," he said emphatically. "We have no facilities for visitors."

I just stood there for a few moments, not saying anything more about a telephone call. I began to respect this NCO and to be grateful for his quiet and unassuming style of leadership. With all the fuss I was making, I was surprised he was so calm. He could have raised his voice, rebuked me, ordered me out of his office, or confined me to quarters. *I* was the one who was roiled. The sergeant was unaware that I was slowly coming around to accepting his decision on this matter. But I wondered whether his story about the lack of facilities for visitors was true.

The ship's topkick seemed to be thinking about something. He looked at my nametag a third time and then at me before he spoke.

"Are you . . . Jewish?" he asked hesitantly.

I nodded. He obviously put it all together—my German name, my being from New York, my obsessive concern for my parents, my inclination to question authority, my pushiness.

"How would you like to be one of the Chaplain's assistants? We need three, one from each faith."

I said nothing. I still wanted to make the call.

"You wouldn't have to do any other work," he went on. "No KP, no cleaning latrines, no scrubbing the deck, no detail of any kind."

"Okay," I replied softly, accepting his offer without another word. I welcomed the reprieve from shit duties on the boat to Germany. I knew it was a bribe of sorts. It was obvious he wanted me to forgo my pursuit of a telephone call without saying the temporary duty was tit-for-tat. I played the game too. I let the issue go without *saying* I was letting it go. In the face of what he said, it seemed unlikely I could leave the ship or use its telephonic equipment for my purposes.

"Good," he stated, turning me toward the door. "If anyone tries to put you on detail, tell him you are the Chaplain's assistant and are excused. Report to the Chaplain's Office on the first deck day after tomorrow at o-nine-hundred."

The E-9er patted me on the back gently as I left.

The *Rose* was all set to sail on the afternoon of the twelfth, Lincoln's birthday. It was an interesting coincidence, and perhaps a good omen, since I was a graduate of Lincoln High School. That morning, before lunch, I was passing the time in the recreation room for the troops on the quarterdeck near the stern. I was sitting on one of the ping/pong tables, listening to soldiers as they talked, when an announcement came on the loudspeaker overhead.

"Private David Streiber, report to the visitor's lounge," the monotone voice uttered, "repeat, Private David Streiber, report to the visitor's lounge."

I jumped off the table and hurried to the bow of the ship. Two Navy SPs were standing at a gate that separated the troop area from the officers and dependents. They let me pass when I told them my name was called over the speaker. I was directed to a catwalk that connected the inboard side of the pier to Building A. I crossed it and came to a large room where senior NCOs and officers were hugging and kissing and conversing with their civilian loved ones. My mother, grandfather, and sister were waiting for me. The nice top sergeant did not tell me the truth about facilities for visitors after all.

It was thrilling to see my family once more before shoving off. I had given up all hope of seeing them at the dock. The week before, after I received my orders, I telephoned home and gave my father the new APO address to which he should send my overseas bag and I also mentioned my date of departure and the name of the ship. I had no idea plans were made to come to the Terminal whether I called again or not. The emotion of the reunion would have to comfort me for more than sixteen months. I felt special. Of all the military personnel in the visitor's lounge, I was the lowest in rank.

"Papa couldn't make it because he had to work," my mother said.

"Why did you give my rank as private," I asked, as if it made a difference. "I'm a private first class."

"Dovidl, I didn't know what you are. And the shlemiel of a sergeant downstairs couldn't understand Zeyde's English."

My sister was loath to sit still and was hopping about the room with her doll, looking for someone her age to play with. I was given a small white box tied both ways with a red-and-white string, containing two custard éclairs that I liked and a piece of sponge cake, purchased early that morning from Spiegel's Bakery across the street. My mother again implored me not to get friendly with the Germans, not to talk to the murderers of our people. Zeyde again told her in Yiddish not to worry about me, that I am a smart boy. My sister again said she loved me.

I spent less than fifteen minutes with my family before the visiting hour was over. Foghorns blew three times. Authorities whisked everyone out. I went back across the catwalk and stood on deck near the bow and waved to my people as they left. Standing next to me was a schwarze Army captain. He was in Class A greens, white wife apparent at his side, holding up a little tawny girl with curly flaxen hair. He waved her arm in tandem with his at two of *his* people. I could see two elderly smiling black faces looking out an open glass window. The captain told the child "Say goodbye to Grossmutter, say goodbye to Grossvater."

On the top deck of the *Rose*, just before we up anchored, one consequence of postwar German-American fraternization hit me for the first time. A minute later I headed back to my rack. An hour later we passed through Lower New York Bay. Soon we were sailing leisurely out in the Atlantic.

The next few days were physically distressing for me. I was seasick most of the time. The Dramamine pills I was handed in sick bay did little to calm my stomach. Had I known I would be so vulnerable to the ocean waves, I would have petitioned the Army to fly me over. Before this, my only confrontation with the high seas was on the Staten Island Ferry. No matter what I was doing on the ship—lying face up in my hammock, sitting still on a bench or in a chair on any level, pacing slowly about the main deck—a continuous sharp queasiness ran through my guts. The masticated food in my belly and bowels were like molds of volcanic gelatin swishing around, waiting to gush out at either end at any moment. I dared not put down the heavy paper bag we were issued or, if I was topside, stray far from the railing. I even avoided eating, reasoning that if I ingested less I would vomit less. Several shipmates though told me I must eat even if most of what I forced down was soon heaved up, as the body would still absorb some nourishment. By the fifth day, despite gale winds in the North Atlantic, my constitution adjusted to the incessant rocking and dipping of the ship.

My seasickness caused a delay in the start of my job as the Chaplain's Jewish assistant. "Take two days off," my new temporary boss told me upon seeing my whitened face and lethargy. This was one time I did not have to feign illness to bug out of some detail or responsibility.

The Chaplain, a Lieutenant JG, was a Presbyterian minister in his early thirties. He always wore khakis, the Navy's utility uniform all year round for ranks E-7 and above, silver bar on the right collar and gold cross on the left. The Man of God had a youthful appearance, skin unblemished and unwrinkled, except for the fact that he was prematurely bald. His pate was shiny as a polished billiard ball. The ring of fair hair on the sides was cropped quite short and nearly discernible. His green eyes and persistent half smile radiated a sense of compassion and understanding, or so I thought. He personally selected my two Christian counterparts. One, as he, hailed from a small town in the South but had gone to a Baptist college for two years, the other was an Irish Catholic from Milwaukee, a seminarian who had dropped out after the first year. My only preparation for assisting the Chaplain was four years of Hebrew School, Bar Mitzvah training, and a general interest in religion.

My ocean-crossing job was not very taxing or time consuming. It gave me an opportunity to spend most days away from the troops crowded down below and to escape the many unpleasant details shipboard soldiers were selected for at random by noncoms roaming about the decks and compartments searching for idle hands. More than once I successfully dodged some witless task I was ordered to do by simply mentioning the sergeant major's name and directive.

Every weekday from 0900 to 1600, if the Chaplain was away from his office on some mission, I and my two sectarian co-workers just sat around waiting for G.I.s who might come in with a personal problem or religious concern. On this voyage to Europe, we were the military's first call for assistance, un-ordained ministers helping to solve human difficulties. The JG said we were emergency screeners, were to handle trivial matters ourselves but to refer the serious cases to him. Exactly what qualified a nineteen-year-old high school graduate to practice clinical psychology or religious counseling I never knew. If the boss was in his office with someone, the trio of seconds passed the time in the officers' lounge nearby. There were portholes on the *Rose*'s first level below the main deck, and I liked looking out at the vast ocean. As I crossed the Atlantic, I wondered what awaited me on the other side.

The three of us rotated different lunch and break periods and at times were reduced to a twosome but frequently we were all together. Fortunately for those who may have been troubled, my ministerial skills were never put to the test. During my joint or singular vigil no soldier, Jew or Christian, atheist or believer, ever sought the Chaplain's help. When I was on duty with one or both co-workers, or with the Chaplain in his office, the conversations repeatedly turned to religion and/or race, issues of importance to members of the peacetime Army overseas or stateside.

"You know General Rose was Jewish," the Chaplain told me one day when we were alone.

"I thought he might be," I said. "Rose is a Jewish name. I read the plaque about him near the staterooms."

"He was the son of a rabbi. Grew up in Connecticut and Colorado. His folks came to America from Poland in the eighteen-eighties."

My non-Jewish boss apparently knew a great deal about the life of his ship's Jewish namesake.

"My mother's from Poland too," I noted.

We talked for a while about the general and Jews. I learned that Rose had moved away from Judaism after he was wounded in the first war, when he was my age. Evidently that shift was never put in reverse, eliminating any further similarities between us. The war hero was buried under a marble cross in the U.S. Military Cemetery in Margraten, Holland.

The Chaplain wanted to know about my background and what I believed in. I told him I could read and write Hebrew but could not speak it. I believed in God but did not think one religion was better than another, or one faith truer than the next. He asked me what I thought of Jesus and I replied that I did not think anything of him. The teachers in my Hebrew School never mentioned Jesus or Holy Ghosts or anything about Christianity.

"No," I answered in response to specific questions. "I don't believe Jesus was the son of God and I don't understand how he could have walked on water or risen from the dead."

I would never pull a Rose, I told myself, as I listened to the Protestant minister talk about Jesus and Christianity, mostly a repetition of what I picked up on my own from books or from friendships with Gentiles. He nodded approvingly when I said I attended services each week and holidays, but did not shake his head in disbelief when I revealed I had gone out with non-Jewish girls since I joined the Army. The Chaplain seemed to take a personal interest in me.

My religious cohorts and I spent a good deal of time together in the officers' lounge. We usually just sat around, read magazines, made small talk, and observed others. A frequent visitor was the captain I stood next to on the quarterdeck the day we left port, at times in uniform but mostly in civies. I could see from the insignia that he was a medical doctor. When I was still a little seasick, I started to approach him but then turned around. His family came into the lounge too. More than once the schwarze Mann could be seen in a patently intimate exchange with his weisse Frau. He laughed heartily and loudly and played affectionately and physically with his Mischling daughter, in sharp contrast to the mother who sat by stiffly, her sullen face and icy blue eyes baring a Germanic stoicism that seemed to render her uncomfortable with such public banter.

"What do you think of Blackie and Blondie?" the Chaplain's southern aide asked me one afternoon toward the end of our crossing. The interracial couple had just left the lounge and we were alone. For several days he had observed them without comment. However, I saw him cringe every time they were in the same room with us. I was surprised he had not said anything sooner.

"What do you mean?"

I knew what he was driving at but I wanted to drag it out of him.

"Is it rot for a Nigruh to sleep with a whaat girl?" With his drawl, he pronounced right like *rot* with an elongated *o*.

"What do you mean 'right'."

"You know . . . is it *rot*?"

"No, I don't know," I shot back, again trying to get him to voice his own prejudices. This was not the first time I was a party to or overheard whites in the barracks engaged in negative talk about blacks. "You tell me."

The soldier who grew up in a strictly segregated world, where a knotted rope tarried for the black male sexual transgressor, looked at me for a minute before answering. "Black with whaat ain't natural . . . it's against God . . . and it ain't legal where I come from."

My co-worker was correct on one point. Miscegenation was against the law in twenty-four states, and not just those in his native South but some in the North and West.

"In New York where I come from, it's legal," I informed him. "You see it all the time."

"Well, maybe up North you do things different, but down South we don't laak big black bucks spoilin' our pure whaat women."

Now he was beginning to sound like every other redneck I had met in the Army. I thought he was above his backwater Baptist Bubba buddies because he had gone to college, his grammar was somewhat better, and he did not have a mouthful of decayed teeth. It seems I was wrong and I started to take offense at the uncalled for remarks.

"What if the white woman likes the black man?" I put to him, assuming the role of devil's advocate. I thought of parodying the way he articulated like, but there was no need to go that far to rile him.

"No decent whaat woman would go for a nigger," he insisted, changing for the worse his tone as well as his language.

"The captain's wife looks decent enough to me," I said awkwardly, again trying his patience as well as his beliefs. "She married a doctor . . . and he seems decent too."

"You stickin' up for them?" he wanted to know, turning the argument in my direction. "You people are always doin' that."

I was not pleased by his slight about my being Jewish, not to mention my proclivities or associations. "I'm sticking up for people to have the freedom to date or marry anyone they want."

"Well, that nigger captain better stay in Germany if he wants freedom. Back home, we know what to do with his kind."

My prejudiced colleague was correct again. Soldiers involved in mixed-race unions were wise not to continue serving their country on southern posts. And the Army was well aware of this problem. Regulations permitted such men to request and receive a transfer to a state where their marriages were tolerated or not prohibited by law. Two sergeants in my Signal Corps' company at Ford Ord, one white and one black, returning from the Eighth Army with Korean wives, had refused assignments to Fort Gordon, Georgia. Family life would not have been so peachy for them in that state. They would have had to live on the shady side of town and their children, considered illegitimate as well as colored, would have had to attend segregated schools.

"I'm sure that's why the captain's going back," I said.

The American officer no doubt signed up for another tour of duty in Deutschland mit wife and daughter. Like Thomas Wolfe, he can't go home again.

"Black with whaat still ain't rot," the Johnny Reb twice argued, this time more forcefully and with a rhyme. "The nigger lusts for our whaat women. He beats 'em and rapes 'em. He does it because he hates whaats . . . wants to get back at them for treatin' him bad."

"Then whites shouldn't treat Negroes so badly."

He gazed at me but said nothing. My humor did not register yet.

"Don't make them move to the back of the bus," I continued. "Don't put them in separate and unequal schools. And don't force them to use separate and shittier rest rooms."

"What are you, a Communist *and* a Jew?" He seemed angry now.

I was getting mad too. I looked him straight in the eye. "I'll tell you what I am . . . I am not hypocritical about race like you southerners."

"Fuck you, Commie Jew," he lashed out at me, again with the rhyme. My attempt to elevate the civility and phraseology of our talk obviously failed.

"Do you always put bigotry to poetry?"

He ignored or did not understand my sarcasm. "I'm not a hypocrite. I'm a good Christian."

"Then why do you church-going white boys think it's okay to screw black girls?"

He hesitated a moment, then said, with a tight lip, "That's different."

"Different? How?"

"Nigger gals are loose and play easy to get," the true-to-form southerner answered quickly with a silly grin, eager to prove his point. "They come lookin' for us. We give 'em money and treat 'em nice. They don't mind if we knock 'em up. Hell, they want a half-whaat baby. Gives 'em respect."

"And you don't go looking for them because white girls won't go to bed with you before you marry them?"

He started to say something but stopped.

"And you don't take advantage of those 'poor nigger gals,' as you think of them, just to satisfy your needs?"

The grin disappeared from the Baptist soldier's face. He flushed before me. My last questions apparently hit a raw nerve. He stormed out of the lounge without saying another word. I must have impugned his honor and integrity, or rather this white boy's unjust practice of blaming victimized girls of the opposite race for the illicit sexual liaisons he visited upon them.

Was I culpable of the same offense? I asked myself. Maybe. Was my escapade with the black WAC, or the Puerto Rican girl for that matter, any different? Perhaps not. But as a nineteen-year-old soldier, I never made those personal comparisons.

The next day the offended southern gentleman avoided contact with me. I found myself alone with the third assistant. We spent most of the time engaged in chitchat, first in the Chaplain's Office and then in the lounge. This was the fourth day I had known the Catholic soldier, the co-worker I liked better and felt I had more in common with. He grew up in a poor, big-city, Irish neighborhood, with Italians and Jews not far off. His father was sporadically employed, drank a great deal, and exhibited bouts of violent behaveior. The Milwaukee seminary in which he trained to do God's work gave him a scholarship. I never learned why he left in his second year, but I gathered he had a problem with one of the priests and felt unworthy of taking his vows. When we talked earlier in the week, I thought he was trying to convert me. Now he began to question my faith, not just converse with me about it. Baptist Bubba must have said something to him.

"Why don't Jews believe in Jesus," my Catholic counterpart wanted to know.

"Because we don't accept him as the Messiah."

"But Jesus was Jewish," he said, as if that was news to me. "He came to earth to save the Jews and the Gentiles from sin. He took on a human body, he became one of us. Jesus died for us so he could be resurrected. You have to profess belief in Jesus as your Savior," he exhorted me, "to find salvation and avoid eternal damnation."

What kind of bullshit is this? I said to myself, a thought the ex-seminarian might well have read from my facial expressions. "I'm not worried about my soul being lost or my body going to Hell," I told him instead. "The practice of Judaism is concerned more with observances of God's commandments and blessings here on earth than with what will greet us or come to pass in the next world."

Milwaukee Mick invited me to mass but I declined. He reminded me of Spencer Tracy in *San Francisco* and *Boys Town*, a cherubic priest who could do no wrong and who never loses faith in man or God. You would not know it by looking at him, but the son of an Irish pug, raised on mean city streets, was the sensitive type. The quasi-disciple appeared sincerely hurt by my lack of interest in his version of the Gospel. He must have taken the rejection personally.

When I showed up the following day for what passed as work, the other helpers were nowhere in sight. The Chaplain called me in to his office. His customary smile was gone. I waited for him to speak. My mother always told me to listen to what the other person has to say first.

"I understand you disapprove strongly of different races marrying," he put to me.

I was stunned by the utter falsity of the accusation. "That's not true," I declared, leaving out the sir.

Baptist Bubba obviously snitched about the heated words we had and twisted them.

The Chaplin would not listen to my explanations to the contrary, but instead went on about his own attitudes and experiences. "It's a matter of *culture* and not color," he emphasized, trying to convince me of his way of thinking. "If the colored person has the same education and interests as the white, then they have a basis for a lifetime bond." He told me he had counseled many Negro sailors who wanted to bring home Caucasian brides, with and without the woman present. It was his job to disclose the problems they can expect living in the United States, the South especially. Officially he had to make a recommendation to the black bridegroom's C.O. as to whether the wedding with a white woman should take place or not. In most cases, he admitted, the couple's minds were already made up and they wanted to proceed.

The Navy minister sat back in his chair and looked at me. "I also heard you are against school integration."

"That's not true," I said again.

"Well, I'm against it too," he claimed, as if my denial did not reach his ears. "I wouldn't send my children to the same school with the coloreds. I don't want them going around saying 'motherfucker' all the time."

I could hardly believe, let alone trust, Chappy's words or his deeds. First he mouths a positive stance toward mixed marriage, believing I was against it, and then in the same breath endorses segregation in education after tuning out my rejection of the practice legal in the South. The shipbound career officer with family on shore was liberal, or wanted to appear so, on racial issues far re-moved from his everyday life but reserved a dose of conservatism for questions of color invading his own home.

"Streiber, I can't have my assistants fighting among themselves about race or religion."

Milwaukee Mick spilled his guts too. What did I do to offend him? We had an interesting conversation about theology, that's all. I was only guilty, in one case, of criticizing popular racial stereotypes and, in the other, of eschewing a rival faith and defending my own. Was that so terrible or blasphemous? An out-spoken but well-meaning Jew became the scapegoat for the biases and failings of non-Jews.

"I'm going to let you go," the man who supported God's benevolent view of man said without emotion or kindness. "The arguments must stop."

Chappy's two Christian elves did me in. There was no use debating the matter. The JG's mind was made up. He was not concerned with truth in the abstract or my side of the story. I was the source of the trouble in his shop and he had to put me out the door. It was that simple. The fact that I was the non-Christian did not make the decision more difficult for him. The compassion and understanding I thought characterized the churchman obviously were mistaken judgments on my part. His interest in, or attachment to, me was more transitory than the ocean voyage joining us narrowly in time.

This was the first time I had been fired from a job, in or out of the Army, and it did not sit well with me. The work was unofficial and temporary and insignificant but still I felt a great wrong had been done to me. I would feel the same way, even more so, almost a year later when another military officer told me my services were no longer needed. However, I tried not to let the unjust dismissal upset me too much. Before long, we would be docking in Bremerhaven.

The last two days aboard the *Rose*, without a cockamamie job to occupy much of my time, I spent many an hour just staring at the ocean I so often swam and bathed in, contemplating what my life as a Jewish G.I. in a post-Nazi Germany might be like. Would I run into anti-Semites? Are there any Jews left in Germany? Do Germans still harbor ill-feelings toward their American conquerors and occupiers? Is the Geist of Hitler hovering over the people of the Neue Deutschland?

There was a strange affinity between the solitary private first class standing on the quarterdeck and the dead two-star general whose name the ship bore. Both were American-born Jews. Both came from a parent or parents who were born and raised in Poland. The two were forty years apart in age and their respective parent or parents immigrated to the United States four decades apart. Both had enlisted in the Army at age seventeen.

Major General Rose was the highest-ranking Jew in the Army in 1945. His troops were called the "Spearhead in the West," the first Allied force to punch through enemy lines and enter Germany. After Rose's death, it was rumored that the Panzersoldat who killed him knew he was Jewish, but the G.I. in the jeep with him lived to tell a different story.

Had he survived the war, the 3rd Armored Division Commander, his apostasy notwithstanding, might very well have made an important contribution to the denazification of Germany. After all, in the eyes and the laws of the Third Reich, so long as Rose had one Jewish great-grandparent he was nicht nicht-jüdisch.

I anxiously awaited the conclusion of my troubled shipboard sojourn.

# PART II

# COMPANY ASSIGNMENT
# AND
# FRÄULEIN COMPANY

## CHAPTER 11: NIGHT TRAIN TO STUTTGART

Late in the evening on the twentieth of February the *Rose* passed through the English Channel, slipped into the North Sea, navigated above the East Frisian Islands, steered toward the mouth of the Weser River at the bottom of Helgoland Bay, and dropped anchor in Bremerhaven. U.S. troops were stationed in the port city, located in the former British zone of occupation, to protect military and commercial shipping. USAREUR division command centers and Seventh Army garrison forces were considerable distances away, spread out over thousands of square kilometers in the southern half of West Germany. Docked in Deutschland that Friday night but unable to see anything in the dark or go ashore, I slept very little.

Early Saturday morning, before going to breakfast, I went topside. Some German civilians were busy with various work activities on the ship's quarterdeck. I said "Good morning" to them and "How are you?" in Yiddish, trying to make it sound more like their tongue. They smiled and I was sure they understood me. Out of more than two thousand G.I.s on board, I was but one of a handful who climbed the long stairways at that hour to take a first peek at the Old World and our new home for a spell. I was wearing my fatigue shirt, without an overcoat or field jacket, and the frigid air went right through my body. My teeth chattered and I was shivering all over. Richie was right. It *was* fucking kalt in Germany.

By mid-afternoon I was on deck standing at ease ready to disembark. I was in my Class A greens, OD overcoat, round dress hat, and black leather glove shells with wool OD inserts. Bunched up with all the other troops, I spotted my three buddies from Monmouth and Ord on lines ahead of me. We planned to stay together in transit if possible. Finally, my turn came and I walked down the shaky gangway, duffel bag on one shoulder with arm around it, fingers of the other hand clasping the handle of my AWOL bag. I sounded off my name and serial number as I passed the master sergeant on the dock holding a clipboard and pen. Not thirty feet from the water's edge, a military transport train stood on one of two sets of tracks. Like other soldiers, I did not lodge onto the train via the end car but trudged along the outside looking for a compartment with an empty seat.

"Dave . . . Dave," I heard someone call out in front of me.

I looked about in that direction and saw it was Steve, the only buddy going to Böblingen with me. He was standing on the first step of the second car up from where I was, waving his arm wildly.

"We got a place for you," I heard him say as I moved in closer. "Come on."

Steve helped me with my bags into the compartment he secured with the other two we knew. I felt comfortable traveling with guys I had served with for most of my enlistment, from New Jersey to California and back. For the past three weeks I had had enough of strangers at Dix and on the *Rose*. My duffel bag fit nicely sideways on the floor under the seat and my AWOL bag was just the right size for the metal rack fixed to the wall near the ceiling. Compartments accommodated up to six passengers but we limited ours to four by telling those who popped their head through the sliding door that all the seats were taken.

The train ride to Stuttgart would traverse most of Germany from north to south and take all night I was told, a good sixteen hours. I unbuttoned my jacket, loosened my tie, slid down on the cushioned bench seat, and stretched my legs. My buddies were talking and joking about the Army and their experiences on the ship. I watched them as they settled in for the long haul to our new posts. I settled in too. I thought about the four young men whose lives were connected the past sixteen months, and the two whose lives might remain connected the next sixteen.

I knew Steve a little better than the other two, but I would not say we were close companions. It was just the luck of the draw that he and I would be headed to the same company in the same battalion in the same city. Murphy was on his way to the 72nd Signal Battalion in Mannheim, while Bigelow would soon be a part of the 34th Signal Battalion in Ludwigsberg. Each one of us could have received the Seventh Army dispatch of the other. The Army's impartial personnel assignment system was inexorably moving two unsuspecting G.I.s toward a firmer friendship.

Steve was just six months older than I but had been to college already. He skipped a grade in junior high and completed his first year of college before he enlisted. Why he cut loose from his California campus he never said exactly and I never figured it out. My budding Böblingen buddy frequently talked about resuming his higher education career when he gets out. On both forts I served with Steve, I noticed he liked to brag about his collegiate days. He was eager to impress his barracks mates, no more than high school graduates, with what he thought was his superior knowledge of the world. His casual comments at times turned to invectives, attacks upon a soldier's choices in life or relations with other people.

"That was a dumb thing to do," I once heard Steve say to a spec four at Ord who had just re-enlisted.

Everyone knew the E-4 signed for another hitch because he was depressed over getting a Dear John, did not want to go home and face his family, and needed the bonus to pay back those he had borrowed from in order to send money to his former girl-friend.

"Why put in three more years for a broad who clipped you and dumped you and is screwing someone else?" Steve crudely and cruelly put to the soldier who outranked him by one pay-grade.

We all felt sorry for the poor bastard and Steve's account of the situation was probably accurate, but the expression of those sentiments in that way was uncalled for.

Steven C. Goldbaum was his full name. He was born in New York City, but his parents moved to Los Angeles when he was a baby and he grew up there. Despite his name, Steve was not Jewish. His father and paternal grandparents were but he, like his mother, was raised as a Protestant. The grandparents were born in Germany but the father grew up in Washington Heights on the Upper West Side of Manhattan, a very Jewish area before the war.

Steve was often mistaken for Jewish, and it was not just because of his name. He wore horn-rimmed glasses and looked bookish. He often voiced strong opinions and did not hesitate to criticize authority. He moved his hands forcefully when he spoke. And Steve would not take no for an answer if he wanted something badly enough. At Ord he once went over the platoon sergeant's head, and marched straight to the captain's home off post, when he was not allowed to switch guard duty schedules with another soldier in order to attend a family function in L.A. The officer with two bars was not impressed with the enlisted man with one stripe breaking the chain of command.

If being mistaken for Jewish bothered Steve, he did not show it. Indeed, his own speech mannerisms gave him away. At times he affected a Yiddish accent, something I dared not ever do. Steve would say, "So how's by you?" when greeting someone—me, another Jew in the company, or a Gentile. He liked to make references to religion, the Jewish and the Christian, comments that were uncomplimentary to Jews and easily misinterpreted by Gentiles. "Ask the mess sergeant to make you gefilte fish," Steve might josh, especially on Yom Kippur. Or, if a soldier did a silly or stupid thing, he would wisecrack threateningly, "We'll have to nail you to the cross."

For some reason, I was never the butt of any purposeful or inadvertent joke or affront by Steve's doing. My school and company mate's apparent identity confusion, I reasoned, explained his misplaced efforts to mimic Jews and fault religious life.

Murphy was a southern boy from Biloxi. He seemed out of place in New Jersey with everything very different from back home—below freezing weather in winter, whites divided by ethnicity, the races co-mingling in public facilities. We used to call him Mississippi Murph. I was sure he approved of the segregation in his parts but I still liked him because he did not speak badly of, or use derogatory names for, our black barracks buddies behind their backs. He was quiet and unassuming and made few friends. When I learned he had never eaten New York style food I brought back for him, after a weekend at home, a hard salami and provolone sandwich on Italian bread, with a potato knish on the side and a slice of cheesecake for dessert. Until he came into contact with me, he had only heard of Jews.

In my class at Monmouth, Murphy was the best repairman. It took him no time at all to trouble shoot and fix the bug one of the instructors planted in a piece of radar equipment. He just turned a few dials on the oscilloscope, fiddled with the voltage meter, measured in microfarads the electrical charge in capacitors, tested the ohmage at the ends of resistors, and, voilà, he knew exactly what was wrong. I was very good in the classroom with lectures covering theory, mathematics, and physics. But I was not much interested in the nuts and bolts, or rather the tubes and wires, of electronics. My adeptness in the practical end of the course left something to be desired. More than once Murph assisted me with the workbench exercises.

Bigelow I also liked. He came from a Polish-Catholic working-class family in Springfield, Massachusetts. With his light hair and complexion, he looked more German. Perhaps two or three generations back, before the Bigelowskis left the shipyards of Gdansk for a better life in New England, there had been some ethnic mixing with Poland's neighbor to the west. Despite differences in our backgrounds, Big and I made similar choices in life at our tender age. He enlisted after high school, wanted to be an electrical engineer, picked radar school as the first step in that direction, and was planning on college after the Army. Occasionally we hung out together.

I remember seeing *Frankenstein 1970* with him at Monmouth's central movie theater, a belated implausible sequel to the 1931 classic starring a bloated Boris Karloff. On the ticket line, Hollywood posters with that future date in the title stared back at me behind glass windows and I wondered what I would be doing in twelve years.

"In nineteen seventy," I said to Big, "you'll have thirteen years in the Army." I kidded him about making a career of the life we both discounted.

"No," he replied at once. "In nineteen seventy, I'll have ten years *out* of the Army."

I would have given the same answer to my own loaded question. Two eighteen-year-olds were already projecting their lives well into the future.

A few hours passed. The train-traveling troopers were all comfy in their compartment talking about girls, playing card games, and eating the K-rations given to them.

"How did you make out with that high-yellow WAC?" Big asked me out of the blue, not taking his eyes from the hand that was just dealt him. He could only have been referring to the mulatto girl I met at the EM club the day after Thanksgiving that I dated for a few weeks. She was the only WAC or black I ever went with.

I stalled a few moments before answering, not looking directly at him. "You mean did I get into her?"

"Yeah . . . what else would I be talking about?" Big said lifting his head.

My three buddies gawked at me with all smiles.

"I spent one night with her before I left Ord," I answered simply.

"She must've been wild?" Murph commented. "Those Nigruh gals really move."

"Looked more white than Negro to me," Big added.

"She was all right." That was about all I cared to say on the matter.

"Come on Dave," Steve implored with a smirk. "Give us a blow-by-blow description. You're among friends."

If my radar classmates expected me to talk about my boundary-busting tryst, my private affair in a California hotel one night that I will long remember and hold dear, they were surely going to be disappointed. I felt no need to boast about my intimacies with that girl or the last time I was with her. And I had no desire to get into a conversation about race or color so soon after the confrontations I had on the *Rose*. I tried to say nothing more about the matter. I liked her too much for that.

Big spoke next when I did not. "Did you tell her you'll soon be packing your duffel bag?"

"No."

"Did you tell her you and your three buddies she met will be going to Germany?" Steve remarked.

"It never came up."

"That's a shame," Steve added, this time bordering on offense. "I'm sure she would've liked to hear about the lily white frauleins you could be getting into soon."

"Did you tell her how old you really were?" Big wanted to know.

"No."

"Did you tell her you're Jewish?" Steve inquired.

"She didn't ask."

"What in hell *did* you tell her about yourself?" Murph put to me.

"Nothing much."

Steve leaned forward. "Don't feel bad, Davey boy," he quipped, the smirk still on his face.

Steve always called me "Davey boy" when he was about to say something silly or impudent.

"You might be playing the same game in Germany before you know it." Then he said with characteristic coarseness, relying on a Yiddish word he knew I would readily understand, "But over there you won't have to stoop to that kind of shtup."

The train stopped in Frankfurt after midnight and it woke me up from a light sleep. I put my jacket on and stepped out of the compartment. I stood in the corridor and looked out the window. There was a lot of commotion on the platform with so many troops getting off here and lining up. Some of the boys in OD's or greens were en route to Friedberg, a small town northeast of Frankfurt. A dark brown military bus was waiting to take them to Ray Barracks, home of the 3rd Armored Division, which now had another famous soldier in it. For the past five months PFC Elvis A. Presley was rocking and rolling inside a Patton tank in General Maurice Rose's old combat unit. If the Cold War ever turned hot, the teen idol with his comrades in armor would form a veritable "Spearhead to the East."

There were MPs throughout the train and we could not get off unless this was our destination. I wanted to walk around the station, perhaps buy something to eat, but since I had no German Gelt the restriction made little difference.

Mannheim was the next stop on our night train to Stuttgart. Murph had to get off here and we said goodbye to our Mississippi buddy. He was told to wait outside in front of the station where a deuce-and-a-half will pick him up and take him to Hammonds Barracks, one of the two U.S. Army camps in Mannheim.

We arrived at the Hauptbahnhof in Stuttgart on Sunday, Washington's birthday, shortly before 0600 hours. I doubted the American holiday meant anything to people in the foreign land I was now in. Standing on the platform near the first car was a burly staff sergeant, clipboard rested on his left arm, whistle around his neck, calling off last names in alphabetical order. Names were at times called more than once. He made check marks on his roster every time a trooper with his gear passed by and shouted a first name and middle initial. Every few seconds the staffer yelled a command and motioned the men to keep moving away from the tracks and into the open area of the main railway station.

Bigelow left the compartment first, then Steve. I was the last of our foursome off the train.

## CHAPTER 12: PRIVATE AFFAIR

The platform leading into the Stuttgart station was quite long and I had to wait a while before my name was called. That first morning in Germany turned out to be, as I sensed it might, the last time I saw Bigelow. I thought of him and the question he asked me hours earlier. It was not an unreasonable query. In the Army it was all too common for one young man to inquire about another's female exploits. Perhaps I should have responded more than I did.

It was Bigelow's doing that I met the WAC at Fort Ord. "Come with us to the EM club," he entreated me the day after Thanksgiving. "They're throwing a party." Had he known whom I would be meeting there, he might not have been so inviting. Half a dozen other Monmouth buddies from our platoon were going as well.

"All right," I said to Big, deciding to do something out-of-character for a change. I had never gone to the EM clubs on any of the three posts I was stationed. I was not a drinker and I had no call to hang out on my off-duty hours with those who boozed it up. At Dix and Monmouth, I went home on weekends; at Ord I usually hopped on a bus by myself to Monterey or Salinas to catch a movie, drop in to the USO Club, or just stroll around town. Providence ruled when I accepted Big's offer that Friday.

The EM club was bustling with a live band breaking eardrums for the most part with fast-dancing music. The large room was dimly lit and the cigarette smoke further clouded one's vision. There was a crowd of E-2's and 3's hoofing it up on the floor with WACs in uniforms bearing no stripe or one small one. A few noncoms were raising elbows at tables with the peons. It did not hit me right away but after a piece I was conscious of the fact that only white faces were smiling at this club. Soldiers on the other side of the color line, I was told, took their seats with drinking buddies at a different EM club on post.

"The coloreds don't come to this club," Big said in response to my question about the segregation I observed. "They don't play that jigaboo shit here."

"Off duty the Nigruhs keep with their own," Murph added.

"It's more than spook music and birds-of-a-feather flocking together," Steve said with a  straight face. "The white girls  here won't dance with them."

Toward the end of the evening there was a dance contest. Anyone wishing to enter went out on the floor, stood around for a few minutes, and was matched with someone not of one's choosing. Big dared me to try my dancing feet and I did. I was teamed with a private first class whom I found attractive. She was the height I liked, about five-five, six inches my shorter, and had the thin body frame that appealed to me. I saw right away she was not Caucasian but her skin looked almost white and her hair was straight. The nose was not broad, her lips not thick. The cherry lipstick and rouged cheeks were enough to fool most people from afar in a darkened room. Her green jacket was unbuttoned all the way down and I could make out the size and shape of her melons. On the floor she followed my lead well, especially with the faster dances.

"Where are you from?" I asked her. I did not inquire as to why she was frequenting this EM club and not the other.

"South Carolina."

No wonder she fell in with my steps, especially with the faster numbers. My partner was doing the Shag, a dance popular in her region, which had the same basic movement as the Lindy we New Yorkers did, two sets of triple-steps with the girl then swinging out. I never lost control of my twists and turns on the slippery polished wood. We won second prize, a ten-dollar coupon good for food and drink at the club. The girl kissed me she was so excited.

The coupon was an opening to make a date with the WAC the following week. I had never gone out before with someone of another race. My buddies chided me about planning to see the off-color PFC again. None of them asked to be introduced to one of her friends. Had I been on my home turf, in full view of my parents or friends, I probably would not have sought out her company, despite a young man's desire for new experiences.

As it turned out, we dated every Friday or Saturday night in December. We met at the EM club and danced up a storm. I would then walk her back to her barracks on the other side of the post from my unit. We always sort of stopped short of her building. I would nudge her to an out of the way spot and nestle with her up against a tree or wall. We would do mouth-to-mouth intensely for a while as I ran my hand over her bulgy boobs but never beneath the blouse. I

113

pushed my body up against hers, making sure she could feel my hardness.

On the fourth date, the day after Christmas, in the middle of a prolonged and sweet embrace, without any provocation on my part, she lowered her hand and touched me. First she rubbed me gently, then she squeezed me boldly, guided only by the contour in my trousers. Had I been willing to risk blowing my Army career, not to mention the stockade, I would have jazzed her right there on the ground.

"Why don't we go into town tomorrow," I said with some reserve. "We could get a room . . . in a hotel."

"Okay," she whispered without hesitation, much to my surprise and delight.

This was the first time I had ever asked that of any girl, let alone one not of my own race. It was a bold act on my part, a move I doubted any of my buddies would have made. Perhaps I was playing out a scene I recalled from a war movie, an Aldo Ray or Robert Wagner closing in on a demure foreign girl. We planned to meet at the Fort Ord bus station at five. I would have to wait until the next day to find out whether one soldier misread another's intentions.

The WAC appeared at the bus station as she said she would. I did not tell her right away about the new development that could put a crimp in our plans for the day, or, I should say, her leanings for the night. I wanted to tell her that I had just learned I would be going to Germany in two weeks, it was only right that I should tell her, but I decided to wait for a more opportune time.

"Let's go to Salinas," she said.

"Okay," I of course answered. It did not matter to me where we had our encounter so long as we had it.

My date explained she did not wish to go to Monterey because it was too close to Ord and too small a town to get lost in. Seaside, right outside the post, all four blocks of it, was out of the question. On the way to Salinas, I tried to imagine how she might react if I told her that after New Year's I would be shipping out. Honesty may be the best policy but I had no way of knowing if she would follow the path we had chosen for the day or turn around and go back to the base. So I said nothing.

An eerie silence hovered over the young mixed-race couple sitting together with hands clasped, strangers for the most part, on the road to engaging in the human species' most intimate of unions. The girl whose rank was equal to mine was out of uniform, as I. She did not ask me what my religion or nationality was and I volunteered no such information. I held back trying to find out if it was her Mammy or her Pappy who was black and she passed on telling me of her own accord. Her views on miscegenation or intermarriage were never expressed. I wanted to ask her what it was like growing up with Jim Crow, but kept still. She said nothing about segregated schools or lunch counters, rest rooms or waiting rooms for colored only, or moving to the back of the bus when white folk demanded her seat. When we did talk, it was about the Army or impersonal matters.

"I'm a secretary to a light colonel," she said, when I asked her what she does. Her words initially startled me but then I realized there was no racial intimation intended.

"My MOS is radar repair," I offered, "but I don't do the kind of work I was trained for."

"How old are you?" she asked, and, before I had a chance to respond, added, fortunately for me, "I'll be twenty-one next month."

"Twenty-two," I told her.

She never said why she joined the Army but I gathered she did it for many of the same reasons as I did, to escape a not-so-propitious home environment. In Carolina, what could she do? Chop cotton? Housekeep for whites? Wait tables at a greasy spoon? Down South, who could she marry? A black mill hand? Colored sharecropper? Mulatto good-for-nothing?

From stories I read or heard I fancied what the alluring, not-quite-white soldier gal next to me must have looked like years earlier. Visions of a skinny little girl with nappy hair parted in the middle, long woolly pigtails tied at the ends with small yellow ribbons, crossed my mind. A cute picaninny playing with rag dolls and broken toys in front of a tarpaper shack on a dirt road came into focus.

We walked around Salinas for a while before taking a room over a tattoo parlor two blocks behind the Greyhound station. That would have been a good opportunity to lay myself bare, let her know the most important facet about me now, something she ought to hear, but again I failed to speak.

Salinas was in the heart of a one-hundred-fifty-mile long valley which grew more lettuce and other produce than anywhere else in the United States. Almost all the streets had Spanish names. Most people I saw were Mexican. The men were short, some heavily built, with sun-baked bronze faces, and rough and curled hands. With a brood of children at their side, women walked a few paces behind the men. Conspicuous in this rodeo town were Anglo men decked out in full-brimmed cowboy hats, wide belts and buckles, and pointed-toe leather boots with carved panels. Although Salinas was the capital of Monterey County, Monterey had the advantage of the Presidio and its ocean location. To me, Monterey was the more esthetic and more inter-esting place to visit.

My date waited outside the three-story hotel we decided on while I went inside and registered. The desk clerk looked at me funny I thought when she came in and we went upstairs. It was a good thing I was packing three rubbers. I would need all of them.

The room was plain and simple—a double bed, small dresser and mirror, end table, lamp, and closet. We had a partial view of the street below from a triple window that faced a back alley. Not long after I locked the door, she responded to my touches and we quickly undressed and slid under the covers.

I could not say who was more nervous, she or I. She kept rambling on about being afraid and I kept telling her not to worry, all the while reaching for one of the rubbers I stashed in the top drawer of the table next to the bed. I slipped it around my tip, then took one of her hands and guided her so that she could roll it down. I worked my fingers with hers, which provided a kindled boy added stimulation and, it was hoped, would alleviate a girl's fears of impregnation.

In a flash I was in the saddle, riding hard and fast, weighing down a mare that dug into my back and played kissy ear. While she was accumulating epidermis under her nails and wax on her tongue, I was getting heart palpitations and pistol shots off.

"Oh, you came," she suddenly whined, turning her head from side to side. She could not have felt my generous flow. Undoubtedly she was aware of the tension and then relaxation in my body. "You *came*."

I had never been with a girl before who expected that. What did she want me to do, wait for her? "I thought that's what I'm supposed to do," I explained meekly, after I turned over onto my back and caught my breath.

"What about me?"

"What about you?" I asked without thinking.

"Finish me. Use your hand."

I was in store for a lesson in lovemaking. I feared she might conclude from my inexperience that I had lied to her about my age. I moved halfway on top of her. She took my right hand and put it where she wanted it, partitioning her legs and then grabbing hold of my fingers. With her hand over mine, she found the right spot and began stroking, up and down, like we were sanding a piece of rough sawn wood. The rapid action evoked more passion by the second for both participants. Comfortable with my deftness, she took her hand away and flung her arms around my neck, drawing me to her chest.

"Oh, oh, oh," she shrieked, tightening her grip on me.

Her whole body quivered under mine. It seemed like an explosion went off in-side of her. I continued to stroke her, this time slowly and gently. I extended my touching to include the raw fleshy unseen parts, not bothered by the clamminess I found in her. She thanked me as she moved my hand away.

"I'm very sensitive down there now," she said.

We cleaned up, got dressed, and went downstairs. We had something to eat, walked around Salinas again, and came back to the room. It was getting dark. We sat and talked for a while.

There was nothing for us to do but return to the bed for Round 2. It was apparent we were now both more at ease with each other after bridging the natural gulf between two unfulfilled lovers, consummating the act of reproduction. There was no rush for carnal knowledge this time. We moved our hands and fingers carefully, exploring the unknown recesses and curvatures of our bodies. Our mouths were wet and one. Abruptly she sat up and swiveled around on the bed. She held me with one hand and braced herself with the other.

"Don't come in my mouth," she told me politely.

I imagined these same time-immemorial words were uttered this very minute in many different languages by innumerable women all around the world.

I watched her as she opened wide and clamped down on me. I pulled her hair back to get a better view and caressed her neck. Now she was playing kissy cock. What's next? I wondered. Kissy cunt?

Did she want me to move my face to her middle and burrow into her? I had never done that before and made no gesture toward that end. I think I would have reciprocated had she asked. For the moment, though, she could not ask anything.

"You'd better stop," I advised her, mindful of her admonition. I lifted her head a little.

"Get a baggie," she said, struggling to get the words out.

I had never heard the word used that way. For a moment I thought she was referring to baggy pants. Maybe that was the way WACs or southern girls talked about men's devices.

"Shouldn't we wait? I'm close to coming."

"Just have it handy."

She swung herself around to be flat on her back and rested her head on the pillow. She lifted her knees toward her chest, took my hand and began to stroke. This time I used my thumb and two fingers, rubbing the outside while probing her inside, one complex motion to please two erotic bodies.

"Oh, oh," she wailed. "Now . . . do it now."

I fetched the rubber I placed on the bed and put it on quickly. Fondling her kept me hard. I closed in on her. The two soldiers coupled in a civilian bunk joined forces and rocked in cadence. The noncombatants fielded double-time maneuvers. Under the sheets, they engaged in target practice. One PFC fired his rifle, the other took the rounds in her bull's-eye. They got their discharges together.

Resting in bed in a tangle of body parts, we slowed our throbbing hearts. Before long we were fast asleep. I let pass all openings to divulge the truth about my situation. I felt bad about that but not so ashamed of myself that I would spill my guts now. I could not risk spoiling our relationship, or companionship, or friendship, or whatever *ship* we were cabined on together.

Hours later I woke up in a cold sweat. It was still dark outside and the strange room at first disoriented me. Leaning on my elbow, I peered at the young woman beside me, enamored by her girlish beauty and by thoughts of the intimacies we just shared. Until a few hours ago, she was not much more than a dancing partner. Now we were two P's in a pad, two first class privates having an affair, stumbling through life and what passed for love in dingy quarters.

Why did she come with me to a hotel for the night? Was this her way of getting me involved? Did she just want to marry white or did she want *me*? Racial differences aside, I really liked her and I felt nothing but tenderness for the person who was so loving towards me. I kept looking at my Saturday sweetheart while she slept, as though she and I had lived together as man and wife. But united for life I knew we would never be. Pretty soon I would be leaving Fort Ord and she would be the girl I left behind.

The Tony Curtis character in *Kings Go Forth* came to mind. An arrogant Jewish G.I. in war-torn France wooed Natalie Wood—a half-black, half-white fille of American parents—away from his buddy Frank Sinatra by his good looks, then shtupped the vulnerable girl for weeks with false promises of marriage. The ruse exposed, an uncontrite Curtis claims the miscegenation was just a "new kick," a worn Wood waddles suicide, and a smitten Sinatra swears revenge in blood. Hollywood gave new meaning to the term "film noir."

Was I pulling off a cocky Curtis? Well, maybe. I did not steal the mulatto maid I met in postwar America away from a G.I. Joe, black or white. I made no vows of love or betrothal to lure the free spirit into the sack with me. But I kept silent about my new orders. And I did not beseech her to put in for a transfer to Germany. I was confident she would not try to kill herself because I planned to tell her later on that I received word of my transfer the day *after* our night in town. The worst scenario I imagined was my southern siren singing, like a young Ethel Waters in an early talkie, "Am I Blue?" A memorable send-off from California was all I wanted.

She opened her eyes and saw me staring at her. "What's wrong, sugar?" she asked innocently.

"Nothing," I said. "I just like looking at you." The second answer was no lie.

Tugging me close to her, she whispered in my ear. I reached for the last rubber in the drawer.

# CHAPTER 13: WILLKOMMEN IN DEUTSCHLAND

The main railroad terminal was an imposing early twentieth-century structure. During the war it had been hit by Allied bombs but the building as a whole with its high arched tower was not destroyed. Thick steel girders in crisscross patterns reached upward forcefully toward the domed ceiling. White light gushed through the paneled glass windows on the exterior walls in narrow beams that hit the expansive floor. Citizens of the New Germany did a good job restoring the architectural integrity of their Hauptbahnhof in Baden-Württemberg's biggest city.

This was the first time I set foot in another country. As I entered the Stuttgart station, I could see everything was different. It was interesting just to walk around the ticket and loading areas, taking notice of the odd people and alien environment. I saw mostly American soldiers. There were few indigenous travelers this early in the morning on a Sunday. German men carried briefcases and wore long, dark double-breasted overcoats and hats with folded down brims. Stocky, older women with bags in both hands affected a racked walk and looked plain in their colorless coats and dresses. The porters were white, which surprised me initially. Short, middle-aged plump men in rumpled jackets and trousers, wearing boxed hats angled to one side, carried suitcases and pushed half-empty carts with trunks and pieces of luggage.

Both of my buddies' names came up long before mine on the roll call and we got separated. Steve and I going to Böblingen were instructed to wait outside the station at 0730 in front of pick-up point #3 where an Army truck would be waiting for us. I looked around for Steve but he was nowhere in sight. Bigelow went to another numbered rendez-vous. He was headed in the opposite direction, to Krabbenloch Kaserne in Ludwigsburg, straight north of Stuttgart.

There were some bright lights coming from the food shops near the entrance and I walked toward them. I took a pass on standing outside in the cold for close to an hour. It looked like the bakery was just opening. A rosy-cheeked young woman with dark blond hair pinned up in a curl put on a full apron, tied it behind her back, and moved around several trays of pastries and cakes. I rested my duffel and AWOL bags and went up to the display cabinets. The colorful and odd-shaped desserts on top of and inside the glass shelves and windows were enticing but unlike the cheese Danishes or custard éclairs I often picked out in New York bakeries. I leaned forward and then bent down to read the unfamiliar German script on little white tags beside the sundry sweets. I tried to figure out what they were and the cost of each in dollars or cents. I was hungry for something, for anything in front of me.

"You just come from the States?" a voice called out from behind me. I turned around and saw an American soldier. He was looking at me and smiling. "You seem lost," he said.

"This is my first day in Germany?"

"This is my last," the stranger added, broadening his smile. "Been here nineteen months. I'm going home today."

I just stood there and looked at him. I did not know what to say to the short-timer.

"You want one of those cooken?" he asked, jerking his head in the direction of the trays in the enclosure I had been eyeing.

I knew he meant Kuchen, or cakes, but he pronounced it without the *ch* sound. "I don't have any German money," I told him.

"No sweat, buddy. I'll give you some."

The soldier who adopted an air of friendliness had one stripe on his sleeve. On his left shoulder he had the blue, yellow, and red triangular Seventh Army patch, the one I would soon have to sew on my uniforms. The design in the yellow portion consisted of seven gradations of blocks on either side of the triangle. I had heard it was called the "Seven Steps to Hell" patch, signifying the fierce and bloody ground battles U.S. troops waged against the Wehrmacht and Waffen SS the last months of the war.

Both of us were in Class A's but looked part of different armies. The PFC sported the olive drab uniform with its waist jacket and brown shoes. I was still garbed in greens, with the longer jacket and black footwear. The two suits of OD's I was issued were in my duffel bag and I would soon just hang them in my wall locker. I seldom wore them anymore since I purchased the new greens and dyed my boots and shoes black. It must have been confusing to Germans to see their erstwhile enemies in two different colored and styled winter uniforms as well as the khakis, or light browns, worn in summer. Soldaten in the Wehrmacht and Bundeswehr only had one style of gray uniform.

I reached into my trousers for some change. "Here, I'll pay you for it." I did not like someone I did not know treating me.

"No, let me," he insisted, pulling out a few strange coins from his breast pocket. "My train leaves in an hour. If I don't spend these marks, I'll have to throw them away."

"Okay," I said. "How about this one?" I pointed to a square piece of yellow cake of some sort with chocolate icing or cream and crushed nuts on top that looked good to me.

The overseas veteran addressed the young woman behind the counter as "Schatzie" and said something in German. I noticed she scowled as he pressed his index finger on the glass window in front of the item I wanted. He handed her a coin about the size and color of a quarter. She gave me the cake in a thin piece of waxed paper, then deposited three small copper coins in my benefactor's hand.

"It was only seventy pfennigs," he remarked. "Seventeen cents." To my astonishment he added, "Kraut money ain't worth shit."

I thanked my Seventh Army associate and started to dig in, ignoring for the moment his negative comment. The little something was sweet and tasty, exactly what I needed to give me a boost of energy on a morning with little sleep the night before. I enjoyed eating my treat and I did not mind having an American, soldier or civilian, to talk to.

"Where are you from?" I was asked.

"New York."

"City?"

With a mouthful I nodded.

"I'm from North Dakota myself. Grew up on a farm."

The PFC felt the need to talk about himself and the Army he would soon be discharged from. The vision I got was of a teenage boy milking cows and feeding pigs before heading off to school in the morning, then baling hay and plowing fields until sundown. He said the local draft board took him at twenty-one, despite his father's pleas for a deferral until after the harvest. Before entering the service he seldom came into contact with people of other races, religions, or nationalities. I told him how different his background and experiences were from mine. He bitched about spending all of his time in Germany in a tough Ordnance detachment. He disliked his unit and its work intensely. Had it not been for a mean mother of a first sergeant who favored his own kind, he would have made spec four.

"I didn't brown nose blacktop," he stated, "so he wouldn't put me in for the bird." The weapons-handler was emphatic in his belief that he was denied a promotion because he was white.

I listened without reacting to his every complaint. What could I say to someone I just met about things I knew nothing of?

"Germans are stupid and puny people," the soldier went on, casting aspersions on the country and Volk he was about to kiss off. "No wonder they lost the war. And after they couldn't defend themselves against the Russians without our help. We're the ones who built Germany up again. You should see them when they stand in line, like at the movies or the streetcar stop. They got no manners or respect for others. They push and shove and think it's okay to cut in front of someone ahead of them."

I wondered whether such negativism was characteristic of Americans who have served in Germany, whether I might be saying something similar in a year or so. My cake was all gone and I wiped my mouth and fingers with a handkerchief. I was interested in hearing about Germany. I waited for him to resume talking.

"Where are you headed to?" he asked, changing the subject.

"Boblingen."

"Been there many times. I know the barracks too."

He explained I was on my way to Panzer Kaserne, a German tank base built just before the war. Patch Barracks was where he was stationed, formerly called Kurmärker Kaserne, near Vaihingen, not far from Böblingen, the home of another Panzer regiment. Both bases were constructed simultaneously and were connected by a cobblestone road, Panzerstrasse, designed to withstand the heavy traffic in tanks and resist damage from the metal cleats on their tracks. Kurmärker's regiment in August 1939 was moved to East Prussia and then to an area near the Polish border where on 1 September it crossed over with turret guns blazing. The German tank unit had also taken part in the successful campaigns in Luxembourg, Belgium, and France.

"What's Boblingen like?" I inquired. I was eager to hear anything about my new home.

"It's a small town, but nice."

"Is there much action there?" I asked the soldier.

I had no idea if a Dakota farm boy would understand my big city terminology and, if he did, how he felt about such matters. My nearly twenty months in the Army taught me one thing. There are all types of young men around, the prudes who never use scatological words and turn away from any mention of sex as well as the most foulmouthed imaginable, whose every third word is either sucker or fucker.

"There's plenty of poontang all over Germany," he said simply and assuredly. "A G.I. can get it wherever he is."

My new-found friend's knowledge and proclivities were immediately apparent. This put me at ease and I asked him more about the most important thing on a peacetime soldier's mind. He took my casual questions as some sort of cue and began advising me on a number of points.

"Go into town in civies. Most Germans will spot you as an American from your clothes and haircut, but out of uniform you won't call as much attention to our victory over them or stir up any unnecessary animosity."

I had gathered that much myself. My overseas bag with my civilian clothes, I thought, should be waiting for me in the mailroom at the 176th right now.

"Don't change money in the bars or clubs in town. They pay only four marks to a dollar. The American Express on post gives four-point-two."

"Not a big difference," I noted, without calculating it.

"Two extra marks on ten bucks. Two beers in any bar or club."

Perhaps it was a big difference, at least to soldiers who drank a lot or lived off post. I knew I was in the grips of someone who needed very little prodding to give a newcomer tips. He asked me if wanted another Kuchen, perhaps interested in extending our early morning conversation. I declined politely.

"When you go looking for a piece of ass," he then went on about what he seemingly knew best, "stay clear of the Bahnhof Annies."

"Who?" I must have sounded very naïve.

"The old bags walking the streets around the train station since the war. They only charge ten or fifteen marks but your father or grandfather could've shot his wad into them."

Ten or fifteen Marks, I mused. How cheap love was over here.

"And if you're in a big city, be careful if you wander onto Schweinstrasse."

"What?" I asked.

"Schweinstrasse. It means Pig Street in German. The pros sit in the front rooms of their apartments near the window half-naked and call men in. Middle-age Germans mostly go there. The street's off limits to G.I.s. If the MPs catch you, it's a court martial offense."

I wondered if my Bahnhof buddy ever went to such a street himself or if he was just repeating what he had heard from *his* buddies. This was probably the first Strasse many American soldiers rushed to not long after they landed in Germany, the risk of the stockade notwithstanding.

"You're better off going to G.I. joints," he continued. "But, don't be taken in by the bargirls."

"Taken in?" I inquired again naïvely.

"You don't always have to pay them. Many will put out for a few beers or a glass of schnaps and a good time."

I took notice of what he was saying, not displeased by this confirmation of the greater opportunities for gratis or low-cost sexual encounters in Germany. He told me to get a steady, to try to date the young women who work on post, at the PX or snack bar, the "snatch bar" as it was often called. But, he pointed out, chances are the one who caught my eye would already have a G.I. paying the rent and brown-bagging her.

The USAREUR maven took delight in clueing in a novice. I was getting indoctrinated into amerikanisches Deutschland, more than I asked for. Most Fräuleins, I learned, toil for low wages, cannot buy or even obtain the food they like, and are attracted to American culture and soldiers who are rich by local standards and free spenders. A typical trooper seeking to escape the boredom of Army life and frustrations with authority is easy prey to almost any one of them.

Listening to him talk about women peaked my curiosity about what he called the shop girl. "What does schatzie mean?" I asked, remembering that Richie used the word too.

"It means honey or sweetie, like for a wife or girlfriend. But when you say it to a German girl or woman you don't know, she's insulted. It's considered very vulgar. But that's why we do it."

Now I understood the face the shop girl made but not the soldier's reason for provoking her ire.

"Why should Americans want to insult German women?" I asked.

"Because we like to fuck them but we don't respect them."

I looked at the rural Midwesterner standing in front of me, confused by the manner in which he expressed himself in a public place to a fellow G.I. he just met. No provocation on my part was needed to elicit further talk on this subject. He reproached German women for selling their bodies to Americans, for marrying them just to come to the States. They flock to bars and clubs G.I.s were known to frequent, congregate outside the gates of Army posts, dog the troops on field maneuvers.

The stranger's most colorful and acrimonious remarks were reserved for the Hildas and Helgas who bedded with the black buddies, bleached blondes who lived openly with their shaded lovers and defiantly walked down the street holding hands with and touching lips to the most non-Aryan of men now in their homeland. These postwar pariahs, abhorred by both Germans and Americans, were often questioned by MPs and arrested for prostitution by the Polizei.

"A lot of gals here go for dark meat," he added judgmentally. "And not just for the money."

I was somewhat taken aback by this kind of talk about German women, and by proxy certain American too, but I wanted to hear more of this lesson in foreign female familiarity. "What do you mean?" I asked. I was reminded of the interracial couple I saw on the ship.

"Some frauleins give their cunts to coons as a means of rejecting their land and people," he explained with some insight but arguably more plebeian New York than bucolic Dakotan language. "They know most Krauts are racist. They hate their Nazi past, the Germany they lived through, and the hardships they suffered."

"Well, why don't they just date white G.I.s?"

"We won't go near them," he said, personalizing and generalizing his answer at the same time.

"Why is that?" I was still puzzled but I should have figured it out.

He hesitated a moment, then responded with what by now was a predictable mix of sarcasm and racism in commingled English and

German.

"Most negerliebend gals are hookers who breeze into town every payday." I knew lieben means to love and figured out the unfamiliar part of the word. "Those who aren't for hire are usually older, in their late thirties or even forties . . . not so shane anymore."

From my Yiddish, I knew he meant *schön* in German, or pretty.

"What about the younger ones?"

The soldier about to depart Germany was telling me the inside dope on its people. He paused again, widening his eyes and extending a childish grin, then answered in a matter-of-fact tone.

"We won't touch them either once word gets out they took in a grosse black schwanz."

Here I was apprehensive about Germans harboring negative feelings toward Americans. It hardly occurred to me that Americans, at least those not Jewish, might be nursing ill-will toward Germans. My self-appointed mentor took a lot for granted, using German words freely with a newcomer to the country. Perhaps this was just the way G.I.s talked in Deutschland. I did not like his racial invectives but I refrained from reacting to them, as he behaved amiably toward me and believed he was doing a fellow soldier a good turn. The young G.I. ready to shove off sounded like the older ex-G.I. fag at Port Authority. Both station strangers who approached me had a mouthful to say after serving in postwar Germany.

There was still time before I had to go outside the terminal to catch the ride to my company. I stayed and listened a while longer. The trenchant trooper in transit offered another friendly tip to the new kid on the block. "Most of all buddy," he said with all seriousness, "don't get married."

I looked straight at him but remained tight-lipped. The day I arrive in Germany I hear the same words as the day I left home. Longtime friend and passing comrade alike offered me the identical bit of gratuitous advice. The matrimonial angle evidently was of primary concern to Americans serving in Germany.

"Dave . . . Dave." I heard my first name being called out twice in a familiar voice just as I was about to explore the matter further with this stranger. I looked around and saw Steve standing near the entrance to the station waving at me with both arms. I moved in closer to him, we both made motions with our hands, and then I returned to pick up my bags.

The short-timer was nowhere in sight. Hardly thirty seconds passed. The OD-clad draftee, who had much to tell about German women and saw fit to counsel a newcomer, disappeared from my life as suddenly and unexpectedly as he had appeared.

Steve and I made it to the pick-up point as the sergeant-in-charge was calling and checking off names of the dozen or so men in Class A's standing by the deuce-and-a-half parked at the curb. The NCO in front of me was short and thin with pallid cheeks that reddened in the cold. His voice was deep and pitched louder as he spoke, an incongruous characteristic given his small frame. But this was not the only anomaly about the man. His rank was that of the new Army, a buck sergeant, an E-5 with three stripes and no rocker, one of the enlisted ranks introduced only eight months earlier, while his dress was that of the old Army, brown boots with fatigues.

"Welcome to Germany, gentlemen," the bucky said, after he completed the name check. "Or as they say here, willkommen in Deutschland."

His pronunciation of the foreign language I found laughable. He should have made the *w* sound like a *v* and should have known the country he occupied is pronounced *Doitch*land rather than *Dearch*-land. So much for Americans learning German.

"The Army hopes your stay will be a pleasant one," he added. He then ordered us into the canvas-covered two-and-a-half ton truck and we rolled out.

The bumpy ride to Böblingen, the little city twenty kilometers southwest of Stuttgart, was straight down Autobahn 81. Steve struck up conversations with the other soldiers while I just sat quietly on the bench beside him. I thought about the fellow G.I. traveler I just encountered at the station. His words and exhortations divulged a kind of insouciant hostility toward Germany and its people. Oddly, between the farmer's son from North Dakota and the worker's son from New York, there were several polar connections. They crossed paths briefly on counter points in the Seventh Army's duty tour. They were in units on opposite ends of a road that linked their respective barracks. They had antipodal attitudes about Germans and interracial sex.

Panzer Kaserne was five kilometers from downtown Böblingen, on the southwest part of town. The driver got off at Ausfahrt 22 and then took Landstrasse 464 that went right through the town. We passed the wooded area behind the camp and the outdoor shooting range. Both of these sites, fourteen years after the war, were still being used for training purposes, only now by a different army. Panzer, unlike its Siamese-sister Kaserne, had kept its original name. I tried to imagine what it must have been like two decades earlier when German tanks were all around.

We arrived after 0800. The truck circled the barracks, stopping at different companies, letting troopers off. When we came to the 176th Signal, only Steve and I jumped out. We reported to the Orderly Room, mostly deserted this Sunday morning, signed in, picked up blankets and bed linen, and were told to take a bunk in the large room across from the latrine on the third floor.

The CQ was a young spec four. He sat behind the First Sergeant's desk like it was his own, feet resting on a bottom drawer half pulled out, basking in what little charge he had over the quarters for the day. "Lunch is at eleven-thirty," he told us. "The mess hall is two buildings to the left as you come out the front door. Sorry you guys missed breakfast."

Steve and I were out of breath after walking up two flights of stairs with our heavy duffel bags, AWOL bags, and the sheets and blankets stuck under our arms. As soon as we came out of the stairwell and into the third-floor corridor, we knew something was wrong. Two MPs were standing at the other end. When we moved in a little closer, we saw two hospital orderlies in white scrubs wheel a stretcher out of the latrine with a body in it, the sheet over the head. We ducked into the large room, dragging our bags without saying anything.

For a few minutes there was a ruckus in the corridor. With us in the room were three soldiers standing near their bunks chattering among themselves. Two were white and were wearing just T-shirts with their fatigue trousers, one with his dog tags dangling around his neck. The third was in his drawers and shower clogs.

"What's going on?" I asked of anyone.

"Old Mold died in the latrine this morning," one of my new barracks mates informed Steve and me. "First they thought he might have been killed but then they figured out he just croaked."

"The stiff was a lifer," another remarked. "Put in over twenty-two years. Saw action all over Europe and Korea."

"What was he?" Steve wanted to know. "A sergeant?"

"Hell no," the first one said. "He was a private."

"A private?" I repeated, shocked.

"He got busted all the way," the second explained. "Used to be a master sergeant. Took a swing at a second lieuey who insulted his Kraut wife. The Army didn't give no okay to them marrying because of her reputation. Word was half the troops on Panzer knew the color of her pants. She was born in the East and that didn't help her case neither."

"How did he marry her then," I inquired..

"He had a German civil ceremony. The Army ain't got no way to stop him from doing that. But, she couldn't come on post and he couldn't live off post. Only reason they didn't throw him in the can was he had so much time in."

The third man stepped forward and gave his thoughtful analysis of the situation. "Moldie wouldn't retire as an E-two so the mother-fuckers put him on permanent latrine duty. Dumb ass dropped dead mopping the floor."

Steve and I were both somewhat disturbed walking in on this sad situation just as we dropped our gear in a new company. "To die in an Army latrine," he muttered. "How repulsive can serving your country get?"

To me this was the ultimate injustice and humiliation for a career soldier. Poor bastard made his stripes fighting two wars only to kick the bucket in the shit house stripped of all rank. First the Army fucked his wife, then they fucked him.

There was an empty bunk between the two white guys. Steve took it and began to socialize with them. I put my things down next to the Schwarzer. Two other bunks also had their mattresses rolled up. The last bunk in the room, unmade with the blanket half on the floor, was the dead man's. It stood next to an open wall locker for all to see how messy it was. A cracked mirror hung on the inside of the door. The top of the footlocker was raised and the tray lifted from the normal position and placed sideways. A white towel that otherwise would have served as a liner was strewn over the side.

More than an hour later, the CQ and a German about fifty in stained threadbare clothes, hat in hand, came into the room. The local walked aimlessly behind the soldier like a stray dog on a long leash.

"Which is Private Molder's bunk?" the specialist asked.

Someone pointed it out. The soldier called the German "Comrade," motioned him to come forward, and ordered him to pack all the clothes and belongings from the dead man's lockers into boxes. The German seemed to snap to attention. I heard him say "Jawohl." I thought he was going to click his heels too. The bed was stripped, the mattress folded in an *S* shape, and everything hauled out. Suddenly, there was no trace of the broken twenty-two-year combat veteran ever having lived in this barracks or ever having been in the Army for that matter.

Men from several different companies on this side of the Kaserne were served in the mess hall Steve and I had been directed to. At 1130 from the barracks window I could see the long line that was forming in front of the building two away from mine. Soldiers in uniform and civilian clothes were walking toward it from various directions. I wanted to go to chow but Steve decided to hang out with his two new buddies. They said they were going to eat at the snack bar and I could join them if I wished, but I declined. A foursome with two unknowns was not my style of association. I never liked tagging along with strange people.

This time of day it was warmer and I no longer needed an overcoat. I was still in my Class A's, though, but I placed my dress hat on the shelf in the wall locker and put on the more comfortable cuntcap. Remembering what Richie had told me about winter clothing left around the barracks, plus my own natural instincts for such things, I stood my duffel bag up in the wall locker, removed the combination lock, and secured the door with it. I took a roundabout route to the mess hall. I wanted to see something of Panzer and also kill some time. I had no desire to stand in line until it thinned out considerably.

It felt funny going to eat by myself on a new post. I almost turned and headed for the snack bar, as I generally disliked Army food anyway. For breakfast the shit-on-a-shingle, chipped beef in cream sauce over toast, curdled my stomach. Lunch was often no better, braised ham dripping in fat or canned corned beef hash with boiled carrots. And dinner, you can forget the battered fried chicken bones or dried up pork chops. Half the time I just ate the bread, potatoes, vegetables, and dessert.

On this day, my first mess hall meal in Germany, coincidentally, was the best that I had in twenty months of downing Army chow. Sirloin hamburger steak, thick and crisp French fries, green peas, sweet coleslaw, dill pickles, fresh-baked rolls, and cherry pie with vanilla ice cream—everything I liked. I wondered whether the food was notches better overseas or some higher power knew I was coming to Germany and ordained a singular heavenly repast.

It was doubly fortunate I did not turn around and break bread with Steve and two strangers in the snack bar. The mess hall had another surprise in store for me. I ran into someone I knew in basic training. While I was eating, I kept glancing at a private sitting two tables away. He looked very familiar. At first I could not place him but moments later I realized it was Whitey Stone. My basic buddy was not looking in my direction and I had no idea whether he noticed me or not. That first day on a new post I was sure I was the more observant of those around me.

"Whitey," I called out.

The young man rotated his head to where my voice was coming from. I stood up and looked right at him. It took only a few seconds for him to recognize me, obvious from the look on his face. I lifted my tray and walked to his table. There were several spaces on the bench across from where he was sitting.

"Jesus Christ, it's good to see you Whitey. How in hell are you?"

We shook hands and I sat down to face the friend I had not seen in eighteen months. His light blond hair was thinner and longer than what I remembered but there was the same pale skin, unblemished complexion, and colorless eyebrows. The nickname Whitey perfect-ly represented his look and facial features. We engaged in some small talk. The two PFCs sitting on either side of him seemed baffled every time I mentioned the only name I ever called him by.

"They don't call me Whitey here," he said after a while.

"What do you mean?"

"I don't go by that name."

"Oh no."

"No."

"Then what do you go by?" I asked. I could not see why he would be called anything else.

"Billy . . . my real name."

"I thought you liked the name Whitey."

"I do." He looked over both shoulders briefly and then lowered his voice. "But the coloreds in my outfit don't like to use that word, and they're the majority."

"Then why don't they call you Weissey instead?" I said sarcastically without much thinking, pronouncing it with a *V*

As a kid I used to hear that sobriquet all the time on my block, what everyone called one of Mrs. Mittler's boarders, a man in his late seventies with a full head of solid white hair. Whitey either did not understand or did not appreciate my remark. I made no effort to curtail my use of the term Whitey, despite the sensibilities of any Schwarzers within earshot.

My friend and I reminisced and brought each other up to date. He told me after basic he went through eight weeks of auto mechanics training and then came right over. For the past fifteen months Whitey had been in the 96th Transportation Company, repairing and driving vehicles for Infantry units in the field far more than if he or the vehicles were in garrison.

Whitey was in for three years too, but he did not use his enlistment privilege to select an Army school, even a lengthy one, as I did. He chose an overseas assignment instead. Whitey was slated to go back to the States in November, after completing the two-year tour of duty. But he planned to extend his time by four months, so that when he does return he will have fewer than ninety days left and will get an immediate discharge. That was Army policy. I would have to serve the full three years. He had been a PFC but got busted to private for disobeying a direct order.

We also talked about our squad and platoon in basic. "Remember Quinn, the Irish kid who acted tough all the time?" I asked.

"Yeah. He was always getting into hot water for one thing or another."

We both recounted how Quinn made wisecracks in front of NCOs and officers. Nothing very serious at first but before long it bordered on insubordination. When he picked fights with trainees, he came out swinging.

"He never messed with the coloreds," Whitey pointed out, instinctively looking around again.

"You're right. I guess he knew better . . . or maybe he wasn't so tough after all."

"Quinn wasn't a bad buddy. He was the one who took up the collection for Willie Owens."

"I remember," I said. "It was after we got paid, that last day before we shipped out. Willie's wallet got stolen while it was lying on his bunk. We never found out who did it."

"It was Jo Jo Robson, the drummer from Newark, who copped the wallet." This time Whitey did not look around the mess hall. "He was the only squad member near Willie's things that day."

"I thought it was Tony Petrosini," I added.

"No. Tony talked big but he was no thief. Besides, he never bothered with the coloreds either."

How do you like that? I said to myself. One poor Schwarzer stealing from another.

The PFCs next to Whitey got up and left the mess hall. While we were talking, many of the others around us had left too.

"You been to other places besides Boblingen?" I nonchalantly asked my friend, changing the conversation. I had no idea what kind of an answer was forthcoming.

"I was in Lebanon last year . . . from August to October."

"Lebanon?" I repeated, quite surprised, even alarmed.

"Yeah, President Eisenhower sent eight thousand troops from Germany . . . plus the Navy and Marines. We were supposed to protect the Lebanese Christian government and the Americans living there from Arab nationalists."

"Did anybody from the one-seventy-sixth go with you?" I wanted to know. I was curious about my new outfit.

"The whole company went. They were lined up in the quadrangle with full combat gear."

"Gee," I remarked, "I'm glad I wasn't here then."

"You wouldn't have gone with them," my friend said straight out with great earnestness.

"I thought you said everyone went." Now a bombshell was about to hit me.

"Everyone except the Jewish personnel."

"*What*?" I let out, astounded by this revelation.

Whitey explained that the United States had some kind of un-written agreement with the Lebanese government not to send Jewish soldiers. When the 176th was in formation, the First Sergeant called off a few names, obvious Jewish ones. If your records indicated you were of the Jewish faith you stayed behind, not doing shit for three months as it were. Company Jews who at induction left the religion question blank probably regretted it.

My record contained no such omission. Ironically, I felt a sense of anger and relief at the same time. I was not pleased that America's elected officials pandered to the Arabs but I realized how fortunate it was for me not to have to fight in the Middle East if another conflict broke out.

"Did you see much combat," I asked in an afterthought.

"There was no fighting . . . but one soldier got killed by a sniper. We just sat around all day."

The mess hall was closing and Whitey and I got up from the table. We put our empty trays and cups on the conveyer belt that led through an opening into the kitchen area. I could see Germans in there, men and women, wearing high rubber boots and aprons, scrubbing pots and pans over steamy sinks, mopping yellow puddles off the floor, dipping metal baskets of silverware into soapy water. I heard the mess sergeant call one of the men Comrade as he ordered him about. Whitey saw me staring at the kitchen workers.

"We don't pull KP in Germany. Krauts do all the dirty work on the kaserne. They work cheap and we have to give them jobs."

This particular advantage to foreign duty made me feel good about coming over. I hated KP, and did it on many occasions at all three forts in the States, although I preferred wet hands in the mess hall to muddy boots on field maneuvers or loaded rifles on guard duty.

Whitey invited me back to his room and we walked to his barracks building on the other side of the quadrangle. He shared a private room with one person, typical quarters for soldiers on permanent assignment in these former Wehrmacht facilities. His roommate was on weekend pass so we had some more time alone together.

"Why do you call German men comrade." I recalled the situation with the CQ as well.

"It's the word communists say to each other. In German it means friend or party member."

"Aren't they called Gerry anymore?" That was the slang term I remembered hearing in war movies. The veteran at Port Authority who wanted to take me in mouthed it too.

"No. Probably not since the war."

"Do they like being called comrade?" I wanted to know.

"Shit no. But, we could care less what they like. They lost the war. It's our way of rubbing it in and the fact that half of Germany is communist."

Americans, I learned from Whitey, thought very little of the German men seen on base or run into in town. They were defeated in battle. They do menial jobs. They struggle to feed their families. They pick up American cigarette butts from the floor or on the street to smoke. They get arrested for black marketing. They pimp their Schatzies. They compete with alien occupiers for the affections of their own women. The biggest blow to their self-respect is their inability to stop our black men from sleeping with their white women.

Whitey painted a bleak, or perhaps I should say black, picture of race relations in Germany. He talked about the strained contact he has with the coloreds, as he preferred to call them, on post and the lack of contact with them off post.

"Until fifty-six," he told me, "some companies in Germany were still segregated. They lived and worked on one side of the kaserne, we on the other. We still have problems with them, especially at the EM club. The whites can't take the mixed dancing there. Sometimes fights break out. In town it's worse."

"I never read anything about that," I said.

"They don't print that stuff in the *Army Times* or the *Stars and Stripes*."

All this took me by surprise since the Army was integrated when I joined. And I witnessed no racial conflicts in the towns outside any of the three forts on which I was stationed. But, of course, in the States I did not socialize in bars and there are plenty of black women to go around in every city, with few white men having any interest in them.

I did not press Whitey for futher details on the color question. It twas not difficult to figure out what the schwarze and weisse troops were fighting about on and off post.

Whitey and I spent the rest of the afternoon together. We played ping/pong and shot some pool in his company's day room, took in a movie, and then had a bite to eat at the snack bar.

By the time I got back to my barracks, it was past 2100 hours. Up in the room, Steve still wanted to schmuse with the two guys he apparently befriended. I tried to talk to him, to tell him all about my day with Whitey and the conversations we had, but I could not get his undivided attention. This was typical of Steve, jumping into casual relationships with barracks mates he just met or hardly knew.

I noticed that Old Mold's bed was made up and the wall locker next to it was closed with a key lock on it. While I was out, another soldier had come in and apparently no one told him that was the bed and locker of a man who died a few hours earlier. I certainly would have taken one of the other available places had I been told about the stiff who was carried out on a stretcher.

At 2200 it was time for lights out. I moved around in the dark to unpack my fatigues and prepare my things for the next day. I polished my boots in the latrine where the lights stay on all night, and then shaved and showered. As I lay in my bunk, trying to fall asleep, the ghost of the dead soldier I never knew seemed to fill the room. Well, I lamented, at least Moldie doesn't have to get out of bed at 0600 for reveille any longer.

This was now the Ende of my first full day in Germany. I had a fine welcoming committee, a disparate group of three soldiers, a trio of passersby. A caustic draftee ready to step out of Germany warned me about falling in with its people and customs. A dead lifer busted for protecting his Frau's honor spoke to the problem of G.I.-German unions. And a Fort Dix buddy answering to an achromatic name called attention to a color-conscious Seventh Army.

I braced myself for living my dream of duty in Deutschland.

# CHAPTER 14: LIEUTENANT FINSTON AND COMPANY

On Monday morning, the week after we arrived at Panzer Kaserne, Steve and I were told to report to Lieutenant Finston, the personnel officer, after lunch. We would receive our company assignments at that time.

For several weeks I had assumed Böblingen would be my station for the duration. I saw its position on the map, found some statistics on the city, and imagined what it would be like living there. Not long after reporting to my new unit, however, I was told I most probably would be sent to another location.

The 176th Signal was spread out all over West Germany. Its organizational structure consisted of twenty-four repair teams under six warrant officers. Two teams were in Böblingen, the headquarters, but I could wind up on any one of the other teams at different Kasernes or installations. Our men were on a kind of permanent TDY, attached to other branches of the Army—such as the Infantry, Artillery, or Engineers—to fix and maintain their electrical and electronic equipment in garrison shops or bivouac facilities. Teams of ten to twelve members often lived in a corner of a barracks building relatively independent of the home company's, and their host's, authority and supervision.

I felt fortunate to be in the 176th. It was a good-duty outfit situated in many larger and more exciting cities than Böblingen, places a New Yorker would prize. I might go to Stuttgart or Munich, München in German, Frankfurt or Darmstadt, one of the "*be*rgs" such as Heidelberg or Bamberg or Nuremberg, Nürnberg as they say here, or "*bu*rgs," Würzburg or Augsburg or Regensburg.

The nightlife in these cities is jumping and dollars go a long way. Soldiers enjoy a great open field for fraternization with Fräuleins. Bars and clubs and Gasthauses are vented for business twenty-three hours a day, with an hour set aside for sweeping up the litter G.I.s leave behind. Young German women flock to these establishments every evening after sundown, eager to keep company with their former enemies and conquerors. They drink and dance and laugh with Uncle Sam's troopers until the wee hours. They do quickie dates with boys who better be back by bed check at twelve o'clock, then traipse home again with a pick-up on overnight pass. The first of every month, scores of somewhat older women from all over the Federal Republic descend on cities with sizable American cohorts and camp in for a few days.

But I also felt wary about my new assignment. I could be sent to a small or isolated town with nothing much to see or do, where the Germans may not be as friendly toward Americans, where the population of female fraternizers is bounded. I might go to a team whose chief NCO or warrant officer does not live off post and exercises much greater control over its members. Or, I can get attached to a unit that more often than not is away from the Kaserne and where passes to go into town are hard to come by.

Lieutenant Finston's office was off to the side of the Orderly Room, its front door accessible from the long corridor that ran along the downstairs south wall of the building. Steve and I sat on the bench outside his office at 1300 hours and waited to be called in.

The U.S. Army in Europe, I learned from orientation classes the previous week, had an interesting history. A month after Pearl Harbor a command post was opened in Belfast for a few thousand American soldiers in the U.K. In June 1942 the number had swelled to 55,000 and the headquarters shifted to London. A two-star Eisenhower was the commander for a short time. By the end of the year 135,000 troops were amassed in Britain for the eventual retaking of Europe. Ike was bumped up to lead the Allied invasion of North Africa, while USAREUR, or rather its forerunner with a different acronym, was to oversee the buildup and training of combat forces and to support them with logistics and administrative services. On the sixth of June 1944 there were one and a half million men in the Army poised to cross the English Channel to Normandy.

By war's end, HQ, now outside Paris, prepared to occupy Germany. American combat forces were comprised of four field armies plus scores of groups, corps, and divisions. Almost two million men were on the loose in the summer of 1945, their bodies and souls directed from Frankfurt. The first casualty of the occupation was Ike's policy of non-fraternization. It was verboten for Americans to so much as shake hands with Germans, let alone enjoy relations with their women. G.I.s could not billet with German families, visit their homes, or marry their daughters. When hostilities were over, such restrictions were unenforceable. The Supreme Allied Commander's five stars could not point the hordes of horny young men away from a Frau or Fräulein whose husband or Schatzie was dead or taken prisoner.

A collapsed economy transformed German women from victims of invading enemy armies into spirited fraternizers for material goods or sexual gratification. Not six months after V-E Day, both Ike and the policy had fallen out of Germany. Intimate encounters were now thought of as necessary to assist the German people in gaining back their place among the free and peace-loving nations of the world. By 1947 soldiers were encouraged to fraternize with Germans, to pass along the American way of life.

Only a year after the war, troop strength was reduced to fewer than 290,000 men. Most of the American Zone was under the control of the Seventh Army. A Constabulary was formed, a police force with a mission to maintain law and order in the occupied territory. The G.I. cops had their own shoulder patch, a large blue C on a circular yellow shield pierced by a red lightning bolt. Their use of horse cavalry units, the last ever in the U.S. Army, to patrol borders and quell riots in refugee camps earned them the moniker "Circle C Cowboys," but to the not-so-affectionate Germans they were the "Blitzpolizei."

In 1948, when the British and American Zones were merged, European HQ was moved to Heidelberg. Despite the Soviet Union's hostile actions against the West—their blockade of land routes to Berlin, occupation of Czechoslovakia, and detonation of an atomic bomb—in 1950 only 79,000 of my uniformed predecessors remained in Europe. The outbreak of the Korean War was a clarion call for America. The president ordered a rapid redeployment of armed forces. On 1 April 1951 my company was activated. USAREUR's mission moved from postwar occupation and reconstruction to the all-out defense of Western Europe, West Germany in particular. The Seventh Army went from a "keeper of the peace" to a "shield of democracy." By the time I arrived, there were more than 250,000 G.I.s posted to protect the eastern flank, the borders with East Germany and Czechoslovakia. The riders on patrol now along the Iron Curtain were saddled inside M48 tanks, the military Triggers having been pulled years earlier.

Despite the Army's warning to avoid emotional involvement with German women and to exert self-control regarding sex, the occupation created a new social problem in Germany, the birth of tens of thousands of American orphans, many of mixed-blood. Women could not be kept from climbing through the windows of the Kasernes at night or from dogging the troops in the field from one encampment to another. It was impossible to prevent carnal contacts with locals since we were billeted in former Wehrmacht barracks taken over after the war, compounds often in the centers or on the edges of populated towns and cities.

On off-duty hours, all an action-seeking soldier had to do was seize his pass from the CQ after hours, skip out the main gate, hop on a nearby streetcar, and jump off at the Bahnhof in four or five stops. There he could fire his weapon into any deutsche doll walking the street or dancing in one of the G.I. joints on the town's equivalent of La Place Pigalle. The military's own practice of employing German women, in jobs on post face-to-face with their American occupiers, blasted holes through the doughy wall they erected to prevent communion.

Fräuleins who fraternized with soldiers, with or without stripes or brass, were thought of and treated differently by their respective national groups. To Americans they were objects for physical pleasure, foreign toys to experiment with, companions for love, brides to bring home. Germans deemed them to be outcasts dishonoring the memory of husbands, brothers, sons, and lovers who sacrificed their lives and limbs for the Fatherland. Such women were seen as willful partners in a pattern of sexual transgression that underscored Germany's military defeat and loss of national sovereignty.

In the wake of our victory and occupation, German men came up empty and short in their traditional roles. It was their women who now put food on the table and the American conquerors who put their women in a family way. Female fraternizers were roundly criticized in church sermons, the media, and official documents. It was rumored that a private Presley had a secret German sweetheart. No doubt Elvis was all shook up about what the publicity might do to his post-discharge singing career. Women who gave birth to an interracial child, by and large out of wedlock, were special targets of public scorn in Germany.

The continuing presence of such a large number of G.I.s stationed across the Rhine was a D-Day landing of sorts. This time we were armed with our hometown values and customs instead of government-issued rifles and tanks. The invasion of American culture affected almost all aspects of life for ordinary Germans. Fraternization took on a whole new meaning, no longer simply the association, sexual or otherwise, with the occupiers but the catering to the wants of the soldier and the adopting of his style of music, dance, dress, speech, and manners. Favorite son Elvis on the scene as well as the screen only heightened the mania German youth already exhibited for their cousins from America.

In the Germany I was privy to, there was no shortage of Fräuleins willing to bed down with their occupiers. A good portion of the women in their twenties or thirties had no man to meet or marry. Tales of dollar-rich Americans and the search for a better life attracted young females to Army camps for employment or marriage. Our boys in brown or green had another advantage over German men aside from the demographic and economic imbalances. German women often found their Landsmann unattractive as potential mates or life partners since so many were missing a limb, demoralized from losing the war, or in ill-health due to combat and years of captivity in Russian POW camps. G.I. Joe did not need to be as rich or as handsome as Elvis to be able to say love me tender to a Fräulein and procure a bedding response.

The Army lectured us about holy matrimony to "indigenous personnel," as the distaff natives were called. Before a wedding could take place a G.I. had to fill out a lengthy application and visa questionnaire. He would have to submit birth certificates of both parties, secure the approval of his commanding officer, and if under twenty-one have written permission from his parents. If the Frau-to-be has been married before or has children, records of divorce decrees and/or live births were needed. The marriage-minded soldier would have to attend a counseling session with a chaplain, and expose his woman to an intelligence and morals investigation.

Applications for marriage might take six months or longer, depending on the loved one's sexual history and her and her parents' place of birth. Naturally, such a period of time was disconcerting to the many expectant wife-wannabes that wished to crank out a legitimate baby. The Army was in no hurry to embrace wily women from the East sent to pull soldier boys with wet jocks into back alleys or bedrooms to pump for information or push into espionage. Ditto for women with thick criminal records for solicitation, hot to marry and trot to America just to cut the long arm of German law.

A jowly sergeant, tongue in cheek, advised us to be especially cautious with the ordinary Fräuleins we might meet off the beat, girl-next-door Teutonic types who were neither prostitutes nor spies. Such females love to get their legs around naïve Americans to help feed the family, raus Germany, and get Mutti und Papi out too. By the end of my first week overseas, I knew why Richie and the PFC at the Stuttgart station warned me against following the nuptial trail.

In the indoctrination I was put through, much to my surprise, the topic of interracial conjugations never came up. The composition of the audiences I sat with suggested otherwise. But the Army of my day, top and bottom heavy with soldiers from a segregated South, was not known for its balanced approach to situations involving color. Blackies coupled with Blondies, to adapt an apt utterance, was just as taboo in Germany as in the States. In the film shown of simulated social contacts with German women, no blacks in uniform, light or dark, were staged. The problems with the company kept by thirteen percent of the troops here, so transparent to anyone on and off post, were whited out.

Understandably, the big brass played the race theme in a low key given their pitch for a New Germany and euphony to practices extant in an all-white society. The wartime policy of non-fraternization was in peacetime dead for whites but unofficially kicking for blacks.

The company clerk, a tall and thin spec five with sandy hair, who always wore a yellow ascot with his starched fatigues, came up to me and Steve. He was a draftee who made his rank within the two-year hitch, a promotion unusual even for an enlistee serving an extra year. One of the few college graduates in the 176th, he exuded a kind of quiet confidence in his handling of tedious paper work. He was going home in a matter of days, another reason to be envied. The word around the company was that he rose so quickly because he was personable and was in the Orderly Room every day under the captain's nose, or, as others put it, his nose was under the captain's ass. To me it seemed a waste to move someone up to E-5 who was not a career soldier or who had not re-enlisted. But it was contempt that I felt, not envy. I was sure there were dozens of company team members in distant repair shops more worthy of an umbrella over their bird that never had the opportunity to impress the C.O. with their good performance.

"You can both go in to see the lieutenant now," he said softly.

Steve walked into the office ahead of me. We came to attention in front of the heavy wooden desk, saluted the first lieuey, stated our rank and name, and stood at ease. The room was small with a double window off to the side facing the back of the building. A large map of Germany, almost from ceiling to floor, with different-colored pins stuck in it, hung on the wall behind the young officer. He could not have been more than six or seven years my senior, not a very ripe age for making important decisions over soldiers' lives, I thought.

"There are two openings on different teams," Finston said, looking up from the paper in his hand.

Steve and I gazed at the man with the silver bar on his collar but did not speak.

"One is in Nuremberg, the other in Fulda. Take your pick. You both have the same MOS."

Nuremberg I had heard of but not the other city or town. I had no idea where either was located in Germany. Steve turned toward me and whispered he would like to take the Nuremberg assignment. I did not respond in words, but my facial expression must have signaled a tacit acceptance of his choosing first.

"I'll go to Nuremberg, sir," Steve said with a strong voice.

The lieutenant looked at me. "Is that all right with you?"

"I guess so," I answered meekly, not sure if I really meant it, and quickly added, "sir." What would he have done had I said no? Flipped a coin? The outcome might have been the same anyway.

"Okay, then," the lieutenant continued. "It's settled. Goldbaum to team five, Streiber to team twenty-one."

He wrote something on the paper he held, swiveled his chair around, and used a pointer to show us the location of the two cities. The one I was going to was farther east than Steve's. "I'll cut your orders day after tomorrow."

Steve and I saluted again, did an about face, and walked out. A minute later we were both up on the third floor in the building, our sleeping quarters. Four other soldiers were in the room milling about, two spec fours, a PFC, and a private. The two with birds, I remembered, were at the end of their tour of duty, processing for return to the States. The other two had just arrived in Germany.

"I'm going to Nuremberg," Steve announced proudly to anyone who would listen. "Team five."

"You're lucky," one of the spec fours remarked.

"Why? Were you there?" Steve asked.

"No. I was on another team but I used to pick up equipment and parts from Nuremberg. You'll be at Merrell Barracks, right in town. It's a pretty big city, and very old. Has a lot of history. Lots of tail running around too."

That last statement caught my attention.

"What's the duty like?" Steve wanted to know.

"It's good," the same one answered. "Better than most places. The team hardly goes away from the kaserne. You'll be with the Second Armored Cavalry. They don't bother us one-seventy-sixers. Mr. Barry is the warrant officer there. I heard he's not too chicken shit."

Steve sat down on an empty bunk and put his feet up on the springs. "What kind of work do they do?"

"They fix mainly radio sets and headphones, some microwave equipment."

"Any radar?" Steve inquired again.

"No. But they're supposed to be getting them soon, and pieces from guided missiles . . . NIKE's I think."

The other soldier on his way out of Germany stepped a little closer to me. I was standing next to Steve, listening carefully to all of this. "You going to Nuremberg too?"

"No . . . Fulda."

The spec four I only met the day before and did not know on a first-name basis looked straight at me and spoke directly and confidently. "You don't want to go to Fulda."

From his eyes I could tell he was dead serious. A chill ran up and down my spine. "Why not?" passed from my lips, but I was afraid to hear the answer to my own question.

"Fulda's on the East German border. One of the worst places you could go. There's nothing good over there."

A vague terror seized my person with these remarks, as if some unseen and unknown force was gathering against me. The realization that I had just made a terrible mistake and would pay dearly for it the next sixteen months disturbed me greatly. Without so much as a question or objection for the lieutenant, I acceded to Steve's assertiveness. An opportunity to say something was given to me but I let it pass. I did not have to ask the experienced team member before me why Fulda was so bad.

"They have alerts night and day," the young man I did not know told me of himself. "You'll be on maneuvers with the Infantry most of the time. No hot showers, no passes to town, no weekends off. And the attachment outfit fucks with us."

I gulped. "What do you mean?"

"They make our company guys stand inspections and pull guard duty. They treat us the same as their own troops, like shit."

Now I was panicky about the assignment I was just given. I perspired, I felt hot all over, my heart pounded, my head tightened. Thoughts of escape were swimming through my mind. How can I change what already happened? Everyone knows the Army hates to reverse a decision. The lieutenant said he had two different posts to fill. Steve picked the plum, I was left with the pit. What else was there to say or do? I knew I had to get out of going to Fulda, the end of the earth from what I had just been told. But how? *How?*

The spec four who clued me in did me a favor but I, and probably he too, did not know it at the time. I should have thanked him but in the state I was in I could not think about protocol. In the barracks room, I just kept to myself. Steve was chitchatting with the others and I moved farther away from them. Some time elapsed. Five, ten, fifteen minutes, I lost track. I knew the only thing to do was to go back and speak to the lieutenant before he wrote his report or did whatever he usually does to make the Fulda posting official. But, what would I say to him? What *could* I say?

I went downstairs to the Orderly Room. It seemed hopeless, but I had to at least *try* to get a different assignment. I simply could not spend the next sixteen months in a shitty place. The company clerk was at his desk typing when I came in. He looked up as I approached him.

"Can I see Lieutenant Finston?"

"What about?"

"I need to talk to him."

"And I need to tell the lieutenant what it's about," the E-5 said smugly.

"My assignment."

"What about your assignment?"

For someone leaving in a few days, he was taking his job awfully seriously. He obviously had little concern for my feelings or needs. "I'd just like to see the lieutenant," I said.

He started to say something but then got up from his desk and went into Finston's office through the Orderly Room. He left the door open and I could see them talking but I could not hear them. He came back within a minute and said I could go in. I started to walk across the Orderly Room as he did when he stopped me with an outstretched arm.

"Use the lieutenant's front door," the clerk told me, as if I were stepping on hallowed ground or invading his private space. "Knock first."

I went around as I was told, in no position to disobey an order even if the person giving it had no authority over me, and knocked. After Finston said come in, I repeated the ritual with the salute and rank and name business. I stood at ease, my boxed fatigue cap in my hand behind my back, but I was not comfortable.

The Army officer who held my fate in his hands looked at me with a poker face. Whether he saw this unplanned meeting as an intrusion into his work and time schedule or thought nothing of it was beyond my powers of interpretation. I only knew there was no way he could be partial toward me or to the purpose of my visit. He knew nothing of me and could not know what I was about to ask him. I myself did not even know what I was going to say.

"What is it you wanted to see me about?"

I knew it would have been foolhardy to say straight-out that I did not want to go to Fulda. And I was sure that telling the lieutenant why I did not want to go there would only lead to the *opposite* effect that I sought. So asking him to switch my assignment with Steve's would surely spell doom for me. Then what could I possibly say that would sway him to send me someplace else? *What* someplace else?

"Sir," I said resolutely, finding the thoughts and the words at the very last moment. What the spec four asked me minutes before rang in my ears. "Would it be possible for me to go to Nuremberg too?"

The lieutenant looked at me. He squinted a little, but kept silent. Had I asked for too much too soon?

"I heard Nuremberg is getting radar equipment," I explained before he had a chance to reject my brazen request. "And guided missiles." The words of the other short-timer upstairs served me.

The lieuey did not say anything. I'll have to pour it on, I thought.

"I enlisted in the Army for radar school, but so far I haven't worked my MOS. I want to get practical experience in the latest electronics so I can get a good job when I get out."

That was a white lie at best. I was planning to go to college, but not for anything related to electronics. Then again, who can tell what I would do once I'm back at home?

"You heard Nuremberg is getting radar and missile equipment?" Finston said, breaking his silence.

"Yes sir."

"And that's why you want to go there?"

"Yes sir," I repeated.

"What else have you heard?" he asked cagily.

"Nothing, sir." I feared he saw right through me, that my composure gave me away.

The lieutenant suddenly got personal. "Where are you from, Streiber?"

Now I took notice of the fact that he pronounced my name right for the second time.

"Brooklyn, sir."

"Whereabouts in Brooklyn?"

"Coney Island."

Finston thought for a moment, then commented, "Your neighborhood's been going downhill lately, hasn't it?"

"Yes sir."

"I'm from Queens myself. Forest Hills."

"Yes sir," I said in agreement again, implying I knew or knew of the place he grew up in. I wondered if he thought I was also acknowledging I was aware of the fact that his neighborhood was classier than mine. I could do little but go along with the person I was asking consideration from.

The man with a silver bar on his collar took a breather and sat back in his chair. He looked away from me and moved his head from side to side as if he were searching for something on his desk.

"Well," Finston finally uttered, apparently coming to a decision. "It so happens the OIC in Nuremberg requested *two* new people. And the Fulda team can go another week without a replacement."

A glimmer of hope flashed before me, but I dared not show any emotion or mention Mr. Barry by name. I waited for the first lieuey to finish.

"Okay. I'll send you to Nuremberg."

"Oh, thank you sir. Thank you." I should have said thank God.

He raised his hand slowly as if to return a salute. I took this as a signal that he wanted to end the conversation. I wanted to end it too before he could change his mind. I saluted him, up and down quickly, did an about face, and left the room. I was sure the young officer from New York noticed there was a bounce in my step.

Steve did not believe me when I told him I was going to Nuremberg with him. I had to repeat it three times. Neither he nor the two spec fours in the room could figure out what I said to the lieutenant to induce him to change my assignment. I kept quiet about what words or strategy I employed with Finston. I was headed to Nuremberg, the much better place. That was all that mattered. Let them wonder how I did the impossible.

Why did the lieutenant grant my appeal? It was now a moot question, but I could not get it out of my mind the rest of the day. Did Finston feel sorry for me? Was he just helping out a fellow New Yorker? Did he want to do something for a poor boy from the next borough? A poor *Jewish* boy? He must have figured I was a member of the tribe, I concluded. Finston . . . Finston, I repeated to myself over and over. Suddenly the answer dawned on me. It was so simple, even silly. His Tateh or Zeyde must have anglicized the German name *Feinstein* to Finestone, and then dropped the two *e*'s. The family's house of worship might have been changed as well.

That night I went to bed thinking how lucky it was for me that Lieutenant Finston, or one of his progenitors, might be another General Rose.

# CHAPTER 15: A ROOM WITH A VIEW

"That's Zeppelinfeld up ahead on the left," the driver said, motioning with his hand.

The E-2 from the Merrell Barracks motor pool came to Panzer Kaserne to get Steve and me. The ride northeast from Böblingen was bumpy and boring most of the way. There was nothing much to see out the front or sides of the three-quarter-ton Army truck save cow fields, meadows, and open highway. The two new assignees to Nuremberg squeezed in alongside the driver. The five bags in the back shifted positions every time the vehicle hit a curve or changed lanes. My buddy from two stateside forts did most of the talking, but with the private he just met. I sat quietly, content I was on my way to the second largest city in Bavaria, far from the East German border and the Iron Curtain.

We entered Nuremberg from the southeast off of Autobahn 6 and headed north on Landstrasse 8, turning onto Zeppelinstrasse that veered around to the west. The driver told us he took that route so he could show us the city's most famous landmark. He sought our attention as we were passing a vast desolate area, some kind of parkland. I turned my head and looked forward.

Before me was the side and part of the front of a huge white stone or marble monument with tall colonnades and lengthy reviewing stands beside a lake. The breadth of the structure stood imposingly as the primary quarter of an immense rectangular field. The other three legs consisted of sections of bleachers wrapped around the perimeter, broken up by dozens of equally-spaced identical short towers. Overgrown grass and a wire fence cut part of the area off from street access.

"What's that?" Steve asked.

"Never heard of Zeppelinfeld," I added.

"That was the Nazi Party parade grounds before the war," the driver told us. "Originally it was an airfield for Zeppelins. First used about fifty years ago." On the way up he mentioned he had been in Nuremberg for almost a year.

"Zeppelin Field in English," I said.

"That's right." Our nascent tour guide knew some German as well as local history.

"Seems deserted now," Steve observed. He sat between the driver and me and got a better view of the purported historic site than I did.

We drove past the back of the monument. The driver glanced out the window on his side and then turned to look at us.

"This was called the Tribune. The Nazis built it for their demonstrations, to show off their power. Tremendous rallies were held every year." He pointed again to the left. "Hitler spoke to crowds of hundreds of thousands of people sitting in the stands . . . plus the regiments of soldiers standing at attention in the quad."

"I saw this in a TV documentary," I noted. "The troops were squeezed together like sardines. You could only see their helmets."

"We took it over at the end of the war," our private instructor told us. "Nuremberg was bombed heavily but the Tribune and the stands survived. Since forty-five we've used Zeppelinfeld for our parades."

"Is that so?" I said, more as a comment than a question.

"Yeah. But of course we changed the name."

"What's it called now?" Steve wanted to know.

"Soldiers' Field."

"Like the name of the football stadium in Chicago?" he inquired again.

"Sort of," the driver said, "but with an *s* and an apostrophe to make it plural and possessive."

"Why'd we pick that name," I asked.

"The first American soldiers at Merrell played baseball here in the open field. They called it that and put up a little cardboard sign. The Army then made it official and painted the name in big black letters across the front of the Tribune . . . by the speaker's platform."

So this is where Hitler and his party hacks spewed their lies to the German Volk and world. How ironic, I thought. Americans march and salute the Stars and Stripes on the very spot where twenty years earlier German spectators handed Sieg Heils to the Führer and swastika flag while jackbooted Soldaten made with the goose steps. Off-duty U.S. soldiers play sports where Nazi military leaders once sounded warnings for global war.

We passed the lake. On the other side stood a huge circular building. As we moved closer, I could see it was actually shaped like a horseshoe, unfinished or damaged in the center. The driver signaled and made a left onto Bayernstrasse. "That's the Congress Hall," he informed us. "The Nazis never completed it."

"Looks like the coliseum in Rome," Steve noted.

"It was meant to . . . and also be bigger. Would have provided seats for maybe fifty thousand. The world's largest glass roof was supposed to go on top of it, but the war put a stop to that."

Steve sat back and looked away from the round structure and the street we were on. "Just another reminder of a fallen empire."

"A tomb for Hitler's bones," I followed, putting my two cents in too.

The driver seemed surprised by the tone of our casual but biting comments. I took notice as well. This would not be the last time the two electronics men would be on the same wavelength, would say something in tandem patently critical or disdainful of the Army or Germany.

"We're coming up to Merrell Barracks . . on the left over there." Our truck crossed over the tramline tunnel as we fed into Franken-strasse, then slowed down. The private floored the brakes and turned left. "This is home for you guys. What do you think?"

"It's not the Hollywood Bowl, that's for sure," Steve quipped.

"Doesn't look like Panzer Kaserne either," I remarked.

In physical appearance my new camp was very different from the one I just departed. Instead of a number of little matchbox-like buildings concentrated in two tracts with a considerable space in be-tween, Merrell was an immense red brick four-story structure trimmed in white stone in the shape of an H with an elongated center and extensions on both ends. From the front it was hard to tell what kind of overall form it had. I was immediately struck by the scores of small holes in the brick façade and the many large cavities where whole chunks had been gouged out, the result no doubt of American machine-gun fire and mortar shelling.

The Army either wanted to preserve these grim reminders of vic-tory or did not wish to spend the money to erase the memory. There had been no attempt in fourteen years to patch up our defacement of the building. Obviously the Germans barracked here chose not to surrender. Who were these young men who threw away their lives for a lost cause? Why did the Kaserne's erstwhile soldiers follow or-ders from a demented Great War corporal over their own survival in-stincts?

We stopped at the guardhouse and then drove through. The main entrance resembled an opening to a tunnel roadway, wide enough for only one vehicle to pass at a time. A white sign with black letters identifying the compound hung high above the barrel vault. Several smaller buildings stood in the back and on either side. The driver turned right and pulled up to a double door at the top of six steps. It was HQ for the 2nd Armored Cavalry Regiment. He parked the truck in front, near the sign with the unit's crest and insignia. Steve and I jumped out. It was 1030 hours on Friday, 6 March.

The First Sergeant was tall and lean and hunched over slightly as if he had curvature of the spine. He paced around the Orderly Room with a straight pipe in his mouth, raising his left hand to pull it out every time he spoke. A blue ascot, tucked neatly beneath his starched fatigue jacket, covered his long neck. Steve and I dropped our bags and waited for instructions.

"You fellas are with the one-seventy-sixth, I see," the lanky top-kick said, looking down at the papers we handed him. "You'll be with a nice bunch. Never give us any trouble. Their shop is around back. They always fix our equipment right."

"Yes, sergeant," Steve was quick to say, as if he were trying to make a good first impression.

"Your team bunks in the East Block, on the first level. The two of you can share a room. The corporal here will get you your blankets and sheets and show you where it is."

A thirtyish soldier with two stripes on his sleeve got up from his desk and came toward us. His rank, the lowest of the NCOs, was not seen too often anymore. Almost all PFCs who get promoted, regardless of MOS, are made spec four rather than corporal. The Army, I heard, wanted to reduce the number of G.I.s running around giving orders. The specialist grades introduced after the Korean War were supposed to be for soldiers with specialized technical training, such as in communications or weaponry or mechanics, to reward them with higher pay but not necessarily greater authority over others. But, before long, birds were flying out, and then birds with yellow umbrellas, to clerks, cooks, mess aides, supply handlers, infantrymen, hospital orderlies, MPs, truck drivers, you name it, to anyone regardless of skill. The clerk corporal probably had a great deal of time in grade, judging from his age. If he was boosted now, I reasoned, he would get spec five rather than a third stripe.

"Follow me," the two-striper said as he grabbed his field jacket and led us out the door. He seemed to enjoy his petty prerogatives.

The corporal did not lend a hand to Steve with his two bags or me with my three. He walked us around to the other end of the massive building, letting us stop twice to catch our breaths. We went through a narrow passageway that was cut right out of the back portion of the structure. A large square-shaped courtyard, perhaps a hundred feet in either direction, four sections of barracks all around, appeared before us. We were led to a single door on the side facing east. Thick metal railings piled into concrete stairwells that went down to the basement flanked the door. We followed him up one step, through the opening, and up four more steps before we landed on the first floor. Our room was across the hall and a little to the right. The thumb latch had no lock fastened to it.

"Leave your things for now," the junior NCO told us two seconds after we entered the room. "I'm supposed to bring you to the shop before chow."

"Shouldn't we lock our bags up," I asked.

"Don't sweat it. Nothing ever gets stolen around here."

"I got all my civies with me," I said. "Let me just put my over-seas bag away."

Before the corporal could say yes or no, I opened one of the wall lockers. It was double-wide like the kind NCOs have in their private rooms in the States. I placed my overseas bag sideways in the open space on the right and used the combination lock from my duffel bag to secure it. Steve left his bags out in the open.

"Let's go," the nervous two-striper let out, as if he thought the First Sergeant was timing his absence from the Orderly Room.

"I have to take a piss," Steve declared.

The corporal took us to the latrine across the hall from our room to the right, past the outside door. He waited for us anxiously. I thought he was going to wet his fatigue trousers. I too had to go after the long truck ride, and Steve and I both relieved ourselves. After watering out, the corporal whisked us to a small building in the back of the compound the other end from our billet and told us to go in. As the old two-striper left, I could see it was now *he* who was relieved.

154

The 176th Signal Company's repair shop was cluttered with several rows of workbenches, high stools, and testing equipment. Large wooden crates with electrical devices dangling about occupied the center of the room. My new roommate and I waited inside by the door. A man sitting at a desk on the far end saw us standing there, got up, and approached us.

"I'm Sergeant Doss," he said with an earnest smile, holding his hand out. "I'm the team leader. You must be the two new guys. We heard you were coming today."

The sergeant was plain looking and of average height. He wore glasses with the Army-issued clear plastic frame, which blended well with his nondescript physical appearance. Every ten or twenty seconds, as if he had a tic, he would push the frame back to the bridge of his nose with the middle finger extended, making what could be interpreted as an obscene gesture. He certainly could have benefited from a tighter-fitting pair of glasses. There was a rumpled look about him that, in my mind at least, did not make subordinates feel threatened by his stripes. With his wrinkled fatigue shirt coming out of his trousers, boots not bloused with a metal spring or cut butt can, and scratched belt buckle, he did not seem ready or willing to bawl commands.

Doss as an NCO was noticeably and refreshingly different from the spit-and-polish starchy types in perfectly pressed fatigues often seen behind desks. There were three stripes and two rockers on his sleeve. I guessed he was an E-6, sergeant first class according to the old system of ranks. He did not strike me as a new SFC, an E-7. If my hunch was correct and he was not promoted in three years and four months, he would have to sew on a new patch with only one rocker and report as a staff sergeant.

"Nice to meet you, Sarge," Steve said as he shook hands. I was not surprised by the quick informality given Doss' appearance.

"Glad to be here," I added. The sergeant could not possibly know how much I meant that.

"Let me introduce you to your teammates."

The team leader took us around to each bench to meet the guys one at a time. We only spent a few seconds with each one, long enough to shake hands, read a nametag, and bear a face in mind. Besides Doss, I counted ten repairmen, five PFCs, four spec fours, one who said he was going home in three days, another in two weeks, and a spec five. One spec four who was not a short-timer was much older, late thirties I guessed, retirement age if he had his twenty in. Two were from the South, judging by their accents. Four had Italian, Irish, German, or Polish surnames. The rest seemed more middle-American, not from any particular region or nationality group. There were no Jews that I could discern by name or appearance and no Schwarzers. Steve and I, a Protestant from California and a Jew from New York, rounded out the all-white team.

Doss told us to go to chow with the others or to the snack bar if we wanted to and then take the afternoon off to get squared away. We should report to the shop on Monday at 0730, and then later he would take us to the Area Office to meet Sergeant Bentley and Mr. Barry. Steve and I went with four of the guys to the mess hall near the East Block. Lunch was nothing special.

We walked back to our quarters. I was still a little disoriented in the new surroundings. The room was about nine by eleven feet. Two single bunk beds were at the far end against the inside walls, separated by a double-paned window that opened inward. I had never seen windows like this. I turned the handle and pulled it toward me, then released the catch at the base of the other pane and swung it out too. The window faced directly east and offered onlookers an impressive panoramic vista of a corner of Nuremberg.

I had a clear view of almost half the round portion of the forsaken Congress Hall and part of re-named and re-treaded Zeppelinfeld. I was standing no more than two kilometers from where the most evil men in history, murderers of millions, stood not two decades earlier. In a few minutes I took my eyes and mind off these bygone landmarks, now little more than decaying symbols of a forgettable era.

What a strange field the Army put one of its soldiers in. A Jewish-American was posted to a German barracks whereby he could awake each morning and behold two remnants of Herr Hitler's dead dream of a thousand-year Reich and the triumph of his National Socialism.

Steve claimed the bunk on the left as you face the window, and the vacant wall locker on that side of the room. We unpacked our things and made our bunks. Underwear, shirts and shorts, rolled military style, and toiletries went in the footlockers. Uniforms, jackets and trousers were hung in the right side of the wall locker, with long and short left shirtsleeves facing front in overlapping order, bearing rank and Army patches. Boots and shoes were polished again and placed side-by-side under the beds. Shelves on the left half of the double wall locker had sufficient space for the clothes I brought from home. Steve had no civilian clothes with him. For the first time in the Army, I had a modicum of privacy and space, a shared room and a roomier locker. Already I was beginning to enjoy my final tour of duty.

After getting squared away, Steve started to read but I wanted to walk around the building. I first climbed the stairs to the second and third floors and moved up and down the corridors. All I saw were rooms for two or more soldiers and latrines, exactly what was on my floor. I tried to imagine within these walls young blond men with blue eyes in gray uniforms with black belts speaking German as they performed their mundane duties, some with Lugers holstered at their side, others restraining Dobermann Pinschers on a leash.

There was no point hitting the top floor so I went back down and kept going until I reached the basement. It was dark and dirty with an eerie quality about it. Doors were all shut, some secured with thick metal grates. I found an opening with a staircase that led down to another level, a sub-basement that was darker and dirtier than the one above. There was a musty maze of narrow passageways and turns leading in different directions.

When I came to yet another opening with descending steps, this time with no visibility whatsoever, I called my foreign-camp hunt quits. The 176th did not have to send a search party for me. I found the path back to the first floor but with hands running along the walls most of the way. I emerged into the light with blackened hands, a dry mouth, and a stuffy nose.

Steve was inattentive when I came into the room. I grabbed a towel and bar of soap and rushed out again without saying a word. When I returned from the latrine, I told him about my wanderings in the building.

"Three basements?" he said in disbelief. "What for?"

"Beats me. I couldn't see much."

"What was this barracks during the war?"

"Beats me," I repeated, shrugging my shoulders. "Ask one of the guys from the shop."

With the past identity of our Kaserne unable to be resolved by either of us, we took a break from any additional activity and rested on our bunks. Steve continued reading while I stared at the ceiling.

What lay just outside the window filled my thoughts. I recalled those last days on the quarterdeck of the *Rose*. I was sure my apprehensions were not the symptoms of Baron Munchausen disease. I traveled more than three thousand miles only to land on a foreign military base with peculiar parallels to my own domestic residence.

The Brooklyn apartment on Mermaid Avenue and my Nuremberg barracks off Zeppelinstrasse were both footsteps away from two of the most crowded spots in the world at one time. Rear windows opened to scenes, past or present, of more humans per square mile or Quadratkilometer than could be found anywhere else on earth. On Coney Island beaches and in Nazi Party bleachers, great masses of people gathered for *rec*reation from work and the *re*creation of spirit.

So long as I roomed in the East Block of Merrell Barracks, de-composing monuments from Hitler's failed reign would be projected onto my front wall every day at first light. I was certain this was not a view my mother wanted me to wake up to.

## CHAPTER 16: G.I.s AND FRÄULEINS

On Saturday, our first full day in Nuremberg, there was a knock on our door in the early afternoon. Before either Steve or I could say come in, it swung open. One of the teammates we met the previous day popped his head inside, then his whole body. It was Danziger, the one who was going home in two weeks.

"Hey, you guys. Want to join us in the other room?"

Danziger was about my height but thinner. His light hair was cropped very close, especially on the sides, like he was still in basic. I'm sure he had no fear, as I usually had, of an officer or NCO suddenly coming up to him and ordering him to get a haircut. But, he was no spit-and-polish type either. His fatigue shirt and trousers fit loosely around his slim body frame like they were a size too big. From what little I saw, he seemed a pleasant fellow, intent on helping others if he could.

"What's in the other room?" I asked.

"Repairmen who want to celebrate."

"Celebrate what?" Steve injected.

"La Pinza's last weekend in Germany. We're going into town later. You two can come if you like."

La Pinza was the one who was leaving on Monday. He was very short, literally, not just figuratively. At the workbench sitting on a high stool, his feet did not clear the bottom rung. La Pinza was somewhat chunky and looked typically Italian with his dark complexion and thick black hair slicked back.

"Can we go off post tonight?" I inquired.

"You bet. Doss said he called the Orderly Room and told them to make out passes for you guys."

"Lead the way," my roommate said with a smile. Steve was always one to go along with others and party.

We tailed Danziger down the hall on our side into a much larger room. There were four beds but one of the guys from the shop who slept in the room was not there. The bunks were not made. Footlockers were not in the normal horizontal position at the foot of each bunk. They were placed, it seemed, more for others to sit on than for the one whose locker it was to get at its contents easily. There were a few chairs and a table with boxes of cookies and crackers and a jar of peanut butter on top. Two wall lockers were open and I could see cans of drink and food on the shelves. The clothing inside, Army and civy, were not laid out in neat format resembling anything what Steve and I had just effected. As we had been told, Merrell Barracks apparently was not chicken shit for the troopers of the 176th.

Danziger broke open a small bottle of whiskey, poured shots into small plastic cups, and passed them around. I knew alcohol in the barracks was just as verboten here as in the States.

"Prost," he said, lifting his right arm in a near Nazi salute. He made a toast to short-timers and the Fräuleins they leave behind.

"I'll drink to that," La Pinza responded with a happy face.

The little man was wearing a baseball cap tilted back on his head such that his pompadour was visible. He hailed from upstate New York and accented his words differently from the downstate italiani I was used to hearing.

I took a sip and looked around the room again. "Don't you have inspections around here?"

"Hell no," Jones said, or Jonesy as he was called, a southern boy who spoke with a heavy drawl and whose language proficiency left much to be desired. He was a stoutly hulk with a crew cut and several missing teeth that showed when he spoke or smiled. He always seemed to be wiping his brow, his extra poundage obviously not a prophylactic against perspiration.

"The second cav don't bother us none," Jonesy continued. We don't have no bed check neither. It's like they don't know we is here."

At Panzer I learned that in Germany bed check was twelve o'clock every night except Saturday when it was extended by two hours. If there were no forced return from town, the senseless or immature soldier would stay out all night carousing and whoring and then would have great difficulty getting up in the morning for work or details or drills. Not a very effective way to run an army.

"If you stay out after midnight," La Pinza added, "don't come through the main gate until six-thirty or seven the next morning. Otherwise, the guard will write you up."

"What if you can't wait until morning?" Steve put to them appropriately.

"Then you come through the hole in the fence around back," Danziger advised us.

"Where's that?" I wanted to know out of curiosity, not that I was planning to stay out that late.

"Walk past this building, away from town," Danziger said, motioning with one hand. "Follow the fence about fifty or sixty yards. You'll see the hole."

"He means sneak past this building," La Pinza qualified. "When you get off the strassenbahn, stay across the street. Don't let the guard see you."

"Strasswhat?" Steve said as he turned his head toward La Pinza.

"Strassenbahn. The streetcar. It stops on the corner."

The five of us sat around for a while and talked. The other guys got refills but I passed. Steve and I were clued in about certain practices that went on at the shop and the idiosyncrasies of the two sergeants and warrant officer we would be dealing with. The conversation then, ineluctably it seemed, drifted toward what was on every young American male's mind in Germany.

The three teammates stressed that female company was the most important aspect of a peacetime G.I.'s life overseas. Relationships with fellow soldiers take a back seat. Sexual involvement with Fräuleins, they all intimated, will come to define our whole experience in Deutschland. From what I was told prior to landing at Merrell, I had no reason to doubt the veracity of this trio of concerned barracks mates.

Danziger spoke of the older gal he has been shacking up with for six months, her four-year-old daughter left with grandparents, and his plans to still be single when he boarded the boat in two weeks. La Pinza bragged about the puttane he picks up on streets around the Bahnhof, all much taller than he is even in flats, and the gyrations they did together in bed. Fat Jonesy told how he guzzles beer in Gasthauses for hours, then takes off with anything in a skirt, sometimes paying for his pleasure, sometimes not. It seemed our new-found buddies cornered us purposefully to apprise us of the situation we would be facing with the locals. Evidently this ritual was an out-of-manual SOP, a means by which company men with many months and days crossed out on their calendars introduced new arrivals to the Fräulein kultur.

"There are three kinds of women in Germany," Danziger said with a solemn face. "And one kind doesn't mix with the other."

Jonesy stepped forward. There was a gleam in his eyes, as if he enjoyed the telling of these tales. "First there is them what is called nice German girls," he blurted out bluntly. "They never went with no G.I., won't never invite you into their home, and won't take down their drawers for nothin'."

Steve and I listened but said nothing. What could we say?

"Those pure pussies are way out of our ball park," La Pinza pitched at us. "You couldn't slam bang one if you had the only bat in town." He had better grammar but the same barracks crudeness. "A damn Kraut soldier couldn't get into her dugout," he added with a hand gesture characteristic of the Italians I knew in Brooklyn, fist and forearm rocked back and forth with thumb and pinky extended.

I was intrigued by, but did not readily accept the veracity of, the free lesson about German women I was getting, not the first since the night before I had to report to Fort Dix. Why can't I meet a nice German girl? I asked myself. Why are the Seventh Army sophisticates so dogmatic about what is not available to me? How do they know what I could or couldn't do in this strange land? There must be some unspoiled creatures on the other side of the barracks fence willing to break the ice with an American soldier. So what if I'm in a foreign army? We're the foreigners who saved them from the Russian beast. They should be grateful to us.

"I don't believe I can't meet one of these girls you're talking about," I said.

Steve joined me in my quest. "Yeah, where can we meet the classy stuff?" I was sure he too was bucking for a positive answer.

"You just can't," Danziger again said with assurance.

"You better believe it, new boys," La Pinza remarked.

For a moment, I thought he said *Jew* boys, implying that nice German girls would not go out with Steve or me if they thought we were Jewish. That would have been an interesting wrinkle in this impromptu briefing, postwar German youth obeying outlawed prewar racial codes. Either way, from what I was just told, there was a self-imposed non-fraternization policy in effect for the highest caste of women.

"How is you gonna meet a fraulein ain't bopped a buddy before?"

Jonesy jumped in, keen on setting us straight. "In the bars? . . . on the streets . . . on post? All these gals done spread 'em for ten or twenty swingin' American dicks already. Many have a kid and most dropped one or two."

I wanted to convince them that their generalities did not apply to me. Perhaps I needed convincing myself. "I'll wear my civies when I go into town . . . I won't hang out in G.I. joints."

"Hey, where will you go?" La Pinza put to me, jerking his head upward in typical Italian fashion.

"I don't know," I said, shrugging my shoulders slightly. "Don't they have socials for young people, like dances in schools or community centers?" In New York I always went to dances to meet girls.

Now Steve stepped in against me and I knew my argument was getting weaker by the second. "You're dreaming, Dave. G.I.s couldn't go to events like that even if they had them here."

Danziger explained in no uncertain terms that I would not be able to mingle with Germans who stayed clear of Americans unless I spoke perfekt Deutsch. It was impossible for me to meet, let alone stick it to, German girls in the top order. They live at home with their folks, have fathers who would forbid them to see me. The Polizei or MPs would be summoned if I tried to come in the front door. Had I happened to meet such a Fräulein, she wouldn't go to bed with me since she isn't looking to marry a G.I. and doesn't want to leave Germany. She knows if she gave herself to me or to one of my compatriots, ipso facto, she could not be "nice" any longer. Relatives, friends, and neighbors would banish her to a lower level. Her whole life would change.

"Then which girls can I go with?" I asked, playing along with my sociability advisers. I still had not resigned myself, however, to my presumed ignominious fate. In the alien community just outside the guardhouse, I might have to take what I can get.

"The question is which girls *should* you go with?" Danziger said and La Pinza echoed.

"What do you mean?" Steve asked. He was listening as intensely as I was.

Jonesy edged closer and lowered his voice a notch. "They means you should only make for the frauleins that doesn't go with the jigs."

"The second kind," La Pinza clarified.

Here it was at last, the unvarnished classificatory schema G.I.s in Germany devised for the female population. Germans themselves probably employed it, I reasoned. The whites-only Fräulein fraternizers comprised a middle-tier group. I did not need to ask which members of the opposite sex were situated at the bottom. My instructtional teammates got around to them soon enough.

"Any whaat G.I. datin' a nigger-lovin' gal ain't worth shit," Jonesy went on with little reserve. "Kissin' her is like suckin' black dick."

"Your buddies won't be your buddies anymore," La Pinza warned.

The third kind, we were told, sometimes dabbles with soldiers of both colors. The scenes they do turn out well for the dark but not the light. Such women were plentiful in Germany, a boon for the minority of G.I.s who could not hide their hide hue and were estranged from the people around them. For the majority of G.I.s who had no trouble blending tones with the homogeneous popula-tion, double-exposure types were anathema to their sense of decency and order.

"Where do we meet the prejudiced types in Nuremberg?" Steve asked. "The ones who go white only."

"Any of the bars or gasthauses on Luitpoldstrasse," Danziger answered him. "Downtown, near the bahnhof. We'll take you there later tonight. We usually hit the Luitpold first."

Steve looked directly at Danziger. "Is that where you met *your* girlfriend?"

"We call girlfriends 'schatzie' here."

"Where did you meet your schatzie?" Steve asked again.

"I was introduced," Danziger said. "She used to go with another guy on the team. He went home six months ago."

"How about introducing me before you leave?" Steve asked unabashedly. I was quite surprised by this seemingly desperate move on his part. Steve was not bad looking. He certainly could have found a sweetheart in his own right.

"If you want," Danziger answered unemotionally.

"I want."

"Don't worry," La Pinza quickly pointed out to Steve with a silly grin. "That other guy . . . if he was Italian they could've called him

Bianco. No kinky hair coming out of his head."

I was sure Steve understood the racial analogy but he did not react to it.

"She's twenty-five," Danziger advised Steve.

"That's okay."

I was surprised again that Steve did not mind she was six years his senior. That old a gal certainly did not interest me—unless, of course, she was extremely attractive.

"She wants to get married and come to the States," Danziger advised again. "But she won't leave her kid behind."

"That's okay too. I know how to hold women off."

I was surprised a third time. It seemed nothing could dissuade Steve from making this play for a hand-me-down local girlfriend.

"Steve, are you sure you want to get involved so fast?" I said. "You don't know anything about this German gal."

"I'm sure," Steve said to me. He then turned to Danziger. "What's her name?"

"Ursula."

There were a few moments of silence in the room, as if the conversation among the five 176ers was drawing to a close. Steve and I should have felt very fortunate. We had a fine how-do-you-do to the wonderful world of women in this new land we were now part of. One class of potential intimates was beyond our reach, another was quite available but for a price either in cash or a coupling, while a third had a social disease that rendered them untouchable by the likes of us.

Danziger got up from his chair and looked back at Steve and me. "If you guys want to come into town with us, meet us in the front parking lot at nine. Wear civies if you have them."

Jonesy faced me. "You wanna hook up with a fraulein too?" he asked with a serious expression. "There is many I know? I can takes you to 'em."

The bloated unprepossessing soldier must have thought I wanted to see his fat face and full figure every time I made love in Germany.

I shook my head. "I'll find my own, thank you."

## CHAPTER 17: A TASTE OF AMERICA

I went with Steve to the parking area near the front of Merrell Barracks' main building at 2100 sharp as Danziger had said, ready to venture into downtown Nuremberg with three of our teammates. This was our first time out on the town in Germany. After chow, we shaved and showered and spruced up for the big night ahead. I put on the crew neck maroon Shetland wool sweater I had purchased in the PX at Fort Monmouth, my favorite, careful not to stretch the small opening, my striped chino trousers with buckle in back, and the tan desert boots I owned since my senior year.

Steve had no civies and had to borrow different pieces. He was about my size, slightly bigger, and I let him wear a pair of my chinos and a V-neck sweater. A shirt and jacket, though ill fitting, he picked up from other guys. With his Army-issued black dress shoes and matching socks, he was all set.

Our three buddies were waiting for us. Jonesy was the one with the automobile, a '54 Chevy not in the best condition but roomy enough for five. La Pinza, who should have sat in the rear seat because of his stunted stature, sat up in front, a small concession given to the soldier whose home-going we were celebrating. I sat between two full-sized bodies, occasionally elbowing my way to get a better view of the strange-looking structures outside the door windows.

"Where are we going?" Steve asked impatiently. I was at ease to just wait and see what develops.

"Mom's," Danziger said.

"Mom's? What's that?" Steve asked again.

"An American club we always take a new man to," Danziger explained.

"What's it like?" Steve wanted to know.

La Pinza looked around to us. "It's different," he said with a faint smile he could not conceal. As he turned his head away, it looked as though he was covering his mouth with his hand.

"Different from what?" I asked.

"Other American clubs over here," Danziger simply told us.

"Ain't much different from what we got in the States," Jonesy added.

I had no idea what they were alluding to or where we were going but I sat patiently as we wound through a number of side streets in what looked like a remote area. Presently we came to a free-standing building that resembled an old road house like something on the back lot of a Hollywood studio. Jonesy pulled the vehicle around to the rear door and stopped.

"You two go inside," Danziger said to Steve and me sitting on either side of him. He pointed to the door. "Get a table. We'll park the car and be there in a minute."

Steve and I got out of the car. We were about to be the butt of a standard prank pulled on newcomers to Germany, soldiers of our genus anyway. Neither of us suspected anything. There was nothing about Danziger's instructions that was unusual or called attention to the impending horseplay. As we neared the door, I could hear loud music going. We went inside, I first and Steve a close second. Without looking around carefully I just continued moving toward the center of the floor. I got about ten feet when I heard Steve mumble behind me.

"What the fuck."

By then I had taken notice of the surroundings. I fell dead in my tracks. Steve bumped into me as he stopped short too. It was as if both of us were struck dumb. Expressionless, I just stared at the fifty or so people in the large room—at crowded tables, in the dancing area, standing or sitting around a U-shaped bar. The jukebox blasted away with sensual Rhythm and Blues sounds that penetrated my eardrums. A scuffle broke out in the corner. Two MPs stood by as if they were manning battle stations. The women were not of my age group, late twenties to even early forties I would say, most a trifle plump to quite portly, all lily white with heavy make-up, naturally blond or bleached hair in a poodle cut or long and straight. Many wore tight-fitting slacks, smoked long cigarettes, and chewed gum vigorously. The young men, a few in uniform but most in garish civies, were all coal-faced, their pairs of eyes fixed on Steve and me, white balls shining in the darkened room. We had stepped into a black-only bar.

One of the MPs came over to us. "You G.I.s?" he demanded to know.

Steve and I both nodded.

"You looking for trouble?" the tall white soldier cop wearing a helmet liner, armband, and shoulder braid asked sourly.

Neither Steve nor I responded.

"You two better hightail it out of here if you know what's good for you. Go somewhere else. There are plenty of white joints in town."

We turned around and headed for the same door we came in. The MP's command was superfluous. Steve and I would have left anyway in a matter of seconds, once the shock of learning the true nature of the establishment abated. The three pranksters were leaning against the car, waiting for us, all laughs and giggles.

"Why'd you send us in there?" I complained. I did not like being on the wrong end of a crude joke.

La Pinza composed himself. "We wanted to show you the real Germany."

"Mom's kinda reminds y'all of home, don't it?" Jonesy gibed.

Danziger, the least offensive of the three, changed the subject. "Come on. Let's go to the Luitpold," he said with a straight face. "We had our fun."

Jonesy drove around to the front to get to the street. As we passed the shabby building I looked out the window and caught a glimpse of the flashing red, white, and blue neon sign above the main entry. "Mother Tucker's" it read. This brief encounter with Mom's, as Americans of both races dubbed it, turned out to be the only time I ever ventured into such a bar in Germany.

The drive to the Bahnhof area took about fifteen minutes. Steve remained quiet, as I, but perhaps for different reasons. He probably chalked this up to a Signal-one-seven-six initiation rite and I saw no reason to voice my irritation toward teammates I would probably never go to town with again. Two would be gone in a matter of days and a third I had next to nothing in common with outside of an Army uniform.

Danziger did most of the talking aimed at the two neophytes in his outfit. He explained that during duty hours, white and black soldier together in work assignments and military exercises with little or no outward appearance of any enmity. Off duty both colors enjoy equal access to on-post facilities. Anyone can go to the movie theaters, snack bar, PX, swimming pool, barbershop, or service club. The only times problems crop up is at the EM or NCO club when there is integrated dancing. Any skirmishes involving partygoers of the same or opposite sex, however, are quickly put down by willful exits or military sanctions.

"Bunkin' with boogies in the barracks," Jonesy cut in, "don't mean we wants to drink with 'em or watch 'em gets close to our women."

Off post, Danziger continued, is another story. Once you walk out the gate, it's a different world. Whites want nothing to do with their darker comrades in arms. In German towns where troops are located a strict pattern of separation exists. Certain entertainment sites are reserved for white only. If colored happen to wander in, before long they are warned to leave—by waitresses, white G.I.s, or club owners. Why would they want to stay after being told they won't be served drinks and the Fräuleins won't dance with them? If the unwritten-norm-violators don't beat it, the whites beat them. Sometimes the fights are so bad the whole interior of the bar is wrecked. The MPs called always side with the whites, who are seen merely defending their territory, and take away G.I.s the bar owner wants removed. Since the Polizei have no jurisdiction over American soldiers, they refuse to protect the non-white troublemakers.

In Baumholder a few years back, we were told, all hell broke loose one night. Some soldiers were killed. The only black and white co-mingling was in the red blood running in the gutter.

"The nigs play in a different league," La Pinza said, this time without his baseball cap on. "We don't run after their babes, they don't come to bat for ours."

Danziger remarked how beneficial it was for the colored troops to have their own joints to hang out in. The segregation, he argued, facilitated their search for sexual favors in a foreign land with no females their own kind. Most of them never got near a white woman before they set foot in Germany. A post-Nazi society, seeking to redeem itself for past racial misdeeds, conferred upon the descendants of American slaves emancipation from the discrimination they faced across the Atlantic. The bright lights atop black-only bars might very well have spelled "Colored Only," but to those about to enter the words were a proclamation for freedom to fornicate with belles heretofore outside the perimeter drawn for them. When the black buddies mosey onto a plantation like Mother Tucker's, they know every white sister sauntering about is willing and ready to tuck them in. Such unshackling opportunities for love or pleasure most certainly could not be found in many bars or clubs in the good old USA.

"The Krauts like it thataway too," Jonesy noted. "They wants the nigger bars separate. Easier to keeps their daughters away from and easier for the po'leece to pinch the prosts."

Jonesy was not the most sophisticated or thoughtful soldier I met overseas but here he was on the German mark. Many Germans developed friendships with the Negersoldaten occupying their homeland. Black G.I.s rented apartments from them, shopped in their stores, passed out chocolates and chewing gum to their children, and often made a greater effort than the Amerikanersoldaten, as the white G.I.s were called, to learn their language and customs.

It was no secret that German tolerance ended with interracial relationships, in spite of postwar legislation that specifically prohibited racial discrimination. The clear demarcation of establishments catering to blacks helped citizens of the Neue Deutschland to dislocate this affront to Aryan sensibilities and protect their women Volk from the sexual transgression and spontaneous violence that transpired on those premises. The Polizei also liked it when the Negerbars were known and confined to certain areas. They presumed only Prostituierten would frequent such forbidden places. So long as American vice was color coded, Germany's anti-prostitution laws were not difficult to enforce.

Danziger stressed that off-post segregation is here to stay because the Army doesn't do anything about it either, and doesn't want to do anything about it. The brass see it as just an extension of what goes on in the States, a voluntary social cleavage that is good for the morale of the majority of the troops and avoids inevitable physical confrontations with the minority. The MPs know where the Sambo Spots are. They can black them out anytime they want. But it suits their purpose to keep them on-limits, to target them for periodic raids in order to show German officials that Americans are cracking down on their homegrown vice. The fact that the military itself was segregated up until a few years before did not endear those with the stars or stripes toward foreign civilian integration. Besides, as any

U.S. officer will tell you, segregation in the community is a problem for the German people to deal with. Our government assumed no responsibility whatsoever for the thousands of American orphans, white or Mischling, toddling around Germany. So why would it work to eliminate the racial divide that contributed to the population growth?

Listening to my new buddies talk, I got the impression that over here color prejudice was still at attention in the hearts and minds of most whites wearing fatigues or Class A's. G.I.s from the South like Jonesy must not have suffered culture shock when they left their bases and entered a partitioned world similar to the one they grew up in.

I wondered how Elvis might have reacted to the segregation he undoubtedly saw when he popped his head out of his tank. Friedburg was probably no different than Nuremberg. In his pre-Army days, the vocalist/guitarist was known to have mingled with blacks in Memphis, learned to play their style of music, and sang the Blues with them. A private Presley, in or out of uniform, prob-ably would not patronize the clubs and pubs in the ghetto part of his garrison town. Boozing and shmoozing off post with the 3rd Ar-mored's darker squads would mean unnecessary risks to a public Elvis bent on doing his time and resuming his singing and acting career without controversy. One jailhouse rock was enough for the poor southern boy who, both on and off the screen, tried to stay out of trouble.

Thanks to my three teammates, I was given a taste of America on my novice night out in a faraway country. Like Coca-Cola and Campbell's soup, Jim Crow had been imported to Germany. I swallowed hard, but the lump in my throat was not food for thought. It was a good thing the WAC I knew back at Ord was not handed her own orders for the Seventh Army. Which set of bars would she grab hold of off post? With so many chalky Damen in Deutschland ready and willing to dote on men of both complexions, not many black buddies would pine for a pale sister. The young white soldiers might let her just . . . fade away.

Driving away from Mother Tucker's, I had no reason to believe that the German-American fraternization I witnessed on the other side of the color line would in short order come to affect my chase for carnal contacts.

## CHAPTER 18: IN SEARCH OF GOOD TIME

Luitpoldstrasse was Nuremberg's answer to La Place Pigalle in Paris. It was a short street, running from Königstrasse to Sterngasse, not very far from both the German National Museum and the Hauptbahnhof. The block-long strip of bars, clubs, Gasthauses, cafés, restaurants, cheap hotels, Pensions, and a movie theater stood in the shadow of the Old Wall, the sixteen-foot medieval cobble-stone bulwark that warded off enemies of Franconia's largest city for centuries. Colorful neon signs gracing every entertainment establishment flashed garishly from sundown to sunup.

Women fortyish and then some paced back and forth in the passageways of the hotels, or outside on the street, in their extra high heels, tight skirts falling above the knees, and unbuttoned waist jackets. G.I.s in uniform or civies approached the women with open wallets in outstretched hands. Stocky men in suits and ties, faces like bulldogs, patrolled in front of the doorways to some clubs. The street was filled with American soldiers and young Germans of both sexes in search of fun and frolic every hour of every day.

That Saturday night the five of us were headed to Luitpoldstrasse with Jonesy at the wheel. I tried to put Mother Tucker's, and the forked system of off post pleasure-seeking my schwarze comrades in Germany lived by, out of mind. He parked the car across from the main station, headlights toward the Old Wall in an unmarked space, and we all walked around the medieval tower on the corner. Steve and I tagged along with our teammate guides who pointed out and gave brief reports on the goings-on at various places of interest on Luitpoldstrasse to a young soldier in a foreign country.

I was sure Steve felt as I did, immensely excited and eager to take everything in on our first foray into Nuremberg's naughty nightlife. My stateside buddy stopped to talk to one of the women standing alone, even touching her on the shoulder in a gesture of friendliness, but Danziger pulled him away. I could not help noticing an intoxicated and laughing private in OD's, cuntcap pushed back awkwardly on his head, in the open hallway to one of the Pensions. Leaning over with one hand against the building, the other holding his exposed pecker, he was pissing away in full view of everyone who happened to walk by. A yellow puddle gathered around both of his shoes.  This American ambassador of good will apparently had little or no interest in endearing himself to our German hosts.  At the curb in several places two or three soldiers in uniform stood next to or surrounded a young woman more modestly dressed than the hotel hookers loitering about.

Our gang led us straight to the Luitpold, one of the most popular Gasthauses in Nuremberg.  It was situated on Luitpoldstrasse's northern side, in the middle of the block.  All those seeking the company of the city's young German women frequented this place and others like it.  We took a table near the dance floor.  A band was playing music unfamiliar to me.  People were dancing in the middle of the room.  I saw only white faces here.

Most of the G.I.s, like we, were in civies, easy to peg by their American-style casual clothing and short haircuts, heads sometimes shaved on the sides and back.  The young men with long light hair over their ears and shirt collars, dressed more formally in strange suit fashions, single-breasted jackets with wide lapels and padded shoulders, baggy trousers with high cuffs, were obviously German.  Waiters wore black vests with gold-colored buttons, waitresses short-sleeved blouses tucked beneath pleated skirts.

La Pinza raised his arm to call a waiter over.  "Comrade," he said in a disrespectful tone.  "Funf bier.  Schnell."  He was in a hurry to start drinking and seemed eager to show off his German language skills.

Danziger paid for the first round with a ten-Mark bill when the waiter returned a minute later with a tray of five Steins.  He lifted his glass by the handle and held his hand above eye-level to Prost his drinking buddies.  The rest of us did the same in what I could see around the room was a common convention.

"The beer's warm," I remarked with surprise after taking a sip.

"That's how Germans like it," Danziger explained.  "Room temperature.  Besides, they don't waste money on refrigeration."

"It's stronger than American beer," Steve added.

"You think this is strong?" La Pinza said.  "You should taste the black beer over here.  The women like it too."  I wondered whether he was making another one of his snide racial comments.

We spent almost an hour in the Luitpold.  The guys ordered two more rounds of beer but I had them count me out.  La Pinza and

Jonesy ordered Steinhäger too and downed their beers as a chaser, apparently de rigueur in Deutschland as much as prosting. Not many people were dancing to the droned music. Waiters and waitresses moved about the room depositing various brands of bottled Wein on the tables, replacing a Stein of beer here and there, changing dollars to Marks but not vice versa, carrying trays of food and empty plates to and from the kitchen.

"Let's show these guys the Flying Dutchman," Danziger suggested, looking over to Steve and then to me.

We left the Luitpold and walked directly across the street to the Flying Dutchman, another hotspot popular with G.I.s. This Gasthaus on the inside was a bit smaller, with its long and narrow L-shaped room, but I immediately was struck with a feeling of greater intimacy. Tables were pushed closer together, the music was more American and louder, the people seemed merrier, the ones dancing were more animated. We sat down at a table away from the dance area but I had a full view of everyone in the place. The guys again ordered beer and before long were guzzling the second round while I was still sipping from the first.

"I've got to take a leak," Steve revealed.

"The head's thataway," Jonesy noted, pointing to the door marked Herren on the opposite wall from where we were sitting.

"I'll go with you," I said, sensing my own need to relieve myself in a little while anyway.

The men's toilet in German bars or clubs was an experience unto itself. I almost did an about face soon as I walked into one. I thought I had inadvertently entered the *women's* wash room. An elderly woman was sitting inside by the door in front of a small table with a change box, a plate of coins, and a stack of souvenir cards on it. She was collecting for use of the toilet as well as selling pictures of nude women.

"Zwanzig Pfennig," the sweet old lady would say with a smile and nod to each man that came in as she pointed her finger at the plate. She held a few cards in her other hand and flashed them at the men while saying something in German as they entered and left. Steve dropped a dime in the plate for both of us. Just then another grandmother type appeared, with bucket and mop in one hand and plunger in another. I had never seen women in a men's room before.

174

I looked around for a urinal but saw none. "There's nothing here," I commented. "Where the hell do you piss?"

Steve looked over toward the backs of several men standing in front of us. "Against the wall."

"What?" I was still puzzled by this strange toilet.

"Piss against the wall. That's what those guys are doing."

I presumed Steve was right as neither one of us could see what was going on in front. He found an opening in the line, unzipped, took aim, and began emptying his bladder. I squeezed in next to him and followed suit. We stood about a foot and a half from a blank wall with tile running halfway to the ceiling. At the base, a small curved trough not quite level with the floor carried the fluid to a drain in the corner. As we were spritzing the wall, two Germans came up and rudely elbowed positions on either side of us. We both had to move sideways a few steps while still holding ourselves. The one next to me was shooting with such force I could feel some of the ricocheted spray against my leg. In Germany, evidently they are not big on privacy or modesty when it comes to toilet training.

"Where do you take a shit?" I asked Steve as we were leaving.

He looked around for a moment. "Over there," he said, nodding at what looked like a closet with no door in one corner of the smelly room.

I moved toward the unknown facility. The curtain was open and I could see there was no stall inside. I did not realize how true my thinking about Germans was until I took this peek for myself. On the floor in the back was a round hole filled partly with water. In front of it were cutout patterns for two shoes, toe and heel opposite to me. Suddenly I realized how this makeshift commode operated. A man would enter the stall, turn around, drop his trousers and shorts, squat down with his feet in the shoe cutouts, and take his dump. Not a very sanitary, let alone private or modest, means of moving one's bowels. But these facilities were not much worse than those in older stateside barracks buildings, with their long sink-like urinals in the latrine and several commodes in a row with no partitions. In Germany I had better get used to calls to nature being more of a public affair. I wondered what receptacles for human waste lie behind the door with the word Damen on it, what indig-nities women in this country have to go through tending to them-

175

selves away from home. I was confident, though, that there were no male attendants, old or young, cleaning up, collecting money, or pandering pictures of nude men in the female sanctuaries for personal hygiene.

"How do you like German johns?" La Pinza asked facetiously when Steve and I got back to our table. "Did you guys handle yourselves okay?"

"We did all right," Steve let out with a smirk. "It wasn't hard."

"We held our own in there," I added. No one seemed to get our double-entendres.

"Ain't like America," Jonesy said, comparing the two cultures for the second time in one day. "Here the Krauts piss on a wall and shit on the floor."

I looked around the packed room at the Germans enjoying themselves and thought for a moment about Jonesy's comment. The people here readily absorbed the Jim Crow practice of female fraternization we exported, since it was compatible with their own racial tendencies and it would cost them dearly not to. Our former enemy, however, was unwilling or unable to replace their primitive patterns of urination and defecation with our more sequestered, more dignified, and certainly more expensive civilian style of public toilet construction.

Half an hour went by with more drinking. La Pinza seemed to be in good spirits and was enjoying his final fling in a foreign land. At the next table there were three young women. La Pinza got up and went over to one of them.

"Tanz mit mir, schatzie," he commanded and, without waiting for an answer, grabbed her hand and practically dragged her to the dance floor. They made an odd couple, she almost a head taller than he, but they danced well together, spinning and turning to every beat of the fast tune the band was playing.

La Pinza's actions were a call to arms for me. I approached one of the other two at the next table. Without saying a word I simply extended my palm. The girl smiled, got up, took my hand, and followed me to the dancing area. We did three dances, two fast and one slow, without talking. She spoke no English I gathered. She did not ask me my name and I did not ask her any questions. Like an American girl her feet were in synch with mine.

"Danke shane," I said with a half smile and nod when I brought the girl back to her table. I wondered if I pronounced it correctly.

"Bitte schön," she replied, with a different pronunciation for the second word, and sat down.

Jonesy slid his chair a bit so I could get to my place. "You dance pretty good, Strahber." After twenty months in the Army, I was used to the southern pronunciation of my name. "Where'd you learn them dances, in New Yawk?"

I nodded as I lifted my glass and took a sip. "The fast one is called the Lindy, the slow is the Fox Trot."

I had taken my first step in Deutschland, albeit a tiny one, and it was successful. Bolder moves were now in order, I thought, as I looked around the room. Two Fräuleins were sitting at a small square table on the edge of the dance floor but I could only make out one face. She had straight blond hair, cut short, part on the side, with a lock dangling over her forehead. I caught a glimpse of her profile and then saw her in a three-quarters view as she moved her head. From a distance she seemed quite attractive to me, more so than the girl I just danced with. The other one had her back to me. All I could eye was long wavy bleach-blond hair that flopped onto narrow shoulders.

"You see those two girls by themselves up front?" I said to my three company companions.

La Pinza looked over to where I motioned with my head and finger. "What about them?"

"Do you know them?"

They all shook their heads.

"I like the one on the left, with the short hair."

"Well, why don't you go over to her," Danziger said.

"What should I say?"

La Pinza grinned. "Ask her to eat your wiener."

"Tell her you wants to lick her schnitzel," Jonesy said as he broke out in a hearty chuckle.

"You think they're hookers?" Steve asked.

La Pinza hedged his answer. "Maybe . . . maybe not."

"If they are, how much would they charge?" I wanted to know.

"Twenty or thirty marks," Danziger said. "As much as forty on payday. But, the broads could just be out for a good time."

"Same as you, Davey boy," Steve remarked, and then goaded me. "Go ask the one you like to dance. Cozy up to her. Buy her a drink. Ask if you could take her home."

For someone who was planning to get acquainted with a German girl via introduction, he had plenty of suggestions for me to nab one on my own.

Without saying another word to my buddies, I got up and cautiously walked over to the two Fräuleins. I faced the one that caught my notice. "Would you like to dance?" passed softly from my lips. I tried to be polite and I wanted her to know I was an American. I leaned forward and held my hand out to her I was so sure she would take it.

She raised her head to gaze at me. Just as I surmised the one I liked was very pretty indeed, had a nice round unblemished face with good features. From a sitting position she appeared to have a knockout body too, shapely and well proportioned where it counted. But there was a hardened look about her and a feminine toughness that detracted somewhat from her otherwise enviable face and figure. I could see she was in her mid-twenties, four or five years my elder, but that was no impediment to my interest in her.

"No," she said simply and emphatically and then averted her eyes from me.

I was stunned by the unexpected rejection. Young German women came to an establishment such as this, I was led to believe, to meet young men and dance the night away, whether their motives were commercial or not. I found that out for myself minutes earlier. So why did she not want to spin around with me a few times? Did I look like a baby to her? Was I homely in appearance? Did she have a grudge against Americans? I was ready to head for my table, tail between my legs, but instead instinctively turned and repeated my proposal to the other gal sitting right there. My mother always told me to look before I leap. I should have also known to look before I speak.

"Yes," this one responded without hesitation. She stood up and moved toward the dancing area just as I was getting a good look at her.

My fall-back choice for a dancing partner was no Elizabeth Taylor. She was tall and wiry, a height and body type I was not crazy about. Her longish face, bumpy nose, and beady eyes did not impel any romantic notions in me. The most disturbing facial characteristic, to an oral-oriented young man especially, was her slightly protruding two front teeth, visible even if her mouth were partially open. The tits too, in terms of cup and crest, left much to be desired. The uncomely Fräulein I snagged by happenstance was a far cry from her friend at the table I was quite smitten with. Had the stand-in dissented too, had she been affronted by my blatant beckoning to dance only on a rebound, I would have been better off, or so I thought. But she seemed eager to leave the table with me and I could not bow out gracefully. I resigned myself to the mishap.

This would not be the first time I danced with a dog. We found a spot on the floor where we could cling to each other. For the moment, I regretted having to tangle with this titless and tasteless tart, but just twenty-four hours later I would think differently of the situation.

"What is your name?" my not-so-schön Schatzie-to-be asked as I held her almost at arm's length.

We were doing a slow dance and it was not difficult to talk. "Dave."

She looked at me funny. "Short for David," I explained. She seemed to understand my full name better. "What's yours?"

"Elsa." After a pause, she added, "Where you are from?"

"New York."

"How long in Nürnberg you are? I not see you before."

"I've been here two days. I was in Boblingen for two weeks."

She continued questioning me. "Where you stay? Pinder Barracks? Darby Kaserne?"

I had never heard of those bases and did not know where either one was. "No. I'm at Merrell Barracks."

"I know it. Yes."

It was obvious that Elsa liked me, was not just making conversation, but that incentive was not enough for me to take my mind off the blond beauty at the table. Every so often I sneaked a peek at her when Elsa's back was turned.

"What's your friend's name?" I asked reluctantly.

"Marianne."

"Why didn't she want to dance with me?" I chanced inquiring. I knew I might be hurting this one's feelings by showing interest in the other, but I really wanted an answer. While we were dancing I observed Marianne turn down another guy as well.

"Marianne does not know to dance."

"You mean . . . she can't dance at all?"

Elsa nodded. "She see you dance. If she go with you, she know she look bad."

I was heartened by this revelation. Marianne noticed me creditably prior to my appearance before her and her declination to dance was less a rebuff to me personally than an avoidance of an embarrasssment to her. Being in a clinch with Elsa now seemed worth my while, but still all I could think about was getting my arms around, and legs between, Marianne. I wanted to change partners but not for dancing.

The music picked up. I continued twisting and turning with Elsa. She was not a bad hoofer. But we must have looked comical together, with our combination of German and American steps and dances. I put my hand around her waist and she swung her arm on top of my shoulder. She would bump into me and I would then give her a whirl. At times I was going into a do-si-do while she was coming out of an allemande left.

After a while the band took a break and I returned Elsa to her table. I offered to buy the two Fräuleins a drink, but Elsa said no and Marianne shook her head. Perhaps my ploy to connect with the one I really coveted was too transparent.

"Not tonight," the ugly duckling added. "Maybe tomorrow." The bonny babe sat silently, looking at me with deep blue eyes but expressing no emotion.

I found myself in a precarious position. I could not figure them out and I did not know what to say or do next. Were these two hooking on Saturday until Sunday morn or were they just a pair of good-time Charlizes? Was I in the company of sorority sisters who booked threesomes and/or covered each other's appointments or were they merely a dull duo doling it out free. I made no move on either of them. I did not offer to take one or the other home and I certainly did not ask if or how much they tabbed for their time. I had no inclination to accompany Elsa to her place or to set up a future date. But if I offered to leave with Marianne or proposed to see her again, with the chum I danced with not two feet away still catching her breath, I was sure I would get thumbs down.

"Thank you for the dance," I said to Elsa as I turned to Marianne. "It was nice meeting you too." My first remark was a gratuitous one, the second arguably an understatement. I walked away feeling good that I completed another, more personal contact with a German girl but I left feeling bad that it was with the wrong girl.

"How'd you make out?" Steve wanted to know before I even sat down.

I shrugged my shoulders. "Nothing much. They didn't want me to sit with them. The one I danced with said to come back tomorrow. The other didn't say anything."

"Did they tell you they charge?" Danziger inquired.

"No."

"Did you offer to pay?" Danziger asked again.

"No."

Now Jonesy stepped in true to form. "Strahber. Ain't you never paid for pussy before?"

I did not answer that question.

Danziger got back into the conversation. "You know why she said come back tomorrow, don't you?"

"I got a clue."

"She likes you," Danziger explained. "Sunday night's not so busy. She can't afford to see someone for free tonight."

"I didn't ask to see her," I said.

"She was just covering her bases in case you do," Danziger went on.

"Yeah," La Pinza reckoned. "She's not giving away home plate just yet."

"Well, I wouldn't have paid to score with her anyway," I admitted, following the analogy. "It was the other one I really wanted." I paused a moment before speaking next. "I wouldn't have paid that one either. I liked her too much."

"Then you better kiss them both goodbye," Steve concluded.

"Yeah," La Pinza said again. "Looks like you struck out the first time you swung a bat over here." The tiny italiano was true to his form too.

My buddies, old and new, were right. I couldn't pay for love with someone I was *not* attracted to and I couldn't pay for love with someone I *was* attracted to if it meant standing in line.

Some time passed and I finished my drink. "When are you guys going back?" I looked at my watch. "It's after twelve already."

"Bed check ain't till two," Jonesy reminded me. "The hell-raisin' is just startin'."

"I'm leaving now. My head feels funny. I need to get to bed."

"You only had two beers," Danziger recalled.

"I know. I'm not used to drinking."

"You know how to get back?" Danziger asked.

I shook my head.

Danziger gave me directions as to how to reach the base by street-car and what stop to get off. He told me what to say to the conductor, but it was not Merrell Barracks. When I heard it, a chill ran up and down my spine. He said most Germans in Nuremberg still refer to our Kaserne by its former name.

I left the Flying Dutchman, turned right, walked to the corner, turned right again around the tower, and caught Strassenbahn Nr. 8 at the next street corner. In the middle car I found a seat toward the back.

I watched the conductor as he strutted slowly down the aisle saying a few words to people, punching tickets, and acting authoritatively. He had on a worn dark blue uniform, boxed hat with a badge, and unpolished black shoes. A metal coin dispenser was belted around his waist.

"Merrell Barracks," I said to the petty civil servant when he approached me. I wanted to test Danziger's theory about Nurembergers' knowledge of the American occupation of their city.

The pudgy middle-aged German looked at me with a blank face. "Was, bitte."

"Merrell Barracks," I repeated.

He then said something to me in German that I did not understand, but I was sure he was asking me where I wanted to go.

"Nix verstehen," I said in corrupted German like a foreigner, feigning ignorance of what he was saying. I shook my head slightly to drive home my point.

The conductor again said something in German and then turned to others around me. "Englisch . . . englisch, bitte," he cried out.

"Merrell Barracks," I said for the third time.

I knew this would annoy, if my mother's reasoning about Germans was correct, the erstwhile Nazi, but that did not bother me. Damn, I thought. How can this dumb comrade not know what Merrell Barracks is? It's written in big bold letters across the front of the main building. The streetcar passes right by it, for Christ's sake.

No one came forward to help the poor man. He kept rattling on in German. His face reddened and perspiration began to drip from under his hat. Now I knew Danziger had told me the truth. Enough is enough I decided.

"SS Kaserne," I said finally, holding back the lump in my throat.

"Ach so!" the little fool let out nodding his head and giving me a familiar smile.

Fortunately for me, the conductor was totally unaware of the game I had played at his expense. Had he realized an American occupier was jerking him off about a German landmark on his own work route, I was sure he would have grabbed me by the arm and thrown me off his streetcar. My mother would have been proud of me for giving something back to the good Germans. The object of my disaffection ripped off the top thin paper ticket from his booklet, punched a hole in one of the squares, and handed it to me with the change from the Mark I had given him.

The ride back to the base was four stops and took less than seven minutes. I thought about Marianne more so than Elsa. At the time, though, I had no idea that the two women I just met in the Flying Dutchman would come to play important roles in the life of a horny young soldier before he boarded the boat back to Brooklyn. Separately and for different reasons, meaningful encounters with both were in the cards.

My first night out on the town set the stage for later developments. My tour of duty in Germany, opposite gender-wise at least, was destined to be an interesting one.

# CHAPTER 19: HITLER'S FAVORITE CITY

"Where's Pinder Barracks?" I asked Danziger Sunday morning. "And Darby Kaserne?"

I was fast asleep when Steve and the others came back from the Flying Dutchman shortly before two. I had no recollection of him coming into our room, turning the lights on, banging his wall locker door, and playing the radio. According to Steve, he said something to me and I sat up in bed, mumbled a few words, and then dropped my head back on the pillow.

That day I awoke with an odd sense of place. My name was not Daniel but I felt I was in the lion's den. Just hours earlier I learned the U.S. Army installation I now called home had been a barracks during the war for the infamous SS, the Schutzstaffel. They were the Protective Guard, the private police force of the Nazi Party, staffed mainly by tall, blond, Aryan-looking men who were insanely loyal to Adolph Hitler. They ruled by intimidation, terror, and violence.

It was the SS, not regular Wehrmacht troops, who operated the factories of death. Newsreel footage I had seen in the movies or on television flashed before my eyes—human skeletons standing behind barbed wire fences, bodies dangling lifelessly from rope nooses, naked men and women being herded into gas chambers. The words Auschwitz, Buchenwald, Mauthausen, and Treblinka rang in my ears. The squadron of bullies, thugs, and murderers was led by nondescript Heinrich Himmler, one of the most powerful men in Germany throughout the war, but a rat who turned tail and betrayed his Führer at the end. The room I was sleeping in could have been the former quarters of concentration camp guards who tortured and slaughtered members of my own family, not to mention fellow Jews.

"Why do you ask?" Danziger said.

He and I were sitting in my room talking. Steve was in the latrine shaving and showering, getting ready to head out with Danziger to meet Ursula. He sensed I was concerned with all things military and German that pertained to my new barracks and life in Nuremberg.

"That girl I danced with last night asked me if I was stationed at those bases."

"The one you didn't like?"

I nodded, hoping I was not earning a reputation for making a play for a Fräulein I did not like.

"Pinder is in Zirndorf. A small town about thirty clicks from here straight west."

Clicks? I repeated to myself. So this was the way American soldiers referred to kilometers. Danziger did not pronounce the Z correctly as a *Tz*, German style.

"The barracks was named for John J. Pinder, Jr.," Danziger explained. "Many of the camps we took over were renamed for dead G.I.s who helped win the war."

"Who was Pinder? I never heard of him."

"He was a tech sergeant. Fifth grade, I believe. They did away with technician ranks in forty-eight. Pinder was killed on D-Day in Normandy. Hit three times trying to get a workable radio on shore. They gave him the Medal of Honor . . . after he was buried, of course."

In wartime, it seems the deeds of dead soldiers, more so than the living, that are deemed brave enough to warrant the highest award. "And Darby?"

"Darby Kaserne is in Furth . . . where the main PX is," Danziger went on. "Northwest of here. It's closer than Zirndorf. Furth is a much smaller city than Nuremberg but Darby is a much bigger barracks than Merrell."

"Merrell's not that big?"

"No . . . but it's the best barracks in this area. We're the only one in Nuremberg . . . and not far from the bahnhof either, where all the action is."

"Who was Darby?" I inquired. "Was he the one from *Darby's Rangers*? I saw that flick at Ord."

Danziger gave a nod. "William O., a bird colonel who started the commando unit. They fought in North Africa, and Sicily and Italy. Darby got popped by an artillery round the day after Mussolini was hung upside down. Darby died for nothing. The Germans in Italy already agreed to surrender."

"That's a shame. Did he get the Medal of Honor too?" I thought James Garner was pretty good in Hollywood's take on Darby.

"No. They gave him brigadier general. Promoted him when he couldn't pin his star on."

"What about Merrell? Was he brass too? A sergeant maybe?"

"Hell no. He was a peon like us. The lowliest soldier they ever named a kaserne after."

Danziger's telling of the story of Merrell Barracks intrigued me. It made me feel more positive about my new home in spite of its former SS affiliation. Joseph F. Merrell was a nineteen-year-old private from Staten Island who lost his life leading a one-man attack against vastly superior enemy forces. He literally opened the route to Nüremberg for the advancing American ground troops. The young man assumed command after all the officers and NCOs in his company were killed. For his courage he was awarded the Congressional Medal of Honor posthumously. I felt a strange sort of kinship with the namesake of my barracks. Joe and I both grew up in New York City and we both soldiered in Germany at age nineteen. It was gratifying to know that a buck private can share kudos with, and rest peacefully next to, a general.

Steve came back in the room with nothing but a bath towel wrapt around him, squeaking his way across the floor in his rubber shower clogs. I had never seen him in such high spirits. The noticeable bulge in the middle of his towel suggested he was agog with lascivious thoughts of his impending introduction to a maid-to-order Fräulein. He laughed and joked with his procurer of sorts and me. Steve paced back and forth between his wall locker and bunk. He dressed for what he anticipated would be a promising day ahead, promising, that is, if he were undressing later on.

"Hey, Monmouth good buddy," Steve quipped, bouncing from foot to foot. "How's by you?"

"I'm okay." Obviously he was more okay than I was.

"You going back to the Flying Dutchman tonight?"

"I don't know."

"Well, don't wait for me," he said with that silly grin of his whenever he was about to proffer a double entendre. "I'll probably be all tied up."

I was in no mood to return a comment in kind.

Danziger looked at his watch. "Let's go," he urged Steve. "Ursula will be at the gasthaus in ten minutes. It'll take us fifteen to twenty just to get there."

"What are you planning to do this afternoon?" Steve got off as he was halfway out the door.

"I don't know," I said again. "I may go for a walk."

The new barracks on the south side of town was christened by the Third Reich, appropriately, the Süd Kaserne. It was built to be near the site of the Nazi Party rallies. The SS in 1937 wanted to be represented in Nuremberg year-round and partake more fully in the annual celebrations. The construction of the Kaserne was completed in early '39, in time for the annual rally, meant to be the grandest yet. The SS's dreams of goose-stepping at old Zeppi's field that year, unfortunately for them, were never realized. The ten days of festivities were all set to begin on September 2. But on that day Hitler's SS men were cracking a war in Poland, not polishing leather jackboots and pressing black uniforms in Nuremberg's South Barracks. Dubbed, ironically, the Party Day of Peace, history rendered the 1939 rally the Reichsparteitage that never was.

With no parades or marches in store for the SS, the barracks was employed chiefly as a training school for radio operators, some of whom were summoned to tune frequencies and broadcast directives in the long and futile siege of Leningrad. The SS Kaserne, as everyone spoke of it, its official calling apparently not catchy enough, earned its ignominious repute in '41 and '43 when inmates from the Dachau and Flossenbürg concentration camps were deported to the facility to do dangerous work. SS troops also commandeered POWs from the nearby Langwasser prison camp for forced labor on extravagant buildings a delusional Hitler ordered for his Rally Grounds right up to his shoving a muzzle in his mouth.

By the time I landed at Merrell, it was twenty years after the Süd's opening. Yet its Nazi nickname still passed from the lips, and I'm sure was lodged in many hearts too, of the townspeople. The denazification program the Allies cut out for Germany evidently failed to hemorrhage Heini H.'s hold on a postwar Nuremberg. I suppose it was only natural for Nurembergers to choose to remember the now illegal SS in lieu of the heroic young American who killed twenty-three German soldiers two days before their city's liberation.

Adolph Hitler's favorite city symbolized German nationalism and Nazi glory. The medieval town had once been the economic crossroads of Europe, had a rich cultural heritage in trade and the arts. The Führer selected Nuremberg personally as the site for the annual

Reich congresses. Propaganda speeches, party pageantry, military demonstrations, and memorials for fallen Soldaten all took place on a vast open meadow southeast of the city center. The capital of Franconia was steeped in German history and culture. Built in the old Gothic style, its cobblestone streets, narrow and crooked pathways, houses with red-tiled roofs and gabled arches, pyramid fountains, bell-tower cathedrals, and spire churches evoked nostalgic feelings and Romantic ideals. The city's place in the minds of its country's people reached a peak in the nineteenth century with Richard Wagner's composition, *Die Meistersinger von Nürnberg*. The anti-Semite's opus about German myths and legends, Hitler's avowed favorite, played at the Nuremberg opera house the first day of party rallies. Its overture blasted through tall loudspeakers around Zeppelinfeld all week.

Nuremberg suffered badly during the war because of its manifest ties to Hitler and the Nazis. More a commercial than a manufacturing center, the city and its environs had few significant war-related industries. But, of course, that did not stop the unrelenting bombing of the whole area by the Allies. The devastating air assaults were initiated by the British, part of the RAF's payback to a number of German cities for the Luftwaffe's Blitzkreig on London four years earlier. The Americans soon followed with thousands of heavy bombers of their own. The claim was made the bombing was necessary for the protection of the foot soldiers making their way across southern Germany to Austria. Thanks to Army Air Corps raids, Nuremberg became one great wall of flames. Gray ash and stone rubble supplanted fourteenth century structures with stained glass windows and cross-vault ceilings. Barely ten percent of the city's dwellings were still intact when it surrendered. A prewar population of 450,000 was pared to 160,000. The battle-spent people—without food, water, electricity, or gas—were axing horses and netting cats and dogs for the stew pot.

By myself I went to lunch in the mess hall, the small building right next to my wing of the barracks. I did not seek the company of any of the other guys in my outfit and I did not see any of them in the hallway. On Sunday I suspected they sleep late and much of the day eat at odd times in the snack bar.

After chow I decided to take that walk. This was my first free day in Nuremberg. I had to see up close in detail what I could only partially make out through my window two kilometers away. It was a sunny day, a little chilly but no clouds above. I simply went east along Bayernstrasse. Not far from the Kaserne and before I got to the unfinished Congress Hall and upper part of the ice-covered lake, on my left I could see vestiges of the Luitpold Arena, the original staging area for mass ceremonies beginning in 1927. The spot where Nazi officials rallied crowds of 150,000 did not escape the cross hairs of Allied bomb sights. The once proud grandstand with its three commanding seventy-eight foot overhead swastika banners hung between steel pylons, the speaker's platform, and the spectator stands. Now it all lay in ruins.

Before long I was passing the Congress Hall on my right, the largest architectural relic on the rally grounds. This roofless modern version of Emperor Nero's circus could easily pass for an amphitheater. The prodigious horseshoe-shaped building had archways and entrances set a few feet apart on all three of its levels. The torso, which would have been completely concealed had the biggest hall in the world been completed, was an empty hull of inner courtyards and crumbling stands. I followed Bayernstrasse around and then forked right onto an unmarked side street that fed me right smack into Zeppelinfeld on the northeast corner of the forsaken clearing for party parades. The slow step from Merrell Barracks took almost twenty minutes.

The Tribüne stretched all the way across one of the longer legs of the rectangle that was Zeppelinfeld, the one that abutted the road. It was a stately white marble structure, thirteen hundred feet in length and eighty feet high, with stone seating for tens of thousands on either side of a grandstand at its center. From the road I could see the back of the grandstand, the four doors leading into it, and the top where a great gold-painted swastika once loomed menacingly. I walked around to the front of the Tribüne and then stood in the reviewing area for a few minutes. I looked at the immense silent monument to a Nazi past designed in the neo-classical tradition that invariably inspired a sense of awe in anyone dwarfed by its presence.

The grandstand was flanked by attached colonnades and with two rows of thirty-six tall pillars, one hundred forty-four round supports for the superstructure in all. Fastened to the back wall were ten pilasters with cornices atop the entablatures. There were two tiers of stepwise stone bench seats on the grandstand with an open doorway on its central promontory. I could almost see a mustached Chancellor in military dress being driven in his bullet proof Mercedes right up to the rear, walk in one of the street-level doors, ascend several flights of steps, strut through the doorway, descend the upper-tier steps, and take his place on the small speaker's platform. The platform, with a low iron railing on three of its edges, protruded from the upper tier. The faint outline of a plaque once affixed in front was unmistakably that of a swastika. Across the Tribüne were bold six-foot-high black letters spelling **SOLDIERS' FIELD**, one word on each side of the platform.

I turned around and got a panoramic view of Zeppelinfeld. I counted thirty-four tower-like short structures uniformly grouped around the periphery of the field, visible markers separating sections of the spectator stands. The Tribüne and the bleachers on three sides were built in 1936 by Albert Speer, Hitler's official architect, who put twenty years in Spandau Prison after the war for his collaboration with the Nazis. This architectural monument, Speer claimed, was designed to convey Hitler's time and spirit to future generations. Like his Axis collega Mussolini who could point to the crumbling edifices of the Roman Empire as symbols of Italian honor and power, Hitler wanted Germans at the end of his thousand-year Reich to see the Congress Hall and the Tribüne, even in a state of ruin or decay, as reminders of his glorious reign.

Not another living soul was in sight. I was the lone tourist on Adolph's old stomping grounds that Sunday. An eerie silence hovered over the whole area. Before me was a desolate and deteriorating abandoned tract of city property, so boundless that there was nothing as far as the eye could see. Speer's proposed 400,000-seat sports stadium was never begun. Other Nazi construction projects went unfinished. The last man standing on some distant planet I could have been. I had set foot on what was left of a prewar theatrical propaganda arena postwar Germans preferred to look away from, wasted land that might be used someday for more constructive purposes.

I positioned myself on the barren grandstand. The parade grounds were peaceful, the monument tomblike. I could almost hear the staccato Sieg Heils hundreds of thousands of spectators once shouted in unison. I tried to envision what had lain before me just two decades earlier, the endless formations of marching SS and Wehrmacht soldiers and Hitler Jugend, the hundred beams from flak searchlights around the field shot a thousand feet into the night sky. I moved up to the Führer's rostrum. The small speaker's platform was gated on three sides, roomy enough for just one person. I hesitated a moment but then walked onto the ground that not too long before was hallowed by most Germans.

My mother should not know that I was on the very spot where Herr Hitler made his threatening speeches, reviewed the shoulder-to-shoulder troops, and extended his right arm to adoring crowds. I dared not raise my arm in like fashion. A victorious G.I. in fatigues and helmet did just that on 22 April 45 from atop the Tribüne, parodying the Nazi salute just before the Army dynamited the huge swastika in full view of the Signal Corps' motion picture camera. A still of the smirking American made the cover of the May 14th issue of *Life* magazine the year the war ended.

On that Sunday afternoon I could have been standing in the evanescent boot prints left by der Führer himself at the party rally in 1935 when he read aloud for the whole world to digest the three laws enacted days earlier by a special session of the Reichstag held in Nuremberg. The first abolished the old Imperial flag and decreed the swastika the official emblem of the Third Reich. The second relegated Jews to second-class German citizenship, requiring them to have the letter *J* stamped on their passports. Hitler was heard saying that if this law should fail to regulate the Jews, then the problem must be handed over to the Nazi Party for a final solution. The third prohibited marriage and extramarital sexual relations between Jews and Germans.

Zeppelinfeld's new name aptly characterized the Deutschland I remember from so long ago. Fourteen years after the fall of the Reich, Uncle Sam's soldiers were on a different field of battle. During the occupation, we proudly held our parades on the site of the former Nazi showplace. These demonstrations of the victory of democracy over fascism I was sure were lessons not lost on the defeated Germans. Lying in ruins before me was Hitler's chimerical plan a quarter century earlier of a permanent site for displaying Nazi might and conquest. It was the triumph of his will, as Leni Riefenstahl so masterfully portrayed on film for all to behold, especially the scene at the beginning of Hitler in his airplane descending from the sky to his beloved Nuremberg, like a God coming down from the heavens. The millenarian Nazidom the deranged dreamer foresaw took its toll on humanity for a dozen years by the tens of millions of lives lost. The former German soldiers' staging area was now an American one, albeit for events far less dramatic and enthralling.

Perhaps one day what is left of the Tribüne and Congress Hall will be transformed into a memorial or museum, I remember thinking to myself. When the foreign troops are long gone, when the SS Kaserne is back in German hands, the good people of Nuremberg might resolve to resurrect what they for decades labored to bury. Would the city that hosted the Reich's historic warmongering Party Days tax itself millions of Marks to recreate for future generations the time and place of its morbid fascination with violence, terror, and death? I was sure unborn Germans and non-Germans alike would appreciate the instructional as well as nostalgic value of such Nazi-era exhibitions.

The vastness of Zeppelinfeld and its environs suggested that there was room for a whole new town or village. On this irreverent morsel of earth, where Adolph Hitler's dreams of world domination fluttered about, citizens of the New Germany might construct Appartement-hauses and Supermarkts and Kinos to stand for the remainder of his thousand years. Such a satellite city southeast of Nuremberg could be called, fittingly, Bad Führerland.

## CHAPTER 20: SUNDAY NIGHT AND MONDAY MORNING

We left the Flying Dutchman a little past eleven. Elsa put her arm through mine and directed me across the street and to the right. We walked half a block to Königstrasse and turned left, away from the Hauptbahnhof.

For the past hour I was with Elsa at her table. We danced a few times. She downed three drinks to my one. Marianne showed up for a little while but then took off with a plumpish, balding German who wore small rimless glasses. It was either Elsa or no one that Sunday night after I came back from the parade grounds. When Steve had not returned to our room by nine o'clock, I decided to go into town alone. I walked around a bit first, interested in my new and strange surroundings, but careful not to stray too far from the only street I was acquainted with. Inevitably I was drawn to the place I knew someone I knew would be.

"Where are you taking me?" I asked my female escort.

At the Flying Dutchman I played down my interest in Elsa. She was alone at her usual table up front when she saw me come in. She flashed a smile and that was enough of an inducement to sit down with her, to forget about connecting with a prettier Fräulein this late in the evening on my prime solitary outing in Germany. It was already past ten and I had to be back at midnight for bed check.

When Marianne breezed in, she still looked very sexy to me with her strong Nordic features and coiffed hairdo. She walked around the edge of the dance floor, did not take off her coat, ignored several G.I.s in uniform who tried to talk to her, and soon cut out with some fortyish, plain-looking comrade out of arms. Elsa and I hoofed it up on the floor but for most of the hour I was with her she preferred to sit and listen to what passed for music by a three-piece band. I did not ask her any questions about herself or what she was planning to do the rest of the evening, and she did not ask me anything of a private or military nature. After Marianne parted ways, I refrained from asking Elsa if she too was going to leave with one of my, or one of her, countrymen. Knowing she liked me, I was content to just stay in the picture with her and wait to see what develops.

"Not far from here I live," Elsa answered me.

"Oh," I said simply. With that information I was sure very soon I would be engaged in either some enemy action or friendly fire.

She led me through a narrow side street, still holding onto me. I had no clue where I was or where we were headed. Suddenly she stopped and let go of my arm. "Here wait," she told me.

Before I could say anything Elsa walked off by herself, un-buttoning her coat and starting to lift her dress. I watched her as she left the sidewalk and deftly climbed over piles of rocks and stones. She disappeared behind a damaged section of a brick wall, all that remained of a bombed-out roofless building. Several structures on this block of Nuremberg, not far from the main train station, were still in ruins after fourteen years. Either the Marshall Plan over-looked this corner of the city or the ravages of war needed more time to be erased.

At first I thought Elsa was going to call to me, to get me to stick it to her in the dark standing up against a breached wall, but in less than a minute she was moving toward me over the rubble lowering her dress and buttoning her coat. She grabbed my arm once more and off we were to her place.

Elsa lived on the top floor of a three-story house that had been rebuilt. The stucco on one side did not match exactly that on the other. We entered the building with a key and were halfway up the staircase to the second landing when the door to the apartment on the first floor opened. A squat, middle-aged man in rumpled clothes ap-peared. He said something in German and Elsa responded. The only word both of them said I could clearly make out was Gelt.

Elsa's apartment was tiny, just one room. On the left as we entered was a narrow bed, comfortable enough for only one person, unmade at this late hour. To the right was a single sink full with dishes, a little icebox with the handle missing, and on the shortened counter top a hot plate with two burners. I presumed the partially open door beside the bed, with a white robe hanging from a hook, led to the bathroom. Next to the kitchen area was a small window set in a dormer. The sloping roof on one wall naturally did not amel-iorate the dwarfed feeling one got to the whole apartment.

"Who was that man?" I asked Elsa. "What did he want?" I thought he might have told her she had to pay to bring me in.

"He is the Vermieter. How you say . . . the landlord. The rent he want."

This was the eighth of the month. I supposed she was late in paying, perhaps not for the first time. "How much is your rent?" I said, still curious about things German.

"Hundred twenty Mark for month."

Thirty dollars, I calculated to myself, almost half of what my parents paid in New York for seven rooms. Apparently Germans were still shelling out for the bombs we dropped on them. I started to reach for my wallet when she spoke again.

"He is Jew, you know. He only want money. He too much charge."

I moved my hand away from my back pocket. As sympathetic as I may have been moments earlier toward the seemingly high price she had to bear for a patently substandard domicile, I now felt no compulsion to ease her financial burden.

"If the rent is too much, why don't you move?" I put to her.

"Where I go?" Elsa complained. She removed her coat and hung it on the outside of the closet in the corner of the room. "Not all Vermieteren in Germany say okay to men I take upstairs. I must fuck four or five only to pay rent."

The frankness of the woman, her ready admission to putting a price on her body, and her crude American way of expressing it, surprised me. She did not proposition me but I would have guessed this part of her life was something she might wish to conceal or simply not talk about. The pretense of her not living off the favors parceled out in this apartment to an assortment of men was the scenario I much preferred.

"I take not money from you," Elsa went on. "Today I see who I want."

The compliment was taken in stride without my saying thank you. It was good to know I was rated above my American comrades and German peers. Still I was far from enamored with her face or her figure. But that did not mean I would turn down what she was offering up gratis.

I looked at my watch and saw it was almost eleven thirty. "I must go in five or ten minutes," I told her, now that we were on the subject of impending intimacies. The freebie also had to be a quickie. I knew I would have to bug out real soon if I were to make it to Merrell Barracks by midnight.

"You have not overnight pass?"

"No . . . but my company doesn't have bed check. I either have to be in my camp in half an hour, or I have to stay the whole night. I can't walk through the gate until after six in the morning."

Elsa looked at me intensely. "It good you stay."

"Are you sure?"

"Yes, for sure . . . bestimmt." She stressed with words what she already said with her eyes.

"Okay. I was just asking."

I felt good about what was transpiring. I learned a new German word and shortly I would learn what a German woman was like. But I wondered how we could make love, much less sleep, in that bunk-size bed.

Elsa reached behind her, unzipped her dress, and stepped out of it. She took a nightgown from one of the drawers and put it on, then ran her hands under it to remove her bra, slip, and panties. I took off my tan raincoat with heavy liner and draped it over a chair, then stripped down to my shorts and T-shirt. My first Fräulein climbed into the bed, positioned herself sideways with her back to the wall, and beckoned me with her hand.

From my watch that glowed in the dark I could see it was past four thirty when I woke up. Elsa was still soundly asleep, pressed hard against my back with her arm wrapped around my waist as if she were trying to stop me from leaving. In my cramped condition I was able to doze off but I could not sleep very long. Her bed was not meant for two.

My Sunday night maiden foray into strange territory was less than enrapturing. Apparently German women do not shave their armpits, never heard of underarm deodorant, go for days without bathing, forget to brush their teeth before retiring, and seldom douche their cavernous part. Elsa's anatomical essence, aromatically untoward from mouth to middle, was striking but not offensive to me. My olfactory sense must have been partially blunted by horniness erected from the previous six loveless weeks spent processing at Dix, crossing the Atlantic, and tarrying in Böblingen.

Elsa's uncomely face was not the main detriment to my gratification. One tit was smaller than the other and both were not much to grab hold of. Touching her got me more breastbone than fatty meat. Her lower front orifice was the size I could fit four fingers in. When she spread her long legs and brought her knees to her chest, I entered her effortlessly but felt semi-detached from feminine flesh. With her thin frame I was in contact with her pelvic bone more than any other part of her body. Without the usual friction it took me longer to come but come I did. I gushed a load copious enough for her to gripe about. She leaped from the bed and dashed to the bathroom I made her so sticky and wet.

When she returned, towel in tow, she looked like she was coming at me with her mouth. I greatly enjoyed what the beauteous black WAC back at the Hotel California and the pretty poultry-proximate puertorriqueña in Nueva York did for me, but I was not sure if I would have gotten off again on a buck-toothed Bavarian babe blowing me.

As it turned out, I never got the opportunity to compare the African-Spanish/German connection. Elsa did not move her lips to my middle but rather moved my hand to *her* middle. She liked hard and fast action, every so often synchronizing her hips to my digital motion. Since I was not one of her paying clientele, I could not demand what she generally might charge extra for. The only thing coming out of her mouth was corrupted englisch.

Elsa and I engaged in a little pillow talk after I satisfied her. She told me of her own volition she was twenty-seven, was born in Nuremberg, and lived here all her life. All I did was ask her what it was like in Germany after the war and she chattered away for almost an hour.

"On Ludwigstrasse in the Altstadt we lived," Elsa told me. "Me, my mother, my sister who was older. In a house together with other house, on second floor."

I understood that Elsa and her family resided in some kind of an attached building or row house in the Old City. This was the area Allied bombardiers targeted for obliteration. Not far away every structure along the Pegnitz River lay in ruins. Their house, fortunately for them, was among those only slightly damaged. The house two doors down took a direct hit and the common wall with the next building collapsed, leaving two rooms in Elsa's apartment without a ceiling or outer wall. The three women took refuge in the basement bomb shelter the night of the air raid in April 1945 and escaped death or dismemberment. Their good German neighbors were not so lucky. The sunshine on V-E Day revealed mounds of rubble at times ten-foot high along every street in Nuremberg's city center. As a thirteen-year old, the woman lying in bed next to me learned to scale the bricks and broken stones of once solid dwellings. No wonder Elsa was quick to take a piss on a pile of rocks instead of waiting until she arrived home. She was treading on familiar ground.

The first winter after the war was the coldest in decades. Germans froze to death huddled together in roofless buildings. In the ten percent of houses in Nuremberg untouched by British or American bombs, there was precious little coal or wood for the stoves and furnaces and people still died of exposure to the cold. The medieval city was left with no public utilities, no postal service, no industrial production.

Those still alive looted warehouses for food. Elsa's mother organized hoarding trips to the countryside to exchange material goods for farmer's crops. Starved Germans cooked hot dogs that were not the kind you stuck in a bun and topped with mustard and sauerkraut. Their daily food rations barely sufficed to sustain life. The average weight for both women and men fell to less than one hundred pounds. The knowledge that the empty-bellied postwar legatees of Germany's physical destruction and economic downfall tasted the concentration camp diet the Nazi's dished out to millions of innocent internees during the war did not make me cry.

"My mother and my sister . . . Trümmerfrauen," Elsa said, throwing out a new word that was soon explained. "Me also at thirteen."

The three survivors of the war became part of the legion of women forced to clear the rubble in what was left of German cities. Someone had to do the brick and mortar reconstruction of a once great nation gone awry, and that duty inevitably fell on the shoulders, or rather the delicate backs, of the women left standing. Men were is short supply. The Russians were not very cooperative with the Allies after hostilities ceased and held back more than three million German POWs, to form labor battalions to repair the damage their leaders inflicted on the Soviet Union. Soldaten who did return often appeared on two crutches and one leg, or with one sleeve dangling from a jacket or coat, men hardly able to perform the limby work of lifting chunks of stone, pushing wheelbarrows of bricks, and sorting reusable building materials. Military occupiers rounded up all available women, even teenagers, to endure the spine-testing job of rubble clearance. Elsa told me how she would stand on the broken rocks from sunup to sunset, in sweltering heat and in bitter cold, helping her sister and mother with the lighter tasks, fetching them water and food during time outs.

The first few years of the occupation were extremely difficult for all Germans Elsa stressed. There was never enough food, the housing could not be rebuilt fast enough, Hitler's Marks lost most of their value, refugees poured in from the East, necessities proved hard to come by, luxury items were unheard of.

It was Elsa' ssister who saved the family from starvation. Six months after the war, with the ban on fraternization lifted, the eighteen-year-old hooked up with a G.I. from the 122nd Transportation Battalion, the first outfit assigned to the renamed Merrell Barracks, a hick from Georgia I gathered. She met him at the Army Hospital where she was working part-time as a nurse's aide. Every other day she was dressing the leg wound he sustained in the final days of the war but before long every other day she was also undressing her legs for quickies in the hospital bed.

When well enough to leave the hospital, the white southern boy soon became the family's provider and protector. He came to Elsa's damaged house regularly with bags of groceries, cartons of cigarettes, boxes of nylons, and fistfuls of rubbers. After dinner the mother would take Elsa by the hand and retreat in silence to what used to be the living room. There they sat on a water-stained couch for up to an hour, with half a roof over their head and near a wall ready to crumble, while the young couple had their privacy in the room behind the kitchen used as sleeping quarters, with just a curtain for a door.

When mother and younger daughter heard movement in the kitchen, they knew it was safe to exit their unsafe hideaway. I wondered what the middle-aged German woman might have done if it started raining before her ears picked up footsteps in the adjoining room. She likely would have forced herself and Elsa to endure the naked wet weather lest their stream of meal tickets be punched out.

By 1950 the sister was keeping company with her third American soldier. "He bring food, she give him good time," Elsa said unapologetically. "We care not what neighbor say."

Number 3 was bagging it for the now *four* hungry householders Living in the fully rehabilitated building but whether she would become a wife and sail for the States was still up in the air. For the churchgoing Pittsburgher, balling a Schatzie who had dropped one child was one thing, toting a Teutonic tart and her two-year-old tot back to Ma and Pa was another.

Little Elsa was now a grown woman and followed in her sister's footsteps, or rather the sibling's bedroom strides. Elsa began to date, if you could call it that, young G.I.s from different Nuremberg-area Kasernes whom she met in the bars along Luitpoldstrasse. She hoped to snare a husband and an emigrant pass too. When she brought home the find of the day, they headed for her bedroom while Mutti, Schwester, und Baby dawdled in the kitchen or living room.

One night one of her marks left twenty Marks on the dresser after pulling up his pants. Elsa was very pleased by the surprise gift, and thankful for what it could purchase for a needy household. Pretty soon she was requesting contributions from the American haves for the German have-nots, compensation for that which she had previously consigned free of charge. She preferred to think of it as reverse war reparations, the victor paying the vanquished. Thus began her career as a good-time girl.

Elsa described that day in 1953 when there was a knock at the front door and she answered it. The man in the tattered Wehrmacht overcoat with sergeant's stripes coming undone standing before her was not immediately recognized. Gaunt, bald, sallow complexioned, eyes recessed, the former soldier was obviously in poor health and had a dispirited look about him.

"Mein Gott, mein Gott," Elsa's mother screamed running from the kitchen when she heard his weak voice.

The man was Elsa's father. For eight years no one knew if he was alive or dead. He fought on the Eastern Front and was taken prisoner after the bloody battle for Stalingrad. That was the last anyone ever saw or heard of him. The Russians, of course, denied that they had any German prisoners at all, so they could not very well present the Allies and occupation authorities with lists of captured soldiers to be repatriated. For the better part of his absence Elsa's father slaved away in the Ukraine minefields.

The returning POW was hardly the type to resume his normal spousal and paternal duties. He failed to find work, blamed the United States for Germany's woes, felt abandoned by his country, could not get it up for his wife, and resented his daughters' fraternization with the foreign troops. Most difficult of all for the struggling New Germany family to accept were the spent man's anachronistic utterances of Nazi epithets directed against the dark Americans now enjoying themselves in his land and the Jews who did the German people in.

Elsa's sister soon set up house with a white G.I. who was willing to take in the baby. Elsa likewise could not stand living with a demoralized and fascist-leaning father. She saved a little money and moved to this small apartment where she has lived by herself for almost five years. The former Trümmerfräulein apparently felt that lying on her back with Americans was a better way to support herself than straining her back in the workplace with Germans. I wondered how many others had bounced around in this bed before I came to it, and came in it. My guess was that she probably brought more than five hundred new shooters and repeat payers home with her, an average of two dicks every week.

Elsa's English vocabulary no doubt was picked up from her American suitors, and suited her chosen life style to a T, or I should say an F, a favorite word judging by the frequency with which it fell off her tongue. The sad account she told me of her family after the war was riddled with coarse, slang, lewd, and impolitic words and phrases more commonly heard among soldiers in the barracks than sweethearts in the bedroom. None of the girls I knew before coming to Germany, the virginal as well as the carnal knowledgeable, those wearing a cross or star, spoke like that in front of boys. The lass' lingo to some extent affronted even my sensibility, a lad used to hearing tall tales of sexual conquest on New York streets and in Army barracks.

Elsa woke up and saw that I was awake too. She reached up and touched my cheek not facing her, then moved her face to mine and kissed me several times on the other cheek, holding me like in a vise. The warmth of her body felt good. The unexpected embraces of an avowed hooker and older female started to arouse me but were somewhat disconcerting.

"Schatzie. Did you much sleep?" she asked.

"A little."

Now I knew she really liked me. I was her beau, not just a nightly pickup. I was comfortable with the velocity in which unpaid intimacy can be achieved in Europe but not so comfortable with that kind of a deal if it was going to be fastened to an emotional component.

Elsa ran her hand down to mine and moved it to her middle. Without panties to deal with, I fingered right in to accommodate her need for a second round of stimulation. Soon she was moving with the rhythm I set, short and quick strokes up and down her clit that awakened her ardor. She separated her legs a bit more. I took that as an invitation to paw her on the inside as well. Then she grabbed hold of me and started jerking back and forth. Elsa was now very wet from my dexterous action. I knew *I* would soon be very wet from *her* dexterous action if I did not slow her down or stop her.

I pulled my hand away from her. "Get on top of me," I said, surprised by the commanding tone I assumed with someone who had thus far commanded me.

She straddled me without saying anything, acquiescent to my new role as occupation authority it seemed. She reached under her, clasped me with her fingers, fitted my tip in, and pushed down like a plunger. This time she was tighter even though she needed no lubricant. As she rocked, Elsa worked her legs under mine, as if to lock me into her movements. I did not have to do anything but lie there. She did all the work. My hands on her hips were in motion more than my torso. She stopped rocking for a moment, lifted her nightgown above her head, and moved my hands to her breasts. With her hands over mine, she made circular patterns like she was waxing the hood of a car. It seemed odd that Elsa on the road to her climax craved human touching the most on that part her body endowed the least. She was now pumping fast and hard and began to moan.

"Stop not, stop not," she wailed.

Stop what? I said to myself. I was doing very little, only hand-to-tit action. The first time we did it Elsa did not come when I did. She wanted her completion afterward. That is what she probably was used to with the parade of other G.I.s who marched into this apartment for over half a decade. Boots on, boots off, either way made no difference to her. But now she wanted her own satisfaction in unison with me, and it was up to me to give it to her or, more accurately considering my relative inactivity, let her get it from me. I held back coming and remained stiff, something not too difficult for me to do on second rounds. She pumped faster and lifted herself higher. I almost slipped out. Finally, the moment was upon her.

"Jawohl, jawohl," she cried fittingly in her own language in the heat of passion.

Yes indeed, she was telling me, she got off. Elsa quivered at first but then relaxed and remained in a squatting position on top of me. I moved my hands to her hips and did some thrusting of my own to finish myself off. My body really felt good after that.

Frank Sinatra was right. Love is lovelier the second time around. Not-so-pretty German women were not so bad after all.

Elsa told me which way to walk when I left her place in order to get back to the Hauptbahnhof where I could catch Strassenbahn Nr. 8. She helped me dress by buttoning my shirt as I sat in a chair putting on my socks and shoes. I had my hair combed and face patted too.

"Maybe you come again," she said with an innocent look about her when I was standing in the doorway. I was sure she did not realize the pun in English. "See me at Flying Dutchman."

"Okay," I said simply. What more could I say after I banged her twice in one night?

"Please Friday or Saturday not."

"Okay," I repeated. There was no need for me to call attention to why she excluded those two nights of the week.

Riding on the streetcar back to Merrell, looking out the window at the break of dawn in Nuremberg, I could not help thinking of the overnight pass I was handed by one of the city's native daughters. My first time out alone looking for love in Germany I scored two hits, on Sunday night and Monday morning. Most soldiers I imagine would award themselves a medal for that feat. With the day's early light, however, I could see it bothered me that I did not make it instead with the more beautiful babe I eyed. Marianne I coveted but

Elsa I bagged. I had little desire to go home again with Cinderella's stepsister, my parting word to the homely creature notwithstanding.

My body felt whole from the dual releases of reserve energy but my soul was wounded from the dual compromises of intercourse and discourse with a fowl-featured and foul-mouthed Fräulein. A single with Marianne I imagined would be more wunderbar than a double with Elsa any day of the week.

I made it back to the barracks before six thirty on the first day of work in my new company. The troops were just waking up, showering, and going to chow. Exactly as my teammates had advised on Saturday afternoon, there was no problem walking through the main gate. The guard, in fitted Class A's and shiny black boots, MP helmet liner on his head and .45 semi-automatic on his hip, did not ask for my pass or I.D. and hardly looked at me as I whisked right through. I guess in my civies I had "American soldier" written all over me. For all he knew I could have been a Russian or German spy who bought his clothes on Kings Highway in Brooklyn.

Steve was still asleep in his bunk when I entered our room. He too had a thin smile on his face.

# CHAPTER 21: THE SHOP

That Monday morning, our first day at work in Nuremberg, it was five to eight when Steve and I moseyed into the shop with the other guys on Team 5 who bunked in the barracks. Already at their workbenches with cups of coffee were the three other teammates who were married and lived off post, one with a brown thermos next to him. Sergeant Doss was at his desk in the left corner of the room looking at some papers. He too lived off post with his wife and two kids and, I found out later, was often the first one in the door. Although Steve and I were told on Friday to come in at seven thirty, our barracks buddies said not to sweat it, that Doss is not chickenshit about his boys all being there at the official start of the workday. There seemed to be a quite leisurely atmosphere in the shop.

"Goldbaum . . . Streiber," Doss called out when he saw us. The sergeant got up from his desk and walked over to where Steve and I were standing. "How was your weekend? Did the guys take you into town?"

"We had a few beers Saturday night," Steve answered with a smile. He said nothing about his date with Ursula on Sunday afternoon.

Doss turned to me. "What about you, Streiber? Meet any frauleins?"

"I spoke to a couple at the Flying Dutchman."

I saw no need to render to a sergeant over me a blow-by-blow description of my romantic encounter with Elsa sans overnight pass that could have gotten his new boy busted and him in trouble too. I had not even told Steve about it yet. And I knew nothing of how he made out either, but I could make a pretty good guess.

Doss was his usual self. Boots not spit-shined, yellow scarf not tucked in all the way, fatigues a trifle furrowed, and every so often pushing his eyeglasses back to the bridge of his nose with the middle finger.

"Well, okay . . . let's get you guys settled in. Goldbaum, why don't you take La Pinza's place? He's going home today. Danziger, let Streiber sit next to you for the meantime."

Steve and I faced each other on opposite sides on one of the shop's three long workbenches. They were about twelve feet long and four feet wide on the right half of the room as you walk in the door, with shelves along the middle of each bench containing test equipment and electrical outlets. We sat on a high metal stool and our feet comfortably rested on the bottom rung. An array of different pieces of small equipment lay in wooden boxes before us, all radio-related. The first workbench, which Steve and I were on, was set up for the repair of small pieces, the other two for bigger radios and jeep mounts. The huge transmitters were fixed outside the shop, in the radio shack that they were in on the bed of the deuce-and-a-half truck parked nearby.

Unlike many of the other members of the two teams, Steve and I were not radio-trained at Fort Gordon, Georgia. The 33-week radar repair course we completed at Monmouth ill-equipped us to troubleshoot and put back in good order the large and complex units that ended up on the floor on the left side of the shop, often stacked on top of one other. The team leader, disorganized as he may have been in his personal appearance, was wise enough to start the newcomers out with the small and easy stuff.

First there were the headsets that Steve and I worked on. This device consisted of two rubber earpieces with an electric receiving element in each. A wire that ran over one's head connected the earpieces, and a cord plugged into a radio set. To troubleshoot, we used resistance measurements of the elements or put the headset in a test jig. We were told to replace the defective parts, anything worn or dinged that would not pass inspection. A common defect was the frayed rubber coating on the cord. The Army wanted it to look new, even if it worked fine.

Headsets had what the guys referred to as a "banana" plug, or male plug, because it had a piece that stuck out. If the piece stuck way out, my teammates pursed their lips and called it a "bwana" plug. At times we had to unscrew the plugs and re-solder the connections inside. Then there were the microphones. The plastic body had a rubber boot that covered the switch. Inside was an element to send voice messages. Microphones either had a straight cord or a curly one, ending in a banana plug or a twist-on plug with four connecting points. As with headsets, we had to test, repair, or touch up. Ripped rubber boots were the biggest problem with this unit. Finally, Steve and I were given telephone handsets to fix. They came in olive drab or black versions, dubbed, respectively, the Popeye and the Sambo. We mostly replaced the receiving or sending elements or the cord. The handsets frequently came in with cigarette burns on the plastic body so we had to replace that as well.

On the next bench, the more experienced shop repairmen got their hands on other equipment. One unit was the RT-524, a radio transmitter that sat on a mount on the back fender of jeeps. It had a microphone that looked like a lollypop, a stick handle with a "Push" button to talk, and a top part that resembled a ball cut in half. An operator spoke into the flat part of the ball and wore a separate headset.

There was also the AN/PRC-6, a portable handy-talkie used by both the Army and Navy. This miniature battery-operated FM radio receiver-transmitter obviously was designed for short-distance communications. It had a telephone hand piece plugged into the battery pack which had a shoulder strap and a long antenna. The guys around me called this, appropriately I thought, the PRICK-6, since it was an average-size vital piece of equipment needed by every soldier out in the field in Germany.

"Does the PRICK-Six come with a thin rubber cover that slides over the top for protection?" I asked. The guys all laughed.

In our shop each piece type, in the hundreds, was repaired by replacing the elements. Presumably, rubber covers, if they were issued, were replaced often by the G.I.s in my outfit. The third workbench had piles of the PRICK-8 and the PRICK-10 models, man-pack sets with greater frequency ranges and number of channels. These useful pieces of equipment should have been sized a few inches larger for easier visual identification and hand-held operation.

One of the biggest items repaired in the shop, stacked up against the left wall, was the AN/GRC-26, a mobile radio teletypewriter housed in a hut mount on a deuce-and-a-half truck. Nicknamed the ANGRY-26, it had a transmitter the size of a dishwasher and large vacuum tubes. By contrast, the AN/FRT-22 was a fixed-station radio transmitting set. The FART-22, I was told, was the talk of the shop every day after lunch. The O-5C/FR, however, was chatted about all the time. Called officially the Exciter Unit, because the crystal-controlled piece was used to excite the oscillator section of a transmitter for single-channel or facsimile operation, my teammates not surprisingly called it the Excite Her Unit. By skillfully moving the little dials on this device, a soldier can shift the output frequency, and the emission, of a receptive transmitter.

The boys on the bench farthest from me worked on the PP-116A/FRC or Vibrator Inverter. It was a heavy-duty power supply designed for use in mobile installations with a 115-volt, 60-cycle AC. It was called, facetiously I thought, the Vibrator Insert Her as it was used with receivers and intercommunications equipment. When the piece is inverted, the vibrator can be inserted and the voltage will rise during continuous operation.

Around ten o'clock, as I was starting on my third headset, La Pinza showed up in the shop. He breezed in through the door like Superman coming down to earth. He was dressed in fatigues and not Class A's as I thought he might be. It turned out La Pinza was not going straight to the train station and then to Bremerhaven to catch the boat but rather would be en route first to Böblingen, to Company headquarters, to process out of Germany. For 176ers, a bumpy ride in the back of a truck to whence we came was a necessary step before the westerly ocean voyage to the States. The brown-booted G.I. bounced from one foot to the other. His dark features seemed lighter with the broad smile and happy face. Steve and I just shook La Pinza's hand and wished him well as he hopped from bench to bench to say goodbye to his buddies, but others got up from their stools and did more than we did. Danziger, who towered over the ready-to-leave soldier, gave him a hug.

"I can't wait to join you next week," the other short-timer said.

Some guys grabbed La Pinza's right arm in a gesture of good will, or patted him on the shoulder, or ran a hand through his wavy black hair.

"I'll miss you guys," the home-bound soldier shouted for all to hear. "But I'll miss the frauleins more."

"If you don't like the tail back home," someone said, "re-enlist for your old outfit."

"No sireee, Babe," the baseball-minded La Pinza shot back. "This is one game I'm not playing in any more."

Sergeant Doss came over and said something to La Pinza. He seemed genuinely concerned with the fate of the cheerful team member ready to exit. Before long, the small soldier boy sailed out the door and onto a waiting truck.

For a few minutes I too thought about going home and what was just said. La Pinza was saying goodbye to Fräulein Rye, not Miss American Pie. I wondered how I would feel in fifteen months when my time was almost up. How eager or reluctant would I be to leave Germany? Would my first taste of German women savor into a fine full course?

My first morning on the bench consisted of repairing nine small pieces of equipment by replacing wires and soldering parts. I was not working my MOS, not yet a least, but I was finally diagnosing and fixing electrical equipment as I had been trained to do during my more than eight months of Army schooling in New Jersey but failed to do in the five months I spent in a signal company in California. It now seemed that my remaining days in the military would be put to good use, good that is if I wanted to be a radio or television repairman when I got out. But since I had no such post-discharge plans, I wondered if this type of work experience would be useful in the long run, let alone hold my interest in the short run.

So began my first day in the shop in Deutschland. In this American-occupied territory, I was sure activities for soldiers off post would be more exciting than anything happening on post.

# CHAPTER 22: THE TWO Bs

After lunch Doss walked Steve and me over to meet Sergeant Bentley and Mr. Barry. The two Bs managed and operated all ten teams and shops in Area II, our company's region in southern Germany that stretched from Regensburg to Bamberg. They worked out of what was called the Area Office, a little nook on the first floor of the West Block in our immense barracks structure. It was off to the right of the main room that had cubicles of clerical personnel from other outfits on post. There also was a floor-to-ceiling, thick-walled, bank-type, walk-in vault. Twenty years earlier this must have been where the SS safeguarded secret Nazi files.

The B & B work station consisted of two desks, two chairs, a file cabinet, and a small black-and-white chart hanging on the side wall depicting each team's monthly equipment inventory and repairs. One desk was by a window that opened to the outside of the building. If one looked out sharply to the left, a part of our shop was visible. Another desk was in front with space enough between for just the swivel chair.

The man sitting quietly by the window was a warrant officer. He was in fatigues and I had to strain my eyes to see the silver bar with two black stripes on his right collar and on his left the Signal Corps insignia with two crossed flags. The bar indicated he was a Chief Warrant Officer 2, the second from the lowest of four ranks in his Army classification. The noncom behind the desk in front stood up first as we approached.

"Sergeant Bentley," Doss said, a little nervously it seemed to me. "These are the two new team members . . . Goldbaum and Streiber."

Bentley took a few steps toward us and extended his arm. He did not have to ask who was who as our last names stenciled in black on white textile strips above the right pocket of our fatigue shirts were clearly visible. Bentley was somewhat shorter and a few years younger than Doss, but stockier and one grade higher. On his apparently size-Small fatigue shirt, the patches of three stripes and three rockers on both sleeves appeared larger than what they actually were, bending in the middle as he lifted his elbow. His hair too was shorter than Doss', cropped low on top and shaved on the sides, shaved high as if to avoid any possible criticism by officers that the strands above his ears were too long. Bentley's head resembled an orange with a peeled lower half.

The master sergeant smiled at us. "How y'all doin' boys."

The southern white's accent was thick and unmistakable. Bentley shook hands with Steve and then me. His palm was soft and dainty, almost effeminate. I was sure he never had to tote dat barge or lift dat bale along the Mississippi like the men on the soulside of town, the darker denizens of the Delta. And if he got a little drunk, he probably did not land in jail either. The handshake was weak and irresolute, uncharacteristic of someone of Bentley's rank.

Standing next to Doss, the contrast between the two noncoms was glaring. Bentley's fatigues were tailored, starched, and pressed. There was a mirrored-polish on the tip of his black boots. The finely-knit cloth belt was cut exactly to specifications, with no black showing next to the shiny gold buckle, only the gold metal piece on the end. Bentley's yellow scarf fit perfectly around his small neck and was tucked in just right. With flying colors he would have passed any inspection.

Barry got up and came over to us. He was the tallest of the trio of Army men positioned above me, about my height, an inch more perhaps. Lean and somewhat lanky, the CW2 had regular features and a regular haircut, top not long and sides not shaved.

"Welcome to Area Two," he bellowed with no regional accent.

The veteran soldier's type of rank, appointed by warrant from the Secretary of the Army and not commissioned as an officer by the President, was used for technical experts in specialized military operations. Warrants were in-between master sergeants and second lieutenants, neither plebeian enlisted men nor privileged West Point, O.C.S., or academy gentlemen.

Steve and I saluted, called out our ranks and names, and shook hands. At the time I did not think much of the fact that Barry welcomed us to his area of command rather than simply to Team 5, but months later when I saw that guys in the shop were transferred to other teams I realized that the warrant had no qualms about shifting the personnel under him around, the interruption to their personal lives never considered as a mediating factor.

"Where are you from, Goldbaum," our new leader inquired.

"California, sir. Hollywood."

"Oh . . . Movieland," Barry said in a way that sounded silly. "See any stars lately?"

"No sir."

For a moment I thought Steve might say something to brown-nose the boss, but my roommate did no ass-kissing that day. In the barracks back at Ord, the soldier raised in the movie capital of the world used to drop names of stars he had seen in front of the Brown Derby, or walking down Vine Street, or on the sidewalk by Grauman's Chinese Theater.

Barry looked over to me. "And you, Streiber?"

"I'm from New York, sir."

I did not think it was necessary to specify Brooklyn, much less Coney Island, as Lieutenant Finston back at 176th HQ wanted to know. I presumed the two Bs would know I meant the *City* of New York.

Barry glanced at our nametags. "You two must be Jewish," he said, evidently not skittish or embarrassed to talk about religion.

I wondered if he would be as loquacious if the subject was race. The warrant officer probably put one-and-one together in identifying Steve and me, but got more than two. He could have schmoozed to himself "I know lots of Hebes live in New York and all the movie people in Hollywood are kikes."

"My father's Jewish," Steve answered first, "but he doesn't practice any religion. My mother is Protestant. I'm an agnostic, sir."

Both Barry and Bentley seemed taken aback by this, as if they could not fathom someone not being Jewish who looked Jewish and had such a common Jewish name. Doss was unfazed.

"An agnostic," Barry repeated. "You mean you don't believe in God . . . any God?"

"That's an atheist, sir. An agnostic is someone who doesn't know if there's a God, someone who is not committed to any religion or belief."

I thought Barry might be perturbed by this little lesson in religion from a subordinate, but he was not, or did not seem to be. Bentley was the one who continued this line of conversation.

"Are you an agnostic too, Strahber?" he cut in sarcastically with his mispronunciation of my name, smiling a bit. I was sure he knew I was a bona fide member of the tribe.

I shook my head. The comment did not rate a verbal reply.

"You're Jewish?" Barry asked, just for the record.

"Yes."

"There are no Jewish services here at Merrell," Barry advised me. "Your services are held at the Palace of Justice downtown. That's where all Jewish personnel in the Nuremberg command go." He nodded toward Doss. "Sergeant Doss will tell you how to get there."

"Thank you, sir," I added, not to be impolite. My new boss was making a big assumption about my religious needs and practices.

"You two came from Monmouth, did you not?" Bentley said, changing the subject. "You both have a radar repair MOS."

"Yes sergeant," Steve answered quickly for us.

"Well, we don't have any radar equipment here," Bentley revealed. "Mostly different kinds of radio pieces and power supplies."

"I'll be glad to work on any piece of equipment you have," I said like a good soldier. I could very well have said I was glad to be working in Nuremberg and not Fulda on any piece of equipment. "I'm sure I can learn a lot here. At Fort Ord, after Monmouth, we didn't repair anything at all."

"What outfit were you in at Ord?" Barry wanted to know.

"The Forty-first Signal, sir," Steve answered.

"What did you do there?" Barry asked again. "I don't know that outfit."

"Nothing important, sir," I said. "Every day we were assigned to different details, like policing the area or cleaning the barracks. One of our Monmouth buddies became battalion mail clerk. They had no electronic equipment to fix. It seemed our radar repair training was wasted."

"We were fortunate to be transferred," Steve added. "Everyone in the Forty-first said you have to go overseas to work your MOS."

"We were fortunate our transfer was to Germany," I qualified, since Steve was speaking for me too. "At Ord, half the guys who came with us from Monmouth got shipped to Korea."

Bentley budded in again, looking over to Doss. "They're the lucky ones, aren't they?" he said, obviously meaning the contrary. "We know. We were in Korea for that war. The Army still has only huts for the troops . . . and far away from any city."

Doss smiled. "Don't forget the frauleins, sergeant." It seemed a bit obsequious for one sergeant to be addressing another sergeant as "sergeant." I would have thought there was more equality between the E-6 and E-7 ranks.

Bentley quickly agreed. "Yes. They're prettier than the gook girls."

I gathered Bentley was not among the thousands of G.I.s who brought home a Korean wife with their duffel bag. That went for Doss and Barry too, given the frankness and crudeness of the comment.

"Okay," Barry said, glancing over toward Doss, changing the subject of race. "Thanks for bringing in the new men. I'm sure you have work to do in the shop."

"Yes sir," Doss replied, saluting the warrant officer. I thought he was going to click his heels too.

"Doss," Bentley said as we turned to leave. "Get me those numbers I asked for by tomorrow. Write it up."

"Yes sergeant."

We left the Area Office and returned to the shop. I departed with the knowledge that apparently courtesy for military addresses in my new outfit was a one-way street, going uphill.

I wondered what the two people I had just met were really like. And Doss for that matter. My life in Germany and the rest of my time in the Army might be determined by my relations, good or bad, with this three-ring set of superiors, one near and two not far away.

Before long, the roles would be reversed and the two Bs would be the superiors near.

# CHAPTER 23: GIRL IN THE SNACK BAR

There was something about her that caught my attention the moment I laid eyes on her. She moved gracefully over the floor and around the room that extended from one end of the elongated building to the other, like a great fish swimming in the ocean depths. I watched her as she deftly picked up dirty plates and empty glasses on the tables, as she carried stacked trays off to the kitchen cleaning area. My eyes followed her bodily shifts as she added coffee beans and replaced filters in the hot water dispenser, set up rows of cups and saucers on the counter in neat formation, and filled shiny silver containers with crushed ice. Some of the soldiers sitting and eating said something to her with a smile or simper when she stopped to clean their tables or clear things away, words she invariably ignored as she casually walked off without responding. One went so far as to put his hand on her ass and run it down a bit as she bent over to wipe with a rag. I saw her pull his hand away without any ado whatsoever, as if this sort of harassment was a regular occurrence, and artlessly proceed to another table.

It was a week before Danziger was set to leave Germany. He asked Steve and me to join him for lunch at the snack bar. Jonesy and two other guys from the shop were going too. Danziger wanted a lot of company when he said goodbye to Army chow. I told him I would come along, pleased that those I worked with presumably have accepted me into their inner circle, but Steve took a pass. I was also eager to try the only culinary alternative on post to Merrell's mess.

The snack bar was on the second floor of a small two-story sideways Z-shaped building located in the west-front area of the Kaserne, over the PX. The building was on the other side of the rectangular open space adjacent to the west wing of the base's main structure. The one-story movie theater was at the far end of the Z. The five of us got to the snack bar at a quarter to twelve and fell in at the back of the line which by then extended out through the ground-floor door for twenty or thirty feet.

Danziger seemed somewhat anxious, shifting his weight back and forth from one foot to another as we all chitchatted. Jonesy was his normal self, uttering poor grammar and equally poor judgment on broaching topics of conversation. I participated here and there, often gazing at others on the moving chow line, but did not speak as much as I usually did. Dombrowski stood by stiffly, almost at attention, but when he talked was quite animated, swinging his arms up and down. He replaced the teammate Danziger's Schatzie had lay down for previously. I thought Dombrowski might have asserted some sort of seniority or superceding right to be next in bed, to bump Danziger as it were. But, the second son of an unemployed coal miner from Wilkes-Barre, Pennsylvania, who at nineteen enlisted to learn a decent trade, was probably too much the "dumb Polak" others called him behind his back, albeit in jest I believed, to have thought of it. Westhill took a place after the four of us and did not seem to be paying much attention to what was being said. He was an interesting fellow, not very loquacious but one who could deliver a catchy or pithy phrase when he did venture to talk. Westy grew up in East Texas and was a true product of his region. Exposed to two cultures, he exuded both western and southern attitudes and behaviors when it came to issues of politics or race.

This was the beginning of my third full week at Merrell Barracks and the first time I would be eating out with the boys.

By five past twelve we finally reached the serving portion of the line. On the jukebox in the middle of the room, one of my favorite tunes, Lloyd Price's *Personality*, was playing. I was sure the hard of hearing outside the building hearkened it as well. Behind me was Westy, the other three directly in front. I glanced at the slices of pies and cakes on little white plates laid out on two glass shelves along the counter. Cups of different sizes and ice-filled glasses were on the counter farther down from the desserts. Off to the side was a coffee and tea dispenser but the soda fountain was behind the counter. Frankfurters and hamburgers were steaming on the large black grill, the French fries crackling in the vat of oil.

Three Germans, two men and a woman, white aprons tied around their waists and wearing paper caps, were preparing the food. They spoke in what passed for English, asking troopers what they wanted and making inconsequential comments when handing over edible items as if they were practicing their vocabulary. I ordered two hamburgers for fifteen cents each. A portion of French fries cost a dime, ditto for the glass of coke. An additional fifteen cents.was the piece of apple pie I grabbed

"It's not too bad in Germany," I remarked to Dombrowski in front of me. "For sixty-five cents I can get a whole meal."

There was an unoccupied square table in the middle of the dining area and the five of us fitted ourselves around it. The guys talked as they ate, oblivious to the dozens of other soldiers mostly in fatigues who encircled us and were doing much the same. I enjoyed my modest meal without saying a whole lot, comfortable just to look about the room and observe the German workers and their American patrons in their daily routines. A soldier went up to the jukebox, put a coin in, and pushed a button. A moment later Bobby Darin was crooning his latest song, one he wrote himself.

> *Every night I hope and pray*
> *A dream lover will come my way*
> *A girl to hold in my arms*
> *And know the magic of her charms.*

The girl working in the snack bar was exceptionally appealing to me, more than Marianne back at the Flying Dutchman. I just could not look away from her. She had a delicate beauty that simply captured my imagination. The Fräulein was about my age, a year or two older probably, and, from my sitting position, seemed the right height for me. Her yellow hair was pinned up in back but I pictured it was the shoulder length I liked and that she let it down after work. I did not pay much attention to the melody or the words in the background.

> *Dream lover where are you?*
> *With a love, oh, so true*
> *And a hand that I can hold*
> *To feel you near as I grow old.*

The girl came to our table. She squeezed in between Jonesy and Danziger in the corner directly across from me, then leaned forward to do her work. Her skin was pale and exquisite, like ivory, without a blemish of any kind. She needed no cosmetic to conceal pimples, acne, birthmarks, or unwanted hair. Her eyes were a deep blue that radiated both warmth and seduction. The ruddy cheeks gave her a girlish appearance. To me her facial features were nearly perfect for a young woman—eyes set just right, mouth small, nose straight and short, chin not cleft or protruding, hairline high and level. I focused on her while she cleaned up in silence and averted eye contact with the five of us at the table. I even played Superman, feigning x-ray vision through her apron, blouse, and bra to make out the firm and full pair of tits, the consummate size and mass for a young man to get his hands and mouth on. She then turned away and walked briskly to the next table. My line of sight followed her winning figure—the slender waist, strong shapely legs, slightly curved hips.

My eating companions must have detected I was staring at the girl. She was not a fleshy copy of some Greek goddess immortalized in stone but for my money her every facial and bodily feature was quite the ideal.

"That's the type I like," I said forthwith after the Fräulein left our table, nodding my head in the direction she was walking. "I'm getting a boner just sitting here." Such a boast was uncharacteristic of me. Perhaps Germany as a trooper's terrain for female frolicking was stirring me.

In a move redolent more of instinct than intellect, I got up and started after the girl. A half-eaten burger, a few fries, and an untouched pie were left behind. At that moment I was quite oblivious to my comrades but later I would recall that as I walked away Jonesy had said, "Bet it ain't good enough for her." Dombrowski uttered something too and grabbed my wrist but I did not hear him either and pulled loose. The four Merrell sophisticates must have marveled at the cold, determined look on the face of the newcomer to their camp's snack bar.

My Teutonic Venus was at the hot water dispenser, crouched down almost on her knees looking for something in the cabinet underneath. I walked slowly up to where she was and stopped beside her on her left. It so happened I was facing my buddies but I did not look over to them for their approval or to see if they were watching me.

What should I say to the fair lovely before me? I asked myself. What could I say to an attractive German girl working on an Army post to arouse her interest in me, a total stranger, a soldier who at first glance she would likely peg as just another boorish American seeking to get into her pants. One thing I did know. I dared not call her Schatzie. In the position she assumed, I was sure she did not notice me standing next to her.

"Hello," I said finally, worried she might sneer or snicker at me.

She glanced up with surprise but did not raise her body or say anything to me. The innocent look on that baby face and contour of her folded legs made her all the more alluring. I could see I interrupted her concentration but she did not seem annoyed. It occurred to me I could have whipped it out and gotten a blow job her head was that close to my middle.

"Can I help you?" I added for lack of anything better to say. Maybe this will engage her to talk.

"No thank you. I can do it."

Her voice was soft and sweet, her English pronunciation less accented than her compatriots behind the counter. The girl turned her head from me and continued moving cardboard boxes and metal bowls around on the two shelves in the cabinet.

"Do you work here every day?" I asked in a last ditch effort to continue what little conversation we had.

Was my coming on to her too transparent? I feared. I was sure she did not think I was doing an employment survey for the military.

She closed the cabinet doors and stood up with a large metal bowl in her hands. The height I hoped she would be she was. That certainly was a relief to me. My heart pounded a little faster now that I was standing close, just about touching distance, to my Miss Perfekt. I gawked at that endearing face and figure, trying to gauge her interest in me.

"I do, yes," she answered, glancing at my face, nametag, and then sleeve.

The way she transposed parts of sentences reminded me of the way Anna, my sixth-grade classmate, talked. I was pleased the object of my affection was speaking to me and spoke my language.

"I haven't seen you here before." I omitted explaining that this was my first time in the snack bar.

"Sometimes at night I work." She was now looking at me more intensely and down at my nametag again. I certainly did not mind her doing that. Let her think my parents or grandparents came from

Germany. That would only help my case I reasoned.

"Would you like to go out sometime?" I posited promptly and directly with raised eyebrows and a dainty smile. I knew I had to make my play right away. At any moment she might tell me her boss was watching us or she has to go back to her duties. "I could pick you up after work."

After some hesitation, she answered simply, "I have a boyfriend."

She seemed taken aback by my naked effort to hook up with her, as if I forded across some unmarked boundary or marched through a door that she had shut. Was her Schatzie German or American? I wondered. In either case, the look on her face told me she was uninterested in or unimpressed by strangers approaching her.

"Oh," I sighed ruefully. "I'm sorry I bothered you."

This was not the first time a girl I liked very much and tried to steer my way turned me down because she was already taken. But I was disappointed just the same.

"That's okay," she said before turning to walk away. She flashed a half smile as if she were flattered by my unanticipated attention. "Maybe I see you again."

I watched her as she distanced herself from me, still enamored with her physical appearance and, from the brief encounter, now comforted by her not unpleasant disposition. She could have said something nasty to me or even given me the air. I interpreted the girl's words favorably, preferring to believe she was holding out a sliver of hope for a future get-together should she be free. I felt gratified that I made the effort to secure the company of a girl who so moved my being.

Bobby Darin's singing voice filled the room in a second playing of the new hit. As I returned to my seat, his lyrics again passed right through me.

*Someday, I don't know how*
*I hope she'll hear my plea*
*Someway, I don't know how*
*She'll bring her love to me*
*Dream lover until then*
*I'll go to sleep and dream again*
*That's the only thing to do*

*'til all my lover's dreams come true.*

Back at the table, all in the gang-of-four were looking at me funny. Their jaws were half dropped, sullen expressions were written on their faces, all eyes fell silent.

"What's the matter?" I asked.

"Not here," Danziger replied, scanning the troopers around us. "We'll tell you later."

What was so secretive I had no idea but I did not push for an answer. I waited patiently until we left the snack bar about fifteen minutes later and all piled into Jonesy's car. He had to move it to the parking lot near our sleeping quarters. I sat in the back, huddled between Dombrowski and Westy, facing Danziger up front who had turned his head toward me.

"I asked that girl out," I mentioned casually to my silent and solemn companions. "I . . . ."

Danziger cut me off before I could tell them how drawn I was to her. "Man, you don't want to go out with her."

I looked at him in amazement. What was he talking about? How could he think that girl was not worth getting into?

"Why not?" I asked.

There was an eerie stillness for a few seconds. Then Jonesy said over his shoulder, "Hell, she's colorblind."

"She's *what?*" I questioned without thinking, tilting my head a little. The real import of his words escaped me momentarily. I assumed he meant she had an eye disorder. My initial reaction was to feel sorry for her.

"She's fucking a nigger," Danziger spit out plainly just as I got the gist of Jonesy's comment myself.

This was the first time I heard Danziger make an overtly racist comment, and it sounded especially crass coming from him. But I was infinitely more stunned by the revelation that the beautiful blond I went batty over, the second Fräulein I fell for, had broken the gravest taboo among G.I.s in Germany. I just could not fathom the object of my affection consorting with a Schwarzer, an idea whose time should never have come.

"Black as shit," Dombrowski qualified, as if I needed a clearer picture of what was being sketched for me.

"He's with the second cav," Danziger continued. "Lives down the hall from us at the other end."

My good work buddies were not going out of their way to spare their new teammate's ego or sensibilities on this most personal of matters in a young man's life. Their best bit of information was yet to come.

"Got a cock the size of your forearm," Jonesy said adding insult to injury. He took his left hand off the steering wheel and slammed it to his right biceps. "I seen that spook in the shower."

A sudden chill ran up and down my spine. In the pit of my stomach there was a gnawing sensation. I was rendered speechless by the bad tidings that just reached my ears. What could any right-thinking white male say when he finds out the fine female he coveted happens to be a crossover cunt? My co-workers must have thought me the complete fool for having run off from the table half-cocked, oblivious to their attempt to restrain me, for shamelessly pursuing a prepossessing maiden whose tastes abased to the pitchy breed.

"Whites call him the Ace of Spades," Westy noted. His laconic remark said it all. I could only wonder what the black troopers called him. The Ace of Hearts perhaps.

"I just didn't . . . " I uttered meekly when words came back to me. "She seemed so . . . ." I was unable to finish my own sentences.

Jonesy pulled up to the parking area on our side of the Kaserne. Sordid snapshots were developing in my head as I walked alongside those who held nothing back in clueing in their babe of a buddy. But I had no yearning to behold the scene of my fantasy fuck in a room somewhere flat on her back spreading those lissome legs to the hilt to fit her big black buck in. And I fought real hard to efface the vision of the indefectible dame I drooled over on a bed up on her knees Frenching her paramour noir, opening that petite bouche ever wider to receive the bulk male. I wanted those luscious lips, up high and down below, to be dilating for me. Now that they were soiled as well as stretched, I knew I would not stand at ease if I ever pressed my lips to hers, at either site, or was encased in them. Fat, ugly, coarse, stupid Jonesy was right. For the German girl who craved oversized overdone putzes, an average white American boy, even a comely one, was not good enough.

A strange feeling came over me as I set foot in our barracks, walking a few paces behind the others. I did not immediately go into my room to bunk down after lunch for a few minutes. All the temperate notions I swallowed about interracial dating and marriage were stirring within me after those close encounters of the white kind with the girl of my dreams. The affair with the black WAC at Fort Ord three months earlier seemed a distant memory, an out-of-body experience almost, nothing to do with me. My liberal comments on the *Rose* to the soldier from the South boomeranged. The favorable words I spewed in the middle of the Atlantic about the mixed couple on board appeared vacuous and childlike in the face of my visceral reaction to the unwelcome unveiling of the snack bar beauty. What I said was good for someone else's goose, not for this gander.

I turns around and looks down da hall toward da other end to where I be told my Negro nemesis keeps. Is my informative friends going to tells me which room he be in? I hopes not. I don't wants to aks or knows who dat motherfucker is. Where he hung out I had no call to be. How he hung out I had no care to see.

Lunch was the last meal I had that day. All afternoon the two hamburgers, French fries, and apple pie stewed in my stomach as I mulled over the jarring turn of events that began when I was taken for a ride. I was quiet and contemplative. But it was more than food that was stewing in my insides. Steve noticed the refraction from my normally talkative self but had no hint of what was eating me. I could not concentrate on anything but the dark images my benevolent buddies so barbarously banged into my brain. The shop repairers passed electrical components to me for testing but all I could do was leave many of them in the tray untouched.

Later in the recreation room at Special Services it was no different. Magazines, newspapers, or a round of pool lost all appeal for me. I had no appetite for dinner at the mess hall and to eat again at the snack bar was out of the question.

It was not until dusk that the howitzer shell fired at me that afternoon reached its target. Back in my room, soon as I plunked down on my bunk I jumped up and ran to the latrine with hand over mouth. Standing over the sink heaving my guts out, I looked away from the reflection in the mirror of the two 2nd Cavalry Schwarzers behind me in the shower.

# CHAPTER 24: JUDGMENT AT NUREMBERG

On Friday morning of the following week, in the shop, I went up to Sergeant Doss.

"How do I get to the Palace of Justice?" I asked.

"Take the streetcar right outside the main gate to the bahnhof, then transfer to the number eleven going in the same direction," he said. "Get off at the sixth stop. It's the great big building in front of you. You can't miss it."

"Okay . . . thanks."

My team leader looked at me a moment and added. "The Palace of Justice is where they held the trials for the war criminals."

"Yes I know," I answered without comment.

I wondered if he would he have told me that bit of information if I were not Jewish? I wanted to say that's where the Nazi bastards were judged harshly and got what was coming to them, but I held my tongue.

After work, I left the shop in a hurry. I went to chow, cleaned up, and changed into my civies. I told Steve I had other plans for the evening. At 1800 I left Merrell, just as the guys down the hall in the 2nd Cav started their G.I. party. It was gratifying to see black and white working together for a change, even if only for cleaning the latrine, halls, and sleeping rooms.

In the States, every Army base I was stationed on had Jewish services in one of the chapels. The chapel buildings were all painted pure white, had a steeple on top, and looked more like a church than a synagogue. But on Friday evenings and Saturday mornings, as well as holidays and holy days, one was converted into a makeshift synagogue, at least on the inside. The tall cross on the altar was carried off and stored somewhere in the back, a portable Torah and a not-so-tall Menorah with little electric lights were brought in, probably from the same storage room, and placed in the center and right side, respectively, of the now bimah. I had no clue as to what kind of religious conversions or accommodations were made for the Nuremberg-area Jewish troops.

It was only at Fort Ord that I attended services with any regularity. At Dix, I did not go to services at all for the eight weeks I was there. Every Friday, after the day's basic training exercises, we had to scrub and clean the barracks and ready its floors, windows, and latrines for Saturday inspection. I could have been excused from this unpleasant weekly chore in order to attend prayers on the base, but I knew my Christian comrades would not understand church on Friday and I did not want to bear the stigma of someone who used religion to bug out of brushing, brooming, and buffing with his buddies.

At Monmouth, I only went to services a few times during my ten-month stay. It was one of the few Army posts that had no work scheduled on Saturday. I just had to be present on my Sabbath if there was a parade. The Army's traditional Friday night G.I. party came a day earlier. As soon as classes and inspections were over on Fridays, and if I did not have to play marching soldier on Saturday, I would pack my AWOL bag, pick up my pass, and dash to the main gate on the Eatontown side of the fort. There I would catch the bus to New York that stopped in front. Most weekends I did not even go to chow I was in such haste to get away.

At Ord, however, being three thousand miles from home, I thoroughly enjoyed attending services, either Friday evening or Saturday morning, occasionally both times. Not that I was observant, but I enjoyed the time off from military duties and the companionship of young soldiers from different parts of the country I had something in common with. By that time I was in the Army more than a year and did not care what my bunkmates thought if I exited the barracks before the party was over or missed a full inspection. Going to the base's hastily constructed Jewish chapel was like a visit with a surrogate family.

The streetcar I changed to at the Hauptbahnhof, the Nummer 11, ran along Fürtherstrasse and, like Doss said, dropped me off right in front of where I was going.

The Palace of Justice was an impressive four-story structure. It had a red-tile, steep-sloping roof with different-sized dormers. The first floor was much higher than the other levels and was fronted by an arcade with a series of arches. A wrought iron ornamental fence about ten feet high, with panels made up of posts with spear points on top, formed a perimeter around the Palace. The main part of the building was set out in front, the side wings cut back. On the top floor there were stone sculptures between every second window. These window-high statues seemed to embody the German spirit of divine destiny. Room 600, where the Nazi leaders sat with their earphones listening to translated testimony about their crimes against the peace of the world and crimes against humanity, was in the center of the East Wing on the top floor. From the street, anyone looking up and to the right could find the window that from 1945 to 1949 let fresh air into the foul chamber of horror stories.

To some extent I was aware of the reputation of the Palace of Justice, its infamy before the war and its fame afterward, prior to this first visit. It struck me as odd, some might say even blasphemous, that Jewish services were held at the place where German courts convening after 1935 enforced the so-called Nuremberg laws against the Jews, racial codes enacted that year in the city. The Palace was the place where more than a decade later many of those responsible for the final solution to the Jewish problem were tried and died.

In this stately building in front of me, the whole world learned of the gruesome particulars of what the Nazis had wrought on the world, the spot where captured films were shown to the international media. From within these walls all could see moving images of bulldozers shoveling Jewish bodies into mass graves, men and women with Star of David patches forced by dogs and rifles onto cattle-car trains, sad-faced children behind barbed-wire fences brandishing tattooed numbers on their arm, naked people herded into locked rooms with shower heads designed to spray Zyklon gas and not water, Jewish dead loaded onto fire-resistant trays and slid into crematoria.

Nuremberg and its Palace of Justice were not chosen at random as the place for the Allied powers to mete out justice to those who executed Hitler's orders or wishes. Before war's end, Secretary of War Stimson drafted a plan for the trial of war criminals, President Truman approved it, and they naturally wanted the trials held in the American zone that was carved out. Nuremberg was under our control and the city, the ceremonial birthplace of the Nazi Party and the site of the annual propaganda rallies, was thought to be the proper locale to mark the demise of Naziism. The Palace in the center of town was also the practical ideal. Largely undamaged by air raids, the building complex contained courtrooms, plenty of office space, prison cells for the Nazi naysayers of culpability, and a private court-yard for carrying out the public sentences ordered by the Tribunal yeasayers of death.

The courtyard hangings were conducted at dawn within days of the verdicts. There was no appeal. Judgment at Nuremberg was final and the Allied victors would exact swift justice on the Nazi vanquished. The case of Hermann Göring, whose ego was only surpassed by his waistline, brought worldwide attention. The testy Luftwaffe com-mander demanded a firing squad, the traditional method of military execution, one he exclaimed was fitting a soldier of his rank. The international panel of judges ruled otherwise. They thought his and his co-conspirators' ethical lapses warranted a painful and undig-nified noose around the neck over a quick and noble bullet through the heart.

Old Hefty Hermie, though, fooled everyone. The night before his date with the hangman, he swallowed a cyanide pill that had some-how been smuggled into his cell. Some said the culprit was the Ger-man doctor who regularly checked the former Field Marshall's bodi-ly signs. Others blamed an SS officer who gave a bar of soap to the unrepentant perpetrator of the Blitzkreig. Then there is the story that Frau Göring must have passed the pill to her condemned husband in a kiss on her last, undoubtedly tearful, visit. A U.S. Army first lieu-tenant was even suspected of betraying his own country, an honor guard it was known Herr Göring had earlier bribed with a watch for the extra food his oversized torso craved.

Of the Nuremberg 12 sentenced to hang, the only other escapee from the ultimate retribution rained on German leaders was Martin Bormann, the Nazi Party Secretary, believed to have bored his way out of the country and into South America. But the Palace was still the place of justice. Some of Hitler's henchmen got their due at the end of a knotted rope. Others were justly carted off to Spandau Prison for life, or confined there for two decades, as was Albert Speer, the Minister of Armaments, for using slave laborers from oc-cupied territories to build weapons. Still other pals of Hitler would certainly swear on a stack of Nazi bibles that justice came out of Room 600, as they were acquitted.

The Palace's infamy weighed on my mind that twenty-seventh of

March when I entered the famous building to attend Jewish services. Coincidentally, it was Good Friday. I was on my way to a mass of a different sort.

Services were held in a room on the main floor not far from the front of the building. A sign directed me straight ahead. I ran two fingers over the mezuzah on the door frame and brought them to my lips. A wooden box full of both black and white thin yarmulkes was just inside the room. I took one and placed it atop my head. I passed by the rack of tallises neatly draped over ascending dowels. Prayer shawls I knew were worn on Saturdays, not Fridays.

I took a seat in the last row of folding chairs. This evening's service had already started. A prayer book was lying in the middle of the seat and I picked it up. The room was almost filled to capacity. I looked around at the assemblage of people in the room, a quite different congregation than that at any of the camp services I attended heretofore. As in the States, there were young men in uniform, both officer and enlisted ranks. And there were young soldiers in civilian clothes, their military status only revealed by their haircuts. But, unlike Jewish services at some converted white chapel on an Army base far from the nearest town or city, here in Germany in a pre-Nazi government building I saw what I presumed were non-military men in their thirties and forties, some with women and children at their side. And I eyed a number of older men who did not look American. There were few older women of any nationality.

With the conclusion of the service, everyone retired to the room directly across the hall for the Oneg Shabbat. Spread out on a long table were wine and refreshments. There were folding chairs strewn about the room, but not enough for each person. We all held up little white paper cups filled with red wine while we said the blessing in Hebrew in harmony with the rabbi. Then the rabbi lifted the white cloth with a gold embroidered Star of David that was covering the large braided challah. With a long cutting knife, he cut the bread into thin slices while he said the Hamotzi, sometimes cutting the larger slices in half. People reached for pieces of challah and marble and yellow sponge cake with their tea and coffee.

I stood by myself in the middle of the room, nibbling on pieces of bread and cake and downing them with the grape juice I helped myself to. I did not know anyone there and did not approach anyone.  Before long, *I* was approached.  A man that looked to be in his early forties, in a dark suit and red bow tie, walked over to me.

"You're new here, aren't you?"

"Yes," I said.

"What's your name?"

"David . . . David Streiber."

The average-looking man with horn-rimmed glasses and slightly pointed nose told me his name and then extended his hand.  "Are you in the Army?"

"Yes," I said again, with a handshake.

The Jewish stranger was an American, I was sure, as he had no accent.  I waited for him to talk first, as my mother had often advised me.  He soon asked me what my rank was, where I was stationed in Nuremberg, how long I have been here, and when I would be going back to the States.  I answered his questions, which seemed harmless enough coming from a home-grown Landsmann, without hesitation.  If a German Gentile his age whom I had just met asked the same questions, I would have kept my mouth shut.  The man did not say much about himself, only that he had been a major in the Air Corps during the war and now worked as a civilian for the Army.  I was nudged around the room, introduced to everyone, and I had a chance to chat for a minute or two with each of my co-religionists.

The Nuremberg Jewish community—a motley crew of Germans and Americans, military and civilian, young and old—welcomed me benevolently into their familial association.  I was sure my mother would not have disapproved of my getting involved with this particular family in Germany.

Rabbi Washer and his wife were a young couple in their mid-to-late twenties.  She hailed from the Midwest, he from New York, and they both donned continual smiles as they greeted people and shook hands.  The Jewish Chaplain was still wearing his white ceremonial robe so I could not see his rank, but he likely was a lieutenant, second or first.  He wore no yarmulke but most other males in the room and I observed that custom.  I recalled he did not wear one during the service either, so I gathered his rabbinical training was in the Reform branch of Judaism.

Military personnel comprised one contingent, albeit varied, at the Oneg Shabbat.  A number of congregants were doctors or dentists who were drafted and commissioned. They worked at the Army Hospital nearby or at clinics in Kasernes in other cities not too far away. The young, lower-rank soldiers were stationed at various barracks in the area, draftees and enlistees who, like I, were not planning a career in the military. There were no Jewish noncoms that I discerned from any introduction, or EMs who had re-enlisted. One person, though, was very interesting to talk to, an Air Force captain in counterintelligence, but of course he did not say anything specific about his work.

Another group of worshippers at the Palace of Justice was made up of American civilians not connected with the military. I met an insurance salesman from New Jersey, a former G.I. who spent almost five years in the Army during the war. He was with his wife and two kids, the boy soon to be Bar Mitzvah. They lived in an apartment on Regensburger Strasse not far from Merrell Barracks. He was an agent with Metropolitan Life, he told me, and could only write policies for servicemen. I thought he was going to try to palm a policy off on me but he did no such thing. On the contrary, he invited me to his home for Passover.

Then there was the Korean War veteran who owned an import-export business, and was married to a German woman. She did not look Jewish to me and I did not ask but she could have been a convert. A lawyer from Boston was in my line of introductions too. The single thirty-something was employed by the State Department and was on leave for two years to help gather evidence for the German government to prosecute Nazi war criminals. He certainly was in the right place, I thought, proximity to evil and redemption. In the stillness within the Palace walls, haunts of the courtroom activities upstairs, guilty verdicts announced, and hangings in the courtyard might provide inspiration for his legal tasks.

It was the older German Jews that intrigued me the most. A well-dressed couple in their sixties, who had returned to Fürth after the war to reclaim the family business, told me they come to services every Friday night. They had fled to Switzerland at the end of 1938 after their property was firebombed on Kristallnacht. A tall heavy-set man with a black beret, who milled around by himself and hardly spoke to anyone, had been a respected judge before the war. I was told he lost his whole family. He escaped in time and waited out the war in Australia and Israel. The jurist the Nazis removed from the bench in 1936 came back because he felt Germany was his home. When I heard that, I thought how nice it would have been for my family had Mrs. Mittler shared the judge's feelings and followed his trail instead of remaining in New York and buying our building.

The cantor for the services, who had a superb singing voice, was also a Jewish returnee, but one from the States. He was a buyer for the PX and reappeared in Nuremberg in 1946 to marry his shikse Schatzie and be with her family. The congregation had one member, a balding man of fifty that spoke English very well, who gave tours of the Palace of Justice. He handed out picture postcards of the War Crimes Trials and had been an interpreter for the British and Americans. The German Jew was a bit of a scribe too. One of his jobs was to take the last testament of those Nazis about to be hanged. Too bad he never got to climb the steps of the gallows to write down Hermann Göring's final words. If a noose had tightened around that fat neck, one can only wonder if utterances of regret would have been heard or choked off. Unless I was mistaken or not very perceptive, none of the people I met were Eastern European Jews or concentration camp survivors.

After the Oneg Shabbat, I rode back to Merrell Barracks on the streetcar with a PFC in the 303rd Maintenance Battalion I met, Stanley Grossman, a twenty-one-year-old from Queens. We both talked about our similar plans after our discharges, I to start college and he to continue. My involvement with Nuremberg's Jewish community began that Friday evening, exactly three weeks after I first set foot in the city. It was to last almost a year.

# CHAPTER 25: THE MOUSE THAT ROARED NO MORE

Merling avoided eye contact with me all morning in the shop. The spec four with more time in the Army than I had sat facing me on the other side of the bench, two seats to the right of my place. Every once in a while I glanced over to him. He either had his head down, focusing on the piece of equipment he was repairing, or was looking to his left or straight ahead. When I was working on a piece and not looking his way, through the corner of my eye I could see him stealing a peek at me. It was the first of April and it was beginning to look like this would be my Fool's Day.

We were paid early that morning. All of us from the shop lined up in the hall next to the Orderly Room with the troops from our host company and inched forward toward an open door. A warrant officer from the 2nd Cavalry HQ sat at a table in the doorway with a gray metal strong box filled with American currency in front of him. When we reached the door we saluted and stated our name and rank. The paymaster counted out our money by laying each bill on the table on top of one another. He then handed us our cash for the month minus any deductions for social security, dependent's allotment, savings, and laundry service. We had to verify the amount and sign next to our name on a long white lined sheet. Back at the shop, I expected Merling to come to me right away or to say something from across the bench but he did neither.

The son-of-a-bitch owed me money. I hardly knew the soldier in my outfit now indebted to me. Two weeks earlier, in my second week in the shop, Merling approached me and asked to borrow twenty dollars. He did not say what he needed the money for and I did not ask.

In front of several teammates, the bitchy bastard begged for the bread. I was not keen on lending money in the Army and seldom did so, but the cash-strapped co-worker made me feel sorry for him. I wanted to appear friendly and cooperative to my new bud-dies. Still I hesitated before reaching for my wallet. Then he quick-ly took out a piece of paper and wrote on it "I.O.U. $20 to be paid on April 1, 1959" and signed it. Danziger was standing next to Merling and without being asked put his signature on the paper as a witness. So, foolishly now it seems, I loaned money to a virtual stranger except for the fact that we both repaired electrical equipment in the same shop.

As it turned out, giving away my next to last twenty in the middle of the month hurt me. A week later, out and about in Nuremberg, I was hard up for that Gelt and *I* had to do without. I loathed asking anyone for money, whether it was to incur a debt or to collect on one. In his time of need I helped out a teammate as an act of good will, to be on top with the guys I had to work with, and now it was I who was on the bottom of this deal.

What the fuck is wrong with that ass hole? I kept asking myself after we both got paid. There I was, busy with soldering wires, testing tubes, and replacing broken parts, and all the while thinking of getting back my twenty. Why doesn't Merling come to me or say something? He promised he would pay me on payday. The other guys heard him. He put it in writing. I had the proof that I forked over two sawbucks and this was the day he agreed to cough them up.

If that wasn't enough to infuriate me, I didn't even like Merling. Before I slipped the cash to him he was not friendly toward me and after he wouldn't help me with a piece of equipment I was having trouble with when I asked him. The ingrate was a mousy sort of guy, even looked the part with his small nose and big ears and two enlarged front teeth, a colorless character who sniffed around for a morsel of cheese in someone else's cupboard.

To me Merling the Mouse was a rat in disguise. He kept mostly to himself, hardly ever smiling at or telling a joke to or exchanging words with a fellow teammate. Stealthy, apathetic, humorless, and nondescript, Merling was not someone I would have welcomed as a roommate or an Army buddy.

Why did the Mouse trap me? I wondered. He could have put the bite on any one of the other guys in the shop, those he knew much longer and better. Maybe he had and they wisely turned him down? Merling must have thought I was an easy touch, that Jews always have money to lend.

By the time we stopped work for lunch, I had had enough. With my temperature rising, I went over to Merling just as he had finished shutting his equipment down. Straight in the eye I looked him.

"You were supposed to pay me today," I spit out in a chilly tone.

It pained me to have to ask for money, and ask in a confrontational manner, for what was rightfully mine, for what should have been returned to me freely and unobtrusively. But Merling was uncharacteristically hostile.

"I paid Danziger what I owed him," he roared back without hesitation or emotion, and then turned his head slightly from me. "He's going home tomorrow. You'll have to wait till next month."

Now I was livid but tried not to show it. Merling's beastly explanation and body language made his utterance sound like a legitimate justification for breaking a contract and prioritizing his payments. He obviously thought he had a right to do that, to decide unilaterally that his debt to me was less important than his debt to someone else.

If Merling had come to me, had asked if I could wait another month because he needed to pay Danziger first, I probably would have said yes. That would have been my choice, I'm the creditor. I did not have a college degree in finance, but at age nineteen I had enough common sense to know that it was not good business to let a debtor dictate the terms of a loan. The way in which Merling soldered his words, that I will *have* to wait until next month, short-circuited the wires in me.

"I want what you owe me now," I demanded as aggressively as he demurred. "You promised to pay me today. What you owed Danziger has nothing to do with our agreement." I pulled out his I.O.U. from my shirt pocket and waved it in front of him.

Merling still showed no emotion and made no hand movement toward his back pocket. I did not expect him to plead for my forgiveness but he could have said he was sorry. He just stood there without roaring anything else, like a lion waiting for its prey to make a move. In effect, he motionlessly and silently maintained his position that he was justified in deciding who should get paid first. My feelings and my financial needs were of no importance to the defaulter. I must have raised my voice more than I thought and started what others saw as a commotion. Danziger and a couple of other guys gathered around us. I saw that Doss was approaching too.

"What's the matter, guys?" our team leader inquired as he positioned himself between the two disputants. "Why all the shouting?"

The Mouse was true to form and waited for me to answer. "Merling owes me twenty dollars and won't pay me. He promised to give it to me today right after we got paid."

Doss looked at Merling. "Is that true?"

"I have the proof," I added before Merling could answer. "Here's the I.O.U." I showed the paper to Doss.

Doss faced Merling again. "Is this your signature?"

Merling nodded.

"Then why don't you pay Streiber?"

Merling spoke up at that point. "If I do I won't have much left for myself for this month. I had to pay Danziger fifty dollars. He's going home. I told Streiber I'd pay him next month."

"I don't want it next month," I injected quickly before Doss could respond to Merling's lame excuse. "I don't want any more promises. I want what is written on the paper."

Doss looked at me and thought for a moment. He pushed his eyeglass frame back to the bridge of his nose. He took out a handkerchief and wiped the corners of his mouth and then his brow. Doss knew my demand was justified but I could not tell from the expression on his face whether or not he would sympathize with my situation or Merling's. The E-6 was not the forceful type, not the kind of noncom who liked to pull rank or order underlings around. But, was the boss man going to play mediator?  Or would the peacetime sergeant take cover from the battlefield staked out by two of his men?

"Streiber, it's only twenty dollars," Doss argued, revealing the role he would assume in the drama unfolding on his stage. "You can wait till next month, can't you?"

Only twenty dollars, he said. Twenty dollars was a tad less than one-fifth of my monthly pay. Twenty dollars was almost one-third of my father's weekly salary. Twenty dollars paid most of my parents' rent for the old apartment in Coney Island each month. Twenty dollars put big bags of food on the little kitchen table in our new apartment next door. Twenty dollars was what I earned in high school on two Saturdays working in a grocery store for wages of seventy-five cents an hour plus tips. Twenty dollars bought a handmade wool suit with vest from the German tailor in a corner room on our Kaserne. Twenty dollars was the price of a full-length, hooded British Loden overcoat sold in the PX. Twenty dollars would buy love four times from any Hilda or Helga pacing around the Bahnhof.

Danziger offered his two cents too. "I'm sure you'll get your money next month."

Talk was cheap for Danziger and I resented it. He should have been the last person to take sides in this matter. I did not see him kick back twenty from the fifty Merling handed him earlier that morning. The short-timer knew better than to raus Germany with a G.I. marker in his fist.

"I don't want it next month," I repeated in the most emphatic voice I could.

I gave no thought whatsoever as to whether my new boss or team-mates would brand me as a hard ass. "I want what Merling owes me now. He promised . . . I took him at his word . . . I loaned him the money on that basis."

Doss stepped back a little. "You're right, Streiber," he said, still trying to reason with me. "But Merling is short this month. Give him a break."

"Maybe I'm short, maybe I need the money too?" I stressed.

Danziger pulled me aside and whispered in my ear. "Merling will pay you interest. He can pay twenty-five, maybe thirty, next month. I only loaned him thirty-five. I'll work it out with him."

It was against Army regulations to lend money with interest and everyone knew it. That was one of the first things taught to new recruits. It was bad for morale, I recalled the basic training noncom saying, bad for establishing trust and comradeship among soldiers in or out of combat.

Nevertheless, the practice of charging your barracks or foxhole buddy interest, at usurious rates, was widespread. A week, even days, before pay day, empty-pursed troopers with hand extended would beseech some fellow in the outfit, and get the needed cash after signing an I.O.U. for a higher sum payable on the first of the month, but without a specification as to how much was borrowed. Like a used car salesman who jacked up the loan value of old junk heaps, the interest was built into the price. This was the loophole the G.I. usurer drove through in order to both clutch a profit and steer clear of a court martial. Fifteen usually got you twenty, a vig of 33 percent for an extremely short-term loan, perhaps 2000 percent interest on a yearly basis, an enviable margin for any bank or finance company to record on its balance sheet.

Doss acted like he did not hear, or did not want to know, what Danziger said to me. But our team chief was anxious to settle this matter between the two warring parties under his command. "Streiber, if Merling doesn't pay you the twenty next month, I'll make good on it. Will this satisfy you?"

"No," I said right away. "I want Merling to pay me."

"Why?" Doss asked. "What difference does it make?"

"This difference. Merling shouldn't have paid Danziger before he talked to me," I retorted. "He should have asked me like a teammate to extend the loan another month, not told me like a sergeant that I must wait to get paid at his convenience."

Merling's lips moved a bit. He started to say something but stopped. What could he say? He admitted he owed me the money and was supposed to pay me that day. And I refused to relieve him of his obligation.

Doss looked like he did not know what to say or do anymore. "Why don't we all go to chow," he said after a few seconds, shifting his head away from me. "Merling, see if you could borrow twenty from someone else." The sergeant then looked back at me. "Streiber, let's talk about this later."

This was a cop out, pure and simple. First someone who owes me money avoids contact with me all morning, then our supervisor who knows the money was owed and was due to be paid that day evades making a decision about the matter and shuns telling a subordinate what he must do. But, there was nothing more that could be said at this point. I turned around, walked out the door, and headed toward the mess hall.

Over lunch, nibbling away at what seemed a less than satisfactory meal, I decided the action I would take if Merling did not pay me. If one sergeant was not much help, I would seek aid from another with more stripes.

In the barracks after chow, before we had to report back to the shop, I confronted Merling again. Steve tried to talk me out of it but I would not listen. I walked right into the room Merling shared without knocking. Dombrowski was sitting on his bunk, writing a letter on top of a box in his lap, and was startled by the intrusion. Merling was standing near the window, facing it, and turned when he heard the door open. He was not surprised to see me. I went up to the person who was causing me all this aggravation.

"Are you going to pay me, yes or no?" I demanded.

"No," Merling said, calmly and deliberately, shaking his head.

"I'm going to see Sergeant Bentley now. You can come with me if you want. I'm telling you this so you can't say I went behind your back."

The Mouse nodded and left the room with me. In silence we walked from the East Block to the West Block of our large Kaserne. Two lower-ranked soldiers a grade apart in the same company were locked in battle with each other, without weapons, over a non-military issue. Our quasi-march took less than three minutes. I wanted my money, and I wanted it now.

Sergeant Bentley was sitting at his desk when Merling and I came up to him, I in the lead. Mr. Barry was also at his desk but was looking at some papers. The E-7 was in his starched fatigues, spit-shined black boots, and yellow scarf.

"What can ah do fo' you boys?" Bentley said, not taken aback by our surprise visit. He stood up, moved a little closer, and faced us.

"Merling borrowed twenty dollars two weeks ago, Sergeant. He promised to pay it back today, on payday, but now he won't pay it." I took out the I.O.U. and handed it to Bentley.

Bentley read the paper and turned to Merling. "Is this true?"

"Yes," Merling said simply without nodding.

"You borrowed twenty . . . not something less," Bentley stated. He obviously was trying to determine if any interest was part of the deal.

"Yes," Merling repeated.

"Then why don't you pay Strahber?" the southerner asked.

Mr. Barry lifted his head from the papers he was reading and eyeballed the three of us standing in front of Bentley's desk. The head man said nothing but he seemed intently interested in the unfolding personnel decision.

Merling meekly explained his situation. "I had to pay Danziger. He's going home tomorrow. I won't have much money left."

"If you promised to pay Strahber today, then you have to pay him," Bentley told the mousy debtor directly and authoritatively.

"But . . . ," Merling began to say.

Bentley cut him off immediately. "But nothin'. You *have* to pay him."

Six stripes, a commanding manner, and the role of ranking non-com in our unit evidently was all it took for Specialist Merling to surrender. He reached into his back pocket, pulled out a wallet, and handed over a crisp new twenty-dollar bill. I thought I'd never see Andrew Jackson's face pass from Merling's fingers. I was relieved I would not have to say kaddish for that twenty after all.

The now sullen-looking holdout turned around and left the Area Office. If he had a tail, it would have been wagging between his legs. I thanked the master sergeant for interceding on my behalf. Bentley advised me not to lend money I was not prepared to lose or wait another month for.

That afternoon back at our bench, Merling continued to avoid eye contact with me. His head was lowered, he spoke to no one. The cockiness displayed earlier in refusing to pay me, gone. Merling was the mouse that roared no more.

## CHAPTER 26: SOUR KRAUT

Seeing the reflection of the hatless German with rumpled raincoat in the glass panel window told me something was amiss. I was standing in front of one of the shops in the Hauptbahnhof while the man was standing behind me and a little to the right. He was looking at my refracted image in the glass. The stranger was thin and tall, six one or two, in his mid-to-late-thirties, and bald-headed except for a small patch in the back. His chiseled features—bony nose, prominent cheekbones, recessed eyes—coupled with a chalky complexion gave him a ghostly appearance reminiscent of a silent Lon Chaney in *The Phantom of the Opera*.

From his clothing alone I could tell the man was a Deutscher. Less than two minutes earlier, as I was walking along the main corridor inside Nuremberg's main train station where the shops were, this odd character was coming toward me from the opposite direction. I could not help noticing him because he jerked his head in my direction when he noticed me. He stared until he walked by, as if he were profoundly surprised or moved by seeing me. My glance at this person through the corner of my eye was with barely a thought in mind. Once he passed, I did not look over my shoulder to see if he was still focused on me.

I continued walking a little farther until I stopped at a men's store to peer at the apparel on the bottom of the display case. When I looked up, I saw reflected in the window the face and figure of the staring stranger that just breezed by me. The sudden and ungainly presence of this head-jerking German who came up behind me I knew was no coincidence. The man I never met obviously reversed his course, traipsed in my footsteps, halted in back of me, and for reasons unknown was resting his eyes upon me.

It was the first Sunday in April and I was out and about by myself. Steve, as usual, was on a date with Ursula. With the twenty handed over by the mouse that roared no more, I had more than a C note and a half in my wallet, lots of dough for a horny young man to play around with off post in any German town for a month. The going rate after payday was twenty Marks or five dollars. That was fine with me if the object of my attention was as young and attractive as the Marianne I tried to dance with in the Flying Dutchman, or the girl in the snack bar, assuming of course the professional worker was on the white side of the color line.

On Sundays I liked to walk around Nuremberg in the afternoon, to take in the sights and sounds and smells of this medieval city. I was always on the lookout for a female to fit in to, one that fit in to my exacting criteria for facial beauty and bodily shapeliness. She could be a waitress in a restaurant, salesgirl in a department store, a Fräulein on line at a movie theater or streetcar stop, a dirty blond feeding pigeons on a park bench. Like in a Hollywood movie, I longed for that chance meeting with a deutsche damsel, for a Blitz bolt to strike two strangers when they meet, for love on a bootleg basis. It was easy to score here in Germany, I told myself. This was the land of plenty for American soldiers, a field of pretty Mädchens for the taking. If Lady Luck failed me that day, I could always march into the Flying Dutchman after dark, capture an available Elsa, and boot her down.

When I left the barracks after lunch, I decided to see the local Schweinstrasse, the street where scantily-dressed women sit in the large windows of houses and entice men to come in. That's what my teammates called it, but I was told Frauentormauer is the official name and that it was opposite the Old Wall. How to get there, I did not know and I would have to ask someone. What I did know was that it was off limits. Stalking on this particular Strasse in any German city could get me walking to a court martial in any USAREUR command. But I still itched to view some unclothed Sally on Prostitute Allee, to scratch this unique sight into my European diary. A trip to the bedroom with any of the Damen on display, and a stint in the stockade after I zipped up, was not the kind of double entry I wanted to write in. I just planned to seek and peek, find out where this street of ill repute was and stroll over to it later in the afternoon before it turned dark.

I spun around and looked at the man who was looking at me. He said something in German that I didn't understand and didn't respond to. Then he switched to English.

"You are . . . American?" he said with a mild accent, hesitantly.

Who is this Kraut I just saw walking away from me? The hairless pate, pallid skin, and piercing eyeballs were a dead giveaway. Why is he following me? One look at my face and the batty Bürgher ties himself to my spoor.

"Yes," I told him. Maybe I should have said nein or walked away.

The stranger obviously wanted to engage me in conversation. But who knows what else? We talked for a while as we stood in front of the window. His English was very good. He wanted to know if I was in the Army and I told him I was. He asked me where I was stationed and I said Merrell Barracks. He thought I wanted to purchase something in the store and offered to translate for me but I told him I was just browsing. He kept asking me seemingly innocuous questions about *my*self, without saying anything about *him*self, and I began to wonder what the German's motives were. I knew he was lying to me. He did not happen to stop to help me when he saw me looking in a store window. He first saw me walking toward him, then turned around and pursued me to the men's shop. There definitely was something screwy here.

What was I to make of this not-so-chancy brush with a local male in a foreign land? What was any young American soldier in occupied Germany to make of a Mann who stares at him, deliberately follows him, and says he wants to help him? I was sure he did not realize I earlier pegged him noticing me, and did not think I knew he deliberately dogged me. Should I tell him to his face that I knew he lied to me? If I did, his very white face would likely turn ruby red and he'd turn around again, this time away from me.

There was nothing stopping me from saying auf Wiedersehen, but I decided to play along with the transparent deception. Why did I not just leave? I really cannot say, not even now, over fifty years later. I probably wanted to find out what he was up to. I was an inquisitive American in a foreign land who earnestly wanted to learn about the local people and their customs. Or it could be I was bored with the uneventful day and was ripe to take in a new, and possibly interesting, experience.

But I would have to be at least a little distrustful, I told myself. This odd-looking male who darted toward me at the Nuremberg train station could be a kindred soul to the Mike O'Brien I ran away from at the New York bus terminal. Did he too want to lure me into a Bahnhofstoilete? That would explain why he was walking around the Hauptbahnhof aimlessly, ready to change course after momentarily eyeing me. It was also possible the first German man I had more than cursory contact with was a spy.

If the German was a Homosexueller, he must have come out of his closet after most homes in Germany had no closets, or roofs or walls for that matter. The Nazis did not look favorably upon sex deviants of any kind. Perhaps he thought I was AC/DC, a male who could plug in to either sex's front or back sockets and get a charge. I neither said nor did anything to indicate that I was or was not a switch-hitter. If not a queer who sought my company, then maybe this Nazi-era German was now spying for the Russians? Or East Germans? He might be trying to *recruit* rather than seduce me. I imagined the stranger could be pumping me for classified information about my company's functions and personnel or for military documents and materiel. The Army warned me to keep my mouth shut with any German who comes on to me in any way. Well, the brass did not have to worry about this soldier. With Herr Fag or Herr Spy, a Mr. Unknown who picked me up on a ruse at the train station, I not only would keep my mouth shut but my buttocks too.

A third possibility came to mind. The stranger could be a regular Josef, an ordinary German just looking to make friends with a G.I., keen on getting his hands and mouth on amerikanische Zigaretten, Kaffee, or Tee, but not me. PX and Commissary goods were cheap, hard to come by on the local economy, and fancied by every German. I heard of G.I.s brown-bagging it for their Schatzies, but here a German man could be doing it backwards, snuggling up to a same-sex American for eating, drinking, or smoking purposes. If this were the case, I did not relish myself in that role. I gave up my part-time job as grocery delivery boy when I joined the Army.

"Do you know where Frauentormauer street is?" I asked him.

I hoped I pronounced it right, rolling the first *r* like Europeans do. The German was as good a person as any to collar for the purpose I had in mind that afternoon. I also wanted to send him a message that I was seeking a female for my kind of love, and not interested in accompanying him to a smelly station stall for any male type of engagement.

"Yes, of course. It is by the Wall, not far from here."

He did not ask why I wanted to know where the street was or if I wanted go to there.

"Did I pronounce the street right?"

"Yes, but in German you do not need to add 'street' to that name. Mauer means wall. It takes the place of Strasse or street."

I thought for a moment and then said, "You mean you don't say Frauentormauerstrasse?"

"No, no. That would be . . . extra . . . not necessary . . . ." He searched for the right word in English.

"That would be *redundant*, we say."

"Yes, yes," he said. "I learn something new in English."

"And I learned something new in German . . . how to say wall." I was humoring him, waiting for him to make the next move.

"I show you Frauentormauer." The stranger smiled and his eyes sparkled. He was obviously pleased to offer to take me somewhere in the city, to further his questionable contact with me.

"No . . . no. That's all right. Just tell me how to get to that street. I'll find it."

"I take you to the Wall," he insisted. He reached for my upper arm and gently nudged me around. "We walk now."

I went along with him, still playing this adventurous scene out. He seemed harmless enough. We walked in the direction he was going earlier, toward the main entrance of the Hauptbahnhof. It was a good thing my mother could not see me talking to, and walking alongside, the sort of character she warned me against getting friendly with.

The German led me out the wide doors of the station, down its five steps, and across the large square, the Bahnhofplatz as he referred to it. Like a tour guide, he pointed to the Grand Hotel on the northeast corner and the U.S. Army Hotel next door to it on the right. He said that before the war the Army Hotel was called the Grand Hotel Guesthouse, built by the Nazi Party as an annex to the Grand Hotel. My Nuremberg navigator explained how the Guesthouse was used exclusively by Herr Hitler for the Third Reich's Party Day rallies each summer. At the end of the war, Americans confiscated the building and converted it into a hotel open to all U.S. forces in Europe.

We turned left toward the Old City and passed the medieval tower at Königstrasse, a round brown brick structure that was well over a hundred feet in height and perhaps thirty in diameter. The German said there are four of these towers around the city, originally main gates attached to the Wall. He then took me through several winding streets in the downtown area.

He stopped at a corner. "I live near," he said. "We go to my flat first. I make coffee. I have cakes also."

So this was the game plan all along. By offering to direct me to Frauentormauer, the German schemed to put us in proximity to where his apartment was and then entice me to scoot there with him for some refreshments. To go or not to go, that was the question. Playing tag-along with a stranger through public streets is one thing, entering an unknown's private part is quite another.

"Okay," I said reluctantly. I wanted to see what housing on the local economy was like.

I was led into a narrow concrete building with a sloping roof and dormers. There was a store in the front of the ground floor just like in the two buildings I lived in on Mermaid Avenue. The roof levels on all of the houses on this block were the same height. We walked up three flights to the top floor. He lived in a small two-room flat.

The kitchen facilities were not in a separate room but off to the side of the living area, which contained a few sticks of old furniture. The door to the other room was open and I could see an unmade bed and a chest with pieces of underwear hanging out of the drawers. But for the separate bedroom, this place was not much better than Elsa's one room. I sat on a squeaky rocking chair while he warmed a torn over-stuffed armchair opposite me. He made no effort to put a pot of coffee on the stove or cut a piece of cake.

We talked about nothing of great importance, just chattered away about ourselves, Americans, and Germany after the war. He smiled occasionally and had a pleasant look about him, content I gathered that I came with him to his personal quarters. Neither of us got up from our seats or positioned ourselves closer to the other. My impression was that he was waiting for me to make a move on him, to get up and touch his hand or neck or face, to say something of an intimate nature about men or his appearance, to give some sort of signal. I did nothing of the kind of course. Since he made no attempt to extract military information, I was sure he wanted what most homosexual men wanted, impersonal sex with a young man he found attractive at first sight. However, he seemed too insecure to move on me, to do something that would get him in trouble with the

Polizei or cause him to lose his job, if he had one.

After a while, tired of playing cat-and-mouse, and that seeing the afternoon was almost gone, I asked: "Why do they call that street Frauentormauer?"

I changed the subject to the purpose for which I tacitly agreed to go with him in the first place. Plus I wanted to dispel any thought or penchant he may have had, now that we were alone in a private place, for getting down on his knees in front of me or bending me over and standing behind me. I knew Frauen meant women, but I heard where the prostitutes stay is just a short strip of the street.

"Frauentor means women's gate. St. Mary's, the women's church, was on this street and it was near the gate of the Wall."

That made sense to me. Like back in Coney Island, the main avenues of Neptune, Mermaid, and Surf were appropriate callings for thoroughfares near an ocean.

"Could you give me directions?" I said as I stood up, making it obvious I was keen on leaving.

Suddenly there was a changed expression on the Kraut's face. The smile disappeared, his eyes narrowed, the cheeks twitched. There was now a sour look about him.

"I take you," he uttered softly with a long puss, and then got up from his chair.

I was as happy to leave his dingy flat as I was to leave my own when I joined the Army. The parting words spoken to me by my boyhood pal and Seventh Army predecessor came to mind. What would Richie say, I wondered, if he knew I *did* come home with a Nazi Schatzie, albeit one of a different gender than he had in mind?

I never got the coffee and cake I was promised.

# CHAPTER 27: THE WALLED OFF

The German and I walked west on his street, Jakobstrasse, about two blocks to Farberstrasse, then turned left for another two blocks. His crabbed face did not mitigate. This time, he did not engage me in conversation about myself. I thought he might ask if I bedded any German women yet, as he was mindful of where he was taking me, but was mum about that topic.

"Here," he said as we reached the corner of Frauentormauer. He pointed to the right on the street I had heard so much about and told me to walk in that direction.

"Is this where the women sit in the windows?"

"Yes, yes," he double-talked in his usual way. "From here to Spittlerstrasse."

"To where?"

He repeated the name of the cross street several blocks away. I thought he said *Hitler*strasse, but that made no sense. Any street named for the Führer during the Nazi era undoubtedly would have been changed at the beginning of the occupation. But calling it Spittlerstrasse was actually very apropos if the street previously was known as Hitlerstrasse. The conquering G.I.s would certainly have spat on such a street and dubbed it Spitonhitlerstrasse. Take out four consecutive letters, *onhi*, and voilà, you have Spittlerstrasse.

I did not have to engage in any storm trooper tactics to get rid of my presumptive admirer. "You don't have to wait for me," I put to him politely. I really meant, I don't want you to wait for me. "I don't know how long I'll be. It could be a while."

The German still exuded the sourly disposition revealed back in his apartment. "Okay," he said resolutely.

I thought he would wave goodbye and say something but he just turned around and walked away. I never saw him again. I too started walking without another word, in the direction he pointed to, only once looking over my shoulder.

The white English-language sign with bold black lettering bolted to the tall stucco building on the northwest corner of Frauentormauer and Färberstrasse could not have been more explicit: OFF LIMITS TO ALL U.S. MILITARY PERSONNEL. There were no MPs around that I could see, and I doubted any were hiding behind doorways or in back alleys. I saw no G.I.s in uniform either. There were some young men with short haircuts in American-style clothes openly pacing up and down the street, all but one white. A few German-looking middle-age men stood huddled on the corner, milling about nervously. I would have thought the johns seeking a surreptitious entry on this block would be the Americans, not the Germans. The Johannes of the city, it seems, were the shy and worried type. Slowly westward along Frauentormauer I walked. There were no sidewalks, only a cobblestone road.

On the north side of the street, there were attached three- and four-story concrete row houses. The uneven roof lines at times revealed a fifth story built from an attic. None of the houses had steps in front to get up to a first floor, or steps leading down to a basement, like the brownstones in Brooklyn or townhouses in Manhattan that came to mind. The first floor was at street level and the houses were fitted with undraped picture- or standard-size windows that anyone from five- to seven-feet tall could freely peek into.

There was no residential south side of Frauentormauer, only the Old Wall. The nine-hundred-year old fortification was about half as high as the houses across from it, with covered walkways on top. Watchtowers reaching the height of the tallest buildings, with doors at the bottom and small windows up the side, were positioned fifty or sixty feet apart. The Wall itself was not smooth or plane, but rather contained a series of blind arcades, solid recessed arches one after the other. Some sections clearly were rebuilt, as the masonry, large stone blocks, was uneven in color and texture. The blocks with rough exteriors were charcoal black, what remained after the Allied fire bombing, while the flat-surfaced pieces of equal size in various shades of gray looked like they were cemented together to re-create the original contour of the Wall.

Mainly I walked in the middle of the street, occasionally moving closer to one of the houses. Burly German men in ill-fitting suits stood guard in the doorways. I was satisfied to simply observe the goings-on of others. The thought of a big black or white MP in polished boots and shiny helmet liner popping out of nowhere, poking me with a Billy club, and parading me off to the pokey would not leave me. Evidently my proximate American comrades did not share such fears. I watched them as they stood on the cobblestone close to the houses and talked to the women through an opening in the first floor window, then went inside and up the stairs with a male escort.

On the second story were the boudoirs to consummate the deal just agreed to. The lone black G.I. was carrying a big brown paper bag with cartons of cigarettes sticking out the top. Several times he was turned down by Frauen who easily looked like they were in their late-thirties and forties. A fiftyish cow of a Frau then waved him in. Schwarzers had to pay dearly to enter a walk-up love nest on white Wall Street in Old Nuremberg.

I was not enamored with any of the women. They appeared to be many years my senior, plumpish and tough in body and soul, hardened by war and postwar deprivation, fattened by relatively good wages earned off young military men and older Germans in a peacetime economy. They wore dark waist-level panties, low-cut bras, and sheer negligees tied around the neck. Chubby legs in high-heel shoes were spread wide apart, at times with feet propped up against the windows. This was not enough to get me to reach for any of the forbidden fruit in this Garden of Frauen. It was not a question of stockade risk. The Frauentormauer prostitutes, stigmatized women walled off from both the city and society, were simply unappetizing to me. Before I hit Spitt, I did an about face and headed back the other way. In my diary I knew I can write that, like Caesar, I came and I saw, but unlike old Julie, I did not conquer.

The movie theater was on the same side of Luitpoldstrasse as the Flying Dutchman. It was sandwiched between a respectable Bavarian restaurant and a cheap hotel. A narrow alley separated the theater from the restaurant. It was barely wide enough for two people to walk through abreast. Glossy black-and-white pictures, frames printed from the film playing inside, were showcased behind glass cabinets hanging to the left and right of the ticket booth and entrance. The film was *Das Mädchen Rosemarie* starring Nadja Tiller and Peter van Eyck. Judging from the building signs, people's clothing, and automobile models, it looked like it was shot in Frankfurt in the past year or two.

I paid one Mark sixty and went inside. It was after seven and I had some time to kill. The Flying Dutchman did not get going until at least nine and I doubted whether Elsa would show up there before then. I needed a rest, or reprieve I should say, from the day's events with the German at the train station who came after me and the women by the Wall who wanted me to come after them. I took a seat in the middle of an empty row halfway down from the back of the theatre.

It was difficult to follow the story line of the film since there were no English subtitles. But I understood it to be about a girl named Rosemarie, a prostitute who shares a basement apartment with two musicians and sometimes sings with them. She then gets involved with a well-dressed businessman and he moves her to a high-rise luxury apartment. The change of residence was probably meant to symbolize a postwar call girl's achievement of upward physical as well as social mobility. I dozed off after Rosemarie was murdered, and it was just as well. The Polizei did not know who did it or why, and in any case the language barrier would have prevented me from figuring it out.

Something rubbing against my left leg woke me up. A girl was sitting next to me, her leg pushed up to mine. With the ball of her foot, she raised and lowered her knee like operating a bicycle pump. The female stranger was wearing a short skirt, bunched up around the middle of her thighs, but no stockings. Her shapely legs were almost completely exposed. She leaned over to me and touched my hand on the armrest.

"You American?" she whispered. "G.I.?"

I nodded. I thought of saying ja, bestimmt, an expression Elsa often used, to get in step with the movie still playing, but I held back.

"I show you good time. Yes?" She moved her hand to my inner thigh.

I turned toward the Fräulein who was coming on to me. There was enough light in the theater for me to see that she was not at all bad looking and rather young, in her early- or mid-twenties. Gauging from my sitting position, she seemed to be the height I liked and I could see she was fully endowed above the waist. I slipped my arm around her back and she snuggled up to me. I cupped her left tit and caressed the meaty soft flesh. She ran her hand farther up my leg, almost touching my balls.

All this was new to me, a strange girl picking me up in a darkened theater and permitting me to touch her. Needless to say, it was immensely more satisfying than having a strange man pick me up in a brightly-lighted bus or train station and wanting to touch me. At first I was hesitant to say yes. The movie on the screen suggested I could be murdered in some basement or wind up in a high-rise apartment with a dead girl. But, if I said no, I would be passing up the chance encounter I had been hankering for all day, surefire sex with an appealing female.

"Yes," I finally said, not worried about untoward consequences.

I grabbed her hand and stood up and she walked with me out of the theater. Seeing her now in the light confirmed my initial impression of her face and figure. She started walking down the alley separating the theater and the restaurant, holding my hand and pulling me like a caboose. Almost at the end, she squeezed in behind stacks of wooden boxes four and five high, and then put her back against the brick wall. I moved in closer to kiss her and touch those bulging boobs with both hands this time.

"Twenty Mark," she said. She reached under her skirt, yanked her panties down halfway to her knees, took my hand and placed it high between her legs.

I went to work on her with one hand, fingers getting wetter by the second, while the other hand reached for the wallet in my back pocket. I did not know whether the twenty was just for a feel or for a fuck. A moment later I got my answer. She put her hand to my crotch and began to rub me up and down. With folded wallet in one hand, I unzipped with the other. She lifted her skirt and stepped out of her panties.

As I was about to pay her, whip it out, and close in under her, a door suddenly opened from the back of the restaurant. Light flashed on us. A young man in a white apron came out into the alley and dumped a pan of water on the ground not far from where we were huddled. When he saw us he stood for a second in surprise.

"Karl . . . komm her," he called back to someone inside the restaurant, smiling a bit.

"Nein, nein," the girl shrieked in total panic, looking alternately at him and then me.

She began to run, clutching her panties in one hand while pulling her dress down with the other. Her high heels made a rapid clicking sound like someone tapping drumsticks on a metal railing. I managed to zip up before anyone else came out from the restaurant, sticking the wallet in its rightful place at the same time. I went after her, but the girl was nowhere in sight. I was sorry she ran away but glad she ran with something in her hand other than my twenty.

I never saw her again. That made twice in one day that I kissed off a German. And that made twice in one day that I did not get walled off love.

Later I sauntered into the Flying Dutchman and found Elsa. She was sitting alone at a table against the far wall, not her usual spot.

"Let's get out of here," I said in a commanding tone. I extended my hand to her.

"Why you not sit down? What wrong, Schatzie?"

"I don't like where you are sitting," I noted with a cold face, but warm to the idea that she thought of me as her boyfriend after only two times together.

Elsa looked at me in complete bewilderment. Nevertheless, she got up from the table and took my hand. We went straight to her place, no stops along the way for pissing on the back street rubble, by her or me. She was bewildered again when I pulled her single bed out from the wall a little before we did anything.

I left about eleven to be sure to return to the barracks prior to midnight. Before I went out the door, I put a twenty-Mark bill on top of her bureau when she was not looking. I knew I did not have to do that, but I wanted to. The Fräulein who fit me in for free still has to buy food and pay rent. The way I saw it, I was simply handing over the fair value for something I wanted and got, when I almost gave the girl in the alley that amount of money for something I wanted but did not get.

Plain and skinny Elsa, my Sunday ace-in-the-hole, in comparison to the aging house-hookers I passed up in the walled off area of Nuremberg, was okay for the day, or rather right for the night.

# CHAPTER 28: OFF THE BENCH

Doss called out to me soon after we came back from chow that afternoon. He was on the telephone and had his hand over the mouthpiece. I put down my soldering iron, hopped off my seat at the bench, and went up to the Sergeant-in-charge at his desk in the corner of the shop. He was just hanging up the telephone.

It was Friday, the first of May. Passover had ended the day before. For the ancient Hebrews in Egypt, enslaved for six hundred years, that was the day they were set free. The celebration of the Jewish holiday in 1959 was a first for me in two respects. It was my first Seder away from home and the first time I attended a communal Seder.

For Erev Pesach, I went to the Seder held at the Palace of Justice. Many of the Jews from the Nuremberg community, German and American, military and civilian, were there along with some non-Jewish guests. Laid out on long tables in the reception room were plates with matzo, the water and egg kind, and little dishes with bitter herbs, parsley, salt water for dipping, gefilte fish, chopped liver, red and white horse radish, roasted eggs, and charoset, a sweet, brown mixture of nuts and fruit.

Rabbi Washer wore the traditional white robe and sat at the head of the table. He recited the service from a large Haggadah, occasionally pointing to and explaining the various sweet and bitter foods to be eaten, symbolic of the twin Passover themes of slavery and freedom. Seder participants were obligated to drink four cups of wine representing the four biblical expressions of deliverance promised by God in Exodus 6:6-7. We all had little Haggadahs and took turns reading passages and asking the Four Questions in both Hebrew and English.

For the second night of Passover, I and Stanley Grossman, the two Jewish boys at Merrell Barracks, were invited to the Silvers' home on Regensburger Strasse, the insurance salesman and his wife from New Jersey. I brought Mr. Silver two cartons of cigarettes from the PX purchased with my ration card. I did not want him to pay me for them but he insisted. The Silvers' twelve-year-old son asked the Four Questions, the daughter sat quietly, and the rest of us in turn read different parts of the service from Haggadahs brought from the

States. I got to play the wise son, Stanley the wicked, the son not deserving to be freed from Egyptian slavery.

That Friday I had been in Nuremberg exactly eight weeks. I spent the time sitting on a stool at a bench every workday for eight hours, testing and repairing various electrical components and disassembled units. Working in the shop was a sort of bondage for me. I labored at something close to my MOS, but not at anything remotely related to what I planned to do when I got out of the Army. Simply put, my job at the 176th Signal Company was extremely boring to me. This was all that I had to look forward to for the next fourteen months. It was better than doing the shitty details at Fort Ord, but I had little interest in passing my time this way.

My teammates all ate this stuff up. They liked to fix the different pieces and learn the intricacies of new equipment. Before long I knew I would be sent out in the field with our attachment company and I dreaded that. I did not want the responsibility of getting Army communication equipment back in working order at critical times on maneuvers. The only consolation for sitting at the bench doing robotic tasks was that it left my mind free. Dull shop work allowed me time to ponder about college.

Doss was sitting down and I standing when he broke the news to me that would change my Army life again. "Sergeant Bentley wants to talk to you," he said.

"Right now?"

"Yes. Go to the Area Office."

"What about?" I asked, without adding 'Sarge'.

Doss was not persnickety about his troops calling him sergeant every time they spoke to him. The spec five in the shop just called him by his last name and the spec fours did that at times, like superiors addressed a subordinate, and he did not seem to mind. The PFCs generally gave deference to his rank, but I avoided it if I could.

"He wants you to come work for him."

"What do you mean? Doing what?" I inquired.

"They need a clerk in the Area Office."

"A clerk? My MOS is radar repair."

"Sergeant Bentley knows that. Mr. Barry too." Doss was always formal about higher ranks.

"Then why do they want me?" I asked, still in the dark.

"They want somebody. Boblingen won't send us someone with a clerk's MOS."

I thought before I spoke again. Doss looked at me. He saw I was confused about this job offer. "Are you sure they want *me* to be the clerk?"

"Streiber, I recommended you. You'll like it over there."

"Okay. I'll go talk to Sergeant Bentley."

What else could I say? I grabbed my field jacket and cap and left the shop. It was a short walk to the Area Office. I had a minute or two to think.

It was not difficult to fathom why Doss recommended me. I was the slowest repairman in the shop, and arguably the least competent. And I was sure my lack of enthusiasm for handling all things electrical and electronic was a signal that emanated from my core. Clearly this was an interesting turn of events, an opportunity for me to get off the bench. Out of the blue a new job, unlike anything I had done previously in the Army, was about to fall in my lap.

Doss was right to recommend me for the clerk's job. He said nothing about the poor repair skills I displayed in his shop. From what I could tell thus far, the team leader was not the son-of-a-bitch kind of sergeant. He did not say insulting things to subordinates or hurt their feelings. I appreciated that kind of courtesy from a superior, rare in the military. Doss had been watching me. I knew it. He saw it took me longer than the other guys to fix the small components. With the large or complicated units, it was obvious I was less knowledgeable and less motivated to learn more about them. I was not crazy about repairing things electrical and he, and others on benches next to or near me, knew it.

My team leader did not, I was sure, recommend me just to get rid of me for causing trouble with another soldier in his shop, as the Chaplain did aboard the *Rose*.

Still I wondered if I should take the clerk's job. I would forgo any chance of gaining more experience in electronics, ostensibly what I joined the Army for, something that might prove useful in the future even though I had no plans to take electrical engineering in college. It meant I would be working closely with two people I knew nothing about, always under their noses for them to discern my work capabilities and character traits.

But taking the job would also put me in a position to learn and master clerical and administrative skills heretofore unknown to me, proficiencies probably useful to a college boy. One fact was certain. A move from bench to desk represented a leap across a cultural divide in any country, in military and civilian affairs, a change from toiling with one's hands to laboring with one's head, an improvement in social status, a ticket to the middle-class.

The two Bs were sitting at their desks when I came in. Immediately I noticed something was different in the Area Office. A third desk had been placed in front of Bentley's, with a swivel chair in between. What little space there was in this makeshift office now was even more cramped. The two bosses evidently had decided on nabbing a clerk to assist them, whether I took the job or not.

Bentley got up from his desk and smiled. In his starched fatigues and spit-shined boots, he was quite the opposite in appearance from rumpled Doss in the shop. "Strahber . . . glad to see you." The six-striper extended his hand to me.

"Thank you, sergeant," I said, shaking his tender hand.

Barry came over. "That goes for me too."

I saluted the warrant officer as if I was reporting to him. "Thank you, sir."

They're soft-soaping me, I thought. They must want or need an assistant real bad.

"Sit down, Strahber, we want to talk to you," Bentley said in a low voice. He pointed to the chair in front of him.

I did as I was told. Bentley slid into his chair. Barry pulled his swivel chair forward to be closer to us. The two Bs acted like troops advancing for a frontal assault.

Bentley spoke first, leaning toward me. "Strahber . . . we were impressed with the way you conducted yourself with Merling last month. He owed you money and wouldn't pay. But you didn't get into a fistfight with him. You came to me to settle the matter."

"You had a personnel problem and you dealt with it through proper channels," Barry added. "We like soldiers who follow regulations and go to higher authority."

"Thank you," I said again, this time to both simultaneously.

"We'd like you to work for us," Bentley said. "We need a clerk in the office here."

"We can't officially reassign you since you don't have a clerk's MOS," Barry explained, "but there's nothing in Army regulations that says a radar man can't do clerical work."

"I've never done clerical work before," I revealed to my higher-ups.

I was perfectly honest with them and did not want to seem too eager. It was better to let them sell me on the idea of a military occupational metamorphosis, even though I had already decided the pros outweighed the cons for the new job.

"There's nothin' to it," Bentley assured me. "You graduated from high school. You can read and write."

"But what would I do here?" I wanted to know, more out of curiosity than for information requisite to making a decision.

The sergeant stood up. He moved toward the small chart hanging on the side wall and placed his hand against it. There was crude writing on the chart, words and numbers written with a black marker, and some vertical lines.

"We want you to make more charts . . . and larger ones. Charts giving graphic information on equipment coming in to the teams we oversee, what needs to be repaired, and how fast we get the pieces back to the companies we service."

"Sort of a timetable and specification of work accomplished by each team," Barry noted.

Such an artistic and numerical endeavor actually appealed to me. In high school, I took an art class and did well in mathematics and liked both subjects.

"That looks interesting," I commented without expressing any emotion.

"You would also type letters and reports, answer the phone when we're not here, and do miscellaneous office work," Barry added. "You can type, can't you?"

"Yes sir. I had typing in junior high. And I did it at home too. My parents bought me a typewriter for my fifteenth birthday." I did not say my hitting of alphabet keys was almost as slow as my repairing of electrical equipment.

Bentley pointed to the file cabinet in the corner. "We'll need to redo our whole filing system."

"That's sounds okay too," I said.

I was sure they thought I would take the job just offered me, but I had not yet verbalized an acceptance.

"You won't have to go out in the field," Bentley told me in an apparent attempt to tempt me.

"And you'll have evenings and weekends off," Barry said to sweeten the deal, with delight it seemed. "Men in the shop sometimes have to work late or on Saturday if equipment has to be repaired in an emergency."

I finally uttered with a little smile what the dynamic duo wanted to hear. "Okay. I'll be glad to be your clerk."

I was also glad neither of them mentioned anything about my questionable electronic repair skills. From now on, I'll be Mr. Chart-It and Mr. File-It, not Mr. Fix-It.

Bentley displayed his pleasure as well as his authority. "Good. Report here Monday morning. Tell Doss I told you to take the rest of the afternoon off."

"Thank you, sergeant," I said as I got up to leave. We shook hands again.

"Oh . . . by the way," Barry threw out. "We put you and Goldbaum in for promotion. You'll get the official notice in a week or two. Go to the PX and buy your spec four patches so you can have them ready."

"Thank you sir." It was nice to know I would be getting my bird. Steve and I both lost time because of the transfer from Fort Ord. It was a good thing I was told about it *after* I accepted the job offer. I would not want my new bosses to think I could be bribed.

I left the Area Office thinking turning points in my life occur right after a holiday, either Christian or Jewish. Two days after Christmas, I learned I will have a new life. My transfer was a miracle and I was reborn. The day after Passover ended, my exodus from the shop began. I would be a slave no more to the 2nd Cavalry's equipment breakdowns. That phase in my life I passed over.

I would have to wait until next Easter, however, to find out that I had another cross to bear in the Army.

258

# CHAPTER 29: I AM A CAMERA

The German man I hardly knew kept looking over to me. I was standing a few feet away from him, back from several other soldiers, listening keenly to his every word. He would move his head to glance in my direction for a few seconds and then turn again to continue what he was doing. The man held a Leica M-3 in his hands, one of the most expensive cameras manufactured in his country. He was twisting it up and down in one motion and explaining its automatic parallax compensation and flash synchronization to the Americans surrounding him. By the third look my way, it was apparent the German had something more than taking pictures on his mind. I had only seen him a few times before on similar occasions, in a crowd of G.I.s eager to learn from him. We had not exchanged many words.

We were in the photography lab at Merrell Barracks. It was Thursday, the twenty-eighth of May. The lab was part of the Special Services branch of the Army, located on the second floor of Building 551's West Wing. No one on post would miss it as it was just around the corner from the main entrance. I passed Special Services every day on my way to work at the shop or the Area Office and again on returning to my room. The facilities for soldiers consisted of a large reading and recreation room with magazines and newspapers on metal racks and a pool table in the center, a classroom for lectures and meetings, a woodworking area, and a separate space with various pieces of photographic equipment.

The German was in charge of the lab. He advised Americans on which cameras to buy or what kind of lens or filter or film to use and assisted them in developing their black-and-white prints. From what I could see, there were no provisions for color pictures or slides. Like many of the other indigenous personnel employed by the military, he earned about one hundred Marks, less than twenty-five dollars, a week. But that was more than he could possibly have garnered toiling in the local economy without resorting to any black market activities. He was far better off than the Putzfrauen who scrubbed floors at the Kaserne and his Kameraden who did the KP, maintenance, and sundry menial tasks.

The German was about seven or eight years my senior, somewhat taller, much thinner, and had sandy brown hair styled in a crew cut that resembled the tops of most of my American peers. He always wore a solid colored or patterned bow tie with a white shirt and kept his sleeves rolled up above his elbows like a tool-and-die maker while he was working in the lab. He was soft spoken and exhibited mildness of temper, behaviors not characteristic of a Landsmann his age twenty years earlier who wore a swastika armband or Nazi uniform.

The German was not old enough to have commanded pride in the Gross Deutschland that Hitler carved out by his expropriations of foreign territories. If there was any inordinate esteem on his part for the divided and dwarfed Germany he now inhabited, I did not detect it. I took his personality attributes as a sign of insecurity or subservience typical of German men of his generation, those whose teen years coincided with the turmoil and deprivation of the immediate postwar period. He was dependent upon his former enemies for his meager livelihood and he knew it.

I only saw this Special Services Mann when I entered his domain on my off-duty hours. Even before I bought a camera, I frequented the lab. I enjoyed listening to him talk to soldiers about single and twin lens reflex models, focal plane shutters, f/stops, and zoom actions. With growing interest I observed his hands-on approach to teaching the basics of photography.

Interestingly, the German often referred to G.I.s not by their name or their rank or their outfit but by the make and model of camera they showed up with at his bailiwick seeking help. Many troopers came to the lab after work as I did, after they changed into their civilian clothes, minus any outward identifying personal or status lineaments other than race. The German either saw no nametags, stripes, or unit patches or remained oblivious to those he did see. To him one American was the Voigtlander Bessamatic, another the Exakta VX, a third the Fujica ML. I was the Retina IIIC.

I had purchased my German-made Kodak camera for $92.50 at Merrell's PX, one of the most expensive sold there, almost a month's pay for me. The brown leather case with adjustable strap was included at no extra charge. Since the list price was $175 without the case, I felt it was a bargain. Many G.I.s picked up far cheaper cameras, with no special or advanced features, but I wanted a model that had everything I most likely would ever need, one I could upgrade later on.

My Retina was the top of the Kodak line. It had a viewfinder and rangefinder combined, built-in light meter, the capacity for inter-changeable wide-angle and telephoto lenses, an f/stop of 2, a shutter speed of 1/500th of a second, and a rapid film advance. It was a relatively small camera, good for traveling and shooting fast. The most distinguishing feature was its compactness. The glass lens, mounted on a base and sliding track, folded in and opened out on a rounded quarter hinge attached to a protective door. I grew very fond on my Retina soon after I placed it on the shelf in my wall locker, before I even started rolling any film. The future photog-rapher looked at his prized possession every day and tinkered with its movable parts.

La caméra, c'est moi, I said to myself, recalling my three years of high school French and adapting a phrase from Louis XIV.

When I landed in Germany my mind was already set on taking up Fotografie as a hobby. My father was the one in the family who owned a decent camera, an old Kodak with bellows and foldout lens that yielded negatives the same size as prints. He was the one my grandparents, aunts, and uncles always called upon to snap pictures of themselves on holidays and their children at birthday parties, Bar Mitzvahs, and weddings. My overseas tour afforded me the opportu-nity to carry on this tradition.

I fancied myself as a shadowy soldier shutterbug, a snooper troop-er traipsing around the capitol cities of Europe clicking away at every historical landmark, tourist attraction, and point of interest that came his way. And I was not alone in this pursuit. Practically every G.I. in my barracks had some sort of black box dangling from his neck, many with lenses of varying lengths protruding from it, when he went on leave or into town on weekends. My company buddies often talked about what new lens or flashgun or filter they bought or hoped to purchase. I was bent on producing *David's Travels*, a celluloid storyboard of Old World scenes to show the folks back home.

The German recommended I pick up a 35 mm automatic. "It is small . . . easy to carry around," he said. "Fits in your pocket."

He also told me it was good for shooting subjects still or in motion, and up to thirty-six times without reloading. Just point and click, point and click.

The PX had an entire section devoted to photographic merchandise. The wide variety of cheap to expensive German, American, and Japanese cameras displayed on wooden shelves against a corner wall and in glass cases in front was confusing to me. I had no idea of which one to buy. There was an array of attachments and accessories as well. Every size and shape lens could be found, some bigger than the cameras themselves. I saw tripods big and little, light meters of different intensities and shapes, lens-cleaning brushes and paper, cable releases, camera straps, lens covers and shades. Stacks of black-and-white or color foreign and domestic slow- to fast-speed film were lined up in neat cubbyholes. Leather and cloth carrying bags, to store and tote the photo-novelties one accumulated, were hanging from hooks. Every time I visited the PX, I found myself in the corner section perusing the full complement of wares. I usually stopped off there right after work and before chow, still dressed in my fatigues and field jacket, eager to put my hands on and learn more about cameras and kindred things.

I was on the lookout for a nice German box. I had heard they were built better, especially on the inside, and easier to cock. One day my quest for the procurement of an appealing Kamera reached a climax.

"May I help you?" I heard a woman say in a German accent. She caught me bent over her middle display case, looking at the equipment she just spread out.

I stood up and faced the salesclerk. Suddenly I felt warm with my field jacket on inside the building. I pushed my zipper all the way down and removed my fatigue cap. The Fräulein was somewhat stocky and not very attractive, in her late twenties I would guess, with short stringy hair and no makeup to speak of. There was a masculine quality about her that did not endear her to the opposite sex. Her voice was deep for a woman. The breasts seemed strapped down, not much of a bulge in her chest. The sallow skin tone would not have brought her an edge in any beauty contest.

"I don't know which camera to buy," I answered.

"What you want?" she asked, stepping forward a little.

"I was advised to get a thirty-five millimeter."

"Reflex oder automatic?" she said, rolling her *r* like Germans do and awkwardly ususing *oder* for *or* in English. .

"Automatic."

The young woman turned around and snatched a camera off the shelf, then leaned forward on the counter, luring me to move in closer to her. She looked straight at me, held the camera in one hand, and reached out with the other. First she brushed back a lock of my hair, a premature gesture of friendliness I thought. Then she lowered her hand to push back my open jacket to better read my name tag.

"Your name is German, yes?"

I nodded.

"You speak German?"

"A little. Wieviel kostet es?" I said, trying to impress her. My mother used to say that all the time in neighborhood stores run by elderly Jews.

"Only twenty dollars," she replied. I got the impression it was against the rules for her to speak German to the Americans in the store. "It is one of the cheapest."

"Is it a good camera?"

"No. It has not a light meter, you can not change the lens, the shutter speed is not fast, and the aperture does not go down small enough."

"Aperture?" I asked, pronouncing it the same way she did. I had never heard that word before.

"The opening in the lens. Here, I show you," she said, picking up a Retina IIIC.

I watched her as she unlatched the little door, unscrewed the lens, set the stop to the number 2, moved the shutter speed dial to the B setting, snapped the shutter and held her finger there, and lifted the camera so I could see the stationary circular shutter blades.

"This opening the biggest." She moved one foot away from the other as she spoke. Then she set the stop to 22, repeated the steps, and placed her feet together again. "This smallest."

"Yes . . . I see what you mean. Is aperture size important?"

"A camera that is good, it has a small opening," she said with a little smile, still eager to keep my attention. "You want a f between sixteen und twenty-two."

"What does an f do?" I wanted to know.

It occurred to me that a good camera was analogous to a good woman. And I certainly wanted a good f.

"You get depth more."

"Depth?"

"In the picture. The back is clear like the front."

The unattractive salesclerk went on explaining about cameras and picture-taking in terms of lens openings and image penetrations, long and short time-exposures, black and white framing, thick and thin adapter rings, quality and cost. She stood between an array of shutter boxes that ranged from under fifteen dollars for a basic American-made job with no special features to more than one hundred fifteen dollars for one of Germany's Zeiss-Ikon Contraflex models that could accommodate almost any attachment.

The lady behind the PX counter let me play with her Graflex Century 35 and Cannon P. Each time she deliberately touched me by placing her hands around mine, ostensibly to show me how to insert accessories into the box. I was sure she wanted to place more than her hands on me but I gave no signal as to my receptivity to any off-post encounter. However, I made no effort to pull away from her either. I needed her assistance in a matter of importance to me. After trying out her Retina IB and IIA, I was eventually sold on the IIIC because of its superior features.

Although I was sure this female Kaserne worker, with knowledge of light and color, could tell black from white, unlike her country-woman in the snack bar, I did not try to connect with her. She was not my physical type, and too old for my taste. There was no doubt in my mind that I would not be the last G.I. the tomboyish touchy-feely Fräulein in the PX might entice into her fold.

The German in the photography lab concluded his demonstration with the Leica and moved away from the others. Suddenly the man I hardly knew turned and looked at me again. He came up to me and without a word nonchalantly put his hand above my elbow, then moved me gently around to the side and away from earshot of the others. He acted as though we were longtime friends and he wanted a private moment with me. I did not know what to make of this but I trusted it would not be déjà vu, the start of the events that occurred at the Port Authority Bus Terminal and Nuremberg train station.

"Would you come with me on Sunday to meet the sister of my girlfriend?" I was asked straight out. His English pronunciation was very good.

I did not answer right away. Why he was asking me to join him on this proposed deutsche-amerikanische double date, I had no clue. But I was relieved he was not asking me to come home or couple with *him*.

"You are not like the other Americans I see here," he said before I could respond.

I took this as a compliment although he did not say, and I did not ask, why he thought I was different from the hundreds of G.I.s he must have come into contact with during the course of his employment. He may have noticed that I did not smoke or act in a rowdy manner or pepper my conversations with sexual or scatological references. He could have been partial toward me because I did not make jokes about Germans or talk about Germany losing the war or address him as comrade. Perhaps too he assumed, from the one time he saw me in fatigues, that I was of German background.

"Yes, I'll go with you," I told him and said nothing more.

I did not ask what his girlfriend's sister looked like or how old she was. And I did not ask about the German family whose Heim a Jewish boy would soon be entering. I was willing to set out on this solicited safari, disposed to just accompany him without any foreknowledge of where he was taking me or what or whom I might be getting myself into. My mother's admonitions about not getting involved with the German people were brushed aside. This could be my chance, I reasoned, to meet a local female as yet untouched by G.I. hands.

"Good. Can you meet me near the Hauptbahnhof on Sunday at twelve hundred hours . . . where the Strassenbahn stops?"

"Yes," I said again, and then confirmed the time, date, and place.

It was a good thing the German did not suggest we meet the day before, on Saturday the thirtieth of the month, our Memorial Day. That military holiday would not be too auspicious for German-American fraternization.

The German had no way of knowing that I very much welcomed the opportunity he presented to me, to have a date, ostensibly, with a nice German girl. This coming Sunday, Elsa would have to go home with some other G.I. or German, whether she fancied him or not.

Later in the day I decided that on Sunday my camera would remain on my closet shelf. The German would have to get to know me by name.

# PART III


# A FOREIGN AFFAIR

# CHAPTER 30: TWO STREETCARS AND A BUS

On Sunday morning Steve asked me where I was going all dolled up. He saw I shaved and showered, splashed on a little cologne, spit-shined my shoes, and slipped my head through a favorite crew neck sweater.

"I have a blind date," I told him, not trying to make too much of it.

My roommate was surprised as well as curious and wanted to know who was fixing me up. I recounted the incident three days earlier with the German in Special Services and his spiel about the girlfriend and the sister. Steve said he met the Kraut once but was not impressed with his capabilities in anything other than photography. My older and wiser Army buddy who had been to college read more than I did into the seemingly innocuous social situation. He voiced concerns in his usual blunt manner, questioning the sagacity of my heading off on a tail trail with some cornball comrade I just met who probably didn't know beans from Bratwürst when it came to women or Americans.

Why would a Kaserne klutz collar a G.I. Jew to jack his Schatzie's Schwester? Steve wanted to know. My friend from posts past was not optimistic about a favorable future for my impending foray into interfaith fraternization.

"I don't know why the German picked me," I said, shrugging my shoulders. "He seemed to like me. He told me I was not like other Americans."

"You *are* not like other Americans."

"But I look like other Americans," I retorted.

"That may be. But either there's something wrong with the Kraut or there's something wrong with the sister," Steve reasoned.

"I hope it is *you* who are wrong . . . at least on the second thing."

"Does the Kraut know you're Jewish?"

"I don't think so."

"Well, don't expect the welcome mat by the door when they find out."

"I'm not worried," I shot back defensively. "I don't usually give out too much information about myself. People can think what they want."

"First you've got to get through the door as an American," Steve advised me. "That won't be easy. But, at least you're white. Then you have to keep from being kicked out when they learn who you are? The Germans still don't like the Jews."

Was Steve being overly pessimistic about the current character of postwar German people? I wondered. Or was I being overly naïve?

"What should I do, wear a cross around my neck?"

"No. But you better not tell them you're Jewish, even if they ask," I was warned.

"I wouldn't lie about a thing like that."

"Well," Steve said, in a last bit of advice as I was leaving our room. "Then I wouldn't count on any cunt."

To get to where I was going that Sunday, I had to take two street-cars and a bus.

What Steve said ran through my mind riding Strassenbahn Nr. 8 the four stops from Merrell Barracks to the Hauptbahnhof. He was acting just like my mother, warning me about getting involved with a German family. It is one thing to be shtupping a Fräulein who lives alone or who is cut off from her parents or relatives and has been involved with Americans before. That was Steve's story and by all accounts he was doing well. It is quite another to be welcomed into a German home and to be breaking Brot and eating apfel Streudel with Mutti, Papi, Grossmutti, Bruder Bruno, Tante Tania, and Onkel Oskar.

The German was waiting for me when I arrived at the Haupt-bahnhof stop at five past twelve. He reached out to shake my hand and did so in the typical German manner, once up and down with a weak grasp, not the American way of several movements in a firm hold. He wore what looked like a new raincoat—dark brown, dou-ble-breasted, and belted—over a suit and tie and a hat with a wide brim. I was dressed more casually in a beige single-breasted rain-coat over a sweater and slacks. No one could mistake our national-ities from our clothing.

We caught the Nummer 21. It was on a different track at the Hauptbahnhof stop but started to go in the same direction as I had been heading from the Kaserne, north along Königstrasse. We soon turned onto Fürtherstrasse. The German said we would stay with this tram, as he called it, for less than half an hour, all the way to the city of Fürth, the end of the line. We sat down toward the rear of the trolley's third car, in a curved seat for two, with me at the window.

The German did most of the talking. First he wanted to know what certain words meant. He pulled a folded piece of paper from his coat pocket containing a list of words he had come across but could not translate exactly into deutsch.

"What does 'mere' mean?" he asked me kindly, and then spelled it out. "I always want to improve my English."

"It means 'nothing but' or 'something little'," I responded right away. He looked at me as if he did not understand. "It's an adjective . . . used to describe a noun." He still looked puzzled. "For example, if you say, 'The man traveled a mere two miles to work,' it means two miles is a small distance. Some people may have to travel twenty miles to get to work."

"Ach so," the German said in his own language, nodding his head.

He had four more words he needed clarification with and I answered all of his questions. He scribbled some notes on his paper. For a change, I was teaching *him* something. I was beginning to think he invited me just so I could play Noah Webster for him.

The German did not ask me anything about myself. This very much surprised me. I assumed he would be curious about who *I* am, other than a camera model, or where I grew up in the States or what schools I attended or where my parents or grandparents were born. Had he known more about me, he might not have asked me to join him on a social occasion to meet a German family. Had he known more about my attitudes toward local women, he might not have asked me to meet his girlfriend or her sister.

"We lived here in the Old City," he said, pointing to the right and twisting his hand to indicate the area north of the street we were on.

My soon-to-be dating companion began talking about his life and the hardships he and his family endured during and after the war, just as Elsa had done that first night. It must be some sort of ritual with young Germans of that generation when they meet Americans, meant to evoke sympathy or understanding perhaps. We passed the Palace of Justice on our right. I thought he would mention something about Nazi crimes and Jewish suffering but he passed on those subjects. He said he was born in 1933.

"That was the year Hitler came to power," I commented, remembering my high-school history. "He was appointed Chancellor, even with his Nazi Party getting less than half the votes."

"Yes."

"Germany changed that year."

"Yes." For a second time, the word passed his lips weakly and unemotionally.

"But not for the better," I added, taking the risk of stirring up something.

"We Germans do not like to talk about that now." A trace of emotion showed.

I did not have to ask him why he said that. After some pause, he continued on his own. His answers were predictable. The German said he did not believe all those horrible things with the concentration camps and the Jews really happened, but even if some horrible things did happen he did not know of them. He claimed ordinary Germans were not allowed in the concentration camps and never went to the occupied countries where the fighting was. He never saw any Jews being killed. He only knows about the bombs dropped on Nuremberg and all the houses on fire.

I looked at the German sitting beside me. He was too young to have fought in the war. He obviously had nothing to do with his countrymen's crimes against the Jews or any other group. But he was not too young at war's end to have witnessed or seen pictures of or heard about the mounds of civilian corpses, the human skeletons trudging out of the camps, the War Crimes Trials going on just blocks from his home, or the Nazi perpetrators in the prisoners' gallery of Room 600. For someone who works with cameras and photographs, he should appreciate as indisputable evidence the pictures taken by his own Germans during the war, and pictures taken by Americans when they liberated the concentration camps.

Here it was at last. What narrators said in documentaries, what I read in books, what other G.I.s have been telling me. *The plea of ignorance.* Germans never saw their Jewish neighbors taken from their homes at the point of a rifle and forced onto waiting trucks. Children didn't notice their Jewish classmates' empty seats one day. College students thought nothing of their Jewish professors not showing up to class and being replaced by a non-Jew. City dwellers paid no attention to the sudden closing of the Jewish-owned shops they frequented. *The denial of individual responsibility.* Even if ordinary Germans saw strange and unusual things happen to their judische friends, neighbors, classmates, and shopkeepers, what could they do about it? It's not my fault, everyone said, the Nazis did it. *The lack of collective guilt.* We Germans did nothing wrong. We are not guilty of any crime. It was all Hitler's doing. *The claim of being a victim oneself.* The world should forget the Nazi atrocities against other nations and the Jews. What was done to the German people is what the world now should be talking about. The Allies should apologize to us for destroying our cities? Reparations should be given to every German citizen.

"My father was not a member of the Nazi Party," he continued, looking away from me, "but he admired those who were."

His answer puzzled me. "Why was that?"

"Because my father believed Hitler was good for Germany, and therefore good for the rest of the world. I remember as a boy hearing my parents talk about such things."

At that point I cooled it. I did not want to say something about Nazis or his country or the war that would so upset him he would storm away from the soldier eagerly awaiting an introduction to a German girl as yet untouched by American hands. As this streetcar scene unfolded, I did not have to say much more. He kept talking about his early life without any further provocation.

The postwar German worker said his father was a worker, a porter in the Hotel Deutscher Hof on Lutherstrasse near the Hauptbahnhof.

"Hitler stayed there for the annual Parteitag rallies. He had his own special room on the second floor with a balcony that looked over the street."

I imagined the Führer standing on his balcony reviewing the marching columns below. Storm troopers in brown shirts, Waffen SS in black shirts, Wehrmacht soldiers in gray uniforms, and teenage boys in short pants, many banging drums, all hoofing in lockstep un-der his nose. The German told me the marchers moved shoulder-to-shoulder along the narrow streets and over the bridge to the city square, named Adolph Hitler Platz from 1933-1945.

Every year in September the father caught a glimpse of the mustached leader of the German people strutting through the hotel lobby surrounded by an entourage of providers and protectors. The father believed Hitler broke down hoary Prussian class barriers, made life much better and more honorable for the working man. The man who lugged luggage for loaded guests thought his son, like the sons of doctors and lawyers, could go to the university and become a doctor or lawyer too.

"My father took me to the nineteen-thirty-eight rally," my Strassenbahn seatmate, who was not quite six then, remembered. His Papi was given the day off, to attend festivities on the Day of the Labor Service, Wednesday the seventh of September. The boy recalled the cold stone grandstand they sat on, the great crowds of people, the soldiers in columns and rows, the loud voices over the speakers, the shouting and saluting, and his father bringing him to the Toilette in one of the short columns around the periphery of Zeppelinfeld.

My first German friend and his porter Papi attended what turned out to be the last Nazi rally. They witnessed the prelude to the greatest war in history. It was named the Party Day of Greater Germany, meant to celebrate German expansionism. Six months earlier German troops booted across the Austrian border and heeled toward Vienna. The ensuing Anschluss was a complete takeover of Austria via military threats and forced plebiscites. Not a shot was fired. Thus was born Gross Deutschland. The German-speaking people annexed to the Fatherland lined the streets waving swastika flags and smiling at their goose-stepping neighbors to the west. Austria, unfortunately, was not the last slice of European territory outside of Germany that Hitler cut for himself.

The '38 rally proved to have greater importance for Germany and the world than the ones preceding it. Radio coverage was expanded to include a nightly two-hour program highlighting the political, cultural, and sports events. For the first time.an American ambassador attended an annual Reichsparteitage. International press coverage was the widest yet. Nuremberg's mayor presented Hitler with a replica of the Austrian crown jewels. Feldmarschall Göring on Saturday, the Day of the Hitler Youth, warned democratic nations not to interfere with German policy toward Czechoslovakia. Hitler held a reception for the press and spoke of the new projects the Party was building for the rallies, a new city not in the medieval style and separate from the old Nuremberg.

On the last day of the Party congress, the twelfth of September, the Day of the Army, Hitler, in his closing speech, demanded an end to the oppression of the three and a half million ethnic Germans in Czechoslovakia. The Sudetenland would be claimed by Germany, he shouted into the set of microphones. Weeks later, troops were ordered into the Sudetenland, Hitler threatened war if Czechoslovakia was not partitioned, England and France gave in to the German leader's bluster at the conference table in Munich, and the territory was ceded to Germany. The little boy, his baggage-toting father, and the world saw Gross Deutschland get even grösser.

We reached the end of the streetcar line in Fürth, got off, and walked a few yards to catch Autobus Nr. 70. There was a bus parked at the curb. I boarded first and we sat down together in a middle seat. Ten minutes later we took off. The ride to Zirndorf lasted almost twenty minutes. I looked out the window for most of that time.

The German I hardly knew talked about the Klotz family I would soon meet. "The father was dead," he said finally, "killed during the war."

I wondered if *his* father survived the war, and if so if the poor man is still heaving his hump at the Hof. One thing was certain whether he was alive or dead. In the Germany after Hitler, the porter's dream of his son going to the university was dead. It was comforting to know that my dream of going to college in the States was alive and well.

The German said his girlfriend's name is Karin and talked about her lovingly. She and her older sister lived with their mother in a four-room flat. They received a small pension from the government. The three women had to make due with the meager Marks doled out to them.

We arrived in Zirndorf a little past one. The German said we could have arrived earlier had we taken the train from Nuremberg. To him, the ninety Pfennig saving was worth the additional thirty Minuten ground transportation time. The bus dropped us a block and a half from Karin's door.

## CHAPTER 31: A KISS BEFORE CRYING

Karin's house was across the street and a block up from the Bahnhof, on Gartenstrasse, just down from Bahnhofstrasse. The train station was a tiny one-story red brick building, nothing like the main terminal in Nuremberg with its three sections, high ceilings, grand archways, pedestrian mall, and shops and stores. Zirndorf was a small manufacturing town and like Nuremberg, its urban hub, had no significant war-related industries. But it too was bombed like any other German city. The stone row house had miraculously escaped damage during the war despite its proximity to railway lines that fed into and out of a major terminus. Some buildings, on side streets a block or two away, still bore the scars of the Allies' air campaigns, nothing but a pile of rubble or fragments of outer brick walls.

The four of us returned to Karin's house just before five thirty. It was beginning to get dark. We had spent the afternoon walking around town and sitting on park benches on the periphery of what my new friends called Zirndorf Woods in English. Karin's sister went into the kitchen to be with the mother. I could see that the German who invited me out that day to meet his girlfriend's sister was mad. He and Karin were standing in the foyer talking in German, I was off to the side.

The tall man's head was lowered, his face pale and drawn, the eyes reflecting sadness within. I said nothing to him or to Karin. I did not know exactly what she was saying to him, but I knew he would not take it too kindly in any language.

I slipped away quietly to go to the bathroom near the kitchen. It was plain to me that my presence in the foyer was unnecessary for Karin and unwanted by my dating companion. I caught a glimpse of the two women sitting at the table. The sister was cutting bread, the mother reading a newspaper. When I returned, Karin was just closing the front door. The German who initiated this Sunday foursome had left without saying auf Wiedersehen to me. I did not get a chance to say dankeschön to the man who introduced me to a nice German girl. I never saw or spoke to him again.

Karin turned toward me and extended a hand. "Come," she beckoned. With her other hand, she opened the door to the sitting room off the foyer on the right as you walk in the apartment. Like a good soldier, I obeyed the one-word command. I took her hand and followed her in. I did not know then that in the months ahead I would come often in that sitting room.

Four hours earlier, I walked in the door to Karin's place. She lived in an apartment on the first floor, a few steps up from the street level, of a three-story building. When the German and I entered, I naturally let him go in ahead of me. From this first visit to the home of a German family I did not know what to expect. The Army's lectures to soldiers upon arriving in Deutschland only dealt with warnings not to get emotionally involved with local prostitutes and Fräuleins too eager to marry G.I.s, or be hoodwinked by black marketers and spies, either German or American. No sergeant or officer ever advised us on how to act with, or what to expect from, a typical Familie in the cities and towns outside our Kasernes.

It was Karin who greeted us at the front door. The German mumbled my first name and I said hello with a nod and a faint smile after being introduced. She was not at all surprised to see me so I wondered what he had told her about me. We stood in the foyer and I got a good look at the girl the German spoke of with warmth, affection, and enthusiasm on the way over.

Karin was short, about five one, had an okay figure, and was young in appearance, my age I gathered. The white polka-dot dress she was wearing, her small breasts, and her look of innocence gave her a girlish image. She had a nice face, not real pretty but one with no detracting features either. Her long hair was the way I liked, wavy and parted off center, but it was dark brown, not the light blond color I was most charmed by. Karin was no match against the taller statuesque girl in the snack bar or stunningly sexy Marianne in the Flying Dutchman, but there was a pleasant quality about her. She was more appealing than wiry Elsa I wrapped around with every week or two. Not many guys would kick her out of bed.

"I happy to meet you," Karin said as she looked at me, very intensely I thought. "You first American I know."

Karin's English was far from perfect but it was a relief to know I could communicate with her easily. The sound and style of the speech reminded me of Anna years earlier in Brooklyn when the refugee girl started to speak my language. It was also a relief not to hear Karin enunciate with a powerful German accent and guttural tone like Mrs. Mittler, the former landlady I despised. Demure, polite, and soft-spoken, Karin was no Fräulein Hitler.

I hoped I would be able to say the same about her sister whom I had not yet met. Pinder Barracks was right smack in the middle of this little town. Lots of my uniformed peers were probably walking up-and-down her street all the time looking to get to know this young German thing and her sibling. But unless the girls frequented the local G.I. joints, and Karin at least did not look the type to do that, their social world was unlikely to include the horny boys in greens or OD's from across the Atlantic.

Karin brought us into the kitchen, a rather large room, where the mother was. It looked like she was just finishing lunch. The three of them spoke in German and I stood there like a dummy. Karen kept glancing over to me occasionally. The mother stood up to greet me, forcing a smile that evoked puzzlement more than cheerfulness. She was wearing a long-sleeved sweater despite the fact that it was not cold in the apartment. The mother was short like Karin, her hair dark too but with strands of gray and thinning with age. The woman could not have been more than 55 but looked 65 with her sallow complexion, deeply-wrinkled face, and weary eyes. The war and its aftermath no doubt took their toll on this widow with two children.

Suddenly, a door next to the bathroom opened and out walks in a creased sleeveless black dress a tall, stout, dowdy, dirty blond female who appeared to be in her late twenties. This could not be the sister, I told myself. She looked nothing like Karin or her mother.

Why would the German think I would want to milk this cow of a Fräulein? Her bulky build alone would repel almost any young man. Fat face, thick neck, broad shoulders, flabby arms, protruding belly, extra wide hips, meaty thighs—who could grab hold of those udders? The ungainly woman wobbled into the kitchen, her body mass shifting clumsily from side to side with each step. But the sister she was, as I heard the word Schwester mentioned twice when Karin and the German were talking. Perhaps he had never met the third person in this family triangle either.

My roommate was right about this deal. Steve called it. There *was* something wrong with the sister. And I was trapped with her for the day. I could not insult these people by heading for the door, even though they were all strangers to me. I would have to play this torturous scene out and hope the curtain falls before too long.

I said something to the sister out of courtesy. I assumed she spoke English too. But I was wrong a second time. My portly prize for the p.m. neither spoke nor understood one word of my language. She looked at me with a blank face until the German translated what I said. Did he not check to see if the person he wanted me to meet spoke some English? Did he expect me to communicate with my blind date through picture drawings?

A few minutes later the girls got their coats and out the door the four of us went. We walked down her hilly street, then over to Fürtherstrasse, and down a few blocks to the Marktplatz. We sat around on benches for a while and talked, I being the odd person out without much to say to the trio of Germans, two of whom spoke English.

Later they wanted a snack. There was an enclosed food wagon on wheels parked on the edge of the square, an Imbiss they called it, with a large wooden window-style board that folded down in front. Customers had to look up to the rosy-cheeked young girl inside eager to serve the German delicacies crackling on the grill. All three ordered Bratwürste, Nuremberg's famous spicy pork sausages. From the smell, I knew this was no kosher hot dog or Nathan's pure beef frankfurter. I told them I was not hungry. The girl put six pinky-sized sausages with sauerkraut and mustard on three paper plates. Bier in a bottle was also ordered.

"Ein Cola, bitte," I said to the girl behind the counter. No one needed to translate that for me. I wanted to show my new friends I could speak some German.

"Aufmachen?" she asked me, holding out the coke bottle she took from the refrigerator.

I assumed she was asking me if I wanted it opened. From Yiddish I knew machen was make, and I figured auf means off. "Ja," I answered. I would remember the new word I just learned.

With my aufmachened coke bottle I watched the three eat and drink standing up against one of the tall tables without stools near the Imbiss. They dipped the little pork sausages in the mustard before mouthing them, occasionally licking their fingers, and then scooped up the sauerkraut with the plastic forks they were given. To me the greasy and smelly Schwein sticks were indigestible. An all-beef hot dog topped with mustard, sauerkraut, and relish is what I would have gobbled down, but Zirndorf was not Coney Island. I was sure my non-Jewish friends swallowed my not-hungry excuse and attached no Naziesque meaning to my not eating pork.

With their stomachs full and my coke downed, we headed toward Zirndorf Woods, a green area three or four blocks from the Bahnhof in the direction of Nuremberg. We walked in couples on several gravel paths alongside the grassy masses, aimlessly circling around in different directions.

First the sister paired with me. I could not help noticing she had much difficulty walking. I talked to her in a mix of poor German and simple English words. She responded in all German, most of which escaped me. Then the sister walked with the German. With Karin I found I did not have to speak slowly or in Pidgin English for her to understand me. She replied in fluent English but with grammatical errors and an occasional German word. She said she had taken English in school after the war. Evidently, in the sister's elementary school days, before and during the war, the language of the British and American enemies was not a mandated part of the curriculum. Karin I understood very well. I spent more time walking with her.

"I born in Leipzig," Karin revealed. "In Osten part of Chermany." I understood her to say her birthplace was East Germany.

Karin told me her family had lived in Leipzig for generations. Before the war her father worked at the city's famous university, one of the oldest in Europe. She never said what he did there but I gathered he was not a professor or scientist. During the war the government made him a guard at the local labor camp. She did not say *slave* labor camp but I figured that is what it most likely was. I preferred to think the lack of specificity was due to her limited knowledge of English rather than an attempt to conceal a foul family past.

"My father not Nazi," Karin insisted.

She said the same thing as the German earlier in the day. Perhaps a father's lack of party membership in the 1930s is what attracts young men and women to each other in Germany in the 1950s.

"They give him job at camp."

I did not doubt her words but I did doubt that it made any difference in his line of work.

279

Leipzig's location southwest of Berlin and on a direct flight path from England to nearby Dresden insured that the Klotz family would not escape their share of suffering. Air raids destroyed Leipzig's railroad tracks and the American POWs confined at the labor camp repaired them. Karin's father could have been a kindly soul or an amoral beast in his treatment and supervision of prisoners. Toward the end, when the Russians were advancing, Karin's parents, like hundreds of thousands of other Germans, fled to the West. They were terrified at the thought of what the Red Army barbarians would do to them and their two children. Karin did not say it but I was sure the father was happy to quit the camp and had planned to tell the conquering Americans that he treated their fighting men with kindness.

The family made it to Nuremberg, thinking it was safe there. Two weeks before V-E Day, however, the former guard was killed. He went out looking for food for his family one morning and was hit by an exploding shell in the streets of the Old City. Authorities found the father's body in three pieces. From the second floor of their fire-bombed building, Karin's sister was forced to jump and broke her ankle. The mother was seriously burned on her left arm, shoulder, and back. The widowed mother grabbed her two daughters and evacuated the ruined city, later finding refuge in nearby Zirndorf. At war's end, only little Karin survived without any physical indignity.

I thought Karin, and her sister and mother, might exhibit some animosity, holding me partially responsible for the death of the father and their pain at the hands of my erstwhile American comrades. No hostility or resentment was apparent, however. Perhaps the passage of fourteen years, plus West German dependency on the United States for protection from the rapscallion revengeful Russians to the East, have dulled any initial ill-will felt after the war.

There was something weird about the relationship between the women. The two seemed uncomfortable around each other, as if some tension or conflict hovered over them. I did not see them walk side-by-side or hear them talk to each other. Karin ignored her older sibling, only walking with and talking to the German or me. It was as if the sisters were putting on some kind of act. They lived together, saw each other day and night, supped at the same table, even double-dated, but behaved as if a partition separated them. Each played a different role in this Sunday scenic scenario, oblivious to one another but performing in the same matchmaker outing. The Schwester had more to say to an American stranger who could not respond to her in any meaningful way than to her own blood speaking the same language.

Karin did not know I had no intention of stepping out with her hard-stepping sister, that this afternoon would be all the time I planned to spend with the older unprepossessing woman. I did not talk about the sister and I certainly did not say anything about the German's romantic feelings for Karin. They were boyfriend-and-girlfriend based on what he had said to me. Moreover, I gave no indication I wanted to step out with normal-stepping Karin. Karin was very nice but she was not exactly the type I was hankering for.

In any event, I never liked the idea of making a play for someone else's girl. It was therefore with some measure of astonishment that I took the news Karin imparted to me. My preconceptions about my new friends were shattered.

"He not my boyfriend," Karin said to me with a touch of apprehension in her eyes.

We were sitting on a park bench. She was facing me. Her back was to the German and sister sitting on a bench more than twenty feet away. I was sure they could not hear us talking. She looked over her shoulder quickly.

"He *think* I his girlfriend," she emphasized, "but I not."

Karin explained that she has known the German for about a year. They were just friends, she kept insisting. They occasionally go out to eat and he comes to see her in her house, but they just talk. With some embarrassment and without a good command of the English language, she expressed as best she could in euphemistic terms that there was nothing sexual between them. She took pains to tell me she never even kissed him. They only touched hands in a cordial way when they said hello or goodbye.

He was too tall for her, Karin said. She wasn't enamored by his looks and it displeased her that he was so shy around women. He didn't earn enough money to support a wife and couldn't pay for a decent apartment. As she confided these personal feelings, Karin looked at me with an intensity I had not known before from a girl.

"You I like," she blurted out finally, "him not."

Nothing that had happened earlier prepared me for this romantic turnabout. A man I hardly know brings me to this German family to meet, ostensibly to get involved with, his girlfriend's sister but before the day is out I'm entangled with the girlfriend while he's left with the sister if he wants her. I just sat there listening to Karin, not knowing what to say or do.

"I go tell him now," she said in an excited state after getting this off her chest, and then started to stand up.

"No . . . wait," I responded right away, reaching out to stop her. I liked Karin, sure, but I did not like being part of any love triangle.

It was too late. Before I could say anything more, or grab hold of her arm, she jumped up from the bench and hurried over to where the German and her sister were sitting. I watched her as she stood next to the self-proclaimed boyfriend, looking down at him while she spoke, occasionally gesturing with her hand. A minute or so later, she hurried back to where I was sitting and sat down by me, a little closer than previously.

"I tell him, I tell him," Karin repeated.

A great burden it seemed had been lifted from her. She forced a smile and her eyes watered a little.

Karin leaned toward me. I took her cue, leaned forward, and kissed her. It was just a simple brush of lips, no hands, but apparently that was enough for her to get emotional. Tears trickled down her cheeks. She cried like a child happy that a lost puppy dog returned home. We sat and talked for some time. With my arm on the back of the bench, I held her hand. I could see she was both relieved and troubled by the positive action just taken.

About five we all started to head back to the apartment. I made sure Karin and I walked well behind the German and her sister.

The sitting room was fairly large, about twelve or thirteen feet square. It abutted the front of the building and there was a double window that opened to the street below. About all anyone could do in this room is sit. An old-style couch for three people, cushioned with wood armrests and legs, stood in the center of the room to the left of, and with its back to, the door. Opposite the couch were two low-back chairs, also cushioned with wood armrests and legs, separated by a dark-stained table supporting a tall brass lamp. A small decorative cabinet with a curved top standing on four legs was against the side wall; the three knobs and dial told me it housed a radio, probably the only medium for this family's entertainment. From what appeared to be a 1920s cabinet, rants and ravings from Herr Hitler about the Jews and Communists and enemies of Germany no doubt had been listened to, by these people or some other German family. There was no television in the room. The cost of the visual and audio form of communication in postwar Germany had not yet fallen to the level of Frau Klotz' means.

After closing the door, Karin slipped off her shoes and sat down on the couch with her legs folded under her. Like a little girl doing a curtsy with both hands, she spread her polka dot dress out over her knees and onto the couch. She motioned me to sit next to her. We talked, mainly about what she had just told the German. She did not want him to pursue her and did not wish to be his girlfriend.

I was uncomfortable with this conversation since I knew I was the proximate cause of her breaking off with the German. The deeper cause obviously was her unwillingness to get involved with this particular man regardless of his feelings toward her. When it became crystal clear to me she had no intention of ever seeing the German again in the way he wanted and that it was I she was interested in, I took action.

I leaned over and kissed her on the lips and touched her face gently, our second kiss as it were. It took just a few kisses more, this time French kisses, for her to get up and sit down sideways on my lap, spreading her dress again. I could feel the warmth of the back of her upper thighs and buttocks through my trousers, even the outline of her panties. Her middle was directly over my middle. Every passing second my romantic passions were rising.

"Your mother or sister might come into the room," I told Karin. I was very nervous about a sudden intrusion into this potentially embarrassing and unfolding intimate encounter.

"No," she said straightaway. "Mutti like read in kitchen. Und Schwester knock first."

That calmed my fears somewhat but I was still not sure how far I should go, or could go, on the couch with Karin this first time together. I wanted to reach under her dress and touch her where it mattered but I dared not so soon in our relationship. Although I knew it was not a valid comparison age-wise, I could not help thinking of the incident with little Anna in her apartment eight years earlier when I touched her middle, how she said nein and pulled away violently. For the moment, I had to be satisfied with just joining mouths and drawing in with my new-found partner.

Whenever we came up for air, I turned toward the door to give a look. No one knocked or came in without knocking. I had a boner and I was sure Karin could feel my hardness. I wanted her to reach down and at least hold me but she made no such move. That did not faze me though as such an advance to a boy just introduced to would have been far too daring for a girl concerned with her reputation, in Germany or America. Unlike twelve-year-old Anna, I was sure Karin knew what a penis looked like and felt like. But that did not mean she had to grab me so soon after we met.

I remembered how it was months before the foreigner schoolgirl acted on her curiosity about a boy's body parts. And it took four dates with the WAC back at Ford Ord for her to touch me down there.

The next step beyond kissing was taken by me. I waited until our lips were locked, when Karin had her arms wrapped around me. I ran my right hand over her left breast several times, caressing it softly. She did not pull my hand away. Then I ran both hands over her and held them there. She leaned back and looked at me but said nothing. I unbuttoned the front of her dress and glided a hand over one breast, then the other, finally working my fingers under her bra. Still she did not do anything to stop me. When I twirled her nipple with two fingers she started to breathe heavily and drew me close to her chest. I pulled one side of her bra down and brought my mouth to her soft flesh and hard nipple. Karin tightened her grip around the back of my neck and head. Sitting down during all this above-waist lovemaking, I remained stiff as a board.

Playing touchy-kissy with Karin was at the same time both enjoyable and frustrating. The same could be said, however, about the sucky-fucky action I had with Elsa, but in reverse. The pleasure I derived from prolonged deep kissing with Karin and touching her bigger cup-size breasts was offset by the pain I felt in my groin from being erect so long. With Elsa, I enjoyed her oral work-ups and the release of my load inside her but had little to feel on her chest and I was loath to bring my mouth to hers.

I needed to stand up and walk around. I slid Karin off of me and onto the couch. She looked as though she did not know why I suddenly stopped kissing and caressing her, but she did not question me. I watched as she straightened her bra and buttoned the front of her dress. I did not want to get up yet since I was still too firm and enlarged not to be embarrassed by Karin seeing the "banana in my pocket," as a risqué Mae West put it in one of her early talkies. So I sat a while longer looking at Karin and holding her hand but saying little. What was there to say? We had achieved a certain level of intimacy, to be continued and raised the next time out.

Later, with a final kiss goodbye and plans to meet on Tuesday at the Hauptbahnhof at six thirty, I left Karin's apartment. It was close to seven-thirty. I could have headed for the Flying Dutchman and tried to pick up Elsa for a quickie, but I passed on that even though my body belonging to the Army badly needed a discharge.

I arrived at the barracks at eight-forty and shot straight for the snack bar. The German workers had just started to shut down for the day, placing chairs upside down on the tables and mopping the floor, but the grill was still open. I asked for two beef frankfurters, well-done, with the bun toasted, like I would get at Nathan's. An older Fräulein working behind the counter prepared them for me.

The young Negerliebend girl I was so enamored with was nowhere in sight. She was probably handling a big and juicy well-done wiener of her own outside the snack bar. At the accoutrements' table, I put mustard, relish, and sauerkraut in that order on top of my Coney Island. My dream lover did not need to put anything, except herself, on top of her foot-long.

Back in my room, I told Steve about the turn of events. He was very surprised to learn that I connected with the girlfriend and not the sister. I told him her name.

"She's a nice German girl. Young, sweet, never knew an American before. I'm seeing her again on Tuesday."

"What happened with the sister?"

"She was fat and ugly, and had a bad limp. I'd never fuck her."

"What happened with the German?" Steve wanted to know.

"He took a hike."

"Seems like you fucked the German instead."

"No. I had nothing to do with it. Karin said he was not her boyfriend. He only *thought* he was. She liked me. She told him to get lost."

"I told you there was probably something wrong with the sister," Steve noted with some measure of satisfaction. "And I said the comrade didn't know his ass from a hole in the ground."

"I felt bad for the German, but what could I do? Karin dumped him and threw herself on me."

"How far did you get with this girl?" Steve wanted to know.

"We made out for a while. I felt her up, kissed her tits."

"That's all?"

It was no secret that Steve was shtupping Ursula on a regular basis. But, she was older and had a kid already.

"What'd you expect me to do? She lives at home. Her mother and sister were in the next room."

"Well, you'll have to wait two more days to see if you can go further," my friend with more experience with German women advised me, "and you may have to take her somewhere."

# CHAPTER 32: DEAR DOVIDL

As soon as I entered my room after work, I saw the letter lying on my bunk. It was neatly placed in the center of my squared-off bottom blanket, tightened to regulations so a quarter could bounce on it. The white envelope stood out boldly against the dark brown of the OD blankets covering the pillow and the mattress. Apparently, Steve had picked up the mail and gone to chow without me.

When I left the Area Office I went straight to the PX to purchase something for Karin. My first thought was to put the letter in my wall locker and read it later that evening or the next day. There was not much time for me to shave, shower, get dressed in civies, pick up my pass, and catch the streetcar to the Hauptbahnhof if I was to meet Karin at six thirty as we had arranged two days earlier.

It was a letter from home and I held it up. I recognized the cursive writing on the envelope right away as my father's. He had beautiful penmanship and his letters were always easy to read, and that made up for the grammatical errors and run-on sentences. When I opened the envelope and glanced at the folded paper, it appeared it was from my sister. It was written in cursive too, but the handwriting was child-like, in a large script on lined paper.

As I unfolded the letter, I saw that the *i*'s were sometimes not dotted and the *t*'s crossed above rather than through the stem. The first words of sentences, if not a proper noun, were not capitalized. There were no periods at the end of sentences, just a space. I soon realized it was my *mother* who was writing to me, in her English as a second language learned in night school. She was the only one who called me Dovidl. I was still her "little David."

There were two yellow-lined pages filled almost to capacity, front and back. I read the letter slowly to comprehend the incorrect spelling, grammar, and punctuation. For the moment my eyes were fixed on these strangely-written pieces of paper. I lost sight of the fact that Karin would be waiting for me in an hour's time.

*Dear Dovidl,*

*Papa made out for me the envelop   he writes so nice   thank God we are all right all in good health   we hope to hear good news from you   the weather here is fair not to cold and no rain   I never wrote* you before in the army   I write now because you are in Germany   I want to tell you things you should know what I never told you before

I didnt tell you everything about Poland when I was a little girl how hard it was and how we sufferd   it was right after the first war my father he didnt have a job   he had to work here maybe there for a few zlotys   our house was small the roof always leakd   on the floor we only had straw   we sufferd because we were Jewish   half the people in our shtetl were goyim   they didnt like the Jews   they took most of the food the solders brought   the solders in our town they were White Russians   I had to stand in line in the cold for howers   with a pot my mother sent me to get soup   I got a piece of bread to but we all had to share it   my father gave the children first then my mother   sometimes he didnt eat   the goyim they made fun of us   the ortodox they wore beards and the women wigs   the goyim cut mens beards and grabed the womens hair and threw it down and then they laffd and ran off   the poleece the Polaks they didnt do nothing   they laffd to   we hated Poland that is why my father left and then we all came to America

America has been good to us   Papa has a job   he works steady now   the children they were all born here thank God   just in time we got out of Europ   who knows what would happen if we stayd someday maybe we will all live in Israel   Israel is Gods chosen country and he will always protect us   God wants all Jews to live in Israel   that is the land of milk and honey just like it says in the bible   but Germany that is the land of Hitler and the nazis and the concentration camps

Dovidl you are in the devils chosen country now   there is blood running in the streets   the blood of our people six million of them the Germans are worse than the Polaks   they hate us more   they wanted to kill all the Jews in Europ   Dovidl do your family a big favor stay away from the Germans   dont talk to them and dont go in their houses   they only want to take something from you   the German girls they got big eyes for the yanki doller   a Jewish boy like you nice looking they want to rope you in   a German girl she only wants to get marreed and come to America   when she finds out you are Jewish she will say bad things about you behind your back God pikd us and gave us a religon   a German girl will take you away from your religon   you cant trust the people who tried to kill

288

*you   they are still nazis all of them   I am praying for you and for all
my children they should have the best always*

*I hate to send emty page so I am writing more on other side*

*God should whach over us and show us miracls   in March was
Purim   you know the story   Hamon talked to the king to destroy the
Jewish people   then Mordechay and Ester changd his mind   that
was Gods will   the Jewish people were saved   the nazis tried to
destroy us to but they didnt   we survived   last month was Pesach
you know how Moses took our people out of Egypt out of slavery   he
gave us the ten comandments   and then we enterd Israel the
promised land   you cant forget 6000 years of hate   the Germans
want to do to you what Hamon wanted to do to us and what the
pharoh in Egypt wanted   God will protect you I am sure 24 howers
a day*

*I pray you will come home next year and will go to colege like you
want   I know you are ambishus and want to get a good job and be
somebody special   Papa said dont worry about the money   you can
live here and go to school   we have a big apartment now   you have
your own bedroom and you can study   for you Papa got a desk*

*a big kiss for Dovidl on kepele   love to you from all of us*


*Mama*


I folded the letter back the way it was and slipped it into the envelope. I found a nice place for it on the shelf in my wall locker in
front of some toiletries. Since my locker doors were always open
when I was in my room, the letter would be immediately visible to
me at all times.

# CHAPTER 33: FINGER FUCK

I had to wait on the corner a block away from Karin's house for some time. It was late, after ten, and I was eager to get back to the barracks and into my bunk before bed check. This hour of the night on a Tuesday the bus from Zirndorf to Fürth ran every twenty minutes. The air was cool and I kept the collar up on my raincoat and my hands in the pockets. Every minute or so I stepped forward and looked to my left to see if the bus was approaching.

My first date with Karin went very well. As we had arranged on Sunday evening, we met at six thirty at the Hauptbahnhof. She was waiting for me in the crowd of people that stood around near the streetcar tracks. I noticed her right away. She too was wearing a raincoat, light green in color, with a dark green scarf tucked in halfway. A bit of a smile suddenly appeared on her face when she saw me walking toward her. Although I wanted to, I did not reach over to kiss her in a symbolic gesture of a lover's simple greeting. With our passionate kissing two nights earlier, I felt we certainly had every right to a quick touch of lips. But I knew this was Germany, and not France or Italy, and public displays of romantic emotions were frowned upon. Karin did not stand on her toes to make an effort to kiss me either. She looked as though she wanted to, or so I imagined. The fact that this was her first official date with an American likewise might have explained the reserve I witnessed.

"Hi," I said, as I stopped less than two feet from her.

"Hallo," she replied with a wider smile.

"Nice to see you again."

"Yes. I also."

I took that to mean she was glad to see me too. "Where shall we go to dinner?"

"I know good place. Not far."

Karin reached out for my hand and led me past the Bratwurst stand in front of the medieval tower and around the corner to the left on Luitpoldstrasse. The German restaurant I was taken to was the same one next to the alley where weeks before I got a free finger fuck with a not-so-nice German girl. I hesitated a moment but then went inside. Surprisingly, it was a respectable eating establishment on a street not known for respectability. It would never be mistaken for the Four Seasons on Fifth Avenue but it was not a rowdy G.I. Gasthaus either.

We were seated at a round table meant for more than two. The waiter came over, a young man in his late twenties, dressed in a white shirt with bow tie and black vest. A small towel hung over his left forearm. I did not have to stare at him to see that he was not the one who came upon me in the alley with my fly undone and the no-panties girl.

"Guten abend," he said with a smile. He handed us two long folded menus.

I looked at the embroidered name written on the waiter's vest. It did not spell Karl. I feared Karl's kitchen mate was a busboy who would soon come to our table.

Karin said something to the waiter in German and he walked away. "What you like to eat?" she asked, opening her menu.

I looked closely at my menu. I did not know the German word for chicken or beef, but I assumed the column marked "Schweine-fleisch" or pig meat was the section for the pork choices. My eyes focused on the other columns.

"You eat in German restaurant before?" Karin inquired.

"No."

"What you like?" she asked again.

"A beef dish is good."

"I order for you," Karin said. I did not know whether it was a question or a statement of intent. She suggested something under the "Rindfleisch" column. She said it came with potatoes and a vege-table. I told her that was okay. I was sure it would be much better than anything the mess sergeant cooked up for the Merrell troopers that day. The price next to the item was listed as "8,50" and I understood that to mean eight Marks and fifty Pfennigs, not a bad deal for a spec four clearing a hundred-twenty-five bucks a month.

Just then the waiter came back. Karin ordered for me and selected something for herself under the column I looked away from. At that point in our relationship, she did not know my last name and I was sure she did not attach any significance to my preference for beef over pork.

Karin and I talked a bit while we waited for our meals. What the conversation was about, I have no recollection. My mind at the time must have only zeroed in on what we would be doing later back at her apartment. I studied Karin's face as she spoke. She exuded a sweetness and naïveté as she struggled with her English. I glanced down at her breasts when she was not looking directly at me, wondering if I would be getting my hands and mouth on them again soon. I could not help speculating if my fingers that evening would find their way under the panties of this nice German girl. I tried to discern where this first relationship with a non-hooker in this country was going.

Would I be getting into someone I did not meet in a G.I. joint or darkened movie theater? I asked myself. Would Karin just be a diversionary dinner date before I dashed back to see Elsa on a Sunday? My mother's letter on my locker shelf, and admonitions about German people, were not in my thoughts.

The waiter finally came and we downed our meals. My beef dish was good. Karin seemed to enjoy her dish but I did not enjoy watching her eat Schwein.

We left the restaurant at seven-forty and, after making good connections on one streetcar and a bus, arrived in Zirndorf before eight-thirty. Karin led me into the kitchen where her mother and sister were, and I greeted the two other women in the Klotz family. Then I was shuffled into the sitting room and Karin excused herself. A few minutes later she returned, having changed from her dress into a pair of brown slacks and a white blouse. She smelled nice, as if she just washed her hands and face. I too went to the bathroom to freshen up. When I returned, I sat down on the couch next to Karin. Before long, we started in where we left off two days earlier.

She sat on my lap, we French kissed, I ran my hands over her breasts, but I did not unbutton her blouse. I thought the risk of discovery too great. Instead, I put my hand between her legs, up into her crotch, rubbing the fold with my thumb in opposing motion with my four fingers.

To my surprise but delight, Karin did not take my hand away. She might have had she been wearing a dress and I reached underneath. I was sure that was why she changed into slacks. In any event, I was pleased I had succeeded in that logical next advance. Every step closer to a home run with Karin could be one step back from my practice shots with Elsa.

A half-hour later, I heard footsteps coming toward us and I quickly pulled my hand back and pushed Karin off my lap. There was no knock at the sitting-room door. It swung open abruptly and in sauntered both the mother and the sister. This is what Karin said would *not* happen, but yet it did. The two intruding women took seats in the chairs. The mother switched on the lamp and started reading her newspaper, the sister turned on the radio. Karin just sat on the couch and said nothing. I did the same since I had a banana in my pocket and could not get up anyway.

A few minutes later, Karin grabbed my hand and led me out of the sitting room and into the kitchen. It was a good thing I had gone down a little. She maneuvered me onto a chair near one side of the table, not one I saw her mother or sister use, and sat sideways on top of me. With her arms around me, we continued the deep kissing she seemed to like and I moved my hand again to her crotch. The kitchen chair, with its hard seat and back, was nowhere near as comfortable as the cushioned sitting-room couch, but for the purpose of limited lovemaking it was good enough.

We stayed in that position for a while and I became so hard it started to hurt. It must have been my erectile function that gave rise to my next move. Still kissing, I took my hand away from her crotch and boldly pulled back the elastic waistband of her slacks and slipped my hand beneath, then reached down and inside her panties. My middle finger found its target. Karin was nice and moist and not too hairy. She tried to pull my hand away but I resisted and made a sound while our lips were engaged that could only be interpreted as a strong no. This time from a German girl, I would not take nein for an answer.

Karin surrendered without a fight. She took her hand off of mine and let me finger her as much as I wanted. The soft and wet cavity between her legs would never be off limits to me again. I gambled and triumphed in reaching a higher level of intimacy.

Another half an hour passed and it was déja vu all over again. The mother and sister came back into the kitchen, and Karin and I returned to the sitting room. I walked past the two women like I had a thorn in my shoe, limping on one side, to conceal the bulge in my trousers. We resumed our lovemaking activities for a while longer, this time back on a comfortable couch. My ass felt better but not another part of my body. Fingering Karin was very enjoyable and I felt good emotionally, but my groin area ached a great deal.

"I make all what you want," she said to me when we paused a moment from our continuous kissing. The look on her face was serious, the look in her eyes honest.

I took that to mean that on our next date she would go all the way with me. My push forward, or rather my hand down her pants, obviously resulted in this leap to the finish line.

"Where can we go?" I inquired, eager to follow up on this favorable turn in the conversation. "We can't do anything here." I moved one hand to the couch for emphasis.

"I know place."

"Where?" I said, without thinking, as if it mattered.

"I take you. Next time."

"Okay. I'll come back on Thursday." And then I said "Donnerstag," remembering how my mother referred to that day of the week when she spoke to Zeyde.

"Make me not a baby," she pleaded, looking me straight in the eye.

Karin had that same facial appearance of seriousness and honesty, and I took her at her word. This last comment could leave no doubt in anyone's mind about how far she would go with me. I was only two days away from getting into a nice German girl for a change. And it left no doubt that I'd better return with protection.

With the time, purpose, and qualification for our next meeting firmly established, I left Karin's apartment just before ten. After well over an hour of making love and no climax to show for it, I still had a partial erection and a bad case of blue balls. It hurt, but it was a good hurt.

"Donnerstag," she said, as she kissed me goodbye at the outside door.

The bus to Fürth finally came. I gave the driver a 50-Pfenning piece and he gave me 10 Pfennings back and a paper ticket. There were only two passengers on the bus, an older German and a young white American soldier in uniform sitting in a middle row by the window. I sat down in the aisle seat in the row across from the PFC. Even though I was in civies, I knew he could tell I was an

American and a soldier too. My evening encounter with Karin put me in a talkative mood.

"Where are you stationed, buddy?" I asked.

"Pinder Barracks."

"Oh. That's right here in Zirndorf, isn't it?"

The young man turned toward me and nodded. I noticed he kept his hands in his pocket even though it was not cold on the bus. He had a sullen and hapless look about him, as if he was in a state of perpetual anger, but I did not think much of it at the time. I thought of telling the stranger about the nice girl I just fingered in Zirndorf, but I waited for a more apropos moment.

"I'm at Merrell in Nuremberg," I said instead. "I've got to take this bus and then two streetcars to get back to my barracks. It usually takes me an hour . .. longer this time at night."

He did not respond by saying where he was headed. And I did not ask him such a question as it might be too personal for a stranger to say.

"What branch are you in?" I said to change the subject and to make our late-night exchange more impersonal. He had his Army overcoat on and I could not see the insignia on the epaulets of his jacket.

"Artillery."

"I'm in Signal. Made spec four May thirteenth."

"You're lucky you're not in the Artillery like me."

"Why is that?" I inquired matter-of-factly, not knowing where this conversation was going.

"Because you don't have to handle heavy weapons. A soldier can get maimed in peacetime like in war."

That was a funny comment, I thought. The casual talk we were having suddenly turned a bit more serious. I said nothing as I did not know what to make of it. I suppose it was not odd for one soldier, even a stranger, to talk about the vicissitudes of military life to another soldier. But, what does this have to do with me, a G.I. not in a combat unit on his way back to his new post after a hot date?

The soldier suddenly drew his right hand from his coat pocket as if he were pulling a gun and held it up to me. "This is all I have to show for being in the Army," he let out.

This sudden action on his part shattered any pretense of small talk between us. The first joint of his index finger was missing. Skin had grown over the uneven stump.

"My job was to load shells into the breech of a Howitzer one-fifty-five. Last October a nigger in my battery closed the hatch two seconds too soon. The motherfucker cut my finger off."

Instinctively I looked over both shoulders, but there was no one near us, at least no one who might understand what we were talking about in English. Neither the bus driver nor the German turned around or said anything. Racial slurs by whites, from the North or South, were nothing new to me in the Army. But I still was uncomfortable with a stranger being so forthright with me about so personal a matter. The young soldier demonstrated how his job was to use his index finger to push the round into place.

"I felt a sharp sting," he said. "When I pulled my hand out, I saw the cut tendons hanging. I fainted from the shock and loss of blood. The next thing I remember is waking up in the hospital with my finger bandaged. The black son-of-a-bitch never came to see me and never said he was sorry."

Now it made perfect sense to me why he failed to introduce himself or offer to shake hands when I first spoke to him. And I did not think about it before but I did notice he only used his left hand when talking to me and kept the other in his pocket. What else could I say to this angry young artilleryman I just met and probably would never see again?

"The Army fucked me," he went on. "They said the missing joint on my finger wasn't a serious enough injury for a medical discharge. They wouldn't let me out early and they wouldn't let me re-enlist either. I'll get a ten percent disability pension when I get out. Big fucking deal. Not even twenty bucks a month."

I empathized with the poor fellow as he now seemed less of a stranger. I knew the details of the most important event in his life. Finally, I found some words to say. How comforting they were, I would not know.

"At least you didn't lose your whole finger or your whole hand. Be grateful for that."

He looked at me for a few moments in a solemn mood. His eyes told me he was reflecting on what I had just said. I thought he was going to say you're right, but then he turned negative again.

"I can't be grateful. The loss of one finger joint was enough to ruin my life."

"You don't look ruined to me," I said. "I see many Germans around town with only one arm or one leg."

"I had a schatzie. I even lived with her for a while. Wanted to marry her and take her to the States. But after my injury, she left me. She said when I touched her down below it upset her."

"There are other girls."

I thought of saying you could finger fuck with your left hand, which was something the bastardly battery black might have said, but I stopped myself in time.

"I'm sure you could meet someone who wouldn't be bothered by your finger."

"Yeah, girls who are disfigured themselves. Who wants them?"

"It's really only minor," I reflected, trying to take the edge off his anger.

Ironically, I identified with what he was saying, as I felt the same way about Karin's sister.

"It's major to me."

"Well, maybe you'll feel better once you're home?"

"I doubt it. My advice to you buddy is don't get married in Germany. The girls here either fuck the jigs or they fuck you."

Again with the don't get married. That's all I've been hearing since I left home. Now there would be no apropos moment to tell this stranger about the nice German girl who lived near his barracks that I met and planned to continue dating. On this seventeen-cent bus ride, I had to listen to a disaffected G.I. tirade against the Army, another G.I., and German girls.

I got back to Merrell about eleven thirty. Steve was still up, lying in his bunk reading a book. When I came into the room, he put the book down and smiled.

"How'd your date go? Get your finger wet?"

"As a matter of fact, yes," I shot back without hesitation. "And I learned about another kind of finger fuck too."

There was no need to tell Steve what I meant by my last remark.

# CHAPTER 34: NO SPLENDOR IN THE GRASS

Thursday, the fourth of June, was my one-month anniversary of clerking in the Area Office. I liked the new job very much. Bentley and Barry were cordial toward me and did not overload me with work.

The first week they just wanted me to familiarize myself with their filing system and the different equipment reports tucked away in the file cabinet rather haphazardly. I was asked to go through the reports, place the loose papers in Manila folders, and develop a method of classification. In the second week, my promotion came through. My new bosses congratulated me with a handshake and a pat on the back. The same day I went to see Bruno, the German tailor in the barracks, and for one Mark he removed the single yellow stripe from both sleeves of my fatigue jacket and sewed on the blue patch with the head of a bird that I purchased in the PX. I told Bruno I would bring all my uniforms in for patch-changing soon.

I could now answer the telephone as *Specialist* Streiber. In recent weeks my duties were to type letters, prepare reports, and think about making those charts Bentley spoke of. All in all, I was pleased I went through the military makeover. After almost two years in the Army, I was beginning to enjoy the life of a soldier on post.

Donnerstag, 4 Juni, was also the day Karin told me she would make all what I want, so long as I made her not a baby. On Tuesday, while sitting on my lap, she obviously was thinking in German when she whispered those enticing words in English. However, while feeling her up, I was thinking of Eros and Aphrodite in any language when I asked where we would go to do what she knew I wanted. I had no idea where she might take me, and it did not much matter. I was beside myself for two days in anticipation of the consummation of our budding love relationship. After three months in Nuremberg, I was beginning to really enjoy the life of a soldier *off* post.

That Thursday my rifle was fully loaded and I was aiming to hit the object of my affection, Karin's centerpiece. I had not slipped it to Elsa in almost two weeks. The past Sunday and Tuesday I played French-kissy, suck-titty, and finger-fucky with Karin for extended periods of time, each night going back to Merrell with high cock and achy balls. I kept telling myself at work all day that this night is different from all other nights, even though I was not silently reading the first line from the Four Questions in the Haggadah. I hoped I would finally fire off my stored bullets of youthful sexual energy an hour or so after I walked out the barracks gate. I did not have my yarmulke on but I prayed I would not have to target Elsa or, if she were unavailable, some other Fräulein pickup this coming Sunday just for the sake of coming. A nice German girl is what I longed to zip my fly down for.

Bentley sensed a change in me. "What's the matter?" he commented late Thursday afternoon. "You seemed distracted all day."

He was right of course. I was preoccupied but not with thoughts of signal equipment reports, letters to sergeants in charge of other teams, or graphic wall charts.

"I have to go somewhere right after work."

"Is it important?"

"Yes," I told my boss without specification or qualification, nodding my head a little.

Bentley did not ask where I had to go or how important it was. He glanced at his watch. "Well, Strahber, why don't you leave now. There's nothing much more to do here today." He did not look over his shoulder to Barry for approval.

"Thanks, Sarge. I appreciate that."

I put the papers spread out on my desk in the top drawer and locked it. I grabbed my cap and in a flash I was out the door, walking back to my room on the other side of the compound almost double time. My ruminations were on something else spread out.

I cleaned up, splashed on a bit of cologne, and snuggled into my civilian clothes quickly. Before I headed out, I slipped two rubbers in my front pocket, one that I borrowed from Steve the day before. I did not wait to go to chow. The Klotz family had no telephone so I could not call Karin to tell her I would be there forty-five minutes early. Nevertheless, I was confident she would be happy to see me at any hour and be ready to go off with me.

The two streetcars and a bus that I took to get to Zirndorf seemed to take longer that Thursday. Karin opened the door when I arrived but she was not smiling. There was a morose look about her. She averted eye contact, did not speak, motioned me to wait in the foyer, then turned around and went into the kitchen.

I could not read any expression on her face. My first thought was that she had a change of heart about making all what I want, baby or no baby. I heard her say something to her mother. A moment later she came out of the kitchen and reached for the green raincoat and scarf hanging on a wall hook in the foyer. I looked at the dress she was wearing.

"Come," she said, extending her hand to me after she put on her raincoat.

That was exactly what I wanted to hear. That was exactly what I wanted to do. The familiar word and gesture put to rest any doubts I had about her being in a different mind or mood. It was ten after six when we left Karin's house. There was still light outside. She held my hand and led me what seemed east and then south.

We walked in eerie silence for about half a mile. Karin looked straight ahead. I turned my head now and then to look at my lover-to-be. There really was nothing to talk about. We were just two young people moving ineluctably toward some hiding place in which to engage in life's most intimate of unions and experiences.

Karin gave me no clue as to where she was taking me. We could be on our way to a friend's house, where we would have a private room and a warm bed in which to carry out our mission. Perhaps she was planning on us registering in some hotel or Pension a kilometer or two from her house where no one knows her. I trusted she was not the type of girl who would be barreling me to some pile of rubble or out-of-the-way alley, ready to stand against a bombed out or solid section of brick wall with her dress up and panties down.

But she might be forking me to a bucolic area outside her small town, a Deutsche Dogpatch of sorts, where like Li'l Abner and Daisy Mae we could sneak into the barn and romp around in the haystack. Karin's mother was pint-sized like Mammy Yokum, and smoked cigarettes rather than a corncob pipe, but when we returned I hoped she, unlike Li'l Abner's mother, would not be throwing me the famous undercut punch to uphold order and decency in her home.

We soon entered another parkland area, more secluded than the place on Sunday the four of us had gone walking. Why Karin was taking me here I had no idea. Perhaps in this vast preserve there was a cabin that locals used for dressing or resting. There could be a bunk bed or couch inside where young German girls give themselves to young German or American boys. We walked for several minutes across an open meadow and to a grassy field, still hand-in-hand, then turned into a clearing behind some tall bushes. Karin stopped and looked at me. Our hands separated.

"Here," she said.

"Here what?" I blurted out instantly. For a moment she lost me.

As a Coney Islander—who knew teenage boys in the city made it with girls on rooftops, in parks, in alleyways, and on the beach under the Boardwalk—I should have known what she meant.

"We make here." She started to unbutton her raincoat.

"On the ground?"

Karin nodded, but without a smile or facial expression of any kind. All this was new to me, but I realized I had to take the lead. If she was willing to make love on a flattened bed of damp grass, I was not about to turn the opportunity down.

I removed my raincoat, opened it wide, and laid it down on the ground. I took her by the shoulders and gently nudged her to lie on her back. I lay down on my left side next to her, resting on my elbow for support, partially on the raincoat. Wild chrysanthemums, brightly colored double flower heads, touched my ear and I brushed them aside.

She waited for me to lift her dress and slip her panties off. I was hot but not quite ready yet. I reached for her crotch, separated her legs more, and worked two fingers inside. Leaning on one elbow and the other hand busy, I could not kiss her or touch her breasts.

Karin covered her eyes with one forearm. "Go make, go make," she shrilled despairingly.

I unzipped, whipped it out, and grabbed a rubber from my pocket. I unbuckled too, to free myself more. Rolling the rubber down greatly heightened my sensitivity and anticipation. Karin brought her other forearm over her eyes. I barely got my head in when I began to shoot off. With bullets firing in rapid succession, I managed to get only a little deeper into Karin. She just lay there, not lifting her knees to make penetration any easier, not moving in unison with me, not reacting to my thwarted pumping action. Karin made all what I wanted, if just letting me stick it partially in is all a nice German girl thinks a horny American boy wants.

I withdrew and saw through the transparent protector the ejaculate in blotches encircling me. I wrenched the thing off and held it up-right. The white liquid drained to the tip. I could see the spent rub-ber had no breaks in it and there was no leakage. I was sure I made Karin not a baby. I threw the sticky roll-down behind a bush when she was straightening herself out and looking the other way. With a handkerchief I wiped myself and then fixed my trousers and belt back to normal. I brushed off the outside of my raincoat.

This first intimacy with Karin was far from the hour of splendor in the grass, of glory in the flower that William Wordsworth wrote about. In our brief romantic tryst, as the poet intimated, I knew we will grieve not, we will rather find strength in what remains behind. She in the grass and I in the flower did not know the radiance which could be so bright, but I hoped it would not be now for ever taken from my sight.

That Karin and I did it, albeit hastily and clumsily, was the impor-tant thing. She was not the virgin I thought she might be but I be-lieved her when she implied she had no carnal knowledge of G.I.s. From here on out, it was only a question of how often we would do it. I wanted Karin to mark me down for Sunday and/or Tuesday as well as next Thursday. The follow-ups, I wished, would be indoors on a soft mattress and not outdoors on hard ground.

We walked back to Karin's house holding hands, again in silence. There was not much to say before we joined bodies, and there was even less to say after. Karin again stoically kept a straight face passing through the streets in her town with a foreign male compan-ion. She could hold her head higher than townswomen whose com-panions were not white but lower than those with males not foreign.

Karin's mother was in the kitchen eating. She prepared something for her younger daughter, a bowl of dark soup or stew with more vegetables than meat. I too was offered a bowl but politely declined, even though I had not eaten since lunchtime. I could not tell what kind of meat it was. Instead, I just had a piece of schwarze Brot mit Butter, as the mother called what she handed me. I figured I would grab a bite later on post at the snack bar.

There was a half-empty jar of coffee with a German label on the table. The mother scooped up a spoonful of granules and mixed it with some hot water in a cup for herself. She spoke to Karin, look-ing back to me several times. Karin translated her mother's words.

"Mutti want know if you bring Kaffee next time you come."

"Yes," I said right away, glad to hear that there would be a next time. "I'd be happy to."

"Mutti like Maxwell House."

"I can get the coffee your mother likes."

Mutti evidently has been around, I thought. She knows American products and knows I'm the one who can provide them for her.

"Kaffee cost much money in Chermany," Karin went on, "and it taste not good."

"I understand," I said. "I'll bring the biggest jar I see."

"Mutti say she pay you."

"No, no. That's all right." I could not very well take money from a frugal fatherless Familie, especially since I felt I already got paid.

"You bring Tee also?"

"I'll bring tea also, I repeated."

Why not? For a little coffee and tea, Karin can have me.

"Mutti say any kind good."

"Yes of course."

I thought they were going to tell me not to bring Lipton Tea because it is from a Jewish-owned company. This German family was laying out the welcome mat but expected me to step back on it carrying a brown bag.

I finished eating what the mother gave me. The piece of buttered black bread, heavy and cut thick, was good. I would have asked for another slice had I thought I was not taking food from needy people's mouths. I excused myself, indicating I wanted to wash my hands, and got up from the table to go to the bathroom. What I really wanted to do was to take a piss and wash something else.

When I came out I told Karin I had to get back to the barracks. My day's work was done, I felt. There was nothing more for me to do here. If I stayed any longer, I'd have to ask for pencil and paper to make out a grocery list. She whisked me into the sitting room and closed the door. Standing facing me, I looked at the Fräulein who had just dropped her pants and spread her legs for me. She smiled for the first time that evening, threw her arms around my neck, and reached up to kiss me. Her lips were moist and sweet. I ran both hands over her breasts.

"I happy I make all what you want," Karin beamed like a schoolgirl.

I did not say anything. I only kissed and touched.

"Now we . . . now we . . . how you say . . . ein Paar," she finally said, failing to find the right words in English.

I had no idea what that meant in German, and she could easily tell that from my facial expression.

"Here wait," Karin pleaded and ran from the room, leaving the door ajar. She came back not thirty seconds later holding what looked like a German-English dictionary. She flipped through the pages. "Ein Paar mean a couple or pair," she let out with a bright face. "Now we like one."

Yes, I thought to myself. Now we are united in body, but I was not so sure we were of one mind. Karin obviously was taking our transitory woodsy liaison more seriously than I was.

"I am happy if you are happy," I said, running my hands around her, front and back.

A few minutes later, we were standing by the door, saying good-bye, when the mother called out to Karin and said something. I recognized one word and knew what was coming next.

"Mutti like American Zigaretten. You bring also?"

"What brand?" I wanted to know.

Karin looked puzzled. She squinted and turned her head slightly.

"What name of cigarettes?" I explained, not waiting for her to look the word up.

"Oh," Karin said and called out to her mother. She then answered, "Mutti say macht nicht."

"Sure, okay," I told my new love. I too should have answered, like the mother but in soldiers' vernacular, mox nix. The old lady said it makes no difference what brand I came back to the house with so long as it was the American-made smokes that she liked. To me, it made no difference what the cigarettes cost me in the PX so long as I came back to this house and had the chance of coming again in the old lady's daughter.

Like any young American soldier during the postwar privation, by thrusting into a German girl, nice or otherwise, I was thrust into the role of brown-bagger.

"Sonntag," was the last word Karin said to me that Thursday. We had agreed to meet again on Sunday.

304

# CHAPTER 35: THE SECOND COMING

"She can't come on post, buddy?" the MP at the main gate to Merrell Barracks said to me in no uncertain terms as Karin looked on in disbelief.

It was Sunday afternoon, three days after that raincoat lay-down with Karin in Zirndorf Woods. I came to the Klotz's apartment a little after twelve. Mutti opened the door and greeted me. She smiled when she saw I was carrying a brown bag.

"This is for you." I handed her the bag containing two cartons of cigarettes, a jar of Maxwell House coffee, and a box of Lipton tea. The cigarettes I bought at the PX with my ration card but I had to pay one of the married guys at the shop five dollars over cost to get the coffee and tea for me at the Commissary.

"Danke, danke," the old woman repeated. She opened the bag and looked inside. Her eyes lit up. "Dankeschön, dankeschön."

Karin came from the other room and met me at the door. She looked happy but did not reach to kiss me in front of her mother. The mother excused herself and went into the kitchen. Karin and I had a date to see a movie and I suggested we go to Pinder Barracks near her. With my pass and I.D., I could get onto any American base.

"No, no," she fired back. "I go to Kaserne you have."

Karin insisted we see a movie at my barracks in Nuremberg, despite the long distance. The lengthy travel time did not faze her. It was apparent she was not ready yet to be seen with an American soldier, even in civilian clothes, in her small town any more than she had to. She said something to her mother and I recognized the word Kino so I knew she was telling her we were headed to the cinéma. I waited by the door while she got her raincoat and purse.

At the Hauptbahnhof we changed to get the streetcar to Merrell. We planned to see the two o'clock matinee. She seemed apprehensive at the prospect of coming on an American base for the first time with her G.I. boyfriend, even though we were now ein Paar. Karin told me she often sees young girls in her town walk through the streets arm-in-arm with soldiers from Pinder, "weissen und schwarzen," as she put it. I got the distinct impression that it was acceptable to her to date a white American from another city, and to enter his faraway barracks. But she would never be seen with, much less lay down for, one of the dark-skinned occupiers of her country on any barracks or in any town or city.

When we got to Merrell, I simply held up my I.D. to the MP as I nonchalantly tried to walk through the gate with Karin. He stopped us cold and ordered Karin to produce her kincard, as he called it. Every German is issued an identity card and was supposed to carry it at all times. With the Cold War heating up, and with East German and Russian spies on the loose, the military naturally was suspicious of anyone not American.

The faux pas was my fault. This was the first time I tried to bring a German national on the base. No one told me indigenous personnel have to prove their identity before they can set foot on American soil in their own country. The MP made it clear he could not let her pass through the gate.

"I bring not Kennkarte," Karin said, frantically searching through her purse, embarrassed at this sudden intrusion into her personal life by a foreign official in her land. "I leave at home." Her face reddened a bit. She acted as though the MP was ready to strip-search her.

I pleaded with the MP. "Can't I just sign for her?"

"No. She has to show her kincard and I have to write her number in the book."

I tried to calm Karin down. I told her that I will accompany her back home, she can pick up the card, and we can come back to the barracks. It will still be early. We can get something to eat and catch the six o'clock show.

"Das macht nicht," I stressed to her in her own tongue. It really made no difference to me. I was pleased just to be spending a pleasant day with my new German girlfriend. It did not much matter what we did. Besides, riding back-and-forth on two streetcars and a bus for more than two hours would give us a chance to get to know one another better.

It was just past two-thirty when we got back to Karin's house. No one was home. She said her mother and sister must have gone to her uncle's for Sunday dinner. They probably would not be back for another two hours. Karin went to her bedroom, while I stood by the door.

"I take Kennkarte," she said when she came back, proudly showing it to me before she put it in her purse.

Something so obvious did not dawn on me right away as I stood by the door waiting for Karin. The MP's rebuff at the Merrell gate, coupled with the happenstance of the afternoon departure of the mother and sister, presented an opportunity for the German-American couple to get to know one another far better than anything they could possibly achieve riding on the streetcar or bus. It hit me when Karin hung up her raincoat, took my hand, and led me into the sitting room. She closed the door and drew the curtains over the window. I took my raincoat off and sat down on the couch.

Karin wasted no time positioning herself on my lap as she had done the previous Sunday and Tuesday. I jumped right into deep kissing and fondling. She did not reach down to touch or hold me. She did not have to. I already was hard as a rock and knew she could feel it. I lifted her off my legs and she stood facing me. This time I wanted *her* to act.

"Take off your panties," I commanded her with a serious look in my eyes.

Without hesitation she lifted her dress, dropped the undergarment to her ankles, and stepped out of it. I unbuckled, unzipped, and lowered my trousers and shorts almost to my knees while still sitting on the couch. She watched me in silence while I quickly took out a rubber and rolled it down.

"Get on top of me," I said in an equally demanding tone and look.

Karin straddled me one leg at a time. She put her hands around the back of my neck and moved her lips to mine. I reached under to guide myself in. I found her opening, fit my tip in, grabbed her hips, and pushed her down on me. Now it was *she* who did most of the work as I jerked her up and down. It felt good, all the way in and nice and tight. She moved with me, almost in rhythmic fashion. Soon my body quivered under her as I released my pent up energy.

The second coming was immensely more enjoyable than the first. I saw more of Karin, I fit in right, I touched as well as pushed, and she did not cover her eyes. The poet's apt words were worth paraphrasing. It was splendor on the couch, glory in the sitting room, a radiance so bright that was not taken from my sight. Karin again made all what I wanted, but this time I felt fully satisfied.

With my trousers half down, I kept the rubber on until I got to the bathroom to wash up. I checked it before flushing the thing down the toilet. Karin came in after me, douched herself with her hand and tap water, and put her panties back on. I thought it was cute the way she bent her knees just prior to pulling up all the way. She too valued a snug fit, and I wanted to touch her once more down there. I stood behind her in front of the sink and gazed at the two young lovers in the mirror. I moved my left hand to cup her right breast, with my arm pressing against the other breast, while reaching down with my right hand. I rubbed the fold between her legs.

Unlike little Anna, my sixth-grade schoolmate, this German girl did not say nein. I kissed her neck while my hands were still busy. Karin seemed to like these tender gestures on my part and did one of her own. She lifted her arm behind her, ran her hand over my face and mouth, then turned around and reached up to me.

"You I love," she said openly and decisively after a prolonged kiss. "Ich leibe dich."

I looked at her without saying a word, either in English or German, somewhat stunned by this raw showing of such strong emotion so early in our relationship.

"Never I love Cherman boy like you."

I had no doubt Karin meant every word she said. She truly felt she loved me, even after only seeing me a few times, and more so than any common comrade or local yokel she might have known in her town. But I just could not bring myself to say anything of a reciprocal nature. I liked her, sure. I liked her very much. We fucked twice. So what? Does that mean I have to say I love *her*? Does that mean we have to *marry*? This girl may want to get very serious with me so I'd better not make her a baby, I told myself. Otherwise my plans for college next year will go down the toilet just like the spent come bag.

"Let's go back to my kaserne," I suggested to Karin. I avoided the topic she raised and what she probably wanted me to address. "Your mother and sister might be home early."

"Yes," she said, apparently agreeing with me on both counts.

We left her house a quarter past three. The Zirndorf bus going east pulled up right after we got to the corner. During the twenty-minute ride to Fürth, we hardly spoke. I did not think she was angry because I uttered no words of love but I did sense she would have liked me to. The silence seemed more a quiet understanding shared by two romantic intimates contented to know that their relationship was both meaningful and growing.

It was almost four-thirty when we reached Merrell. The same MP was on duty and stood outside the little wooden guardhouse. He remembered us. Without waiting to be asked, Karin eagerly opened her purse and handed the Kennkarte to the uniformed American soldier with a pistol on his belt.

"Thank you," he said to Karin. He looked at her I.D. photo and then at her. The MP turned, went in the guardhouse, and wrote in the big ledger sitting on a table.

"Sorry I turned you away before," he apologized, handing Karin back her card.

"We understand." I also wanted to say thank you for turning my girl away, as it gave me the opportunity to fulfill the most important objective of the day early on and without a tiresome trek to the woeful woods. The second coming to Merrell was worth the extra time and trouble.

Karin and I walked through the narrow archway that was the main entrance to the barracks. She marveled at the immense building, looking up and around at the many holes and cavities gouged out from the brick façade. I wondered if she reflected on the fact that only fourteen years have passed since many of her countrymen died defending this structure against the machine-gun and mortar attacks by *my* countrymen. Whether she knew this compound had been, and still is, referred to as the SS Kaserne, I did not ask. How much Karin knew or wanted to talk about Hitler, the war, Nazis, the nearby Party Rally Grounds, or concentration camps, I was afraid to ask or find out.

"Are you hungry?" I said to her just as we came out of the shadow of the archway and into the light. "We should eat something now before the movies."

"Yes . . . I like."

"Let's go to the snack bar. It's just around the right side of the building." The only other place I could have taken her to eat was the EM Club around the left side of the building, but I did not care to go there as it was mainly for drinking and dancing.

As we walked, I played tour guide. I pointed to the East Block and told Karin the room I sleep in was in that part of the Kaserne. When we passed by the West Block, I aimed my finger at the doorway that led to the office where I worked and described what I did. The shop was to our left and I nodded in the direction of the small building and explained the work I used to do there.

There was little activity on post that time of day on a Sunday, but Karin took in all what she saw for the first time. I did not have to elucidate on anything. Her head turned as she peered at the schwarz and weiss troopers in Class A's and civies walking around, the parked Army jeeps and trucks, the many private American automobiles, some German ones like the Karmann Ghia, and of course the young German women next to their American Schatzies.

We scaled the stairway to the snack bar and stood in line. There was only one other couple ahead of us. Karin saw that the men and women employed there were all German. I asked her what she wanted to eat but she shrugged her shoulders. There was no Schnitzel, Sauerbraten, Leberwurst, or Hassenpfeffer behind the counter or on the grill for her to choose from. I suggested what I planned to order, two hamburgers and French fries, and she said okay. For dessert, she did not see any Berliners, German Kuchen, or Schwarzwälder Torte, so she picked up a slice of apple pie after I did but asked that it be topped with Schokolad ice cream. Karin preferred coffee with her American meal rather than the coke I put on the tray.

We sat down at one of the tables for four. The tables on either side of us were unoccupied, as were more than half of all those in the snack bar. After emptying the tray, I placed it on the next table. Karin watched me as I smeared ketchup and mustard on my burgers and fries, but did not do the same. She seemed to be in good spirits, perhaps because she was a long way from home and figured none of the handful of countrywomen around her were from her town or were known to her. I watched her as she ate slowly and deliberately, relishing the taste of the foreign culinary products, while gazing at me from across the table. I too was in good spirits as I could not help thinking about the fulfilling bonding in her flat two hours earlier.

Through the corner of my eye, just as I finished my meal, I saw walking toward us the girl that worked in the snack bar whom I tried to bag. With Karin sitting opposite me, I was afraid to turn my head to look directly at the blond beauty. She stopped at the table on my left and picked up the tray, now filled with my dirty plates and the glass I drank from. Karin still had the coffee cup and saucer in front of her. I thought my dream lover might say something to me but she did not and I rested easy. Either she failed to recognize her sagged smitten suitor or she had the good sense not to step between a soldier and his Fräulein. The color-blind girl then went to the table behind Karin to wipe up. She now stood facing me and I did not have to turn my head to gawk at someone I could not take my eyes off the first time I happened upon. I could look at, even talk to, one German maiden while glancing over her shoulder to steal a pleasing peek at another that so captured my lustful imagination.

She, who a teammate said he would bet my boner was not good enough for, was just as comely to me as ever notwithstanding the knowledge that she had crossed the white line separating the directions American soldiers of different races traveled in Germany. Who knows what goodly dark meat slipped between her legs lately, or how wide she had to open that little mouth of hers? I tried to rid myself of such thoughts. Her endearing face, dandy figure, full tits, and tight ass still greatly warmed my passions. Nice as Karin was, she paled in comparison to my take on feminine perfection poised a few feet behind her. On a clammy Sunday afternoon in a sparsely patronized barracks eatery, an amorous G.I. caught on that he had just put down plain chuck hamburger when he coveted top sirloin steak.

The girl I was eyeing quietly walked away from the next table. I looked at my watch and saw it was five forty.

"We should leave now," I said to Karin. "The movie will be starting soon."

"Yes . . . we go."

We went downstairs and stood in the line that was starting to gather in front of the theater. There was a colorful Hollywood poster in the glass showcase. A Western was playing, *These Thousand Hills*, starring Don Murray, Lee Remick, and Patricia Owens. This would be a first for Karin. She had never seen an American movie in English, only one dubbed in German. I made small talk while we waited for the doors to open.

"Hey Dave," a voice called out from in back of us.

I turned around to look. It was Steve. He was coming toward us with a woman at his side. My roommate was smiling and waving at me.

"Hey buddy," Steve said when he reached our place in line. He put his arm around the woman's lower back and nudged her in front of him. "Say hello to Ursula."

I shook hands with the woman, a simple handshake German-style. She was almost a head taller than Karin and a little heavier, palatable in appearance, with a round face and high cheekbones. She looked only two or three years older than Steve, but still she was not the type I imagined he would go for. They had been together since we arrived in Nuremberg, almost three months, and it would be fair to say they were ein Paar.

"Ursula . . . Steve . . . this is Karin." I tilted my hand toward Karin at my side. She was somewhat stunned by the sudden American-style greetings.

"Nice to meet you," Steve beamed shaking hands with my date and unobtrusively slipping into the line right behind us.

"Grüss Gott," Ursula said to Karin, and she to her, as they touched fingertips delicately.

Steve and I talked a bit in code while our dates chatted away in German, oblivious to what we uttered in our usual military vernacular. Steve knew about the lay-down trip to Zirndorf Woods, as I told him about it when I came back to the barracks Thursday evening. And I knew Ursula had her own apartment and lived alone. Obviously, they did not have to go off somewhere like Karin and I or worry about a Mutti or Schwester barging in on them. Steve must have handily knocked off a piece that afternoon, perhaps about the same time Karin was riding top saddle with me on the couch.

"I thought you were going to take your leave on the home front today," Steve put to me in a low voice as our dates were gabbing.

"My company nixed the local camp for the day's exercises. Our out-of-range base was given a thumbs-up."

"Oh, the backyard wasn't good enough to be seen with a Yank," he quipped sarcastically.

"Affirmative. My company dodged that play."

"Where are you going after lights out?"

"Back to company territory," I said.

"You planning any maneuvers in the field?"

"No. My chosen assignment was completed earlier," I noted euphemistically in case Karin happened to be listening. I did not want her to be embarrassed any more that day, or any other day for that matter.

"Where did you see action?"

"In the German quarters."

"What about the two domestic hounds?" Steve asked.

"They took a hike. We were the Lone Rangers."

"Then you must have had a clear shot at your target."

"You better believe it," I whispered, "and I unloaded my cocked piece."

Just then, the doors to the movie theatre opened and the four of us walked in together. I paid the twenty-five cents for my ticket and for Karin's.

"Ursula likes American cowboy movies," Steve commented as he handed over half a dollar. "The characters speak in simple English, one-syllable words."

"Then Karin will like the movie playing here too, I'm sure."

We found seats in a middle row. Steve and I let the distaff half of our foursome sit between us so they could talk to each other. The two Nurembergers seemed to get along well together. Steve and I left our seats to buy popcorn, candy, and drinks. When we returned, the coming attractions had just started. Karin got excited when the preview of *Fraulein*, with Mel Ferrer and Dana Wynter, came on. She pulled at my arm and almost jumped out of her seat telling me she wanted me to take her to that movie next week. Ursula too indicated a desire to see the American-made Kino missing an umlaut in the title, about Germany at the end of the war and the immediate postwar period, but in her enthusiasm did not knock any popcorn from Steve's hand.

It was close to eight o'clock when the movie of the evening ended. *These Thousand Hills* was definitely not a typical cowboy flick with just shootings, hangings, cattle drives, and train robberies. It felt more like a Western film noir, with social themes that struck a chord. A young man is simultaneously involved with two women, one respectable and the other not, a cowboy from humble beginnings who dreams of owning his own ranch and being rich someday, determined not to be like his father who was a failure and died broke. The poor cowpuncher borrows money for a herd of cattle from his love-struck dance-hall girlfriend, her life's savings, only to later marry the town banker's prim and proper niece. He corrals considerable cash and pines for political office but then betrays his business partner and forsakes the woman who helped him launch his rise to wealth and power. Caught between ambition and loyalty, money and friendship, the rags-to-riches cattleman in the end redeems himself by fighting, against his wife's wishes, for the honor of his erstwhile lover he is indebted to, and is almost killed.

We said goodbye to Steve and Ursula after arranging to meet the following week to see *Fraulein*. I rode the two streetcars and a bus for the fifth time that day with Karin. We got back to her town after nine and we simply kissed at the door inside of her apartment before I left to head back to the barracks. I heard the mother and sister talking in the kitchen but I did not want to go in and say hello to the two people I was glad were not at home seven hours earlier.

Riding the two streetcars and a bus for the sixth and last time, I thought how splendid the day had been, in spite of the extensive, time-consuming public transit shuttling. I had a second and far better core fitting with Karin. The Klotz family's sitting room now doubled as a convenient locus for my future comings. My drool over the dreamy girl in the snack bar delighted me again. I met my roommate's Schatzie and was pleased that she and Karin hit it off. A movie that in some ways paralleled my own status and strivings left an impression on me.

## CHAPTER 36: SUNDAY IN THE PARK

Sunday the twenty-first of June, the beginning of summer, Karin took me for a picnic in the park. She told me a few days earlier to wear a bathing suit so we could bask in the afternoon sun, and said she would pack a lunch and bring a blanket.

In the previous two weeks, we did it a number of times on the couch. These love-ins were schneller as we were not so fortunate as to have the apartment all to ourselves. Within earshot were Mutti und Schwester in other rooms, not eating it up with Oncle at his house. Before we coupled stealthily, I told Karin to go to the bathroom and take off her panties, so that when she returned to the sitting room all she had to do was lift her dress and climb on top of me for a fast fuck. On these occasions, of course, I had to pull up my trousers and zip up my fly *before* dashing to the bathroom. I was sure she did not realize that Sunday we first met, when she held out her hand to lead me into the sitting room, her one word to me would be so prophetic.

From Karin's house we again walked east but much farther than the grassy area she took me to that first time. We crossed over a river and found a secluded spot on the south bank of the Bibert as she called it. In the background I could see a hill covered mostly with bushes. Karin spread the blanket out on a clearing in a field of high grass mixed with composite plants and daisies surrounded by tall cane. Hardwood trees with long branches stood behind the cane and cast a partial shadow over us.

As far as my eye could see, there was no one around. The basket of food was placed on one corner, shoes and a shirt on the other three corners. We both stripped to our bathing suits and lay down on the blanket next to each other using clothing as makeshift pillows. She was in a one-piece Zebra-striped suit. For the first time I got a good look at her figure. For my taste, Karin's hips were a little too wide, tits a little too small, and legs not shapely enough, but her shoulders and waist seemed just right for her body frame.

I leaned over to kiss her and she responded. I had no clue as to how far she would or could go on this partially exposed, though for the moment unpopulated, rustic spot in her small town. The scenario was unique for me and I myself did not know how far to go. Many times I had lain on blankets next to girls on the beach or under the Boardwalk in Coney Island, but that was different because it never occurred to me at age fourteen or fiftteen to do anything more than hold hands with the Jewish virgins, with or without crowds of on-lookers.

I slipped my left hand under the top portion of Karin's bathing suit and rubbed her nipple. She reached down and squeezed me I was bulging out so much. With the fingers of my other hand I moved her suit on bottom back a little and pried her open. Karin suddenly sat up. I thought the German girl was going to pull down the front of my bathing suit and do it French, but she made no such move to satisfy me orally.

"I take off," Karin said, as she started to unzip the back of her bathing suit.

She drew the strap over her head, pulled the garment down to her waist, and wriggled out of it. Turning away from me, she was on her hands and knees for a few seconds reaching out to place her suit on top of her clothes at the other end of the blanket.

For the first time in my life, I saw a girl's twat from behind. In the sunlight, Karin's puffy pinkish labia majora were a shade lighter than the skin on the back of her thighs. From my rear view, the folds starting at the top of her buttocks and running like the letter *J* to her clitoris looked like one continuous line. It was big cheeks over little cheeks. Doggie-style I could have boned into her, a cunt collar I often heard barked about in the barracks but one I never wagged my tail with before.

I took my bathing suit off just as Karin turned around to face me. She lay down again on her back. I quickly pulled a rubber from my pants pocket and put it on. We did it missionary style, the old fashioned way. I lifted her legs around me, stuffed my pleasure part in, and propelled myself in and out. This time too I was somewhat in a hurry to reach a completion. We were in a public park for Christ's sake, not a nudist colony or a stag movie set. I was not worried that Mutti or Schwester would cause a coitus interruptus, but rather any local Fritz or Frieda who happened to be out for a stroll.

As I kissed Karin's face in several spots and pushed harder and faster, I envisioned the Polizei running toward us, slapping bracelets on me, handing me over to MPs, and being carted off to the can. If going all the way without a stitch meant a pinch for indecent exposure, I certainly would have preferred a Frenchie half clothed. Fortunately, this naked city episode had a Hollywood ending, a felicitous release for one and a hasty dressing for two. Karin neither asked for, nor achieved, her own climactic end.

Once back in our bathing suits, thank God, all danger of discovery passed. The sandwich she handed me tasted fine. I did not notice it was ham and cheese until the last few bites.

After lunch, we rested for a while and tried to get a little tan. The tips of our fingers touched as we lie next to each other on the blanket without talking. Later, Karin packed everything up and then led me across the open meadow and grassy knoll to the other side of the park, holding my hand as we walked uphill.

"We go to house of Onkel," she said. "Mutti say he want meet you."

The summer of '59 started out with a bang, and a bare one at that. The sunny-side-up sex, my first ever, was still fresh in my mind as we hoofed it to her uncle's place. If horny troopers at Pinder Barracks enlisted and discharged my off-duty MOS with the town's Fräuleins, Zirndorf's parkland could have become another sort of soldiers' field.

Karin's uncle was her mother's younger brother. He lived alone in a small wooden shack on the other side of the Bibert at the edge of town. One huff and puff and the smokestack shanty could have been blown over. Onkel seemed very happy to meet me, though not surprised by my presence in his extremely modest abode. The middle-aged man smiled broadly, flashing two gold teeth in his upper palate, and extended his left hand to shake my right. He could only greet me with his left for the right arm was missing, probably taken off by an American or Russian tank or grenade or even one of his own German land mines. The cuff on the right sleeve of his ragged shirt was pinned awkwardly to the shoulder. The man was short in stature, stocky, bald-headed in the front and back, with thick fingers that almost crushed mine in the left-handed shake.

No one would ever mistake Karin's uncle for Hitler's ideal Aryan man or Nazi soldier. On top of a metal closet near the front door there rested a Wehrmacht helmet, the telltale curve at the lower end noticeable from where I was standing. I dared not open the closet,

317

lest I would see a bluish-gray Reich uniform neatly hung and black jackboots brightly polished on the floor. The gold in his mouth made me think that if he had been assigned to a concentration camp, his job could have been to pull such valuable teeth from Jewish corpses.

Karin did the talking for both of us. Onkel spoke no English. He looked back-and-forth between his niece and me as she said different things to her maternal uncle, who affected what I thought was a contrived smile. Some of the German words I easily understood. She told him I was an amerikanische Soldat, that I was stationed at the SS Kaserne in Nuremberg, that she went there with me to essen hamburger and see the Kino, that I brought Zigaretten, Kaffee, and Tee to Mutti. The former Wehrmacht soldier's eyes lit up at the mere mention of the word.

"Onkel want know if you bring Zigaretten," Karin said. Walking to his house, I anticipated that request.

"Yes," I responded right away. "Ja," I added, turning my head to look at the man and then nodding.

"Onkle say he pay."

"No, no, that's okay."

How could I take money from the uncle after I had such a memorable time with his niece naked in the park? What he may or may not have done during the war did not weigh heavily on my mind. It was doubtful he could pay much anyway.

The World War II German soldier looked at me and bowed his head slightly in deference to my avowed generosity. I did not want to think his desire to meet me was less to get a gander at the G.I. sticking it to his dearly departed brother-in-law's daughter than to stick his former enemy for free American cigarettes.

It really was not a big deal for me. I was very willing to subsidize the tobacco habit of anyone in the Klotz family who did not take the place of Karin's father and forbid her to see me. The veteran on the losing side did not, and could not, try to strongarm me. There was no attempt to play on my emotions or garner sympathy for a disabled combatant. He simply asked his niece to ask her boyfriend for a favor. She was giving me the favors I sought, so why should I not do the same for a member of her family?

We did not stay very long at Onkel's house. It was just meet and greet, shake and take, talk and walk. Heading back with Karin later that afternoon, I thought of how well I was received by this poor postwar German family. In just one month, I'm shtupping the daughter on a regular basis, shlepping food and cigarettes from the Commissary and PX to the mother, listening for the sister's laborious walk every time Karin and I are in the sitting room, and soon I'll be handing the uncle smokes too.

Maybe I should tell Karin to ask Onkel to invite us to his place once in a while and then take a hike? I was sure the tobacco-deprived German would be happy to do that cost-free simple task for his American provider. After all, it wasn't his leg that was missing.

I went back to the barracks early that Sunday. There was nothing more for me to do at Karin's place.

## CHAPTER 37: SEX, LIES, AND CELOPHANE TAPE

"I try on," Karin said, taking the sweater I had given her out of the plastic bag. There were tears in her eyes. I never saw anyone so happy over so little. She was like a child opening presents on Christmas morning. Before I could say another word, she rushed off to her bedroom.

It was Wednesday, the beginning of July, payday, a milestone for me. For the first time I cleared one hundred fifty dollars, double what the Army forked over two years earlier. The increased cash in hand reflected my E-4 rank, the overseas differential, and my being in over two, minus what was taken out for social security and income taxes. This was cause for celebration, and generosity toward the German family I was involved with.

I arrived at Karin's place just past seven thirty. After work I stopped at the PX, went to chow, showered, and hurried out the main gate. Under my arm was a big brown paper bag. If I had a white beard and red outfit, I could have been mistaken for Santa Claus. I handed two cartons of cigarettes and a jar of plum preserves to Mutti, who said danke with a bright smile. On the kitchen table I left two cartons for Oncle in a small brown bag for him to pick up or be brought to him the next time the Klotz family went for Sunday dinner. My entire ration for the month of July was depleted the first day. I also had something for Schwester, a 32-ounce metal container of sour sucking candies. For Karin, I pulled out a two-pound box of cherry chocolates, a beige V-neck sweater, and a silver locket and chain.

I went into the sitting room to wait for Karin. Mutti und Schwester stayed in the kitchen. In less than a minute, Karin came in and closed the door. "It good, it good," she beamed, running her hands down the front and sides of her upper body to show me how well the sweater fit her. The price tag hung over the back of her neck. I moved my hands to her breasts to make sure the fit was right. She stepped up to kiss me in gratitude, then reached into her dress pocket.

"I put on." Karin fumbled with the locket and chain until I helped her put it around her neck. She acted as if I gave her a diamond engagement ring, her face all aglow with the excitement and emotion of a schoolgirl. "I like, I like."

"I'm glad you like the locket," I told her. I opened it to show her that she could put a small picture inside. "And I'm glad the sweater fits you. I took a guess at your size."

Karin gazed into my eyes and stepped back, still overwhelmed by the three modest gifts I gave her. "Look," she said, as she lifted her dress to show me she had nothing on underneath. She had taken her panties off in the bedroom when she was trying on the sweater in anticipation of our ineluctable union.

It was exceedingly apropos that Karin's come on to me occurred in the sitting room, the best place for me to come on to her. What red-blooded American soldier could resist a German girl's green light? I sat down on the couch and drew her to my lap. Immediately my hands went to work, mostly on bottom. I stiffened up, a rubber was fetched, zipper pulled down, and jumping jack flash we were united. Karin still had the sweater on but I did not reach under it. I climaxed looking at the locket dangling around her neck. As I pulled out, I imagined she might put my picture in the locket and a cross on the chain too.

That evening, I got deeper in the hole with Karin. After the quickie, she sat next to me on the couch. It was apparent she wanted to talk.

"How old you are?" I was asked, just after returning from the bathroom. Karin waited until I had flushed my protection down the toilet and washed up before putting a question to me that must have been on her mind when we first met a month earlier.

I hesitated a moment. I was going to say twenty-one to cover myself. Karin looked about my age but she could be a year older, I thought, two at the most, like the WAC back at Fort Ord. It was a lucky break, therefore, that I did not reply forthwith.

"I twenty-three years," Karin admitted before I answered.

"Twenty-four," I said in an outright lie, swallowing hard. I had never made myself this old before and I doubted whether I could pull it off. I knew I looked a little older but I did not think I could get away with adding *five years* to my nineteen-year-old face. With the light-black soldier-girl, I only had to put on three years to ensure, if my thinking was correct, a continuing relationship. Quickly I mentally calculated what year I should claim I came into this life. "I was born on January thirtieth, nineteen-thirty-five."

"I geboren ten . . . " she responded, holding up the fingers of both hands for emphasis, and then continued in her mixture of German and English, "Dezember nineteen hundert tirty-five."

I had kept the falsification simple, in line with the actual month and day of my birth. "I'm almost a year older than you."

She seemed to buy my lie and I was glad, glad that she did not question me further about age. Perhaps the presents put her in a believing mood. I knew girls did not like to go out with boys who are years younger than they are. It makes them feel insecure, more so than they already are in a man's world. Still I was apprehensive that she might ask to see my I.D. card. I could not very well say I don't have one or that I left it at the barracks, especially after the incident about her Kennkarte with the MP at the Merrell gate. Who would believe a soldier in a foreign country would not have his I.D. with him at all times? The Army told us it was our passport overseas.

Karin moved closer to me and touched my arm tenderly. I was wearing a short-sleeve shirt and felt the warmth of her hand. "I want go marry mit you," she told me flat out, much to my amazement. No girl had ever proposed to me before and I never even *thought* of asking a girl to marry me. The sexual encounter minutes earlier must have warmed her heart too.

What was I to say to a girl I obviously liked and just had my way with after her expression of conjugal intent? She put me on the spot. I looked directly into the lovesick girl's eyes and then away. I could not lie and say I wanted to marry her, and I could not tell the truth and say I did not want to marry her. Karin simply was not the kind of girl I dreamed of or my parents would accept. I did not want to make promises I knew I wouldn't keep, and I did not want to hurt the feelings of a decent girl. I cared about her, sure. I wanted to keep on shtupping her, sure. But I had plans for getting out of the Army and registering for college, not plans for getting hitched and signing for another hitch in the Army in order to support a wife.

I said nothing. It was as if someone grabbed me by the throat. Then, moments later, words came to me, just like that day in Böblingen when I went back to see Lieutenant Finston to weasel out of my assignment to Fulda. "I'll write home and ask my mother," I finally let pass from my lips. I knew it was a lame attempt to stall giving Karin an answer to the matrimonial question, but I could think of nothing else to say. Once again, I was weaseling out of something.

Karin said nothing at first too. She neither suggested I telephone my mother nor inquired as to why a twenty-four-year old man has to ask his mother if he can get married. My answer was not the one she wanted to hear but I sensed she reluctantly accepted the door being left open for a wedding procession. When she did speak, it was apparent she was still interested in knowing all about the foreigner she gave herself to so completely and wanted to spend the rest of her life with. "You are Katholik?" she asked.

"No," I answered simply and directly. I could falsify my age, I could avoid telling the truth about my willingness to marry, but I could not lie about my religion.

Karin sat back on the couch, surprised by my answer. I figured she was Catholic, most Germans in southern Germany were, but her question made me sure of it. She mentally put my figurine with hers atop a seven-layer white cake, now she wants to stick a crucifix in behind us.

"Your parent . . . not from Italien?"

"No," I said a second time to a question about my social background. I could pass for Italian so she assumed I was Catholic.

"Where your parent from?" A trace of disappointment was in her voice.

"My mother came from Poland, my father was born in America but his family is Polish too."

"What your Familie name?" It was a wonder she had not asked that sooner, when she said she loved me perhaps.

"Streiber," I said straight out, unwilling to lie about my name either. I reached for my wallet and took out my pass, knowing that my date of birth was not on it. "Here . . . look." I spelled it out for her too.

Karin took my pass in her hands and scrutinized the English writing on it. "Shtreiber is Cherman name." She pronounced my name in the German vernacular.

"Yes, I know," I replied directly, just as I had done more than eight years earlier when Anna's mother said the same thing, albeit in better English.

323

Karin hesitated this time before speaking. She seemed puzzled. "Your parent from Polen, why they have Cherman name?"

"Because most Jews in Poland have German names. The Jewish people in Eastern Europe originally came from Germany."

I had to tell her I'm Jewish. I couldn't lie about my being, the essence of my self.

Karin's head snapped back in a double take. She looked at me in shock, with total disbelief, as if I had just revealed that one of my parents was African or I was a Communist spy or even a transsexual, a Christine Jorgensen in reverse.

"Never I tink you Jude." She pronounced it *Jewd*, as in English and the book in the New Testament, not *Yudah* as in German.

I should have taken that as a compliment, but I didn't. She had a stereotype in mind and I simply did not fit it. I wondered how many Jews she actually came in contact with in the almost Judenfrei post-Nazi Germany she lived in more than half her life. "Why is that?" I asked.

"You have not big Nase . . . and it has not Kurve." She brought her thumb and forefinger to her nose and effected a curved motion downward.

So, she thinks all Jews have bumper schnozes . . . or beaks.

"You tall," she said.

Another stereotype revealed. Are Jews supposed to be shrimps too? Karin must have seen the Nazi propaganda film *The Eternal Jew* as a young girl in school, a rabidly anti-Semitic portrayal of Jews as rats and vermin preying on the good German people.

"You buy present for Mutti, even Onkel you not know."

Add cheapskate to the stereotype list. And chalk up one more for Joseph Goebbels who never portrayed Jews as bountiful or footing their friends.

"You nice to Cherman people," she added.

Her final characterization was perhaps the most disturbing. "Why shouldn't I be nice to your family? You invited me into your home. I like you."

After some reflection, she said, "Yes . . . you right."

I felt the need to explain myself further with reference to what understandably was seldom spoken about in Germany after the war. "I don't hate all Germans because of what the Nazis did to the Jews?"

Karin's image of Jews was not unlike my mother's of Germans, but I held no prejudices against her. This was the first time I ever talked about Nazis and Jews to a German, especially someone I was intimately involved with.

"Yes," she said, ostensibly in agreement with my last statement.

Karin and I looked at each other. She seemed relieved and moved toward me again. I leaned over and kissed her. Just then, the door opened and I sat back. In hobbled Schwester, a few sucking candies in hand, soon followed by storm-trooping Mutti. They put themselves down on the chairs opposite us and started to talk to Karin. Much of the exchange passed by me, save that it was about Sonntag and Onkel.

"Mutti want know if you come Sunday to Onkel," Karin said. "We all eat."

I was not crazy about downing strange German food, greasy pork swill no doubt. "I don't know. My company is having a Fourth of July picnic on Saturday. I may just want to rest on Sunday." My last comment was no lie, digestive considerations aside.

Karin almost jumped up from the couch. "Oh, Picknick. I want go. You take me?"

I was glad the mere mention of an Army picnic was enough to get her mind off questioning me about my demographics. "Yes, of course. I was going to ask you."

Her eyes gleamed. "What time?"

"It starts at one o'clock. I'll pick you up about eleven forty-five."

"No, no. I meet at Hauptbahnhof. You not come so far on Strassenbahn und Autobus."

Now I knew Karin swallowed my lies and evasions, and was not mad. "Okay. I'll meet you at twelve-thirty."

Before long, with the two watchdogs in the room, I said my auf Weidersehens and headed back to the barracks. "Samstag," Karin reminded me as she closed the front door.

That night I left Karin's place with mixed emotions. In three days, she would attend for the first time an American military social gathering. The 2nd Armored Cavalry Regiment held an annual Independence Day celebration for its troops and those from the attached units, along with their wives and children or Schatzies. My German girlfriend would be meeting my teammates, my bosses and their families, and G.I.s from other companies I hardly knew, black and white. Given the stereotypes she espoused about Jews, I was apprehensive. As it turned out, it was not her biased attitudes toward Jews that I had to worry about.

The next day I came to work at the Area Office a little early, before the two Bs generally arrived. I went straight to the typewriter. I printed 30 Jan 35 on a piece of paper and cut it out close to the edges. I took a small strip of cellophane tape, stuck it over the date, and on my I.D. card carefully lined it up on top of my actual date of birth. The size and shape of the type was not too different from the information typed in. I put the card back in my wallet, but in one of the plastic holders for pictures and not in a pocket where it had been before. If Karin asked to see my I.D., I would simply open my wallet and show her the card through the plastic that obscured the cellophane tape and the altered writing. I banked on her not asking me, as a police officer would do with a stopped motorist, to take the identity card out of the wallet and hand it over.

Thanks to one of my truthful answers to Karin the previous day, I did not have to use silvery duct tape, or any other device, to cover up or change the letter *J* imprinted on my dogtags.

# CHAPTER 38: INDEPENDENCE DAY

The Fourth of July picnic was held in the public park at the Dutzendteich, the dozen lakes on the former Nazi Party Rally Grounds, about a mile and a half southeast of Merrell Barracks. The Dutzendteich once comprised the center of the Reichspartei's military showcase to the world. The Luitpoldarena, Luitpoldhalle, and the coliseum-like horseshoe Kongresshalle stood on the north side of the lakes. Zeppelinfeld with the impressive Tribüne grandstand and reviewing areas and the Städtisches Stadion were constructed on the south side.

The Grosse Strasse, a great road 60 meters across and two kilometers long, the central axis of the grounds, separated the larger and smaller portions of the lakes. The wide boulevard ran from the unfinished Congress Hall at the upper end that was to serve as a 50,000-seat Party convention center all the way to Märzfeld, a German soldiers' parade field and campsite at the lower end named appropriately for Mars, the god of war. Along the March Field perimeter, 24 towers and stands for over 200,000 people were proposed, but only a few of the towers had been built before the war and nothing after its outbreak.

To the west of the Great Road, opposite his Tribüne, architect Albert Speer sought to erect a sports stadium for nearly 500,000 spectators. Work began in 1937 but the war took its toll and by 1944 there was little more than a huge excavation. Only two segments of the stadium as models were built. Groundwater contaminated with hydrogen sulfide soon filled the gigantic cavity, now called the Silbersee. After the war rubble from Allied bomb-ings was dumped next to this Silver Sea, forming a stone mountain.

The 2nd Armored Cavalry Regiment sponsored the Independence Day celebration on the Third Reich's stomping grounds. Everyone from the attachments were also invited, those from my company, the 176th Signal, as well as the 53rd Ordnance and the 39th Artillery. On this day we honored America the Beautiful and the United States' commitment to principles of life and liberty and justice laid out in Thomas Jefferson's Declaration of Independence that the Founding Fathers signed. We held our hearts and pledged allegiance to the Constitution ratified by the thirteen colonies and every president since George Washington swore on the Bible to uphold. As occupiers of a defeated and divided Germany, Americans had an inalienable right to teach the citizens of the former Nazi stronghold the blessings of democracy over fascism, and to set an example for racial tolerance and good will toward all people.

There were no Schwarzers in my outfit, but in the 2nd Cav and other units more than one-third of the troopers were, triple the percentage of non-whites in the United States at that time. For Germans the U.S. Army was the model that black and white, Jew and Gentile, can work together. But for many Germans and Americans alike, racial tolerance was not something that was exhibited on a daily basis either in public or in private.

The festivities were in the Volkspark, a grassy recreational area between the smaller lakes on the south end and the Silbersee.

Soldiers and civilians ate hot dogs and hamburgers and wiped the mustard, ketchup, sauerkraut, and relish off their faces within plain sight of the Grosse Strasse. Herr Hitler many times breezed along this roadway in the back seat of his Mercedes convertible ahead of the military formations, standing up and Sieg Heiling to the fervent crowds of Deutschlanders on both sides of the divide.

Beer, wine, coke, and seltzer were guzzled down looking over to Zeppelinfeld with its ghosts of decades past, faint shadows of goose-stepping Wehrmacht warriors passing by the grandstand speaker's platform under the eagle eye and outstretched arm of the Führer. While munching on potato chips, pretzels, peanuts, and pickles, silent echoes of never-played Nazi sports events could almost be heard emanating from March Field in the distance.

As we swallowed Dutch apple pie and marble pound cake topped with vanilla and chocolate ice cream, a malodorous whiff from the direction of the Silbersee filled our nostrils. Stars and Stripes were waved and firecrackers set off not far from a Congress Hall that, if completed, would likely have displayed swastika flags and had cannon balls fired in front. Americans and Germans, surrounded by the Third Reich's lakeside monuments to unrealized glory, removed particles of food stuck between their teeth with red, white, and blue toothpicks.

That July 4th in 1959 did not turn out to be a day of independence for just U.S. citizens. And, to no great surprise, it did not turn out to be a day where everyone exuded the spirit of equality celebrated.

Karin was waiting for me at the Hauptbahnhof streetcar stop at twelve-thirty like she said she would. I was the one who was a few minutes late. She wore a thin white-and-pink sleeveless summer dress with flower prints and a pair of open-toe shoes, aptly suitable for the warm weather that day. A small black handbag hung over one arm. She seemed glad to see me but I got the impression she had things on her mind other than the picnic that she wanted to talk to me about. We caught the Nummer 8 and sat down in a rear row.

Before she even settled in, Karin asked, "Where is Picknick?"

"Not far from my kaserne . . . at the Volkspark . . . near the Dutzendteich." I did not say Americans would commemorate their good holiday on the evil Nazi Party Rally Grounds.

Karin gave no indication as to whether she, being from a suburb of Nuremberg, knew the connection between the Dutzendteich and the Nazis. She only asked again, "Why Picknick on four Juli?" She pronounced the German word for July as *Yooley*.

"Because the Fourth of July is Independence Day," I explained to this unknowing foreigner. "This is a legal holiday in America . . . even here in Germany for soldiers. We don't have to work. We celebrate the holiday by having a picnic, by eating and drinking with family and friends."

Karin looked puzzled. "What means independence?"

"Independence means freedom," I said.

This was not the first time I explained a word to her in English. More than a month into my relationship with a German girl, I was used to and did not mind playing Noah Webster.

"It means you can do what you want. You don't have to do what your parents want. It also means if you are rich or have a lot of money, you don't have to work if you don't want to."

Karin seemed to understand the dictionary definition I gave, but not how it applied to the United States. "Why America have day for independence?"

The New Germany apparently did not include in the curriculum of its elementary and secondary schools the history of their American conquerors and occupiers. Now I would have to play social studies teacher as well.

"Almost two hundred years ago," I said, adopting a didactic manner that appealed to me, "on July fourth, seventeen seventy-six, famous Americans signed a Declaration of Independence. They declared our freedom from England. We were a colony or part of that country but wanted to break away. England was like our parent. We wanted to form a new nation, our own government. But England didn't want to let us go. There was a war, a revolution as we call it, and we won. America then had its freedom. That's what we celebrate, our independence."

Karin paused a moment and looked at me. I could tell she was thinking about what I just said. "Four Juli like Kristmas," she said, no doubt understanding the word celebrate.

Her connection of the two calendar events was interesting to me, since as a non-Christian I would not have thought of them that way, but it was understandable. Germany had nothing like the Fourth of July . . . or Lincoln's Birthday or Memorial Day. Holidays were religious, not political.

"Yes," I simply noted, unable to disagree. "Everyone is happy, but we eat and drink and have a good time outdoors in the park, rather than around a table in a house."

Karin hesitated again before speaking. She looked at me more intensely, as if she were trying to read my thoughts. "Jude have not Kristmas."

So this was what was mainly on her mind, a comparison of Judaism and Christianity. Her statement was either a comment or ques-tion, or possibly both, and opened a can of worms. She evidently had pondered on my revelation three days earlier, to her utter amazement, that I was Jewish. I treated what she just said as a question.

"No." That was the only answer I could give.

"Where you go to church?" Karin asked, letting another worm out.

"Do you know the Palace of Justice . . . on Furtherstrasse . . . near the Old City?"

"Yes, I know."

"Well, that is where Jewish services are held on Friday nights and special holidays. It is for soldiers and for Americans and Germans who live in the Nuremberg area."

"Cherman Jude?" Karin put to me inquisitively, as if she had heard or thought that there were no Jews left in Germany.

"Yes. German Jews . . . and American Jews not in the Army, and Jewish soldiers like me."

"I want go mit you," she said immediately.

Now I could feel worms crawling all over me. "But you're Catholic."

"I want go," she said excitedly, brushing my comment aside. "I want see what like. I want meet Cherman Jude." She reached to hold my hand. "Katholics think Yesus already come. Jude think Yesus not come yet."

That was one way to characterize the differences between Christianity and Judaism, albeit simplistically. I wondered where she learned that bit of religion. My mother's letter to me was prescient after all. A German girl *was* trying to get her hooks into me. Karin, a Catholic, could only be interested in coming with me to my church, as she mistakenly thought a synagogue was, because she presumed her participation in Jewish services would enamor her to me and pave the way for marriage between us. Certainly I was reluctant to take her to services. It meant an involvement that I was not ready for, but I had to give in on this point or call it quits with a girl I liked and was having my way with.

"Okay. We'll go next Friday. I can pick you up in Zirndorf or meet you at the bahnhof."

Karin flashed a little smile, as if she was pleased with her latest accomplishment, getting me to take her to Jewish services and her starting down the road to independence from Mutti and her Church. Just then the streetcar stopped at the corner before the street the barracks was on. We got off and walked half a block to the left.

A long brown bus was parked to the side in front of Merrell's main gate and we went toward it. The regiment footing the bill for the picnic had arranged transport to the Dutzendteich location for its cavalrymen, its attached troopers, and their Schatzies. Enlisted men and officers who lived off post either had automobiles to take them and their families to the Volkspark or hitched a ride with someone. Parking the Army vehicle outside the gate rendered it unnecessary for German girlfriends, on this national holiday, to present Kennkarten to the guard and have their presence on an American military facility registered in order to partake in the festivities. On our most venerated day of the year, I could have toted Raisa Russikoff to the picnic and no one would have suspected I was fraternizing with a KGB agent.

Steve and Ursula were already on the bus when Karin and I got on board. They saved us two seats in front of them. The girls shook hands by fingers, said Grüss Gott, and chatted away.


At the picnic, Steve and I and our dates mainly socialized with our bosses and teammates, some who came alone. I only knew two troopers from the 2nd Cav and they were sitting and eating with their black buddies and white girlfriends at different tables. It was a beautiful day, clear blue skies and not too hot, with a cool breeze now and then that moved through the trees and shook loose some leaves from the branches.

On the bench next to us at our long wooden table were Dombrowski and Westhill who came without Schatzies. They enjoyed talking to Karin and Ursula whom they met for the first time. Bentley and Doss with their wives and small children were in a different area where families congregated for the seesaws, swings, a sandbox, and jungle gym. Barry, I was told, had other commitments and would not attend. Fat Jonesy was there, he would not have missed all that free food. Surprisingly, given his lack of endearing physical qualities, a not-too-bad-looking Fräulein was hanging off his arm. I watched him stuff his face with so many frankfurters it reminded me of the hot dog eating contest held in Coney Island at Nathan's every year.

Karin seemed to be having a good time. First she talked to and mingled with the white American wives and the Schatzies with white G.I.s. I let her roam about as she pleased, do what she felt comfortable with. I never told her what to do or not do with anyone. Then she ate a hamburger and drank beer at one of the tables for 176ers. Before long, her proclivities popped up.

The two Schwarzers I knew from the 2nd Cav were making the rounds from table to table showing off their chalky dates, proudly traipsing around the picnic site with hands tightly clasped and brushing lips intermittently. At our table, she could see the mixed couples walking toward us.

The black cavalrymen were an odd pair. They shared the large room next to the latrine with two whites in their outfit. Steve played cards with them in that room twice a week and I often went in there to fetch him for one thing or another. Amos Jackson was famous around the barracks. He liked to shave naked at night. When he stood up against the sink, his thick head hung over the rim such that it looked like he was taking a piss. From what little I knew of Amos, he was naïve about the Army and the power plays between noncoms and lower-ranked enlisted men but he seemed honest and forthright. The toilet etiquette of his ragged roommate, Tyrone Andrews, was no better. The hefty trooper always seemed to be on the pot when the latrine was crowded with guys showering and shaving, but with his long shlong over the top of the seat he just farted away between plops oblivious to those around him, smelling up the damn place. Tyrone was more the blustering type, projecting an unwarranted self-confidence and inflated ego. The portly Schatzies at their sides must have been over thirty, not at all attractive with their painted faces, bobbed hairdos, heavy legs, mid-riff bulges, and modest chests.

"Here come Amos 'n' Andy," Dombrowski said in a low voice, employing the sobriquet 176ers coined for these two of a kind in another outfit down the hall from us.

"With a white Ruby and white Sapphire," Westy added softly in his typical sarcastic and succinct manner.

"Can't tell the big nigs from shit or Shinola," Dombrowski said sarcastically.

"Or the fat frauleins from knockwurst or cockwurst," Westy interjected again, as if playing tag with his teammate.

Steve turned around and saw his two poker pals and laughed. He and I well understood the disguised racial slurs, but the analogies to American radio and film characters and a popular shoe polish went right by Karin and Ursula. The sexual innuendos no doubt escaped the girls too.

The six of us just sat there as the salt-and-pepper foursome made their way to our table. Karin was sitting at my side and I looked at her. Her face paled, her eyes beamed straight ahead, her upper body stiffened. Karin's thigh was flush against mine and I was having romantic thoughts of her. But just before the forbidden-lovers quartet sauntered to our table, Karin abruptly got up and walked off without a word. Ursula went after her, but only after first saying hello to the black-and-white pairs, then doing a fast shake with the female crossovers, leaving Steve to gab with the jokers wild and me holding my hot dog.

The denigrating color comments and anatomical annotations were nothing new in the Army among white soldiers, who eagerly and un-abashedly voiced such attitudes outside the presence of their black peers. The frumpy Fräuleins, aside from their color preferences, were not my type but they were Amos 'n' Andy's cotton pickings. On post or in military settings, on Independence Day especially, white and black soldiers and their deutsche dates should be friendly toward one another, or at least give the appearance of brotherly and sisterly love.

Off post, in bars and in town, contacts between the races were another matter. Suspicion and animosity were the order of the day. White soldiers marched to a different drummer and played out southern segregation practices. Ursula was experienced with Army culture, having gone out with two American men that I knew of prior to Steve. She knew how to behave properly in situations where there was a contradiction between the ideal and the real America.

Karin did not have that experience or knowledge and, judging from her avoidance action, was unable to put aside the Nazi propaganda about Africans extant in her society when she was growing up. Whether that judgment applied to Jews as well remained to be seen.

I saw Ursula talking to Karin about twenty yards away. They were standing next to a tree and Karin was waving her hand in a downward motion. Famous Amos and Raggedy Andy and their white dolls had moved on to another table. I was surprised that none of them expressed any indication of being snubbed by a Nazi Schatzie who flat-out refused to talk to them, or touch fingers, because of their skin color, and ditto for their German lovers because of intimate associations. Steve bit into his hamburger and ignored the potentially embarrassing incident. I got up and walked over to where the girls were.

"I like not Neger," Karin whispered when I reached her, having the good sense not to raise her voice. "And I like not Fräulein who sleep mit Neger. Never I make shake hands." She stepped back and put her hands behind her.

Ursula spoke to Karin in German, trying to reason with her I gathered, but it was to no avail. Karin steadfastly declined to be civil to the Americans and Germans she did not know but disliked. This strange scenario pitted Fräulein against Fräulein, German against American. Why was Karin so enthusiastic about coming to the picnic with me if she was going to act this way? Surely she was aware that America was the land of many races and her soldiers came in different colors? Black with white was nothing new to her, for she must have witnessed the dark troopers from Pinder Barracks tramping around Zirndorf with light babes.

"Let's go back to the table," I pleaded, trying to nudge Karin with my hand on her lower back. I did not have to ask her why she left in the first place.

"No. I stay here."

Ursula said something in German but Karin did not respond. Seeing it was hopeless, I turned to Ursula. "Why don't you stay here for a minute while I go and get Karin's food and drink. Then I'll stay with her and you can go back to Steve." Neither of them said anything so I went back to our table to get Karin's plate and cup.

Interestingly, Karin acted as Hitler did at the 1936 Berlin Olympics, when he refused to shake hands with Jesse Owens, the black American who won four gold medals in track and field, at times defeating German athletes. Karin might well have acted like Sonja Henie, the three-time Norwegian ice-skating gold medal winner, who shook hands with Hitler, the future occupier of her country, after giving the Nazi salute. Henie paid dearly in public opprobrium before, during, and after the war for the filmed incident. I hoped I would not have to pay dearly in company respect and comradeship for Karin's declination to shake hands with certain Americans and Germans on Independence Day.

Uneducated and uncouth Jonesy, and the other teammates that clued Steve and me in on G.I.s and Fräuleins that first full day at Merrell Barracks, were right in their assessment. There *is* a three-tier system of females in Germany, and one class does not mingle with the other. Karin was in the first class before she met me. She dropped down to the middle level as soon as she started going out with, not to mention removing her panties and bathing suit for, me. The drop I knew bothered her, since she did not wish to be seen with me in her small town and be subject to gossip and condemnation by her neighbors. No wonder she was so adamant about not greeting Fräuleins at the bottom of the barrel. That was her means of maintaining self-respect and a feeling of superiority over the trashy women in her country. She goes with a white G.I., a look-alike for a German, a cousin from America, not as Nazi ideology would have it some hairy hare-brained ape from the jungle.

"Karin doesn't want to come back to the table right now," I told Steve.

"What's wrong?"

"I'll tell you later," I said.

Steve nodded. I was sure he knew what was wrong.

"I'm bringing her plate and cup to her. Ursula will be back in a minute."

I was just about to return to Karin when I noticed another two-color combo making the rounds. It was the girl from the snack bar and at her side the bulky buck I presumed Jonesy and the others happily described for me. She was wearing Bermuda shorts and a tight-fitting top that revealed her flawless figure. I longed to run my hands over her bust, around her hips, down her legs, and up to her crotch. She was as pretty and captivating as ever with her yellow hair to the neck, fine facial features, immaculate skin, and sweet smile. Twenty Schatzies, Ruby and Sapphire types or not, could not hold a candle to her.

I now had a clear picture of the schwarzen Liebling my dream lover was spreading those beautiful legs for, or opening that appealng mouth to. So this is the cavalryman who keeps down the hall from me whose spot in the girl's bed I wanted to take. He was tall and thin, somewhat muscular, but not handsome in the least. Broad nose, wide nostrils, rabbit ears, curved cranium, protruding lower lip, stubble beard, dark skin tone with a few small white blotches, irregular hairline, eyes set too close, a Sidney Poitier or Harry Belafonte he was not. What my Fräulein Perfekt loved in this blemished baboon, other than what he was packing below the belt, I could not imagine.

"I come back," Karin said, tapping me on the shoulder from behind, surprising me, while I was still fixated on Beauty and the Beast. "I stay at table."

Why this sudden change of heart and mind? Did she notice I was staring at another girl? A very attractive girl but one beneath her in social rank in her country given the company she was keeping? Was she now willing to shake hands indiscriminately? Ursula had her arm around Karin, prodding her to sit down. The talk apparently did some good. Dombrowski and Westy looked on but said nothing.

"Good," I said. I set her plate and cup down on the table.

No other mixed couple came our way the rest of the afternoon. Whether Karin had put aside her Nazi heritage and found some kind of American-style patriotism on this Independence Day was never tested. Fortunately, my bosses did not have dark American wives and little picaninnies, and I was spared the ignominy of my German girlfriend pulling away from them. I could have lost my cushy clerk's job and been shipped out to fix signal equipment in the field in Fulda. Karin would have fucked me rather than the other way round.

The trip back to Zirndorf was a quiet one. Riding on the two streetcars and the bus, Karin and I hardly spoke. She embarrassed me at the picnic, and I probably upset her.

I thought about the film *Fraulein* that Karin and I saw together at the post theater. A young woman in war-torn Germany is falsely registered as a prostitute with the American authorities by a couple operating a brothel, outspoken supporters of the Nazis. She flees and they pursue her, only to be blocked by a sympathetic American MP, a black man. A racial slight is leveled at the corporal and the thankful Fräulein apologizes for her countryman's remark. She later meets the American major who, as a prisoner of war, she and her father sheltered from the Gestapo. He falls in love with her and wants to take her back to his family in New Jersey. When she applies for a passport she realizes she will be rejected because of the registration, but then the corporal, who knows she is not a prostitute, comes to her aid again. The kindly black soldier whites out the prejudicial word on her application. The Fräulein can now marry the American and emigrate. *Fraulein*, with its happy ending of a black

337

man saving a white woman from being blackballed, was definitely not a Hollywood film noir.

The film caught my attention because it showed that some Germans during the war were against the Nazis. How Karin, old enough in the first half of the 1940s to remember the hard times in Germany, felt about the Nazis I had no idea and would not ask. After the war, most Germans implied self-servingly that they were blind, deaf, and dumb about the wartime atrocities. Karin seemed to like the American-made movie because it was a story of a G.I. in love with a Fräulein, he asking her to marry him and come to the States, and she deciding to leave a divided postwar Germany in ruins. Key points in the film about a black G.I. doing good deeds for a Fräulein with urgent needs, and the Fräulein espousing a favorable attitude toward an American of his color, apparently were lost on the prejudiced Fräulein that I knew.

I dropped Karin off at her house without going inside. Our goodbye kiss was a timid one, a palpable deviation from the intensity and aggressiveness of our kissing in previous weeks. When I got back to the barracks, Steve had not yet returned from taking Ursula home. He came into the room when I was already in bed. We did not talk about the day's events that night or at any other time.

# CHAPTER 39: WAITING . . .

Company was kept with Karin on Monday and Wednesday evening of the week following the picnic at the Dutzendteich. As customary, I knocked it off schnell on the couch in the sitting room while Mutti und Schwester were busy in the kitchen. Their voices could be heard faintly through the closed door and that gave me the assurance of committing my spirited love act without fear of detection. Karin failed to climax in such a short penetration time but I certainly did not and that was the most important thing in our continuing courtship. Just pleasing me seemed to make her happy.

The main event of the week, however, occurred on Friday evening when I took my Catholic Schatzie to Jewish services at the Palace of Justice. On Monday and Wednesday, no mention was made of my promise on Independence Day. More mundane things were on my mind and I thought, or rather hoped, she might have forgotten about it. I was wrong.

"We go Freitag," Karin reminded me on Wednesday after I kissed her goodbye. I had one foot out the door when she tugged at my sleeve. I turned around and saw a determined look in her eyes. "I want see Jude church."

She had been waiting to tell me that since Saturday. "Okay," I said, realizing it was futile to try to talk her out of it. "But we don't call it church."

She squinted and twisted her head a little. "What you call?"

"A Jewish place of worship is a synagogue. If it is a very big building, it is called a temple."

Karin looked straight at me with wide eyes. "I want see."

"Okay," I said again. "Can you meet me at the Hauptbahnhof at six thirty . . . eighteen and a half?" I qualified in both military and common German time while pointing to my wristwatch. "If I came to pick you up, we'd be late."

"I meet, yes."

With that taken care of, I finally got both feet out the door.

Back at the barracks, Steve looked up from the letter he was writing when I came in the room. He was sitting in the middle of his bunk in T-shirt, shorts, and flip-flops.

"Karin wants me to take her to services on Friday night," I said. With Steve it was not necessary to say *Jewish* services.

"Will you take her?"

I nodded. "I have to. I promised her." She's been waiting all week for that.

"You don't look too happy about it," Steve put to me. He read my face accurately.

"I'm not."

"Why? Because you think she'll want to convert so you'll marry her?"

I nodded. "Something like that."

"Well, don't worry about it old buddy. Karin probably won't like Judaism. My mother went to synagogue with my father a few times before they got married, and she never converted."

"Yes," I said to my roommate with a straight face, and then pulled the blanket down on my bunk. "But Karin's not your mother."

Steve started to say something but stopped.

"And I'm not your father."

We both went to sleep that night without another word.

I took Karin to services on Friday night, the tenth of July. She wore a plain dress, nothing fancy, and made her face up with just a touch of cosmetics. Flashy or clownish she certainly did not look. She insisted we arrive at the Palace before services began. I knew that when people see her with me, they will know she's not Jewish, but will think I'll soon be filling out marriage papers with the Army. This American boy holding hands with that German girl would not be the only interfaith couple sitting in the makeshift pews.

During the service, Karin was attentive and did not ask any questions about what was going on. She held open the Siddur and silently looked at, perhaps read and understood some of, the translations and transliterations of Hebrew words and phrases on the English language side of the book. I and other congregants mainly chanted in unison from prayers in the original Hebrew on opposite pages. Much to my surprise, she seemed at ease and quite absorbed in the strange incantations from the congregation and the rabbi-led religious practices.

It was *I* who was ill at ease standing and sitting next to the non-Jewish girlfriend I brought with me to Jewish services. I half expected her to look for the holy water to dip her fingers in, or seek a kneeler to genuflect on. But I was relieved to see that she did not cross herself or go up to the rabbi for a wafer to be placed in her mouth, or sip from a cup of wine, in order to receive the body and blood of Christ. This was another first for me, taking a girl, Jewish or otherwise, to shul on a date.

Karin did not embarrass me in the services nor in the Oneg Shabbat afterwards across the hall. She took some coffee and cake like everyone else and sat quietly with me at one of the tables. I offered her a piece of challah the rabbi had cut, with vegetable cream cheese that I spread on it, but she declined and I ate it. After a while, I got separated from Karin when Esther, the wife of the insurance salesman from New Jersey, pulled me aside to talk.

"Who's that girl you're with?" I was asked.

"My girlfriend. Karin . . . Karin Klotz."

"Is she German? A local girl?"

"Yes."

"She's not Jewish," Esther said, more as a statement of fact than a question.

"No."

"Have you known her long?"

"Almost three months," I told my inquisitive but concerned older American friend.

I did not mind this sort of questioning from Esther. Since going to her home for Passover, I became very friendly with her and her husband Sam, the couple with two children. They invited me for Sunday dinner a few times and I brought Sam cigarettes from the PX without him asking. He always insisted I take payment for them.

Esther sort of took a maternal interest in me. Age wise, she could have been my mother. I respected her greatly, mainly because she revealed something personal and it moved me. Once, after dinner, I happened to ask her when she and Sam got married. Sam had mentioned to me that he was drafted in 1940 and served in the Army for five years, seeing combat in France and Germany. Esther said they married right after Sam came home from the war. That made sense to me as I knew their son was born at the end of '46. But I did not know if she was acquainted with Sam before the war. They were both around age forty and could have known each other and indeed before 1940. So I asked Esther, even more causally, if she had known her husband *prior to* his going in the Army. I was just making conversation, never meaning to pry into their personal affars.

"I waited for him for five years," she said without hesitation.

Esther's answer astounded me. How many young women in any country at war would wait five years for their man to come home? Not too many. Most would get involved with a 4F type of guy on the home front, write the forsaken soldier a Dear John letter, and marry some bloke in one piece while she was still young. Esther I'm sure realized that waiting five years would limit her chances of marrying at all had Sam not returned, or not returned unmarried, a fate and choice that fell upon so many young men of their generation. That was really love, I thought. That was the kind of love I wanted a girl to feel for me.

"You're not planning on getting married," Esther put to me, again more as a statement than a question.

Instinctively, I looked over to Karin. She was standing next to a tall older man, the Jewish judge who left Germany before the war. They were talking intensely. I turned back to Esther.

"No. Why do you ask?"

"Because if you said you were going to marry her, I would write your mother and tell her."

"Why? Because Karin's not Jewish?"

"Yes, so your mother could stop you. She would be heartbroken. I know I would."

"I like Karin," I admitted, "but even if she was Jewish I still don't want to get married. I'm only nineteen. I'm just marking time in the Army, waiting to get out and go to college next year. I won't be ready to get married until I graduate."

"That's good to hear, David. I hope you won't change your mind."

I realized then that I had something important in common with Esther. I too will probably have to wait five years to get married. I looked at my respected presumptive protector whom I now had an unspoken bond with.

"Don't worry, I won't," I said, glancing back to my girlfriend who was still talking to the judge. "Excuse me. I should see how Karin is doing."

"Go," Esther said as I turned away, pushing me gently on my shoulder. "But don't make me have to write that letter."

I went over to where Karin was and heard her talking in German, but stood back. Waiting for her to conclude her téte-à-téte, questions ran through my mind. What was she saying to the elderly country-man, but not co-religionist, who was persecuted in the land they both were born and grew up? Was she asking him what it was like under Hitler? What it was like coming back after the war? I wish I could have understood what they were saying. They must be talking about being Jewish in a post-Nazi Germany? I told myself. Maybe she was asking him details about conversion?

Karen and I left the reception room about twenty minutes later, as others were leaving as well. We said goodbye to the rabbi and his wife and a few others I introduced Karin to. They all treated her with respect and no one, Esther particularly, said anything about her not being Jewish or not being welcome to come to services again. On the streetcar and bus to Zirndorf, Karin did not tell me of her own accord what she spoke to the judge about. I very much wanted to know but I held back from asking.

I did take Karin to services again the other three Fridays in the month. She insisted we go, seemed to be waiting for the day all week. She got emotional if I even mentioned that perhaps we should skip one time. It was as if she caught some sort of Friday-night fever. Going with me week after week got both of us more involved with the people there. At the reception, she would talk to the judge and other German Jews, comfortable in her own language. How comfortable she was with the strange religious services I could not say. I wish I could have hidden a tape recorder on her person and later had it translated to find out what was said.

Each time I brought Karin, Esther looked as if she was waiting to say something to me in private. That last Friday in July, I thought she was going to pull a letter from her purse and show me what she intended to send airmail special delivery to 2214 Mermaid Avenue, Brooklyn 24, New York.

## CHAPTER 40: NO GROOM FOR THE ROOM

"Take off your bathing suit," I told Karin, looking straight at her. I spoke in a polite but firm voice.

It was Saturday, the fifteenth of August. Karin and I were at the indoor public pool she had taken me to on Rothenburger Strasse in the western part of Nuremberg, not too far from the German National Museum. She called it the Volksbad. Even if she had not mentioned the name, I could not very well miss knowing it. The eight letters were carved in stone above the front entrance.

The multi-level building with several attached sections was old, pre-World War I it looked like. It certainly was a people's bath, as almost any German could afford the 80-Pfennig admission price. The interior resembled an ancient Roman bathing facility with its barrel vaulted ceiling, series of arches on the first and second floors, blue tile on the walls matching the blue-tiled pool, and elaborate marble tile decorations along the second-floor balcony. Just below the ceiling, the clerestory windows all along the front and back of the building permitted generous amounts of natural light to filter in. Narrow lockers just for clothes hanging and small walk-in changing rooms for men and women were situated on both floors around the pool.

Karin was sitting on my lap in one of the changing rooms. One of my hands was over her breast, the other on her hip. I skulked in there to get back into my street clothes after an afternoon of swimming. When I saw it was fairly roomy, big enough for two people, and with a bench to sit down on, I pulled her inside with me before she could take her own room and latched the door. Karin did not resist coming into the private space with me but she did not seem too happy about it. We kissed a few times standing up, I then sat down and tugged at her to rest on my thighs. Except for the fact that we were in our bathing suits in an enclosed dressing area, the scenario was no different than the times we were alone in the sitting room of her apartment. It did not occur to me that her sensibilities might be offended by my telling her to slip out of her one-piece garment for a purpose she could well imagine. That Sunday in the park she so casually took off her bathing suit for the same purpose without any provocation from me. After gazing at Karin's exposed legs and covered crotch for hours, not to mention those of other young women at the pool, my hammer was cocked and ready to be released.

Karin met me at the Hauptbahnhof at twelve holding a little carrying case. She had told her mother she will be staying with a girlfriend and would not return home until the next day. Whether Karin thought Mutti believed her younger Tochter, I did not ask and did not want to know. She was the one who suggested we spend the afternoon at the public pool and I had no objection. The indoor facility was far from Zirndorf and I was sure she knew none of the young Germans who generally showed up there to swim on a hot summer day.

Later we were to meet Steve and Ursula outside a hotel in the Old City. For the past week Steve and I had planned an overnight stay with the girls. We both wanted an all-nighter, something much more than the quickies we were used to getting for months. Ursula's apartment was small and she did not like Steve sleeping over whereby her nosy neighbors would see him in the morning. Steve did not like to sleep over on weekends even if he could, as Ursula just had a single bed. For Ursula to get away, it was far easier than for Karin. My Schatzie had to tell a lie to spend the night with me whereas Steve's love interest could sleep out as she pleased since her four-year-old daughter lived with the grandmother.

The German girl weighing down my legs looked at me with reproachful eyes. She made no motion to remove her bathing suit but made no effort to disengage herself from my physical hold either.

"Dayf," she finally spoke up, pronouncing my name as she usually did, with an $f$ for a $v$ as in German. "You have me for whole night. Is not enough?"

She was right of course. Her words hit me where it hurt, kicked the cockiness right out of me. I felt ashamed of myself for trying to ball her there and then, in a three-by-four space frequently used by others, smelly with dirty towels and dank surroundings, with people talking and moving about on the other side of a thin wooden door secured by a flimsy two-inch hook. Soon we would be checking into a hotel. What was the rush? Sure she made it with me on the grass that first time, dropped her panties again and again in her apartment when Mutti und Schwester were in another room, and once wiggled out of her bathing suit in the park in broad daylight to fit me in. But that didn't mean she would not be offended by my crass attempt to derive pleasure at her expense in a crowded facility a few hours before we would be tucked away for the night.

"Yes, you're right," I remarked weakly, without saying I was sorry.

I knew I acted selfishly to a girl who was always *unselfish* with me in our relationship. Had I insisted on a quickie at that moment, I believe she would have accommodated me, but I did no such thing.

Karin looked at me but said nothing more.

"We'll wait until later," I added. I should have said *I* will wait until later. I lowered my hand and moved her off my lap. We changed into our dry street clothing. When she started to take off her bathing suit, I turned my head. People were looking at us funny, I thought, when we came out of the changing room.

We left the building and boarded streetcars north and east, toward the Old City.

The Pension was in the middle of Schildgasse, a side street across the Pegnitz River, north of St. Mary's Church, called Frauenkirsche by Karin. It was a small hotel, narrow in front but deep toward the back, four stories high. A green sign bearing the name hung over the entrance three steps above the sidewalk. When we came around the corner, we saw Steve and Ursula waiting for us outside the modest establishment, by the curb, a few meters down from the doorway. She too had a little overnight bag. The girls greeted each other in their usual way.

"How are we going to work this?" Steve said to me, smiling a little.

I shrugged my shoulders. "I don't know. What do you think?"

"Let Ursula and Karin go in first and register. Then we'll go in and get a room."

"Okay," I agreed. That simple scheme sounded fine to me.

We were in conservative Germany, not liberal France. Germans frowned upon unmarried couples renting or sharing apartments or hotel rooms, and it was against regulations. This was not like in the States, where anyone could slap a bill down on the counter and get a room in a hotel with no questions asked. Here a person had to show papers, prove one's identity. If a man and woman sought to register, young people especially, proof of marriage was required too.

Steve and I waited on the street while the girls went inside. Ursula had some money that he gave her to pay for their room. We had agreed to meet *outside* in about half an hour and then go to dinner. We dared not exchange rooms so quickly. After fifteen minutes, Steve and I entered the hotel. We both made a point of showing our AWOL bags to the desk clerk, whom we knew could peg us right away as Americans, so he'd think we were on leave. I paid the fifteen Marks for our room. I looked at the creepy-looking man, a short balding Kraut in his mid- or late forties, as he lowered his head and peered at us over his rimless bifocals. What did this comrade do during the war? I wondered.

Our room was on the second floor. I put my things away but Steve just left his bag on the dresser. We tidied up a bit, and then went downstairs to meet the girls as we had arranged. They were bunked on the third floor. We all looked like the cat that had just swallowed the canary. Ursula recommended a place for dinner and we headed there, careful not to pass by the hotel doorway as a foursome.

It was after nine when we got back to the Pension. The girls went in first. Steve and I waited out front, out of the line of sight from someone at the front desk, and sneaked in a little while later. We got off the elevator on the second floor, Steve grabbed his bag from the room, and walked up one flight. I sat down on the edge of the bed and waited. Not three minutes passed when there was a faint knock on the door. It was Karin with her carrying case. She came in quietly and I made sure the door was securely locked.

Karin and I quickly got down to business. The room had no radio or television and there was little else to do but undress and hop into bed. It was a double bed, meant for two, two of the opposite or the same sex, adults or children or one of each. Before long the sheets felt warm and we were sweating them up.

I thought of Karin's remark and question a few hours before. I would be having her for the whole night, but would it be enough for me? Certainly there would be time for more than one round, and there was also an opportunity to throw different kinds of punches. My mind regressed eight months to another all-nighter, to the memorable date with the WAC in Salinas before I left Fort Ord. Very oral

I was feeling for taking a swing and being swung at.

This was a first for us in a number of ways. First time we did not have to rush making love, did not have to fear Mutti or Schwester busting in on us, did not have to crawl into an out-of-the-way spot in Zirndorf Woods. For the first time Karin and I could explore each other's bodies, pretend we were married, be alone for a ganze Nacht, sleep in the same bed. It occurred to me how fortunate I was that Karin stopped me, or rather *shamed* me, into not pressing her to take off her bathing suit in the dressing locker at the pool. This soldier was now more ready for the initial action, had more bullets under his belt to shoot, and was more likely to stand up for a second or third engagement.

It was all quiet on the German front. As usual, it was up to me to get my balls rolling. Karin looked at me with approving eyes this time. We kissed and she touched my face tenderly. I worked the up-per half of her body with my mouth and one hand while my other hand operated on her lower half. I ran my fingertips up and down her thighs several times before zeroing in on her crotch, first sliding the shaft of my index finger on the edge of her fold, then sticking two fingers two inches inside. My maiden was getting moister by the moment. When I thought she had enough nipple work, I kissed my way south, passing the navel and heading toward the bushy cen-ter below. I did not know about her, but this was a first for me, an action I longed to get in on, a tonguing experience I often heard boasted about in the barracks. I pushed aside some hair and landed a lick. Suddenly my head was jerked back.

"Nein, nein," Karin shrieked, breaking her silence. She had grabbed me by *my* hair and pulled me away.

What's with nice German girls? They cry out "No" in their native language when I crossed a verboten anatomical barrier. Like pre-teen Anna more than eight years earlier, post-teen Karin stopped me cold when I was hot.

"I *want* to do this," I pleaded, looking up at her. The salty taste did not bother me. "What's the matter?"

"I don't like, I don't like."

"Why not?" I tried to say in a sweet tone. "There's nothing wrong with doing that."

Karin sat up and lifted my head away from her private part.

348

"It bad. It dirty."

"It's not bad or dirty. It's an expression of love."

"I don't like," she repeated. "It not love. It bad . . . schlecht."

Getting her to let me go down on her seemed out of the question. I wondered how she felt toward the seesaw we were on dropping the other way. She probably had unclean and dissenting thoughts of that too. But just in case she did not, I rolled onto my back. Now it was *my* private part that was upright and in her sight.

Karin looked down at me but made no movement to hold me or lower her head. I reached around her back and rested my hand on the nape of her neck but did not nudge her. My hand-placing gesture alone should have been enough of a hint for her to know, given our unclothed positions, what I desired at that moment. She still did not move in the direc-tion I had hoped. The girl who told me she would make all what I want either did not know all what I want or did not mean she would make what I want by opening the cavity above her neck to take me in, only the one below her waist.

How does a guy ask a girl to go down on him without offending her? Either she's the type of female who likes, or is not afraid, to take the male organ in her mouth, or one who will not bring her face anywhere near it. The former needs no asking, just lowers her head and opens up, like the WAC in California and the puertorriqueña in New York, and even Elsa a few times here in Germany. The latter type needs asking and prodding and convincing before she, if ever, shakes off a negative preconception and dares to stoop to a new level.

How about doing it to me? I wanted to say to my recalcitrant girl-friend, or how about letting me do it to you? But I held my tongue, for both speaking and licking. Instead I moved my body a little clo-ser to her.

Karin frowned and squinted and pushed back on my hand. "I not do. I not French girl?"

The German girl who never went with a G.I. before, who never even traveled outside her country, obviously got my drift and knew something about cross-national differences in female behavior too. It was hopeless now to expect anything exotic or experimental with Karin. I was in the company of a leg-spreading-only gal. One prize fits all. In this hotel, my ears would not again be hearing words to the effect of "Don't come in my mouth," and my eyes would not again be seeing a girl clamp down on me nor absorb my growing hardness in incremental measures.

"Okay," I said. "Let's just do it as usual."

I guided prim and proper Karin to lie on her back again, slipped on a rubber, lifted her legs, and stuffed it in. I was inclined on the bed, but not inclined to play with her clit to work her up.

After we finished the same-old-love, Karin and I just lie in bed under the covers, still unclad. I had my arm around her shoulder and she rested her head on my chest. We talked for a while.

Suddenly there was a knock at the door. We both remained quiet. I did not get up to open the door and I did not call out to ask who it was. I whispered to Karin not to say anything. She was frightened I could tell. The knocks got louder and more rapid but still we did nothing. Now *I* started to worry. Could it be the Polizei? MPs? The knocking continued. Then we heard a key turning in the lock. It must be the desk clerk creeping in, I thought. Karin stiffened and dug her face deeper into my chest. Slowly the door opened. In the darkened room but with light in the hall, I saw the faint outline of a man's head through the partially open door.

"Wait a minute, comrade," I heard clearly. "Don't go in there."

It was Steve's voice. The door opened a little wider. Now I could see Steve standing behind the desk clerk, with his hand on the German's shoulder, pulling him back from entering the room. The clerk retreated.

"He came to our room first," Steve said, sticking just his head in the doorway, careful not to enter the room. "He knows we switched rooms. And he knows we're not married. He threatened to call the police if we didn't change back. I came downstairs just as he was opening your door."

"I was afraid to answer when we heard knocking," I called to my buddy and now savior, while still under the covers. "He didn't say anything. We didn't know who it was. I thought he'd go away if no one answered."

"Karin has to go back upstairs," Steve said.

It was futile to argue against switching rooms, with Steve or the German. "All right. Give us a minute."

"I'll wait outside," Steve added, and closed the door.

Karin was still frightened but she got out of bed and dressed quickly. I was the one who moved more slowly and just put my shorts on. Karin left the room hurriedly with a bundle in her arms.

Steve got into bed first. He and I had to share a room for the night just as we did in the barracks, but in a double bed instead of twin bunks. It goes without saying that he was not the person I wanted to sleep with for fifteen Marks that Saturday. Now I could guess what the comrade downstairs did during the war. He must have been with the morality police unit of the Wehrmacht.

No sooner did my head hit the pillow that I started to laugh.

"What's so funny?" Steve asked.

"I was thinking of a movie I saw six or seven years ago. *No Room for the Groom* it was called."

"What about it?"

"Did you see it?" I asked my new bed partner who was trying to fall asleep.

"I don't think so. Who was in it?"

"Tony Curtis and Piper Laurie."

"What about it?" Steve repeated.

"Well, it's about this newlywed G.I. who comes home from Korea on leave to find more than a dozen relatives of his wife in his house. He can't find an unoccupied room so that he can be alone with his bride. It was very funny. There was no room for the groom in his own place."

"What was so funny about that?"

"Well," I explained further, "he hadn't fucked his wife yet. That was the punch line of the film. On his wedding night six months earlier, he came down with the chicken pox and the doctor isolated him, wouldn't let his wife stay in the same room with him. The next day he had to ship out back to Korea."

"Go to sleep," Steve said. "Forget that dumb flick."

"I was just thinking. At this hotel, we both got separated from our girlfriends because there was *no groom for the room*."

Steve thought a moment and then was his sarcastic self. "Well, married or not, at least I got groomed in the room before I was kicked out."

"Yeah, me too," I divulged, so as not to invite any intimate questions, but I really felt I was not fully taken care of. Perhaps Karin wanted me to become her groom before finding room in her mind and heart to consummate our relationship further.

Trying to fall asleep next to Steve, I could not help thinking that I should have balled Karin in the locker at the pool when I had the chance, her words to stop me notwithstanding. What she said was actually very prescient, but in reverse. As that Saturday unfolded, I did *not* have her for the whole night and what I did have was *not* enough.

## CHAPTER 41: WEDDING BELL BLUES

"Mind your own fucking business," Steve yapped at me that night after a long talk. His face reddened, he clenched one fist, and he looked as if he was ready to swing his arm my way. I had never seen him so angry. "I don't want to discuss it anymore."

"Okay . . . okay," I said, after he calmed down a little. "Do what you want."

We both climbed into our bunks without another word.

It was two weeks after that all-nighter at the Pension. On Sunday, after we checked out of the hotel, Steve and Ursula informed Karin and me that they decided to get married. He evidently was groomed in the room more than he let on to me. Steve's girl was beaming, eyes all aglow, happy as a lark. Karin was sullen and silent, her long face and closed mouth unable to hide the woeful feelings she must have had.

Every evening when we were alone, Steve bent my ear about his decision to marry Ursula. He rambled on about how wonderful she is and how much he wants to spend the rest of his life with her. Most of the time I could not shut him up and get to sleep unless I turned my head toward the wall and pretended I was not awake. For two weeks I wanted to say something, to try to talk him out of it, but I held my tongue. Finally, I spoke up but my roommate and best buddy in the Army refused to listen to anything I said. No matter what I argued, determined-to-marry Steve had a ready rebuttal.

"She's six years older than you," I pointed out.

"That doesn't matter," he said.

"She has a kid."

"No problem. I'll adopt her."

"Ursula's Catholic, you're Protestant."

Steve shrugged that off too. "I'm not religious."

"What about college?" I reminded the twenty-year-old who had one year under his belt.

"That will have to wait," he replied simply, without any thought given to the benefits of higher education to his, or any young man's, long-term goals.

"What about money? Your parents are divorced, they probably can't help you."

"When I'm married, I'll get the dependent's allotment."

"That might not be enough?" I put to the prospective bridegroom. "Living off post costs a lot."

"The re-up bonus will help."

"Re-up bonus? What are you talking about?"

"I'm planning to take a short and re-enlist."

What Steve meant I understood right away. The Army gave men a discharge, prior to the expiration date of their current enlistment, a "short" as it was called, on condition they re-enlist immediately.

"Steve. That could be another wrong decision. Why do you want to spend three more years in the Army?"

"I enjoy being in Germany. I can extend my tour, spend the whole time here."

"You'll have to get permission from the C.O. on this post," I said, still trying to dissuade him. "We don't even know the noncoms or brass in the Second Cav?"

"The captain's a jerk. He won't stop me from marrying," the hopeful husband-to-be retorted confidently.

"You'll have to speak to a chaplain. Go to counseling sessions."

"No sweat."

"You're not twenty-one. You'll need your parents' permission," I advised him.

"My parents won't stop me."

"What about the Army? Suppose they don't approve of Ursula? Maybe her father or an uncle was a Nazi . . . or is a Communist?"

"Then I'll get married anyway. To hell with the Army's approval."

Steve was resolved to slip a ring on his girl's finger even if it meant a fall from Army grace. "You could be punished for marrying without permission."

Steve shrugged his shoulders and looked away from me but said nothing.

"You won't be able to bring Ursula and her kid to the States?"

"I don't think that will happen," he said, "but if it did I'll cross that bridge when I get to it."

"The Army will check Ursula out. They'll want to know the name of every guy she ever went with, German and American."

This caught Steve's attention. He turned toward me and snapped.

"She didn't go with that many guys. She's a decent girl."

"I know that, but the Army doesn't. They'll assume she's a hooker . . . fucked half the troops at Merrell . . . has VD."

"Cut that out," he said with a raised voice.

"They'll want to know who the father of her kid is. Get him to sign papers."

"I said stop it."

"Steve. I'm only trying to help you, get you to see you could be making a mistake. You could be setting yourself up and Ursula for a big disappointment."

"I don't need your help."

"The Army investigators will even check to see if Ursula hung out in the black bars. Most of those gals have arrest records."

That was the final straw. Steve exploded and told me to mind my own business.

All this was troubling me, it seemed, more so than it did Steve. My best buddy in the Army, someone I thought I knew very well, someone I believed when he said he was going back to college, now was embarking on three momentous decisions—getting married, adopting a child, and re-enlisting—acts I was dead-set against and assumed he was too.

I just did not understand it. A young American soldier empties his rounds into a German girl he likes and before coming to attention does an about face, grabs hold of new battle plans, starts marching to a different drummer, and surrenders positions already secured. This is probably what Richie witnessed in Germany and sought to warn me against.

Steve's proposal of marriage to Ursula may have made him happy but it set in motion wedding bell blues for Karin and for me. His own melancholy would set in later.

Ever since the all-nighter at the Pension, Karin did a lot of talking too. My ear was bent again, but this time by my girlfriend about *us* getting married. In the sitting room of her apartment, no sooner had she hopped off my lap and put her panties back on that she would start in with her Spiel. She was like a broken record. Every night we were together, Karen's words could have passed for the lyrics of a Billboard Top 10 song.

*I love you so, I always will*
*My whole life, I love you still*
*I want marry you, okay*
*I want see my wedding day*
*Always I on your side*
*To you never I lied*
*Kisses and love not carry me*
*Because a wife I want be*
*Wedding bells I must hear*
*Please marry me, dear*
*I be with you, you not lonely*
*Every day, I love you only*
*Come on Dayf, you not lose*
*I got those wedding bell blues*

With sad eyes and a down-turned mouth Karin made the case for marriage. She pleaded she loved me but never asked if I loved her. She stressed she made all what I wanted but forgot about our unconsummated foray into oral endearments in the hotel room. She reminded me that we have been ein Paar for three months but was silent as to whether that was a sufficient basis for a lifetime romantic union. She offered, in a last ditch pitch, to convert to Judaism but did not ask if I wanted her to forsake her Catholic Church.

Everything Karin threw at me was true. Every argument had merit. I believed she loved me. I knew she did all she could to satisfy my carnal desires. I felt a great deal of affection for her. I even felt greatly indebted to her for making the summer of '59 a very memorable one. And I had no doubt that she would indeed change over to my faith.

But what did all this have to do with me getting married? I liked Karin, I liked her a lot, but was I madly in love, no. I appreciated the part-year intimacy she favored me with, but I knew I could not spend the next fifty years showing my appreciation for that. Karin was four years my senior, I desired someone my own age or younger. I had lied to her about my age and if I were to go along with her wishes I would have to tell her the truth, make an admission of wrongdoing, an act anathema to me.

Karin was not a bad looking girl, but enamored of her I was not. For emotional and procreative purposes, I wanted to marry a girl with a more perfect face and figure. The religious difference between us was troublesome but irrelevant since I had no intention of tying the knot. Simply put, Karin was not the girl of my dreams and my family would never accept a German daughter-in-law.

Richie's utterance against returning with a Nazi Schatzie rang in my ears, and my mother's spoken and written words of hatred for all Germans bounced around in my head. If I married Karin, Thomas Wolfe's novel, *You Can't Go Home Again*, would become my mantra. I would be in the same boat as the black captain I saw on the *Rose* coming over who took a white wife.

My roommate's connubial commitment may have cemented his involvement with Ursula, but it caused a crack in my relationship with Karin. All she thought about was wedding bells. Every time I saw her she bugged me about wanting, in her words, to "go marry" with me. I could not tell her a bald-face lie and say straight out I do not want to get married, but I did not want to break off with her either. So I took a middle ground. I told Karin several times, after I zipped up, that I had not yet heard from my mother. Technically that was true, but only because I had not written to my mother about a German girlfriend, let alone anything about getting married. The misrepresentation held her at bay, and that depressed her I was sure. I knew there would come a time when I could not hold back giving her an answer one way or the other, but I tried not to think about the day of reckoning.

I was sorry about the deceit and that began to dampen my spirits. But I believed I was not pulling off a cocky Curtis, not doing a replay of *Kings Go Forth*, and that was some consolation. Unlike the Tony Curtis character in the movie, I was not a soldier who made false promises to a European girl and then lied about putting in papers for the Army's permission to marry just to continue shooting into her. And unlike the Natalie Wood character, Karin threw herself at the American the day they first met, offered to make all what he wanted two days later, and gave her body freely time and again without any verbal commitment. True as that was, I knew it was no justification for my perpetrating a fraud. A nice German girl was going to get hurt because a not-so-nice American boy did not want to give up a steady piece.

I felt bad because Karin was not like the bar-girls at the Luitpold or Flying Dutchman, or Ursula for that matter, local women tempered by postwar combat in foreign soldiers' field of battle, females likely inured to romantic disappointments. Sweet vulnerable Karin would be receiving her answer soon I feared, and that was what I dreaded giving most of all. It would not be the answer the starry-eyed ingenuous Fräulein who yielded to me so completely wanted to hear.

Steve knew I had no plans to marry Karin, that I was against marriage to an older German girl in general. I hoped my roommate disgruntled with me for interfering was unaware of the Frank Sinatra character in the Hollywood war movie, would not play the soldier who forced his buddy to tell the wronged girl the truth. Worrying about how and when to tell Karin that wedding bells would not be ringing for us, that our foreign affair was over, and not knowing how she would react, gave *me* the blues.

# CHAPTER 42: SUMMER SOLSTICE

By late August Karin and I had been going together for three months. I may have felt the blues over her desire for, and my recalcitrance to, German-American nuptials, but I was still fairly content during this time from the good deal of sunshine that came my way that summer.

My off-duty activities pleasingly and pleasantly revolved around my first long-term intimate relationship with a member of the opposite sex. I took Karin to movies at Merrell. She came shopping with me at the main PX at Darby Kaserne in Fürth. We met Steve and Ursula for lunch or dinner at various Nuremberg restaurants. Most important, we coupled two or three times a week on the couch in her sitting room with just my fly down and her panties off. Going at it unclothed that Sunday in the park and that night in the Pension also enhanced my feelings for Karin and our being ein Paar. As a red-blooded young man, my body felt completely at ease, gratified by the frequent release of sexual ten-sion. As a soldier a long way from home, my spirits were the best since I enlisted, lifted by the fact that I had less than a year to go in the Army and by the quasi-family contacts I enjoyed with a local girl.

The summer of '59 was the high point of my overseas tour. My hours away from camp were spent largely with Karin in her apartment. Our sexual encounters multiplied, the relationship solidified, and my contacts with her family intensified.

The very situation my mother and Richie independently warned me against the day I left home, becoming involved with a German family and their marriage-minded daughter, I stumbled right into. Mama's letter repeating those forebodings, resting on my wall-locker shelf and readily seen every day, and my friend's last words to me still fresh in my mind, I all but ignored. June to August was replete with love and companionship, indoor pleasure and outdoor amusement, afternoon jaunts and evening joys.

That year my life seemed to mirror the summer solstice. Like the sun reaching the greatest distance from the earth north of the equator, I deviated astronomically from my central goal. For well over a year I had set my sights on going to college after discharge from the Army. Out of high school for more than two years, I knew I had to prepare myself for the college entrance examinations. I was planning to take the College Boards in early October, given at Darby Kaserne, but that was *before* I met Karin.

The heavy academic work I cut out for myself that summer was cast aside. I found myself burrowing into the nice German girl from Zirndorf instead of the scholarly books and preparatory materials I had gathered, now simply perched on the shelf of my wall locker next to Mama's letter. I chose to spend my free time enjoying the easy sexual favors that were available to me, not learning the hard mathematics problems and not practicing verbal exercises to improve my chances of getting into college.

"How come you're not studying?" Steve put to me the previous day after work as I was getting dressed to go off post for my date with Karin. "I thought you said you need to take that college test."

"I do . . . but not necessarily the one given in October. I can take it in January. There's plenty of time for me to study."

My roommate knew I was procrastinating, trading greater book knowledge for greater carnal knowledge. This was all the more disconcerting since it was I, not two days earlier, who chided Steve about his wanting to get married instead of returning to college. To him it must have seemed I was being hypocritical, but I did not think so since I had no plans to get married, still wanted to go to college, and simply "put off" my studies so Karin can "put out" for me.

In spite of what I thought of my actions, or inaction, it surprised me that I had so readily superseded goal-oriented higher education, preparation for a career in some profession and ostensibly greater lifetime income, for aimless ephemeral good times with a German girl. College was my ticket out of the working class, yet by fooling around with poor Karin I was consciously undermining my aspired exit from a life of horizontal mobility.

On the twenty-first of June, the beginning of summer, the sun appears to rise and stop, then reverses direction after this day. In the cosmos, the solar pause is momentary before a different course is taken. In my life, the knowledge pause lasted all summer and I had no idea if or when I would get back on the course I laid out for myself. The Bavarian merry-go-round I was strapped to with Karin was spinning away from the two brass rings I hankered to catch, gold-painted prizes marked Army Discharge and College Admission. It was a blissful three-month ride but, like the roller coasters in Coney Island that I frolicked on countless times, it too was destined to come to a screeching halt.

This was not my first solstice while in the Army. That occurred back at Fort Monmouth in April 1958, when I decided to go to college. This was arguably the foremost turning point in my life, a pause and redirection of interests and goals of monumental proportion. The stop-and-twirl began before the beginning of summer that year and continued well past the winter solstice, into the summer solstice of 1959. The life-altering event happened suddenly, unexpectedly, casually, and with a perfect stranger.

Today, more than five decades later, the significance of the great change that occurred at Monmouth is still difficult to fathom.

I was sitting in class one afternoon in mid-April, bored to no end with the lecture by a civilian instructor on troubleshooting some part in a piece of radar equipment. He was talking about transmitters and receivers, vacuum tubes and electricity, but I couldn't keep my mind on any of it. I felt I needed a break, just had to get out of there.

The classroom was on the second floor in one of the old two-story barracks buildings toward the eastern end of the post, rectangular wood-en matchboxes with many windows and visible crawl spaces, far from the tall new brick buildings near the Eatontown gate at the western edge. On the pretense of having to relieve myself, I picked up the pass hanging on a wall hook, closed my ears to the instruction I had enlisted for, and walked out of the room. I went down the hall toward the john. On my left I passed the office of the first lieutenant in charge of this five-week section of our course. Out of instinct and not thought I backed up a few steps, knocked, and opened the door.

For months I knew I was not happy with, and did not much like, the training in electronics I was getting. I probably selected the 33-week radar repair school mainly because it was one of the longest I could sign up for, and was taught at a fort closest to my home. The recruiting sergeant at the Coney Island station recommended it but gave me no aptitude test to determine if I was suitable for that line of work in the Army or something similar in civilian life. In my day, if a young man committed to a three-year hitch in the Army he could choose any school offered regardless of his abilities, skills, or interests. In picking radar at Monmouth, I would be able to go home to New York on weekends for most of my first year.

Weeks 1-4 I did like. The beginning part of the radar course was all theory, math and physics, a good amount of which I already knew. In high school I took three-and-a-half years of math, through advanced algebra, and a year of physics. Later sections of the radar course involved hands on, practical stuff—learning to operate, take apart, troubleshoot, and repair different pieces of equipment. Most of the guys in the class "ate that shit up," relished working with their hands and fixing things.

Some classmates were older, sergeants of all stripes with twelve or more years in the Army, veterans of one or two wars, who re-enlisted and selected the radar course in order to have a marketable skill when they left the service. Other than police departments, not too many civilian employers needed ex-soldiers who could fire small arms, handle rifles, throw hand grenades, or load Howitzers.. Even officers in foreign armies, chiefly from NATO or South American countries, wearing strange uniforms, were in classes at Monmouth. It seemed I was the only one sitting in the wrong classroom.

The lieutenant was behind his desk and looked up from the array of papers. He was wearing khakis, the tan summer Class A's, in stark contrast to the green fatigues I was in, the year-round work uniform. He was young, twenty-six or twenty-seven, and cropped his hair short but not in a crew cut. I thought he might be annoyed at the appearance of a soldier he did not know without an appointment, but that was not the case. He smiled when our eyes met.

"What can I do for you, private?"

I did not salute as I was not reporting to him, but stood at ease, albeit somewhat nervously. "May I talk to you, sir?"

"About what?" He pointed to the chair in front of his desk.

I sat down, hesitated a moment, and wiped the perspiration from my forehead. "Can I transfer to another course. I'm not happy with radar repair."

The lieutenant's head jerked slightly. He obviously was surprised by my request. "What week are you in?"

"Twenty-one," I said, leaving out that this would have been my twenty-fourth week.

Each week was a different class, and soldiers at times started in one class but graduated in another. I lost two weeks when I took days off for the Jewish New Year the last week of September and the Passover holiday earlier that month. I also failed a test in March and had to repeat the week.

"That's more than halfway." Now his voice reflected surprise.

"Yes sir," I acknowledged.

He glanced at my name tag. "Streiber," he said, pronouncing my name right. "You enlisted for radar, correct?"

"Yes sir," I repeated.

"Well, what's the problem?" He did not ask what school I wanted to transfer into.

"I don't think I'm cut out to be an electronics repairman. When I get out, I don't want to fix radios or TVs."

I did not mention anything about another course, since I did not know what was available or if a transfer was even possible. I just wanted to talk to someone about it.

"Streiber," he said again, assuming a more personal tone. "Have you been to college?"

"No sir."

"Well, you should start when you get out . . . and major in electrical engineering. That's where the good jobs are. Completion of the radar course will be very helpful to you. It feeds right into that program. You'll have one up on your younger college classmates."

The lieutenant's words stunned me, but struck a familiar cord. It so happened that up until my senior year in high school I *was* planning, like many a young boy of my generation, to go to college and study engineering, as President Eisenhower said we should do in order for the United States to beat the Russians and win the race for space. Hollywood too seemed to glorify the electronics and aeronautical engineer in movies with a handsome Rock Hudson or respected William Holden in Air Force officers' uniform testing jet planes in the sky and solving military problems on the ground.

But I lost interest in college and then started thinking about enlisting in the Army. I wanted to get my military obligation over with, I knew I would not be able to study very well in the tiny apartment my family occupied, Mrs. Mittler was making life miserable for us in the building, and the idea of being away from home and on my own appealed to me.

I tried to shift the conversation back to my dislike of electronics, to the possibility of a transfer to another course, but the lieutenant kept talking about college and engineering. I stood there like a dummy, unable to get a word in edgewise, forced to listen to a sales pitch on a topic I had not anticipated and had given up on. The military man before me dispensing advice could have passed for a college recruitment officer.

In this my ninth month in the Army, the question of my going to college, for engineering or for anything else, suddenly surfaced. I was unprepared for it and was greatly taken aback. It was as if something I deliberately ran away from now hit me smack in the face. The lieutenant rang a bell I could not help hearing.

More than a year earlier I decided against applying for college, but I had friends from high school and the neighborhood in college and that possibility for me, I now realized, must have been dormant in the recesses of my mind all the time. A chance meeting with a young officer, coincidentally just a week after Easter Sunday, resurrected in me the notion of a college education, gave new life to an old career option.

That day at Fort Monmouth the title of a science fiction movie I saw a few years earlier, *The Day the Earth Stood Still*, applied to me. My uncertain plans for the future, my mixed feelings about what I was studying, came to an abrupt halt. The lieutenant's words triggered a solstice of sorts and forced me to reconsider everything I had in my head about myself. A stranger stopped me in my tracks and re-directed me. I knew then that he was right. I *should* go to college when I get out. I should have enrolled in college *instead* of enlisting in the Army.

For the next fourteen months, I could think of nothing but going to college. It was only when I started shtupping Karin steadily that I lost my direction. I did not abandon the new course I chose, I just did not make time to prepare for it. A month later, by summer's end, that would change.

I returned to the tiresome classroom lecture, now with something other than radar repair to think about, and hung the pass back up on the wall. I never got to go to the john.

## CHAPTER 43: AN AMERICAN IN PARIS

The overnight bus ride from Paris to Nuremberg with two rest stops took almost ten hours. I sat in a middle row, near the window, with the seat back and resting my head on a small pillow I found on one of the empty seats. My tan raincoat covering me in front from neck to knees served as a blanket. I tried to get some sleep this Monday evening, the seventh of September. It was Labor Day and I was returning from the City of Light on a three-day pass Sergeant Bentley approved and Mr. Barry signed, hoping to get enough shut-eye so that I could work effectively the next day in the Area Office.

The pass was a present from my two bosses for doing a good job the previous month, for making color charts of equipment repairs that they were impressed with, reorganizing the file cabinet, and getting the typed reports out according to schedule. The three days plus the extra one for the holiday were sufficient for a nice little vacation in Gay Paree so that I did not have to use any of my accumulated leave time.

After work and chow on Thursday I left Merrell and dashed to the Army Hotel across the street from the Hauptbahnhof. There I was told to board at 1930 hours a bus parked out in front that would take soldiers from throughout the Nuremberg Area Command to Paris. The trip was one of a number of planned tours to European cities arranged by the Special Services branches at local Kasernes. The package deal offered was reasonable and included the round-trip bus fare, double-occupancy in a hotel for three nights, two meals a day, and gratuities.

When I went to Special Services at my barracks to pay for a ticket, I feared I might run into the Mann working in the photography lab there, the one who introduced me to Karin and was ignominiously kissed off the same day by the girl he thought was his. The jilted German was nowhere in sight.

The Tuesday before I left I told Karin I would be going to Paris for four days. That turned out to be a mistake. In retrospect, I should have said nothing, gone to Paris, and gotten word to her I could not see her that weekend because my company sent me on field maneuvers.

"I want go . . . I want go" Karin shrieked right after I mentioned it, loud enough for her mother and sister to hear in the next room. She had just pulled up her panties and lowered her dress.

My girlfriend was desperate to accompany me on the tour de Paris, but I did not want any company, not her kind anyway.

"I can't take you. Only Americans are allowed on the trip," I said, not knowing whether it was true or not. "Besides, you don't have a passport." That I knew was true. *I* did not need a passport but she certainly did. My military I.D. was all that was necessary for passage into any non-Communist country in Europe.

"I know why you not take me."

I looked at her but said nothing. The rubber I had not yet taken off after I zipped up was on my mind, particularly since I was going down.

"You want go mit French girl," she quipped in a jealous tone, pursing her lips.

Karin was right of course. My timing in telling her about Paris obviously was wrong too. Her accusation no doubt stemmed from a recall of our disagreement over acts oral that night two weeks earlier in the Pension. In Paris I did have expectations of Frenching as well as fucking but that was not the main reason why I was going. Like any American serviceman overseas, I just wanted to take advantage of my assignment and "see the world." The French capital was often the first place a G.I. in Europe hits when he is on leave or with pass, during war or peace. I had less than a year left before I returned to the States and now was the time to climb to the top of La Tour Eiffel, L'Arc de Triomphe, and La Cathédrale de Notre Dame.

"No," I answered immediately. "I just want to go to Paris and take lots of pictures. I'm not looking for girls."

She knew I had a camera and in the past three months I took plentiful shots of us alone, as well as with Steve and Ursula, all around Zirndorf, Nuremberg, and Merrell Barracks.

"I'm only going to take pictures," I repeated with emphasis, hoping she would believe me.

But Karin did not believe me. She kept saying I was going to Paris, pronouncing it *Pareese*, to meet girls. She even hinted, perhaps too timid or embarrassed to say it openly, that I wanted to get from a French girl what I did not get from her. She was not convinced no matter what I said and we argued about my going alone.

This was the first time we had a sustained row. It was not a knockdown, drag-out fight, and no slapping or shoving occurred, but I saw she was very angry and projected that anger onto me. I was sure her emotional upset was directly related to her wedding bell blues, my noncommittal to marriage after weeks of stalling. Surprisingly, Mutti und Schwester did not poke their heads, or rather big noses, in the sitting room to sniff out what the commotion was all about.

When the quarreling quit, and Karin calmed down, we were still kilometers apart in our stances toward the Paris purpose. At that point, I thought it best to just leave. It was an uncertain departure, neither a final goodbye nor a date to meet again. I left Karin's apartment for the first time without kissing her at the front door. Needless to say, this first-floor scene in Zirndorf was not reminiscent of the balcony scene in Verona in Act II of *Romeo and Juliet*, not the kind of parting that Shakespeare wrote was such sweet sorrow. And Karin, unlike Juliet, did not say to her lover good night till it be morrow.

I never got to the Klotz family's bathroom to flush the rubber down the toilet and wash my private part.

She was about twenty-three or twenty-four, on the short side, with medium-length brown hair in curls at the bottom, a little plump but not fat. Her face was pleasant enough but no one could say she was cover-girl pretty. The young femme I met on a Paris street was two inches taller than Karin, one cup-size bigger, and looked just as demure. I did not think she was a hooker at first because she wore a plain dress and flats and carried a small purse. She was not busting out all over in tight slacks or a short skirt with a low-cut blouse, parading in high heels up-and-down the block and swinging a heavy pocketbook like Hollywood's portrayal of a prostitute. I was standing on the corner with the PFC on the tour whom I was paired with in the hotel. We were discussing what to do and where to go next. The girl was by herself, positioned about fifteen feet away from us in front of one of the shop windows, looking over to me. She finally came up to us but faced me only and began talking in French.

It was Saturday evening a little past ten, the end of my second day in Paris. We arrived early Friday morning. The busload of American soldiers checked into a modest hotel not far from the Montparnasse district, the café hangout during the 1920s of literary, artistic, and political figures. I was given a room with a bath facing the street, but when I looked out the window I did not see the likes of a Hemingway, Picasso, or Trotsky.

My roommate said he was a male nurse at the Army Hospital in Nuremberg, and had been in Germany three months. He came from a small town outside of Kansas City. The local draft board snagged him when he dropped out of college, the pre-med program, because of poor grades. I felt sorry for him. He had big ears that stuck out like Dumbo the elephant and had bad skin, acne and pimples on his face and neck. Not too many girls in any country would find him attractive or want to kiss him. But we hit it off right away even though our backgrounds were very different. I talked to him about my plans for college.

After breakfast on Friday, the trip organizer said we could take in the city by ourselves or sign up for guided tours of famous landmarks at additional cost. My roommate and I decided to go it alone, at least for the first day. We picked up at the front desk, for no charge, a map of Paris and a detailed booklet of places of interest to see and eating establishments.

The first place we hit was Notre Dame. We climbed the cathedral's narrow spiral staircase that would give anyone a headache and along the ascent peered out the grilled windows at the funny-looking gargoyles. The view of the city from the clock tower was stupendous but I did not see any ugly crippled hunchback or pretty Gypsy girl up there. Then we stood in line on the street for over an hour just to get in the Louvre, slowly passing the sidewalk musicians next to open suitcases with different-colored coins and bills, dollars and francs, inside. The huge Medieval and Renaissance paintings on the walls were impressive, but the Mona Lisa was not, a rather small portrait behind thick glass, hard to see clearly with the glare.

Afterward, I walked along the Seine, on the spot where in 1951 Gene Kelly danced with Leslie Caron, where now there were shabbily-dressed men clutching wine bottles urinating against the trees with their other hand, oblivious to those around them.

The Eiffel Tower we got to after lunch. We rode the elevators in stages to the top, walked around the fenced observation deck, and took in the breathtaking 360-degree panorama of all Paris. I over-heard an English-speaking guide tell his group of tourists that this tallest structure in the city, built to commemorate the 100th anni-versary of the French Revolution, was almost demolished in 1909, after the expiration of its 20-year lease. An emplacement of a broad-casting antenna gave it new life. Had Paris' most visible and most famous landmark not been saved, I surmised, the thousands of tons of scrap metal would have yielded a hell of a lot of souvenir pieces for petty Frenchmen to sell.

We took the Métro again, this time to La Place de l'Étoile, where Napoléon's triumphal arch, the world's largest, stands to pay tribute to his Grande Armée and its victorious battles. In the center of the square, I saw France's Unknown Soldier resting peacefully in a tomb below an eternal flame. To get to the arch's summit, we had to huff and puff it up the steps in one of the legs as the elevator was out of order. I looked down at the star-shaped configuration of radiating avenues and the automobiles almost bumping into each other as they sped around the circle.

Friday evening, after downing our dinner, it was Folies Bergère time, a musical and comical revue not to be missed by any young American soldier visiting Paris. The women's costumes were elab-orate, often with a good deal of skin showing, and the songs and dances catered to popular tastes. Had I come to the Folies more than three decades earlier, I would have seen Josephine Baker, the Ameri-can expatriate, step to her famous Danse banane, a highly suggestive dance in a skirt made only of artificial bananas. I might have also gotten a glimpse of Jean Gabin, later dubbed the Gallic Spencer Tracy, in a bit part on stage. After enjoying the female performan-ces, and pushing myself backstage to take a picture of a French doll that caught my eye, I suggested to my Army buddy, who was still ogling the half-naked dancers milling about, that we call it a night. He agreed, reluctantly, and the two horny boys went back to their hotel.

Saturday morning after I woke up I said to my roommate: "Let's go see Napoleon's tomb. We're soldiers . . . it should be interesting."

"Where is it?"

"It's in the Hôtel National des Invalides." I read from the tourist booklet, pronouncing it in the best French I could.

"A tomb in a hotel?"

"Not exactly," I explained, still reading. "It says here it originally was and still is a military retirement home and a hospital for disabled war veterans. It also houses museums, monuments, and burial sites now. We can get there by subway lines eight or thirteen . . . the Invalides stop."

"Okay," my Paris partner said. "You lead the way."

On Saturday after breakfast, we headed out, preferring again to do sightseeing on our own. The PFC was two years older than I, and had been to college for a year and a half, but seemed to defer to my direction in planning the day's activities.

Les Invalides was an imposing structure, occupying an entire city block, with a long façade, a courtyard, wide public esplanade, and tall domed church at the center. Napoléon's sarcophagus lay in a segregated recessed level directly under the stained-glass dome, a comfortable distance from the inquisitive touchy-feely hands of tourists. Some members of the Bonaparte family, officers who served under the small but larger-than-life general, and other French military heroes are interred in different sections. I was sure the body of Alfred Dreyfus, the Jewish army captain convicted of treason and sent to Devil's Island but exonerated years later, the subject of the biggest military scandal in France's history, was refused burial in this hallowed ground.

On the subway map, there was a Métro stop called Bastille and we thought we ought to see the famous prison that was the start of the Revolution. We got off there, went upstairs, and looked around but saw no Bastille. I had the film advanced in my camera and the focus set ready to take a shot. Where the hell is it, I said to myself. After several unsuccessful attempts, I found someone who spoke English and asked him.

"You are a little late," he told us, "about a hundred and seventy years. After the start of the Revolution, the people tore the Bastille down . . . brick by brick."

Still thinking about glorious 1789, we found our way to La Place de la Concorde. I took a picture of the ancient obelisk in the center of the square. And then another of the entrance to the Avenue des Champs-Élysées. This was the site I learned in high school French class where the guillotine stood, between the two monuments emplaced there later. The heads of Louis XVI, Marie-Antoinette, and Robespierre, to name just a few, must have rolled around in the spot where my feet now were.

Paris' most famous avenue was little more than a mile and I could see the Arc de Triomphe at the other end. I tried to envision what it was like in 1940 when German troops proudly marched along the Champs to celebrate the *fall* of France, and in 1944 when the Free French and the American 28th Infantry Division took the same route to mark the *liberation* of Paris. Before going back to the hotel for dinner, we hustled over to see one more landmark, the Assemblée Nationale, the parliament edifice where democracy French-style is famously forged or, as some would say, corrupted.

Saturday night in Paris there was only one place horny young men wanted to go, La Place Pigalle, what Allied soldiers in two wars af-fecttionately called Pig Alley. The Métro map had a stop Pigalle and we headed there. The street with the raunchy reputation was exactly what we had heard, a red-light district of sex shops, striptease joints, sleazy bars, and prostitutes walking around.

Moulin Rouge, the famous cabaret, was conspicuously in Pigalle's center, its huge replica of a red windmill spinning clockwise high above the entrance. Here Toulouse-Lautrec from his nearby studio hobbled on his dwarfed legs to sit at a table and paint the nightlife for his posters. Here the can-can was invented, where a troupe of young women sans panties would dance and at times lift their dresses and hold up one leg to titillate the audience of older men.

My G.I. roommate and I were certainly ready for some action. But we just walked up and down Pigalle, eyeing but not entering any establishment, observing but not approaching a streetwalker in re-vealing clothing. By ten o'clock we found ourselves directly across the street from Le Moulin Rouge, standing by the curb, trying to fig-ure out what's next, when the plain-looking girl who was looking our way came up to us. The mademoiselle smiled at me and said some-thing I did not understand.

"Q'est-ce-que c'est?" I answered, eager to practice what I learned for three years. "Je parle anglais."

"Oh . . . you américain, no?"

"Oui . . .yes," I instinctively said in both languages, nodding my head slightly

"You want good time?" she said in a heavy accent. "I geeve you."

I looked at her more closely now. She really was not bad looking at all, despite her being a trifle plump, and there was a sexy quality about her, no doubt because she was propositioning me. My room-mate stood by but said nothing. He must have wished he was the object of this femme's affection.

"Combien? . . . how much?" I knew that word and I repeated myself again to make sure she understood me.

"Tree tousand franc," she said, holding up three fingers on one hand.

"Trois mille . . . oui . . . je compris." I glanced at the PFC who ex-hibited a blank face. Her price sounded outrageously high but it was only six dollars. "Okay." I nodded again to her. It was fair. It would cost me that for just a few drinks at any bar to try to pick up someone.

"You 'ave 'otel . . . yes?" she said, leaving out the *h*'s.

"Yes."

"Bon . . . we go now."

I looked again at my weekend buddy. "I'm going back to the hotel with her. Give us at least an hour before you come back. I'll take the chain off the door when she leaves."

"Okay," he muttered, yielding to my assertiveness.

"Connect with one of the other gals around here," I advised him, trying to be a pal. "Go with her to her place."

Without waiting for an answer, I got into the taxi that the girl hailed. I reached in my pocket and pulled out the card with the hotel's address. She looked at it and then talked to the driver in French. It was only a ten-minute ride and I played the gentleman. We only clasped hands and I made no attempt to touch her tits, legs, or crotch.

The girl who approached and then propositioned me kept her word. She gave me a good time. In fact, it was the *best* time I ever had with a girl. And she was a lady. She did not ask for any money, before or after. To her I must have had an honest, as well as nice-looking, face.

Soon as we entered my room, she quickly undressed and plopped herself onto the bed I pointed to. I watched her as she effortlessly unbuckled her belt, stepped out of her skirt, pulled the blouse over her head, reached behind to unsnap her bra, and dropped her panties. We did not talk much. My French and her English were both very limited. Besides, what was there to say after I got into bed? I was positioned near the wall, she the unobstructed side of the bed.

The first thing the girl did, in pantomime, was to put the fingers of one hand to her lips and then to my joint that was rapidly standing up. I suppose she did not know how to say "Do you want me to blow you" in English. I said "Oui" of course, and she immediately moved to go down on me.

Frenchie's mouth was moist and she took it all in, rolling her tongue around and sucking like a baby on a nipple. Up and down she went, putz in and out, and then sideways on my shaft. I could see her cheeks collapse as she drew in. It was the most pleasurable oral work-up I ever had. If she bit my skin off, I could not have been more sensitive. French girls really know how to do it. It's not an old boy's tale. Karin had every reason to be worried about me going to Paris by myself.

Before I climaxed I stopped her, then climbed on top of her and slipped it in. She was very moist there too. I was never motioned to put on a rubber. For the first time, I was with a girl who could have been a circus contortionist. She raised her feet way up high above my head, her knees almost to her face, then wrapped her legs around me and pumped rapidly. Her twisted actions forced me to shoot off in no time at all.

The moment I withdrew, she jumped off the bed and dashed to the bathroom, leaving the door open. Catching my breath, I saw her sit on the "other toilet" in the bathroom, the one without a seat around the rim and two handles on the upper end, with her back to me. When I first saw it in this hotel, I had no idea of its purpose, an extra potty for kids perhaps. She turned the handles, ran water into the bowl, and with one hand kept scooping up water between her legs. She was douching herself, something I never saw done before. Karin had no such fixture in her apartment, nor did the Pension we stayed in have one. The French must make love more often than Germans or Americans, and employ protective measures less.

I put on my underwear and reached for my wallet. I handed the girl as she was dressing what looked like play money, three one-thousand franc bills, before she could ask for it. She thanked me,

373

and I thanked her, in French and English. Unlike the black WAC in California and the puertorriqueña in New York, I did not kiss Frenchie goodbye on the lips. She hurried out of my hotel room and out of my life, but not out of my memory.

My roommate must have returned alone after I fell asleep. I was not wakened by him with some Pigalle mademoiselle he snagged, and asked to go down to the lobby.

On Sunday I slept late and missed breakfast. My roommate came back after he ate and his moving about woke me up. "How was that girl last night?" I heard him say as soon as my eyes were open.

"She was okay." I saw no reason to get specific, to give the soldier mostly unknown to me a blowing or glowing description of the good time the girl gave me.

"Why didn't you ask me to come along too?" he put to me inanely.

"I don't like a ménage à trois." That expression I did not learn in French class.

"A *what*?" he said.

"A threesome in English," I told the Kansas hick.

"Oh. I would have waited outside while you were with her," he noted, again being silly.

"I don't like that either."

"What do you mean?"

"I don't like pimping for anyone . . . or someone waiting to take my place in bed."

The night before I left for Germany was different. I did not mind Richie procuring for me or biding my time to get into the Puerto Rican girl after him.

"Oh," he said again, this time with more surprise.

"There were plenty of other girls on Pigalle. Why didn't you go for one of them?"

"I liked the one you were with."

"Well, I'm sorry. She came up to *me*," I said forthwith. "Go back there tonight. Maybe you can find her."

I could see my roommate was angry, surely because I did not help him get laid and he did not get laid on his own. He went back to his side of the room, puttered around, and sulked. When I came out of the shower, he told me he wanted to join the others on a guided tour that day. He did not ask me to go too and I said nothing about my going. Evidently he was insulted by what I said. It had nothing to do with him, but he took it personally.

I spent a quiet and relaxing Sunday by myself, taking in lesser known sights and learning about Jewish Paris, all thanks to the sensitive PFC. First I bought a crunchy baguette, some slices of salami and cheese, a coke, and had my lunch on the grassy area beneath the Eiffel Tower. I then strolled around the flea market at Vanves, looking and touching all the chatzkes on display in wooden trays.

Before long I found myself across the street from the back of Notre Dame, at the Memorial to the Unknown Deportee. Inside were the names of the Nazi death camps where 200,000 French Jews were killed. Nearby was the Jewish Quarter, and I walked around the neighborhood where many of the deportees were rounded up and shoved into trucks, a tangle of petite Medieval streets and alleys. I met an old man who spoke some English and he told me that after the war Jews who survived filed legal actions for the return of their property taken by the Germans and then kept by the French.

On Monday we had to check out by noon, leave our bags with the Concierge, and be ready to board the bus in front of the hotel at 1930 hours, a half hour before departure. All I did that last day was take a picture of the pint-sized Statue of Liberty in the Jardin du Luxembourg, the garden of the French Senate, and enjoy the sightseeing cruise down the Seine as a shutterbug. On the boat there were some young black men but I did not go up to them and say: "Hey man, where are you stationed in the Army?" In Germany, the Schwarzers were American, in France les hommes noir were French, French-speaking Africans from the colonies or the Caribbean.

On the trip back to Nuremberg, my erstwhile Paris roommate took a seat in the back of the bus, far from where I was trying to get some sleep.

## CHAPTER 44: THE LAST TIME I SAW KARIN

"Why you not go see Karin?" Ursula asked me. "She really love you."

It was Sunday, the twentieth of September, almost two weeks since I came back from Paris and almost three weeks since I had seen Karin. We were standing on line at the Merrell theatre, Steve, Ursula, and I, waiting to see the matinee that was playing, a movie coincidentally about a love affair in Paris between an American soldier and a girl he meets at the end of the war. Before I munched on popcorn that day, I had no idea this Hollywood romance would speak to me.

"I don't think Karin wants to see me. We argued before I went to Paris. I wanted to go alone but she wanted to come with me."

Steve jumped in, smiling and turning to look to Ursula for a moment. "I would have gone with you . . . if I wasn't engaged."

I had told Steve about the girl in Paris who gave me the best time I ever had, but I implored him not to tell Ursula. His grin told me he probably said something, but made her promise not to tell Karin.

"She want see you, Dave, I sure," Ursula said and then repeated herself. "Karin love you."

"She told you so?"

I knew the girls were good friends, always talking to each other whenever the four of us went anyplace. But, had they communicated while I was away or since I returned?

Steve's girlfriend stared at me with dead seriousness. "I know," she added simply, without saying how she knew. I did not doubt her or ask for specifics.

"She knows," Steve butted in a second time, perhaps answering the question in my mind.

In Paris, I thought about French girls. Since returning to Nuremberg, I could think of little else but Karin. At the Area Office, my mind wandered in her direction rather than toward the two Bs. After work, I felt no compulsion to swoosh into the Flying Dutchman to hook up with Elsa again or make another effort to bag the Marianne I longed for since I arrived in the city six months earlier. I held back from putting my feet down on the dance floor at the Luitpold, to spin around with some other Fräulein and then hope to spin around with her at her place. And I certainly did not ask Steve to ask Ursula to fix me up with a friend of hers. Karin did not know if I would ever come back to see her again. I wondered if, during the three weeks I was away, she had gone out with another man, American or German.

"Let me think about it," I told my two friends who apparently were concerned about my love life more than I was at the time.

The line was beginning to move and soon we were in the theater, sitting in a middle row, holding boxes of popcorn, and looking at the coming attractions. Two hours later, Steve was taking Ursula home and I was lying flat on my bunk. I was *thinking* about getting into action but he would soon be firing his weapon.

I was also reflecting on the movie I had just seen, *The Last Time I Saw Paris*. Van Johnson and Elizabeth Taylor meet on V-E Day, fall in love, get married, and have a baby. Tragedy strikes when she catches pneumonia one night after a party and later dies because he was too drunk to unlock the door to their home and she had to walk a long distance in the rain to find a taxi to take her to her sister's house. He naturally blames himself for his wife's death, falls apart emotionally and loses custody of his daughter, then runs away to the States, only to come back to Paris a few years later to reclaim his child. I very much liked this romantic story, set in the city I had such a good time in, and its lovely title song written as a paean to Paris after France fell to the Nazis.

The next day I decided to take the advice Ursula proffered. Between typing letters, filing papers, charting equipment repairs, and listening to Bentley and Barry bullshit about their careers in the Army, I made up my mind to head to Zirndorf right after work and chow. I did not take time to shower or shave again, and I packed no protection. But I did make sure to take the two rolls of color slides I got back from Kodak in the mail, neatly packed in plastic holders, plus the little one-eyed slide viewer I picked up in the PX.

The last time I saw Karin, she was angry with me. The thought of seeing her again was a little disconcerting. Has she forgiven me for not taking her to Paris? Would she let me walk through the door? Would she listen to anything I said? Uncertainty held me back from going to see her sooner. I wanted very much to find out if she is still mad, to show her my pictures of Paris, to perhaps rekindle our relationship. For two weeks I restrained myself, but if what Ursula said was true then I should not be afraid to suddenly appear at Karin's front door. Ursula's prodding and Steve's nudging convinced me to do something about the loose ends in the rope that tied Karin to me, to tighten or cut, one or the other.

Karin's sister answered the door when I knocked. She looked at me and then immediately turned around and called to Karin without mentioning my name. Karin came to the half-open door as Schwester was leaving, saw me, and had a look of surprise on her face, not happy or angry, just caught off guard. She was wearing a plain dress and a thin sweater. Even with no makeup on, there was an appealing quality about her, no doubt due to the memory of our making love many times. She opened the door wider with one hand while clutching a cloth napkin with the other.

"Come, Dayf," she said, uttering my name in the way I was used to hearing, after hesitating for a few seconds. She opened the door all the way and stepped back.

I entered and stood in the foyer. "Thank you." I did not take her words the wrong way.

Karin pointed to the sitting room. "Wait. I finish to eat."

"Okay," I said, pleased that I was not refused entrance and that she was speaking to me.

Karin walked to the kitchen, I went into the sitting room. It was after seven and there was still light outside but the room was dark and I just sat on the couch, my favorite piece of furniture. I ran my hand on the cushion where my bare ass moved up and down on a few occasions, and my covered ass on many, and thought about the cute little Fräulein in the other room I was fortunate enough to shtup for four months. What scenario would play next was foremost in my mind.

Within ten minutes Karin was back. I stood when she came in the room. Her face had been touched up. We looked at each other but did not say a word at first. It was as if we had never been introduced, were just total strangers. Finally, I broke the silence.

"Would you like to see the pictures I took in Paris?" I reached into my small carrying case and took out the two boxes of slides.

"Yes," she said weakly, almost without caring whether she saw them or not.

I held the slide viewer and went to the window. I pulled the curtains apart. The two boxes I put on the table next to the window. I took the first slide out, held it up to the light to get a glimpse of it, and set it in the viewer.

"Here, look," I said to Karin, holding it up to her eye level. "This is Notre Dame . . . the Cathedral . . . the famous church."

Karin looked at the slide against the outside light but said nothing. One by one, I changed slides in the viewer, each time telling her what it was a picture of and sometimes adding a few words of explanation, from what I remembered in French class and what I picked up on my trip. Showing her and explaining the Louvre, Mona Lisa, riverbank along the Seine, Eiffel Tower, Arch of Triumph, Napoleon's tomb, the square where the Bastille once stood, Concord Place, Champs Elysees, flea market, Luxembourg Garden, the little Statue of Liberty, and scenes from the cruise ship elicited no emotional reaction or commentary.

She must have learned something about Paris and French history in school, and I thought she would be interested in what I was showing her, but she was not moved at all. Karin politely looked at each slide I put in the viewer, but remained stiff and silent. I was careful *not* to insert for viewing my shots of women at the Folies, sex shops and cabarets on Pigalle, and the Memorial to the Unknown Deportee with its inscriptions of Nazi war crimes. Those color pictures no doubt would have evoked a strong reaction in the German girl who begged me to take her to the French capital.

"We go for walk," Karin said as I was putting the boxes back in my carrying case.

She got her jacket, I grabbed mine, I left the case on the table, and through the door we went. It was obvious she wanted to talk out of earshot of Mutti und Schwester. We walked silently toward Zirndorf Woods, without holding hands, slowly engaging in small talk. Before long, we found ourselves sitting on the same park bench where we kissed that Sunday we met. Now Karin talked freely and weightily. She relaxed a bit, was not as stiff, and her eyes seemed as if they were about to water.

"I hurt you not take me to Pareese. I cry all night when you go way. I think you not like me. You want French girl. I make all what you want and you not want me. I tell Cherman boy who want

379

me I want you. Mutti say you not go marry mit me. You Yooda, I Katholik. Mutti know I stay mit you in Pension all night. She not like."

I let Karin talk herself out, get everything bothering her off her chest. She repeated things and went off on tangents. She even mentioned things about our relationship I had given little or no thought to. When she was done, I tried to answer without lying, but there was no getting around one or two untruths.

"I'm sorry you were hurt . . . but I never meant to hurt you. I couldn't take you with me to Paris."

"Yes . . . I know now."

"I only wanted to see the city of Paris . . . what I saw in movies and read about in books. Every young soldier, American or German, wants to go to Paris."

"Yes . . . I know," she said again.

"All I wanted to do was take pictures of Paris to show my friends and family. I didn't go there to meet French girls."

Karin looked at me but did not say yes this time. Apparently, she still had her suspicions.

"I like you. I always liked you. I never said I would not marry you."

She put her hand on my forearm in a tender gesture. This is what she probably wanted to hear. She moved her head closer to mine. I leaned forward to kiss her and she responded in kind. The back of my hand pushed against her breast purposefully. She did not pull it away.

"You said you wanted to come with me to Jewish services . . . and I took you."

"Yes . . . I know," she agreed with me a third time.

"I never said you have to become Jewish. And I never told you not to go to your Catholic church." Here I was not lying, but I wondered what I was getting myself into.

"Yes . . . you right . . . you not say."

She seemed relieved and smiled at me for the first time that day. A few tears came out. She dried her eyes with the back of *her* hand, with mine still in place.

It was getting dark and there was no one around. This time I ran the front of my hand across both breasts. "Let's go home," I said, without realizing it must have sounded like we were living together or married.

Karin gazed at me with earnest eyes. A moment later she stood up and reached for my hand. We walked to her place in silence, touching palms and fingers nervously. We were of the same mind again, I was sure.

Mutti und Schwester were both in the sitting room when we got back. The door was open, the curtains drawn, two lamps were on, and my carrying case was still on the table by the window. Karin took me into the kitchen. We sat down and she asked me if I wanted some soup and black bread with butter but I declined. When the other two came to the kitchen, Karin paraded us into the sitting room, like we were playing musical chairs. She closed the door behind us. The rest was mostly déjà vu.

Karin and I quickly got back into our usual routine, but this time the route veered off course. She sat on my lap. We kissed deeply. I felt her all over, top and bottom. My cock was a rock, hard and horizontal and hurting. I pushed her back a little, unzipped, and took it out, now being vertical for her to touch, or kiss if she were so inclined. But the German girl did not mouth me of her own accord and I dared not ask for a fast Frenchie. Had she brought her head down, I would not have stopped her from completing the job.

"Take off your panties and get on top of me," I whispered, cognizant of the two watchdogs in the other room. "Schnell . . . schnell."

Karin slid off my lap, reached under her dress, and floored her pink undergarment. When she saw I put no rubber on, she hesitated climbing back and straddling me. "Make me not a baby," she warned me, as she did many times before. The look on her face told me she was afraid.

"Don't worry. It'll be okay. You can wash yourself out right after." I was the one who should have been worried but I had to strike when the iron was hot. My brains were temporarily in a different part of my body.

She still hesitated. I had to grab her by the wrist, pull her toward me, and lift one thigh to position her middle over mine. Our tight coupling occurred just in time. Two seconds more and I would have missed my target and made my deposit in the wrong space.

I pushed her off me. "Go wash now," I commanded. "Clean all of it out what's inside you. Go . . . schnell."

Karin left the room quickly but her panties remained on the floor. I shot a big load and I thought she must be dripping like a broken faucet, but that was not so terrible since she would have less to douche. I heard voices through the door but paid no attention. I used my handkerchief to wipe myself off, zipped up, picked up her panties, and hid the garment in my carrying case.

The voices suddenly got louder and I put my ear to the door. I still could not make out what was happening so I went into the foyer. Karin was standing up against the bathroom door, knocking hard and frantically calling to her sister. The stupid and/or selfish Schwester was not rushing to come out. I was dumbfounded by this familial discourtesy, one sister willing to let another suffer cramps and soil her linen.

I was as helpless as Karin to do anything. I could not very well break the door down and drag the crippled, fat, ugly, dumb blond out, or reveal the real reason Karin had to immediately go in the Klotz WC. The mother too looked on helplessly, unwilling or unable to intervene in the unfolding household sibling dispute and settle it. It must have been a full ten minutes before the bathroom door was unlocked. Karin was in tears, but not the joyful kind that she shed less than an hour earlier on the park bench.

Things calmed down about an hour later and Karin and I were sitting around the table with her mother in the kitchen. The sister was in the bedroom she shared with Karin, hiding out from the other two Klotz's expressions of disapprobation of her baneful bathroom behavior. Karin was now cleaned up and wearing something under her dress. Whether she was in the fertile days of her period, or douched herself soon enough and well enough to prevent fertilization, were questions I dared not ask or think about. I had a chance to wash too. In my carrying case, a sticky and smelly handkerchief took the place of the crumpled panties.

I looked at Mutti, as she was talking to Karin, and wondered what the mother thought of me. She knew I was Jewish. Several times I heard Karin say *Yooda* in her presence with my name, first and last. She knew I was banging her daughter, and in her own household.

Only a fool of a mother would think no hanky-panky was going on behind a closed door, which she consciously refrained from knocking and entering for an hour sometimes, between her young unmarried daughter and the young American soldier. Mutti knew that I made no proposal of marriage to her eligible, marriage-minded daughter after coming in the sitting room for four months. And the old woman knew that Jewish boys don't usually marry non-Jewish girls. If she thought I was taking advantage of her daughter, having a good time with her but not committing myself to marry the poor girl and offer her a better life than what she, her mother, could give her in postwar Germany, she was right. Mutti had every reason to believe that. Karin's mother had lived through the Nazi period, may even have voted for Hitler and his party of criminals in the late '20s and early '30s. Like others of her generation, she must have taken stock in at least *some* of the poisonous propaganda about Jews filtering through her country at that time.

But in point of fact, I did consider marrying Karin. The thought occurred to me a number of times, notwithstanding my comments to the contrary to Esther at the Palace of Justice, my plans for college, my mother's hatred for all things German, and Richie's admonition not to come home with a Nazi Schatzie. I really liked Karin and I knew she loved me. I just could not make a decision.

At Merrell I even hopped over to see the re-enlistment sergeant the week before I went to Paris, to check out what kind of a career I could have in the Army. Bentley and Barry were happy to give me time off for such a purpose. An Army career was not bad, but I was not impressed with it either. Karin, a nice German girl, would make someone a good wife, I was sure, but whether the hubby would be me was an unanswered question.

Mutti lit a cigarette. I did not notice it before but the pack she picked up on the edge of the table was an American brand I did *not* bring her. Either this German family suddenly came into much Gelt or another G.I., perhaps from Pinder Barracks down the street, entered this fatherless household during my three-week absence and became the provider, carrying in brown paper bags with cartons of smokes and other goodies. Did Karin play house with him in the sitting room too? Mutti certainly was adept at turning a blind eye to her daughter's transgressions to facilitate a marriage and ensure the continuous flow of choice tobacco and coveted foodstuffs.

"What you think?" Karin said to me. She saw me staring at her mother smoking.

I tried to be cool and act naïve. "Would you like me to bring more cigarettes? Or coffee or tea?" I was testing them, shaking the backyard tree to see if some rotten apples fall out.

Karin looked at her mother and translated what I said. The old woman shook her head. "No. Mutti have enough what you bring last time."

Last time was more than a month since I toted brown bags to this household, and they were only half full. Neither female gave any indication she sensed I knew the pack of cigarettes lying on the table was different than the ones I brought.

"Okay," I told them, trying to shake a little more. "Let me know when you need cigarettes . . . or other things?"

Perhaps I should have opened the cupboard to see how many jars of Mutti's coveted Maxwell House coffee there were, and what brands the boxes of tea were.

Karin continued talking to her mother. She seemed relaxed and happy, now that we were back together and the Paris affair all but patched up. In her mind, our relationship was surely solid again, cemented by the kisses and touching in the park and, especially, the unprotected coupling on the couch. The business with cleaning up in the bathroom could be forgotten.

I only discerned a few German words—jüdisch, Frau, amerikanisch—but that was enough for me to get the gist of what my girlfriend was saying. She must be telling Mutti that she wanted to become Jewish, become a wife, and become American, take three important steps with the young man sitting at the table the mother may have thought was disreputable. Mutti listened but said little. So flabbergasted she must have been she could have swallowed the smoldering cigarette butt hanging from her lips. I might have had an epileptic fit myself, with Karin making matrimonial plans for me before I rendered an unequivocal commitment.

"What are you and your mother talking about?" I felt compelled to ask.

Karin turned to me. "I tell Mutti I want be Yoodish . . . no more Katholik. And I want go Amerika mit you."

She omitted the part about being a wife but that was implied from the rest of what she was saying. "What did Mutti say?" I wanted to know, more out of curiosity than commitment.

"Mutti say I do what I want."

It was very nice of the mother to say that. She may not be against the Jewish-American soldier who took her house by storm after all. The relevant question though was what did *I* want?

Karin and her mother continued speaking. I got the impression Mutti was expressing herself frankly in German, knowing I would not understand. I suppose she did not want to hurt my feelings, or rather her daughter's chances for marriage. For all I know, Mutti might be telling Karin to hold off, to give her hand to the other possible American suitor. If this was the case, I was sure the G.I. was a blond, Aryan-looking Gentile whose parents or grandparents were born in the Fatherland.

I listened to the foreign language being spoken. Two words the mother said caught my immediate attention: sechs Millionen. Whenever someone says "six million" in the context of a discussion about Jews, it could only mean one thing. I asked Karin what her mother said.

"Mutti say she not believe six million Yooden killed by Nazis. Maybe six thousand she say."

"That's not true," I countered, offended that the mother or anyone would say that. "At the trials after the war, right here in Nuremberg, at the Palace of Justice where I took you to Jewish services, it was proven that six million Jews were killed. They showed pictures of concentration camps and gas chambers." I was sorry that Karin was in the middle of all this but I had to add, "What your mother said is a lie."

Karin translated again, then after the mother responded added: "Mutti not believe much Yooden killed."

"What do you believe, Karin?"

She looked at me with a blank face. "I not know."

Mutti was clearly, and Karin probably, a denier of Nazi atrocities. The elder Klotz must also believe the Jews killed Jesus and caused Germany to lose the first war, what Hitler and Goebbels said to turn the German people against the Jews. What Karin believed I could not say. She never spoke of such things. Like the mother, I said what I believed was the truth without regard to the sensibilities of other people or the possible consequences. Mutti just sat there, smoking another American cigarette, unmoved by the can of worms she may have opened.

Karin wisely indicated we should go back to the other room. I certainly needed a break from hearing lies about my people and wondering what other lies mother and daughter believed. What kind of a family did I get myself into? This would be a marriage made in hell, not heaven. If my Mama and Karin's Mutti ever met, they would be at each others' throats. It seems I came full circle. I joined the Army to get away from one Frau Hitler only to get involved with another.

We sat apart on the couch, holding hands and talking. Karin apologized for what her mother said and I told her to forget it, that it was not the first time I ran into people who believe false and bad things about the Jews. She then climbed up on my lap. I knew it was not to go a second round but only to be closer to me, to talk more intimately. I did not make any movements with my hands but she put her arms around my neck and brought her lips to mine.

"You I love. I want go marry mit you."

I looked straight at Karin but did not say anything. I was still recovering from the maternal anti-Semitism I just witnessed. Karin was spitting out the same words I heard many times before but never responded to in a reciprocal manner.

"I make all what you want."

"Yes, I know, and I appreciate that." That was all I could say but I knew Karin wanted more.

"What your Mutti say? You write her long time now."

Karin put me on the spot. This was the moment I dreaded all summer. I knew the time for pulling off my own version of a cocky Curtis had passed. I had to give her a yes or no answer. The sweet girl who did me no wrong *deserved* a definite answer. I dilly-dallied long enough. I almost choked on the words.

"My mother said no."

The time for lying was over. How could I continue to lie to Karin when I was just the object of her mother's lies about the Jews, whether it was meant to be personal or not?

Karin looked at me with an angry face and pulled her head back a little. She pressured me for an answer and I gave it to her, but it was not what she wanted to hear.

"Why twenty-four years man need Mutti to go marry? You man or boy?"

Karin was right, of course, to criticize me and be mad. A twenty-four-year old man does not need his mother's permission or approval to marry. But I was only nineteen and I needed both. She did not know that and this was not the time or place to come clean about my age. It made no difference in any event.

"I like you, Karin, but I can't get married. It's not just my mother. *I* don't want to. Next year I want to get out of the Army and go to college. I *have* to live at home. That's the only way I could go to college. I have no money or job to support a wife. Where would we live? *How* would we live?"

"Why Steve und Ursula go marry?"

"Steve doesn't care to go to college and he is staying in the Army so he can get married. I don't want to do that."

The unpleasantness in Karin's face intensified and her voice was now strained.

"Why you not tell before? Before I make all what you want. Before I love."

I had no answer to give, not any answer that would deflect her anger toward me. I could have said it was *you* who first came on to me, it was *you* who broke off with the German to be with me, it was *you* who offered to make all I want, it was *you* who took me out in the woods to make love, but I said none of this. Why hurt the girl's feelings, even if these facts about her were true? This time I *was* concerned with someone's sensibilities.

Karin pulled her head back more, sat up straight, and removed her hands from around my neck. Her eyes narrowed and she gave me a cold look.

"Is good what Hitler did to Yooden" passed from her lips, not five minutes after she brought her lips to mine.

Her utterance stunned me. Any good feeling I had toward Karin, who gave herself to me so completely, dissipated at that moment. How could the girl who said she loved me say such a thing? Even if that is how she really felt, it is not something to be expressed openly. All logic and civility seemed to have left the body and soul of the girl who wanted to be my life partner. Sitting on my lap looking at me with daggers in her eyes was a Fräulein Hitler after all.

I lifted the disaffected girl off of me. I grabbed my jacket hanging over a chair and the carrying case on the table. There would be no excuse for me to come back to this household and say I forgot something. In silence I walked out of the sitting room, where I came so often, and whisked out the front door. No goodbye, no good luck, and no good night, in English or German. Our second parting, like the first, was *not* such sweet sorrow.

This love lost scene, with one additional word, could have been written by Shakespeare too. But this departure was not an uncertain one.

That was the last time I saw Karin.

# PART IV

## CHANGE OF SEASONS

# CHAPTER 45: LONG NIGHT'S JOURNEY INTO DAY

The trip from Zirndorf to Merrell, catching a bus and then two streetcars, took about an hour. That Monday night, the twenty-first of September, after I left Karin's house for the last time, the three rides seemed to take *two* hours or more. The long journey back to my barracks afforded me the opportunity to think about what had just transpired in the Klotz household. What it might mean for my remaining nine months in the Army and my plans for the future after I turned in my rifle and helmet and put away my uniforms was not at all clear.

The bus I needed was stopped at the southeast corner of Bahnhofstrasse and Fürtherstrasse. It was not at a red light and could have taken off at any moment. As I turned onto Bahnhofstrasse I saw the bus and instantly imagined the driver was waiting for *me* to get aboard, to take me away from Zirndorf and to a new life without Karin. I ran a whole block to catch it, not willing to wait the twenty minutes this time of night for the next one. Every minute counted, I was in a hurry to begin that new life.

I boarded the bus just as the doors closed behind me, shutting out forever the four months I spent with a nice German girl in her small town. I was out of breath from running, or rather escaping, from this small town and the Klotz family trio. My breathing from now on would be in the life to come.

I took a seat near the rear of the bus, to be separated from the handful of other people. Like Greta Garbo, I wanted to be alone.

That Monday night the long journey to my Army post with my feet on the ground had an affinity with the axial movements of the earth and position of the sun high above me. It was the end of summer and the beginning of fall, the conclusion of one season of a man's life and the opening of another. The breakup with Karin minutes earlier would signal a change in the climate of my daily activities no less important than the shift in temperature of the planet. Summer was gone, and with it the hot and lazy days of time out from work, picnics in the park, and strolls to secluded woodsy spots. Autumn leaves soon would be falling and work calling, picnic blankets put away, and colder weather precluding lovemaking in hidden fields.

Fidgeting in my seat on the bus, I thought this might be another day the earth stood still for me. Like that afternoon at Fort Monmouth when the lieutenant opened the door for me to college, there could now be a halt to everything I was doing and a turnaround in the direction of my life. An unheard of celestial event, an autumnal solstice, was gathering in the sky just for me.

"Is good what Hitler did to Yooden."

Karin's words kept bouncing around in my head, like I bounced around in my seat every time the bus hit a bump in the road. But I fell into a pothole with Karin and we would never travel on the same street together again.

Perhaps I was too hasty in walking out on her. Should I have responded to the comment of an otherwise good German girl on the evil leader of the German people for twelve years? This day did not have to be the end of our affair to remember. I probably used her offensive words as an excuse to let her go when I did not have the courage to leave on my own initiative.

Was it fair to blame Karin for the breakup when it was really my doing that caused it? I was the one who lied, not she, I was the one who misled the other, not she, I was the one who prolonged the inevitable parting, not she. I toyed with her emotions recklessly while I toyed with her body sensually. I derived temporary pleasure without any commitment on my part, free love at the expense of a young woman's dreams for a lifelong intimate relationship.

I looked out the window of the bus. It was the end of the line in Fürth and here I would have to catch the first of my two streetcars, the Number 21 to the Hauptbahnhof.

Had I stayed a little longer in the Klotz household, what could I have said to Karin? That she did not mean it. That she did not know what she was saying. Would she have retracted her vicious statement? Most probably not, unless I promised to marry her. Would I have believed she was sorry for mouthing those ugly words and forgiven her had she taken them back? Not likely, unless she promised not to be angry with me by not marrying her.

Karin could not have meant what she said. First she tells her mother she wants to become Jewish, then tells me she is glad Hitler killed the Jews of Europe. That makes sense only if she was faking her feelings for me and was a bitter anti-Semite at heart. But I did not believe either was true. Her love for me was genuine. But Karin Klotz, KK, knew what she was saying, knew that saying something *for* Hitler and *against* Jews would hurt me. One more K and she could have worn a white sheet and hood. She should have only blamed me as an individual, not direct her baseless words at my people as a whole. The German girl, in effect, treated me like my mother treated all Germans. One bad apple does not a barrel of bad apples make.

For Karin, denial preceded approval. One minute she said she did not know what the Nazis did to the Jews, and the next claimed what Hitler did to the Jews was good. Well, at least she was not like her countrymen at the War Crimes Trials. In Room 600 at the Palace of Justice, which I happened to be passing on the Number 21 this long night, approval preceded denial. Nazi officials who signed and delivered orders for deportations of Jews later claimed before the international tribunal they did not know the deportees were going to death camps. "We were only messengers," they pleaded, "not murderers."

At the Hauptbahnhof I had to wait what seemed like double time for streetcar Number 8.

From what had the ghastly words and sudden breakup proceeded? From the unprotected coupling Karin yielded to reluctantly, from her inability to douche quickly, from her mother's false comment about six million Jews, from her demand for a definite answer about marriage, from my telling her I could not get married at this point in my life? All these events that night surely played a role, but the stage was set weeks before. Karin resented my going to Paris alone, she reproached me for wanting to meet French girls, we argued about it, I left without kissing her goodbye, and our first parting was not such sweet sorrow.

On the third leg of my journey to the barracks, I thought about the movie I saw the day before. The last time I saw Karin could mimic *The Last Time I Saw Paris*. She and I in real life might play Elizabeth Taylor and Van Johnson. I did not want Karin to have a baby with the deposit I left behind. I did not want tragedy to strike and she die of some illness or her own hand. But if that came to pass, would I blame myself and fall apart emotionally? I just walked out on Karin and in nine months I would be going back to the States, but was this running away like the character on screen? Would I seek to learn if Karin was with child, *my* child? If so, would I return to Germany years later to claim my progeny?

The second streetcar I took stopped less than half a block before Bayernstrasse, the street Merrell Barracks was on. It was the end of my long journey from a life I wanted to forget. I got off and started walking. I had not been looking at my watch all evening but it was about the time the movie theater and snack bar were closing. There were soldiers going in both directions, and a few Germans. My thoughts were to get to my room, fall into my bunk, go to sleep, and put an end to the evening's harrowing events. I was in no mood for a winded discussion with Steve about the outcome of my going back to see Karin as he and Ursula advised me.

Suddenly I saw the girl that worked in the snack bar, the color-blind one I was so taken with, walking toward me. She was in plain street clothes, blond hair pinned up, carrying a little bundle under one arm. I had not seen her for close to three months, since July fourth. When she was near me, I felt a rush of adrenalin and emotion at the sight of that perfect face and figure.

"Hello," I said softly when she was a few feet in front of me. I stopped and faced her.

The Fräulein stopped and looked at me. "Hallo."

My heart pounded a little harder, my head seemed lighter. "Do you remember me?"

She smiled a bit and answered, "Yes . . . I do. You ask me out. Long time now."

I looked at the girl with the flawless features, immaculate skin, deep blue eyes, and shape to die for. "I saw you in the snack bar when I first came to Nuremberg . . . over six months ago."

"Yes," the beauty repeated. "I remember. You come to me at cabinet for hot water."

Now I knew she had a good memory and wasn't just saying pleasantries. That pleased me greatly. I must have been the only white soldier who ever asked her for a date. I was very glad she stopped to talk to me. Accidentally bumping into her alone on the street gave me cause for some joy. I still wanted to bump into her in the bedroom. But, what would I say to her now? What *could* I say that would not be offensive and not hurt her feelings? Or not result in a black trooper coming after me with a knife?

"I liked you very much the first moment I saw you," I finally said cautiously. Would she react to my flattery, or was it a come on? "You're the prettiest girl I've seen in Germany."

"Dankeschön." She broadened her smile.

"Bitteschön," I said, returning her thanks.

"I see you at snack bar with girl. And at picnic."

My dream girl had good eyesight too. "Yes. That was my girl-friend. We just broke up."

"Oh, sorry."

"That's okay."

"Why you break up?" she asked.

Was she now interested in dating me? Was there some sliver of hope of getting into her? I might have to bring along a baseball bat, either to satisfy her or to protect myself, or both.

"She wanted to get married and I didn't."

"Why you not get married?"

She gave me a look of surprise, as if she thought every American soldier should marry his German girlfriend. Or was it only every *white* soldier?

I thought hard before I answered. "She wasn't as pretty as you," I said slowly and clearly and unabashedly, focusing straight at her. "And she didn't have the great shape that you have." Now there would be no doubt in the girl's mind that I thought the world of her.

"Dankeschön," she repeated, a trifle flushed.

This time I did not say you're welcome. I wanted to render a bold question, not a perfunctory compliment.

"Do you still have a boyfriend?"

"Yes," she said simply and directly.

I hesitated before opening my mouth again. "Is he . . . . "

"Yes," she cut me off. The smile passed from her lips.

She obviously anticipated what I was going to say. She must have figured I was clued in about the race of her lover boy after I asked her out, or she knew I saw her with a Schwarzer on the Fourth of July. My next statement was going to be very risky, but it was easi-er, emotionally, for me to say in German, imperfect as it was.

"Warum gehen-sie mit schwarzer mann?"

It was a good thing I did not ask this question, given my state of mind and body I felt I had to, in English, as just then a black soldier happened to pass by. The girl I coveted, luckily for me, was not offended or rattled by my egregiously personal and improper question, the answer to which was surely none of my business. She did not cry out for help, slap a soldier who stepped out of line, or turn and walk away from the crude young man who eyeballed her.

"Why you not think I can love black man?" she said calmly, almost stoically.

My question boomeranged. She put the onus on me to explain, and she was right. I probably was thinking too much like an American, not a European.

"Well," I began, with a measure of apprehension. "I see many frauleins go with black soldiers, but they are much older and fat . . . and not pretty at all. White soldiers won't go with them. But you're different. You are young and pretty and have a beautiful figure. I'm sure you can get any white soldier you want."

Her face and voice reflected some strain, and it was I who was surprised this time. I invaded her privacy and she did not have to answer me, but she did. Her response opened a door, but only a crack.

"I went with white soldier. He see me talk to black. He tell everyone I sleep with black but it not true. Then no white want ask me out. You only one."

So that was her story. The Queen of Spades excused her crossing the color line by blaming white soldiers. They dealt her a bad hand.

"I would be happy to go out with you," I said, not really knowing whether I meant it.

Her head turned slightly, the blue eyes narrowed. "Even you know I go with . . . ."

"Yes." This time I did the cutting off. It was not necessary for her to finish her sentence.

"Danke, but I go still," she said with a determined look. "Him I love."

Now she justified staying on the dark side by her own feelings. I looked at her and said nothing, but I was thinking what every white soldier in Germany might think. The Queen wants to be dealt an Ace in the hole. What she loves is not his blackness but his bigness.

"You not believe. You not like what I say?" she asked when I did not respond.

How could I say what I was thinking? It would be an insult to top all insults, and I would be a hypocrite. Even if it were true, that is not something to candidly utter. That is what Karin did with her words to me and I resented it greatly.

"Mox nix what I like," I said instead. "You can go with anyone you want. I just wish it was me."

"Dankeschön," she said a third time, now somewhat less defensively, but did not add that she would date me. She glanced at her watch. "I go now. It late."

Evidently she preferred men who were more appealing below the belt than above the collar, skin color notwithstanding, and I had to accept that. "Yes. I'm sorry I held you up. I enjoyed talking to you . . . and seeing you again." I may have lied to Karin but I was not lying to this Fräulein, or to myself.

"Auf Weidersehen." She turned and walked away.

"So long," I answered, as her back was toward me. The irony of my last words to the girl who never explained *why* she loved a black man hit me later.

That was the last time I saw the girl from the snack bar. I felt close to her now, as she shared her most private thoughts and experiences with me, but I never got to know her name. I also never knew how old she was, where she was born, what faith she practices, how she felt about Jewish people, or what her family did during the war.

This nameless, enigmatic girl was the incarnation of my dream lover. As Bobby Darin wrote and sang, I wanted to know the magic of her charms and I hoped that someday, someway, she'll bring her love to me. We both did something in unison after all. She walked out of my life the same night I walked out of someone else's life, but that was not the kind of joint action I yearned for.

Back in my room, I was glad Steve was not there. He usually did not see Ursula on a Monday night. I assumed he was in the room across the hall playing cards with Amos 'n' Andy and other troopers from the 2nd Cav. The Ace of Spades at the end of the hall, my uncommon uncomely colored competitor, might be in the game and holding another good hand.

I lay in my bunk trying to fall asleep. Soon it would be midnight and the dawn of a new day. Life without Karin was about to begin.

# CHAPTER 46: SOMETHING NEW, SOMETHING OLD

It was Erev Rosh Hashanah, the evening before the first day of the Jewish New Year, the second of October on the Gregorian calendar, almost two weeks after the breakup with Karin and the long night's journey from Zirndorf. I went to services that Friday at the Palace of Justice as I usually did, but this time it was different. At sundown the year 5720 on the Hebrew calendar began, my last in the Army.

When I woke up the morning after I saw Karin and the girl from the snack bar, both for the last time, it was clear to me what I had to do from now on, what my new life should be about.

First and foremost was to hit the books after working hours and prepare for the College Boards given in January. Doing well on these two tests would be my best chance of gaining admission to one of the municipal colleges in New York City, where it was free and I could attend while living at home. I would most likely apply to Brooklyn College, the closest to where we lived, or City College, either the Uptown or Downtown branches, in Manhattan.

Neither my parents nor I had any money to pay for tuition at a private school such as Columbia University or NYU. Applying to the Catholic colleges, Fordham or St. Johns or St. Francis, was out of the question. There I would not only have to pay tuition, but I would be compelled to take courses in religion, not my own. Jewish students from wealthy families went to the private nonsectarian colleges if they did not make it into the City schools, based on a combination of one's high school average and College Board scores. Rich Jewish kids who were brilliant students with high grades, of course, applied to Ivy League Universities. It never occurred to me to try to get into hoity-toity Harvard, Yale, or Princeton.

Since the breakup, I as a soldier put Fräulein fields off limits, a freeze on forays into town for fun or fornication. I stayed far away from the Flying Dutchman and the Luitpold, my old battlegrounds before I met Karin. I avoided hooking up with old Elsa again and new efforts to bag Marianne or another bargirl for the first time. By my own orders young German women working at Merrell Barracks were in the enemy camp, not to be approached for dates or mates or rates. The High Holidays coming up were to be respected. Bentley and Barry said I could take three days off and I wanted to get through Yom Kippur, the Day of Atonement, without feminine distractions. It was bad enough Karin was still on my mind.

At the Palace, services had concluded and everyone in the congregation was in the reception room across the hall. The rabbi was cutting the long twist challah after he said the blessing for the wine and people placed their empty little white cups in the waste baskets. Spread out on the table for the holiday were glass bowls with creamed and pickled herring, gefilte fish, chopped liver, carrot sticks, potato salad, and coleslaw, along with trays of cookies and fresh fruit and slices of chocolate cake, apple pie, and yellow sponge cake.

I saw Esther on the other side of the room and I went up to her, paper plate and fork in hand.

"You can put your pen and paper away," I said.

Esther turned from the lady she was talking to and looked at me. Her daughter was at her side. The little girl, about the same age as my sister but without the beautiful round face, clutched at her mother's long pleaded dress, as if to stop her from running away. The woman old enough to be my mother had a puzzled look.

"What do you mean?"

"You won't have to write that letter to my mother," I told her.

"You broke off with that girl?" Esther voiced right away, remembering her real or imagined threat to me three months earlier.

"Yes."

"What happened?"

"She said it was good what Hitler did to the Jews."

"*What*? She said that?"

Esther was in shock. Her mouth opened, she breathed in, a hand went up to cover the lower half of her face.

"Her exact words."

"Why? What did you say to her?"

"What do you think I said?" I put to Esther.

"You wouldn't marry her."

I nodded my head. "She pressured me for a definite answer and I couldn't lie to the girl." I did not say I couldn't lie to her *anymore*. "She was very angry. I don't think she meant it though."

"She meant it all right," Esther quipped, putting her plate down. She ran her hand over her daughter's head and patted it affectionately. "She wouldn't have said it if she didn't mean it, marriage or no marriage."

"I suppose you're right."

"Well, it's all for the best, I'm sure. You couldn't live with a shiksa who said that, even if she did convert. You're better off without her."

I nodded again. "I'm sure you're right." I was more positive this time.

Esther gave me a hug, a maternal embrace it seemed, and invited me for dinner the following night. It was nice to know that more than five thousand miles from home one Jewish mother was substituting for another.

Monday and Tuesday, the third and fourth day of the New Year, I took off work as my two bosses said I could. I was planning to stay out the following Monday too for Yom Kippur. I spent part of the two days with Esther and her children who were out of school. She made lunch and we talked about my life as a soldier, the new phase *without* Karin and *with* my preparation for college. Esther believed the seemingly nice German girl she met several times at services harbored anti-Semitic attitudes all along and it took a personal crisis in the form of a romantic rejection to bring them to the surface. My surrogate mother indicated that was typical of many postwar Germans she has known, noble on the outside but Nazi on the inside.

I also walked around Nuremberg in the afternoons by myself. I certainly did not wish to hang around the barracks in civilian clothes so officers or sergeants from our attachment company might question me or assign me to shitty details. And I did not want my 176th comrades to notice my absence from work and resent my getting time off for a religious holiday, extra days above and beyond Christmas and Easter which everyone was entitled to.

For much of the time outdoors, I wandered around the Old City. I wanted to see St. Mary's Church again, Frauenkirsche to Karin and the locals, and the big open square in front of it that the elderly German Jews at services told me used to be the Jewish Quarter of the city. From the Hauptbahnhof I walked along Königstrasse, crossed over the Pegnitz River, and could not miss the tall church and the huge square a block away.

Jews in the Middle Ages were permitted to settle along the marshy banks of the river where Gentiles refused to live. Later, Jews were expelled from this area in a pogrom where many were killed and their synagogue destroyed, so that the Christian faithful could build an edifice dedicated to the Holy Mother on the site. Of course all the Jewish property was appropriated and claims from money lending set aside. I wanted to go inside this blood-stained church and see for myself what Nuremberg's medieval Jews died for but dared not on this Rosh Hashanah holiday. Like what Parisians did at Notre Dame, I thought that across the street from the back of St. Mary's the good citizens of Nuremberg should someday put up a Memorial to the Unknown Jewish Martyrs and inscribe the names of the dead and robbed.

The Pension I slept in with Karin, albeit not in the same room because I was not her groom, was nearby in the Old City and I wanted to look at it again too. Seeing the hotel from the outside, in spite of the fact that the desk clerk kicked Karin out of my bed, brought back pleasant memories of love on the run two months earlier.

Walking around some more, I came across a small street named, appropriately it seemed, Judengasse. Christians likely believed that every urban Jewish settlement should have a Jews Lane. A little farther north a street sign caught my attention, Theresienstrasse, and sent chills up and down my spine. I read that Theresienstadt was a notorious concentration camp in Nazi-occupied Czechoslovakia, where most Czech Jews either died or were transported east to Auschwitz.

Standing in the former Jewish Quarter of Hitler's favorite city, I realized full well that I could never have brought home a Nazi Schatzie as my Gentile friend back home wisely warned me against, neither Karin whom I liked very much nor the girl from the snack bar whom I was infatuated with. I could never be sure what her underlying feelings about Jews really were. If Karin and I were fifteen or twenty years older and tried to marry during the Nazi period, we would not have been allowed to. The Third Reich's third Nuremberg law prohibited marriage as well as sexual relations between Jews and Germans. If the Gestapo barged into the sitting room in the Klotz family apartment and caught me shtupping Karin, I could have been shot on the spot. Nazi sympathizer Mutti would likely have been the one who reported me to the secret state police. No truck ride to the nearest concentration camp and possible survival for me.

Karin's comment that last night we were together haunted me as I moved about this city haunted with Nazi ghosts. The following month, right where I stood, would be the twenty-first anniversary of Kristallnacht. The windows of Jewish shops and stores with "Jude" and "skull and crossbones" painted across them were smashed by young men in uniform with swastika armbands swinging night sticks and clubs. Non-Jewish onlookers said and did nothing as they stepped over the shards of broken glass strewn along the sidewalks and streets. A new German word entered into the vocabulary of European languages.

This Yom Kippur I felt I wanted to fast, to strictly observe the holiest day of the year. It was the first time I had ever done so. I used to see my mother not eat the whole day and when I asked her if I should do it she said I was still a child and it was not required of me according to Jewish law. Yom Kippur was a time for introspection, to atone for sins committed against God or man during the past year. Fasting lasts from sundown the evening before until the shofar is blown at the conclusion of services the day of. Not eating or drinking for 25 hours is meant to make the confessor suffer, to symbolize his or her readiness to change for the better.

I attended Erev Yom Kippur services at the Palace of Justice on Sunday, the eleventh of October, just as Jews all over the world were congregating to hear the Kol Nidre. This prayer, centuries old, has a moving melody and is chanted with a sense of emotional anticipation of the atonement to come and promises to be spoken publicly the next day. At the conclusion of the service, as I left, I looked across the hall from the makeshift synagogue. I noticed the door to the reception room was closed. On this night, there would be no bowls or trays with food or drink laid out for hungry and thirsty worshippers. I returned to the barracks alone.

On Monday I arrived back at the Palace for the morning service. I did not make a detour to Merrell's mess hall or snack bar prior to boarding the streetcar outside the main gate. Most of the people who came in the morning, especially the local German Jews, stayed all day for the subsequent services at various times with a break in-between. During one of the breaks, I told the rabbi the German girl I used to come to services with will not be knocking on his office door beseeching him to convert her. And I said to the old man with the beret, the judge who returned to Germany after the war, that the girl from Zirndorf I brought will not be talking to him anymore.

This place of justice more than a decade earlier for Nazi war criminals who denied their unforgivable wrongdoing was now the place of justness for some of their victims who admitted to forgivable transgressions. But was the Palace also a place where a Jew indirectly affected by German crimes could obtain pardon for his sins committed against Germans?

In the afternoon service, I recited the confessional in Hebrew from the right side of the prayer book and read carefully the English translations on the left side. I would not have wanted God to think that I was mechanically confessing to things without knowing what they were. I counted twenty-three different sins in the liturgy, a number of which no doubt applied to me.

I certainly was guilty of *Zadnu*, of sinning intentionally. I cannot deny that I was fully aware I lied to Karin about marriage. As the lying became normal to me, I committed *Tafalnu Sheker*, I desensitized myself to the dishonesty. The sin of lying also involved *Tiatanu*, a misleading of others. Karin told her mother about the possibility of our getting married and so I misled and victimized Mutti too. I myself had fallen victim to my own impulses, was culpable of *Avinu*. I desired instant sexual gratification without regard to the emotional implications for me or for my truthful partner. My errant ways likewise come under *Peshanu*, standards of behavior I knew to be right were broken because of my egotism. Another sin was *Tzararnu*, afflicting Karin who believed every word I said, lowering her self-esteem. And let's not forget *Vihirshanu*, making others wicked. I forced Karin into a destructive response, to say something she probably did not mean and never would have said were it not for my dishonesty. Finally, there is *Gazalnu* or stealing. This sacrilege is not just the theft of money or property but also of time. I stole four months from Karin's young life, an honest girl who broke off with someone just to be with me. I took away from her valuable time to meet a suitable suitor for a lifelong relationship. I suppose I similarly stole from the German who introduced us, robbed him of the possibility of getting back together with the girl he loved.

After Neilah, the final evening prayer, the shofar was blown with several loud blasts of the curved ram's horn. Yom Kippur was officially over. The door to the reception room was now wide open and everyone retired across the hall for the Break-the-Fast meal. It was not long before the bowls and trays with forks and spoons spread out neatly on the long table were empty. I went back to Merrell that night with a heavier stomach and lighter heart.

Come Saturday evening, I headed for Luitpoldstrasse for the first time in months. There would be no more atonement for wrongful acts. Sexual relations, not just eating and drinking, were permitted again in accordance with Jewish law of old. With my sins of the previous year wiped away, I could forget about Karin and the harm I may have caused her. A new start with German women was what I sought and Marianne was most on my mind. She was blond and blue-eyed, attractive in face and figure, the height I liked, I had never gone to bed with her, and I was sure she was on my side of the white line.

I could not figure the object of my affection out though. Her friend Elsa took money from G.I.s but at times, fortunately for me, left the Flying Dutchman with someone she liked and invited him up to her little flat for an overnight stay but would not ask for Gelt. Several times I saw Marianne leave with Germans, not Americans, and I presumed she was the taking type too. But would this fair Fräulein, like her plain friend, be partial to unrecompensed occasional intimacy with a not-too-bad-looking soldier boy from across the Atlantic? Did she possess a heart for love or just a pocketbook for Marks and dollars?

These were questions I wanted answered now that I was presumably free of Karin, the Klotz family, Zirndorf, and guilt over the four-month affair. I hit the Luitpold first, a repetition of the first night out in Nuremberg with my barracks mates seven months earlier. But this time I was alone. Steve of course was with Ursula and I was not a drinking buddy of any of the guys from the shop. I saw no one I knew in the popular G.I. Gasthaus. After downing one beer, I got tired of looking at fat Fräuleins, jerky Germans, and amorous Americans, and sick of listening to the mindless music. I got up from my table, left, and hustled across the street.

The Flying Dutchman at least had a better band, playing more American than Bavarian songs. And the women were thinner. As luck would have it, I happened to walk into a time tunnel. I was right back into an old scene. Marianne was sitting by herself at a table near the dance floor and Elsa was hoofing it up with a dopey-looking Kraut. I waited until Elsa finished her dance and went back to the table alone before I sat down next to the two good-time girls.

"Hello," I said. They both had glasses more than half full so I did not offer to buy drinks for them just yet.

Elsa smiled at me. "You not come for long time here." She ran her hand over mine. "Where you go?"

With a straight face Marianne said nothing but I could not help glancing over to her more than her less attractive friend. "I had a schatzie for the last four months. She lives in Zirndorf. I was with her most of the time."

"You not see more?" Elsa inquired.

"No. We broke up a few weeks ago."

The Fräulein I shtupped before widened her smile. "Willst du tanzen mit mir?" I said in my questionable German to impress the girl whom I knew liked me, and the one I was not sure of.

"Ja. Bestimmt. Danke."

Elsa took my hand and we went to the dance floor. We did a slow one and I held her close to me. "Are you busy tonight?" I said as an opener.

"Tonight no good. Tomorrow come." She touched my face tenderly.

I remembered Saturday night was her busiest, but I thought I'd ask anyway. "What time?"

"Twenty-one."

I understood that to mean nine o'clock. "Okay."

After the dance, we returned to the table. I remained standing and exchanged silent looks with Marianne when Elsa was straightening her chair. I wanted the pretty one to know I wanted her. "Danke-schön," I said to Elsa with correct pronunciation. "I'll see you tomorrow evening."

Sunday night about nine I moseyed into the Flying Dutchman and sure enough Elsa was sitting alone at a small table away from the dance floor. I paid for two beers, we drank and danced a little, then hightailed it out of there and went to her place. This time she did not stop on a side street, climb over some rocks lifting her dress, and take a piss on a pile of rubble. At her apartment building, the Vermieter did not stop her on the staircase so I assumed business was good and she was up to date on her rent. As soon as we got through her door, we undressed and hopped on the bed. I got a good shtup that night, regardless of her physical attractiveness. At a quarter past eleven I left, in plenty of time to get to the barracks before midnight.

After almost a five-month hiatus, I was into my old habit again, banging one Fräulein but craving another.

## CHAPTER 47: THE AUTUMN OF MY DISCONTENT

"I'm sorry you're leaving," I said to Steve.

It was Thursday, the twenty-eighth of October. I was sitting on my bunk, watching my roommate pack his duffel bag. He was busy folding his uniforms and stuffing them into the opening on top. With his thick fingers Steve pushed down hard along the circular edge of the bag to make every inch of space count.

Two weeks earlier he took a short and re-enlisted as he said he would. Neither I, a friend he knew for two years and shared a room with for eight months, nor any of the buddies he worked with at the shop, could talk him out of it. His marriage application was filed and being processed but it would take many more months before Army approval might be forthcoming.

I was there in the Area Office when Mr. Barry, with a nod from Sergeant Bentley, told Steve he could live off post. The re-enlistment and the pending marriage apparently were enough to secure permission from our two bosses who normally did not sign their names to requests for transfers or changes so readily. Ursula had found a larger apartment on Lindenast Strasse, north of the River in the Old City, near the Stadtpark. It was available November first and not too expensive, within Steve's budget with the per diem for food and allowance for lodging he would now be getting. He was very excited about the move out of the barracks and into his own place that weekend, but I was not thrilled about the prospect of having a new roommate.

"I'm not," Steve replied. He bounced around from wall locker to footlocker grabbing his belongings like a squirrel gathering nuts from tree to tree. "You can keep the barracks."

Steve was just expressing what everyone felt. No soldier was really "happy" about living in an Army barracks. You have to sleep on a flimsy mattress in a narrow bed, take care of your personal needs in a communal toilet and shower, eat mass-prepared bland food, go through bed check every night, rise early for reveille, take part in G.I. parties, worry about passing barracks inspections, put up with the lack of privacy, and be ready for alerts that may be called at any moment. If given a choice, what G.I. would *not* trade in his spot in the barracks for an apartment off base where he could eat home-cooked meals and lie next to his wife or girlfriend every night?

"I have to . . . for eight more months."

"Well, don't sweat it, good buddy," he assured me in familiar words. "You'll get another roommate. One of the new guys will probably take my bunk. Maybe you'll like him."

"Maybe I won't."

"Then go back with Karin and get an apartment," Steve countered pointedly, pushing his life plans on me, perhaps still resentful of my trying to convince him not to get married or re-enlist.

My peripatetic roommate's relationship with Ursula was now solid and he wanted the benefits of marriage although there was not yet an official recognition of their commitment to, and love for, each other. In a way, I respected and even envied my best buddy in the Army. He changed his plans and reorganized his life to meet the needs of a Fräulein he cared for deeply, without regard to what others might think, actions I was unprepared to do. I suppose I was more the selfish type, egotistical and self-indulgent, someone who would take advantage of a nice German girl for my carnal pleasures without thinking of her needs or offering anything in return other than my body.

"I can't go back to her . . . even if I wanted to."

I never told Steve what Karin said to me about Hitler and the Jews, an expression of her feelings that irreparably harmed our relationship. Such a statement would dissuade any Jewish boy from marrying a German girl even if he were greatly in love with her.

"I know. You don't want to get married and you don't want to re-enlist."

"Yes," I only said in response, and nodded.

"If you loved Karin you would marry her."

"But I didn't love her," I said honestly. "I *liked* her."

There was silence for a few moments, as if my best friend in the Army knew I told him the simple truth about a relationship he was privy to for four months. "When are those new guys coming?" Steve asked to change the subject.

"Monday."

"Well, good buddy," he said again as he closed his duffel bag and fastened the clasp on one end of the shoulder strap to the hook. "It looks like you'll be sleeping alone for the next three nights."

Steve's comments reflected what I already knew, that everything around me was changing, but not for the better. First Karin is suddenly out of my life and now he too will be a stranger for the most part. Soon another soldier will enter my room, someone to talk to in the morning when I wake up and in the evening before going to sleep, someone I may or may not be friendly with or get along with. Were there other changes in store for me? I wondered.

That last Thursday in October was the last time Steve and I shared a room together.

Two days earlier the telephone rang just after Bentley and Barry left for an afternoon coffee break in the snack bar. They liked to get away from the Area Office occasionally and, so I gathered, wanted to talk about the shop out of range of my or anyone's ears. The last thing they wanted was rumors flying around the shop about personnel changes.

"Area two, one seven six signal, Specialist Streiber speaking sir."

"Strahber," the man at the other end let out loudly.

I recognized the voice as that of Sergeant Branill, the First Sergeant at company headquarters in Böblingen. He only had two or three years on Bentley but looked a good ten years older with his hairless pate and potbelly. Branill sported a diamond in the middle of his six stripes. He recently had been promoted to E-8 but did not have to sew on new patches due to the Army's revised rank and chevron system. Like Bentley, the topkick was a southerner and had even more of that distinctive accent, a Rebel who drawled out my name and his, and everyone else's. And like my immediate boss, he took charge of situations quickly and exerted his authority.

"Yes."

"This is Sergeant Braahnill. Let me speak to Mistah Baarry."

"He's not here, sergeant."

"Then Sergeant Bayntley."

"He's not here either." I did not offer to say where they were.

"When's they comin' back?" toppy said, reflecting his deficient educational background more than his regional dialect.

"In a half hour or so."

"Okay. Tael 'em those three new boys will be there Mohnday. Two replacements fo' team five and wohn new po'zishon fo' team

408

six Ah pulled to get. Ahm cuttin' their orders rot now."

"Shall I tell Mr. Barry and Sergeant Bentley their names, sergeant?"

"Okay," the bald-headed head NCO of the company said again. "Ahll give 'em to ya."

From the awkward way he pronounced their names, I was able to discern how to spell them. I wrote down Hubert J. Isaacson, Richard C. Peterson, and Duncan O. Jameson. The new boys were the three *sons*. A New York Yankee such as I dared not draw attention to his unusual speech pattern by asking him to repeat or spell any names.

"They's all PFCs," Branill added. "Com'pleeted the radio repair cowarse at Fohrt Gordon last month."

"I'll give Mr. Barry and Sergeant Bentley this information, sergeant."

"Okay," he said a third time. "Naace to taalk to you again Strahber. An' keep up yo' good work."

"Thank you, sergeant."

With that politeness from and to a superior, I hung up. Either toppy was just being a southern gentleman of one or both of my bosses put in a salutary word about me after they pirated my ass off the bench. I preferred to think the latter.

When the two Bs returned, I handed the written message to Bentley and spoke to him about this. I knew it was *he* who ran the Area Office and oversaw the teams, at times with an iron fist, with Barry simply going along or rubber-stamping all what was put in front of him. It could be said that I was simply following the chain-of-command, talking to the lowest higher-level person first.

Isaacson and Jameson were put in the room down the hall on my side, where there were two bunks with rolled mattresses. Mr. Barry had Dombrowski assigned to Straubing, a city about 80 miles southeast of Nuremberg, for TDY, as that team was short-handed, and Jonesy's two-year stay in Germany was up and he went home. How long Dombrowski's temporary duty fixing communication equipment in the field near the Czech border would last the Area Officer did not say. I just handed the orders to the Pennsylvania Pole who never questioned why he was picked to go to this less desirable location. The coal miner's son was not too thrilled about the transfer since he was supporting a Schatzie in town and the move would definitely put a crimp in the frequency of his house calls. The dumb Polak feared another Merrell trooper would be taking off his boots near the bed he was paying for. Fat Jonesy, on the other hand, was so taken by his rotation back to the States that he was beside himself; he skipped lunch the day he left, an act out of character for the never-miss-chow soldier.

Peterson bunked with me. Had my room not had a vacancy due to Steve moving off post, the new man would have been placed with a stranger in our attachment unit at the other end of the hall, perhaps a black cavalryman, many doors away from his all white 176th shop mates. My sleeping companion was twenty-two, two years plus older than I was. He enlisted a year earlier after dropping out of college. Peterson was a fairly good-looking fellow, almost six feet tall and medium built, with light brown hair, Nordic facial features, and a muscular frame. Many a Fräulein in Germany would lay down for him. I thought of giving him the dark and dirty dope on the girl in the snack bar, advising him that if he measured up to her size requirement he could be the G.I. who brings the Bavarian blond beauty back across the color line. But I imparted no such advice to the Nuremberg newcomer.

The boys from Branill were a quasi-brood of triplet troopers. In and out of the shop, they horsed around like the Marx Brothers, joking and touching each other like comedians doing slapstick in vaudeville. I always saw Ike, Dick, and D.O., as they were called, go to chow and dine together in the mess hall or snack bar. They even requested their own room in the barracks, a room with just three bunks. One possessed a hairstyle like Hitler, parted on the left side and combed over the right eye in such a way as to invite frequent hand-movements to brush back, as the Führer was often photographed doing. Another went a few times to Soldiers' Field and stood on the speaker's platform mumbling "Achtung, Achtung" with an outstretched right arm. The third in jest liked to place a small black comb on his upper lip, reminiscent of old Adolph's thick but short mustache, click his heels, and give the Nazi salute.

The three *sons* from the same class at Gordon proved to be a disturbing factor in my life that autumn.

After Yom Kippur, I embarked on a crash course of study for the

College Boards. From the library at Special Services, I borrowed books, often novels of movies I had seen, such as *Lust for Life* and *Moulin Rouge* and *Gentleman's Agreement*. I read these works carefully, looking up words I did not know in the dictionary I kept next to me and writing the definitions on pieces of paper for reference later on. Particular attention was paid in my notetaking to the Latin and Greek origins of the English words. I bought a practice book for the SAT in the PX. From the verbal portion, I did the exercises dealing with sentence completion, reading comprehension, antonyms, and analogies. I also worked on learning the vocabulary words. On the mathematical portion, I did not need much brushing up. I remembered my high school algebra, trigonometry, and geometry but I still practiced my quantitative reasoning and problem solving.

The trouble I had with my college preparation was not my lack of motivation or lack of time to study but the lack of privacy. Every weekday evening after chow I would return to my room, lie back on my bunk to read from one of the novels, or sit up and do the verbal and math exercises spread out on my blanket. The ceiling light was sufficient for me but a desk and chair would have been helpful. When Steve was my roommate, he invariably changed from fatigues and left the barracks to be with Ursula soon after work in the shop shut down, often not going to chow. The weekdays he did not see his beloved, he was playing poker in the room across the hall with his black buddies in the 2nd Cav, or, as some of our white buddies in the 176th called them, the Cavalry Coons. I had our room all to myself for hours and I was able to get a lot of studying done.

But now, with Peterson occupying the bunk across from me, I had no such luck for any concentrated thinking. Practically every evening after chow the two *sons* from the next room would open my door to spend time with the *son* in my room. Isaacson and Jameson sat on the floor or Peterson's bunk or the two footlockers to laugh and talk and banter with each other in their usual routines. I tried to shut my ears and ignore the frolicking around me but to no avail. Often I just left the room and found a quiet place on one of the staircases to sit and study for a while. At times I walked to the Special Services building to secure a little nook in the reading room to set myself down in, a comfortable distance from the troopers shooting pool.

I got my studying done that November and December but it was a daily struggle. The lack of privacy in my Merrell room reminded me of the difficulty I had during my high school years doing homework in the small and crowded apartment we lived in. Ironically, to get away from that was one of the reasons I joined the Army. In the coming year, after I leave the barracks forever, my ability to study should be greatly improved living at home in the much larger apartment we have now. At age twenty and a half, I looked forward to having a room all to myself and, as my parents had promised, with a desk, chair, and lamp.

My sex life that autumn wound down considerably. No longer was it two or three times a week with Karin. It was once every two or three weeks with Elsa, and zero with Marianne or anyone else.

Elsa was glad to see me again after more than four months. She seemed content just to have me in her bed—to spread her legs, to kiss my face, to mouth me in private places. She satisfied my need for orgasmic consolation but I was not content with the *quality* of the feminine intimacy coming my way gratis. I could not be as sweet on Elsa, to touch and kiss and look at, as I was on Karin. My willing sex partner's physical attributes were far from the ideal that I longed for. The more time I spent with her on a Sunday night, for dancing and for shtupping, the less I felt good about myself and the more I wanted to change partners. Pretty and sexy Marianne was the one I coveted and Elsa knew it. At times I asked Elsa about her friend when she was not with us in the Flying Dutchman, and when she was there, I tried not to peer but I was sure my furtive glances over to the comely Fräulein were noticeable to the homely one.

Eventually, my Sunday night dates with Elsa became more infrequent. Either she failed to show up at the Flying Dutchman or she came and said she was meeting or leaving with someone else. It was Elsa and not I who took the initiative and phased out our robotic and uncommitted copulation. It was difficult for me to turn down a sure shtup, even if it was less than satisfying to my sensibilities. The additional free time I had plus my unfulfilled erotic desires prompted me to intensify my efforts to mate with Marianne or to get beneath some other seductive skirt.

On Saturday and Sunday nights, when I needed to get away from the books for a few hours, I confined my prowling to three popular

G.I. joints. The Luitpold and the Flying Dutchman near the Hauptbahnhof were hunting grounds from my first night out in Nuremberg, but I also started frequenting the Hillbilly some distance away. It was on Am Plärrer, a transportation hub west of the main railway station, easily reached by streetcar. I would hop over there whenever no one caught my fancy at the other two hangouts. I had heard about this other hot spot but stayed clear of it because I assumed it catered to Johnny Rebs, southern troopers who preferred songs in the County/Western genre over Rock 'n' Roll. The Armed Forces Network often played hillbilly music but I could not stand listening to it and turned the dial on the Grundig radio next to my bunk every time it aired. But I sampled the Hillbilly once and realized I was mistaken. It was actually a good place to sit and drink Bier with buddies or strangers as well as find a Fräulein with a feel for Americans. Hillbilly tunes were seldom heard and the male clientele consisted of an interesting mix of white G.I.s, Germans, Mediterranean workers, and an occasional black G.I. at a table with white buddies. Contrary to my expectations, I witnessed no rebel assaults on the dark trespassers.

For weeks I rotated my weekend outings among the troika of clubs. My efforts to connect with Marianne failed. I spoke to her a few times when Elsa was not around but she was not keen on dating me. And I never laid eyes on a Marianne look-alike. As autumn dragged on, and my romantic engagements waned, the broken relationship with Karin entered my thoughts much of the time. It occurred to me that if I were still seeing the girl from Zirndorf, we would be paying Steve and Ursula a visit in their new apartment. I fantasized taking Karin for walks in the nearby city park after dinner, to look for a secluded site to lay down a raincoat or blanket. Steve's oft-used words stuck in my mind too, that he and I were good buddies, so I presumed he would let me utilize his apartment for lovemaking. If this dream ever became a reality, at the rate I used to make it with Karin, paying Steve a visit might mean paying him rent.

In mid-December, all hell broke loose in the 176th. The shit hit the fan in the shop and in the barracks and some of it even reached me in the Area Office. Bentley and Barry were pissed off at all of the men under them.

For the week prior, all the repairmen, those who lived in the barracks as well as off post, had to return to the shop evenings and on the weekend to prepare for the annual CMI, the Command Maintenance Inspection, conducted by an officer in the 2nd Armored Cavalry. They had to clean and straighten out the workbenches, put the tools in their rightful places and toolboxes in proper order, and make sure all the small pieces of equipment—handsets, headsets, microphones—were neatly placed in wooden boxes on uncluttered shelves along the back wall. The big pieces of equipment—like the AN/GRC-19, 26, and 46, the T-195 and R-392 transmitter and receiver, and the T-4, 76, and 98 teletypes—had to be repaired and tagged ready for pickup or stacked along the side wall with papers attached indicating what was to be done and when. The floor was a mess and needed sweeping and mopping. Men used to soldering wires and testing tubes and replacing parts handled wet rags instead, wiping down all the benches and stools and windows. In the Area Office, I was a one-man team dusting off everything in sight—the file cabinets, desk tops, swivel chairs, and wall charts.

The two Bs came by the shop a few nights that week to see how things were going, and to climb on Doss' back. The poor old SFC could not conceal his nervousness, caught between Bentley's iron fist and the 2nd Cav's chicken shit. I'm sure the two were not pleased about leaving their wife and kiddies home alone, but were oblivious to the discontent of others under them. Back at the office, Bentley ran his finger over the top of the wall charts and behind the cabinets while Barry and I looked on impassively.

As it turned out, the shop failed the CMI and the Area Office received a barely passable grade. A follow-up inspection was scheduled three days later. The two Bs went bananas and their shit, as usual, ran downhill. Bentley blamed Doss and Doss blamed Caplers, the Spec 5 who was in charge of the shop whenever Doss was out. All passes were canceled and all off-post personnel were restricted to the barracks, all except the two higher-ups of course, pending the outcome of the second CMI.

The restriction was especially hard on Caplers, who had just brought his pregnant wife to Germany and needed to be at home with her. I sympathized with him and he asked me to help him, as one specialist to another. I spoke to the bosses, first the sergeant and then the warrant, and asked them to make an exception in Caplers' case. Not only was I unsuccessful, but both Bs resented my interference with their decision-making and assigned me extra duty, the cleaning of the office again even though it passed inspection. As a young man not yet twenty, I suffered my first retaliation for simply exercising my constitutional right to speak. The pettiness of Bentley and Barry, two men I respected, surprised me. They could have just said no. Why was it necessary to take action against me? I did not know it then but this incident set in motion my fall from the good graces of my superiors.

No sooner had we passed the follow-up inspection did another incident occur with our host unit and the two Bs again busted a gut. The weekend before Christmas one of the team members in the room with Isaacson and Jameson, PFC Crouse, was found drunk on the floor of a Gasthaus in town by MPs after bed check and without an overnight pass. They hauled him in, wrote him up, and gave the report to the 2nd Cav's OIC. On Monday morning, December twenty-first, a first lieutenant from headquarters in the West Block came to our side of the barracks to find out why the sergeant on duty at 0200 Sunday had not cited the soldier for not being in his bunk. We were all at work and the Area Office had not yet received a copy of the report. The silver-bar lieuey apparently poked his head in a few of the rooms occupied by the 176th and was dismayed by what he saw.

I was at my desk when the young Cavalry officer stormed in, face all flushed, sweaty as if he had run the entire length of the barracks from the East Block. He passed by me and Bentley without a word and went right up to Barry.

"What kind of an outfit are you running here, Mr. Barry? Who's in charge of your men in the barracks?"

Barry turned pale. He stood up and looked at his superior without saying anything. He had no words because he did not know what the lieutenant was talking about. Bentley, normally the loquacious type, was silent too, just sat there at his desk.

"One of your men was found drunk in town after o-two-hundred yesterday. Your troops on the other side apparently have been escaping bed check. It's also apparent that no one in your company is inspecting the barracks rooms in the morning. I just looked in there and saw beds not made up and wall lockers wide open."

I knew the lieuey was correct but I kept my mouth shut lest one B or the other think I am interfering again. My bunk was always made up in the morning, even on weekends, but many times I was in other rooms during the day and saw sheets turned back and blankets and pillows on the floor. It was a wonder no one in authority noticed it or said anything until now.

"This is the first I've heard of this," Barry said meekly, in deference to the officer four grades higher who was blaming him for the breakdown in military discipline.

"Your men have been getting away with murder," the first lieuey exaggerated. He turned to leave, then looked back at Barry. "But that is about to change." The young officer stormed out just as angrily, before either Barry or Bentley could promise it will not happen again.

All it took was one guy to fuck up and he ruined it for the rest of us. In the nine months I had been at Merrell, our sleeping quarters were on the complete opposite end of the massive building from the 2nd Armored Cavalry's headquarters. The men down the hall at the other end, from that unit, were subject to daily bed checks and inspections, but we were not. "They don't know we exist," my teammates often quipped, proud of getting away with what most soldiers have to endure.

Before the day was out, a messenger came by and handed me a sealed envelope for Mr. Barry. It was an order on fancy letterhead from the bird colonel in charge of the Cavalry Regiment. There were four parts to it. Henceforth all personnel in the 176th Signal Company (Repair) living in the barracks will be subject to bed check, will make up their bunks each morning according to Army regulations, and on 18 Jan 60 will move to rooms in the West Block; all such personnel living on or off post below the rank of E-5, or E-4 with less than four, will report for reveille at 0600.

It was clear from the order that the 2nd Cav was now going to treat us as they did their own. At least it was not necessary for Caplers to ask me again to secure an exemption for him. The expectant father did not have to worry about being AWOL if he remained in bed with his needy wife a little longer in the early morning hours.

The next day our Mr. Barry issued orders too. Crouse was to be transferred to Bamberg and Westheimer to Ansbach, to teams within the warrant's area of command. I, on the other hand, was told I will be heading to Team 18 in Munich, a different 176th area. It was obvious why Crouse was going bye-bye, and Westheimer too, since he had been cited in the CMI report for his fatigue jacket not being tucked into his trousers and boots not polished. But why was I being transferred? Bentley just said the warrant officer and sergeant in Area IV lacked a clerk in their office and I was experienced. He said nothing about how he and Barry would manage without me. All this was to take place, coincidentally, on January eighteenth, the day of the change in our room assignments, by which time we should have received official notice from Böblingen. Our considerate bosses, it seemed, did not wish to interrupt our Christmas and New Year's plans, or, in my case, preparations for Chanukah starting the day after Christmas.

That December twenty-second, when I received notification of my impending transfer to Munich, was also the winter solstice. It was the longest night on the calendar and it marked the beginning of shortening nights and lengthening days. The winter solstice was something to look forward to at the darkest time of the year. It is often recognition of "rebirth" by peoples around the world.

So too my life reflected a winter solstice of sorts that year. It signaled, in the closing days of 1959, the end of the autumn of my discontent and the start of a new season in a new city in a new decade.

# CHAPTER 48: REBIRTH IN VENICE

The ride would take a little more than seven hours. I sat in an aisle seat in the middle of the bus, full with over a dozen young soldiers dressed in civilian clothes as I was, some accompanied by their wives or Schatzies. We left Nuremberg at 0900 and were due to arrive in Venice, after a pit stop and lunch break, in time for dinner at the hotel we were booked in near Piazza San Marco.

It was Wednesday, December twenty-third. I was on leave for six days, approved weeks before the trouble with Barry in the shop, office, and barracks. I had purchased a package tour to Rome. When I went to pick up my ticket in Special Services, I avoided looking around or over my shoulders for I did not wish to see the German from the photography lab. He might come up to me and punch me in the nose for taking Karin away from him and then making her unhappy.

The first night we were to spend in Venice, the next four nights in Rome, and then return to Nuremberg on the twenty-eighth. Like on the Paris tour, I was armed with my Kodak camera and several rolls of color slide film. But unlike Paris, this trip was almost all daytime driving. Too bad I was no longer joined on the couch with my former girlfriend. She would have been thrilled to accompany me to the Eternal City, that is, if she had not already converted to Judaism.

The bus driver was a German who spoke no English. He was medium height and thin framed with a receding hairline, pointed nose, and sunken cheeks. Only one of the women on the trip communicated with him in anything more than simple expressions. The tour guide, who sat in the first seat behind the driver, spoke English fairly well. A heavy-set German about the same height but with a round face and full head of hair, he smiled frequently, but falsely I thought, revealing a gold first bicuspid on his upper-left palate.

Both men looked like they were in their early forties. What they did and where they were during the war I could only guess. The two Germans leading me and other Americans on a pleasure trip to Italy must have been in the Wehrmacht or worse. The driver and guide smiling at us now could have, fifteen years earlier, killed our boys on the Normandy beaches or surrendered to our Russian friends on the Eastern Front or served in the SS as guards at a concentration camp.

I sat back in my seat, closed my eyes intermittently, and mulled over the past week at Merrell when everything went crazy and changes occurred so rapidly. The two Bs were deeply offended by the shop's flunking the CMI. They saw it as a black mark on their record, a big gig that might prevent Bentley from getting appointed warrant in the near future and hold Barry back from his promotion to CW3. My two bosses were likewise not too pleased with the "low pass" they were handed on the office inspection and naturally put the blame on me. And the nasty business with barracks bed check and one of their men being picked up off post for public drunkenness, they knew would not help their careers either. Crouse's binge drinking after he was supposed to be in bed did not endear us to our host regiment as ambassadors of good will to the German people.

Bentley and Barry came down on me very hard, and that surprised as well as hurt me. They liked me I thought. They appreciated the clerical work I did for them, and the wall charts I created. They were pleased with a more manageable administration of the office and felt they could rely on me when they were out. All I did was cause them to receive a lower passing grade on an inspection than what they desired or hoped for, and pleaded on behalf of a needy teammate for an exception to their order on personal grounds.

"Strahber," Sergeant Bentley barked with a cold eye and unsmiling face. Mr. Barry stood in front of the window and looked out impassively, as if he were not involved with this decision. "You're shippin' out to Munich next month. Better get yo' affairs in order."

Get my affairs in order? What was he talking about? The next day I was leaving for a six-day trip to Rome. When I return, it will be just two days before New Years. On January sixth I was scheduled to take the College Boards in Fürth at Darby Kaserne. On the tenth, I start five days of approved time-off to attend the sponsored religious retreat for Jewish soldiers held in Berchtesgaden in the Bavarian mountains every year. By the time I get back, I will have only the weekend to pack my bags and be ready to climb into the three-quarter ton truck for the move to Munich on January eighteenth. The good Master Sergeant probably thought I was still involved with Karin, whom he met at the Fourth of July picnic, or some other marriage-minded Fräulein, and needed a month to either end the relationship or make arrangements to carry her with me to the capital of Bavaria.

The long bus ride to Venice gave me time to reflect on my life at that juncture. I was not happy about my transfer, as I believed it to be some sort of punishment. But the move to a new city and new barracks had an upside as well, an opportunity to meet a new girl-friend and better buddies and have a more enjoyable stay in the Ar-my for my remaining five months. By the time we reached our des-tination, I was not at all sorry to be leaving Merrell. It would be an escape from being pushed under the thumb of 2nd Cavalry officers and NCOs for bed check and room inspections.

As we approached Venezia, as the guide kept calling it, he could not stop talking about the ancient city. He stood up and smiled and faced the rest of us in the bus. With his hands the German gesticu-lated like an Italian, waving excitedly up and down and across. We were told the city's name comes from the Veneti tribe that lived in this region of northeast Italy in Roman times. It is a floating city, a city of canals and bridges, with solid structures built on more than a hundred small islands in the Venetian Lagoon along the Adriatic Sea. Our tour guide winced when he said the original people of Venice were refugees from the undefended countryside and nearby Roman cities who were forced to flee from the successive waves of Germanic invasions. The long stretch of the shallow lagoon was a natural protection against the Huns on horseback.

"How did they construct the buildings on the water?" someone asked, voicing what likely was on everyone's mind.

"That good question," the guide answered, showing that gold tooth more.

The Nazi-era German explained in fair English that Venice's structures were erected on wood piles brought over from the mainland and spaced close together. The piles penetrate sand and mud and rest on a hard layer of compressed clay. Under water, without oxygen, the wood does not decay but petrifies, becomes a stony substance. After centuries of submersion, most of the piles are still intact and serve as foundations for brick or stone buildings, footings for five-story and higher structures.

We crossed the long and narrow Freedom Bridge, the Ponte della Libertà, that connected the mainland to the islands. The guide said it was built more than twenty-five years earlier under Mussolini and originally had a different name. That made sense, as there was not much freedom for Italians under Benito. I saw a sign indicating we were in the Tronchetto district. He turned around and hovered over the bus driver's shoulder, steering him to park in the Piazzale Roma, the public bus terminal, at the beginning of the Grand Canal.

Everyone on the tour bus seemed excited as they hustled off with their baggage and stepped into a waiting vaporetto, the public water bus. The guide handed the ticket clerk a card to punch, presumably the pre-paid discount fare for the lot of us. We took the No. 1 line that sailed along this main waterway in Venice shaped like a backward *S*, stopping at different points and ending at Piazza San Marco.

Cruising down the Grand Canal the view was breathtaking. I grabbed my loaded camera and started shooting. Both banks were lined with scores of colorful multi-level mansions hundreds of years old in the Gothic, Renaissance, and Byzantine style. The impressive homes were built for noble families, meant to display their wealth and art during the glory days of the Republic of Venice.

I saw attached structures of white, red, orange, and yellow brick or stone, with red-tile roofs. We passed under the Scalzi Bridge, the first of three the guide said span the banks. There were outdoor restaurants on the ground floor of buildings at the water's edge, with large awnings covering tables and chairs on terraces, and small awnings hanging over windows on the floors above, all in different colors—red, green, brown. Detached houses in front looked like palaces, very elegant palazzi with colored marble façades, but on the side revealed dull stucco or brick.

I was not just a tourist journeying through one of the most beautiful cities of Europe, I was a *time traveler* like H. G. Wells, but going backward rather than forward. I feasted my eyes on much of what Marco Polo, Cristoforo Columbo, Napoléon Bonaparte, Lord Byron, and Percy Bysshe Shelley marveled at.

A gondolier was tying his gondola with two passengers to a mooring post in the water near a landing on the bank and I snapped a shot. The Rialto Bridge was now before us, the oldest and most famous single-span in Venice, still standing after almost four hundred years. It was a decorative covered bridge with walkways and shops over a bend in the Canal.  Not far from the Rialto were the traghetti, gondola-like boats ferrying a dozen or so people from one bank to the other.  Some buildings in a frontal view appeared to have three tall levels, but after we passed by I saw the side and each level was divided into two floors.

In the last stretch of this snake-like aquatic thoroughfare, we were at the Accademia Bridge, which, like the Scalzi, was uncovered, a simple means for the many pedestrians wishing to get from one bank to the other.  These two bridges were not ornate like the Rialto but functional trestles across Venice's chief divide and, not surprisingly, as with the Ponte from the mainland, date from Italy's Fascist period.  We soon docked on the floating platform at St. Mark's Basin.

We were booked in a small, family-run pensione facing the Rio del Vin Canal in the Castello district, a three-minute walk from the vaporetto landing.  The guide and bus driver led their group of tourists to their hotel through magnificent St. Mark's Square, the city's most famous and recognizable attraction.  We walked down narrow winding streets and across short bridges that spanned a myriad of small canals.  The two Germans acted like Nazi soldiers marching their troops to a garrison in an occupied country.  I thought one might blow a whistle while the other hollers ein, zwei, drei, vier.  I was assigned a room with a Nebraska farm boy my age.  He was stationed at Pinder Barracks with the 22nd Field Artillery.  We unpacked and went to dinner.

"Are you looking for tail . . . local stuff?"

I knew what the artilleryman from Zirndorf was talking about. We were back in our room after eating and on our own for the rest of the evening.  His comment was quite personal and even disconcerting, since we had just met, but it was not out of character for a young soldier in a foreign country.  For all he knew I could have been married or in a committed relationship.

I shrugged my shoulders.  "I hadn't given it much thought."

I didn't tell him I recently split up with a girl who lives near his Kaserne, although at dinner I thought of doing so.  Certainly I missed the steady shtupping I had with Karin, and I had not seen Elsa in more than a month, but it was not just any girl that I wanted. I had to be attracted to her.

"Prostitution is legal in Italy."

"Is that right?" I said, not having given that much thought either.

"That's what I heard. It's only pimping that's illegal . . . and organized prostitution."

My fortuitous roommate was more sophisticated than he let on. He was a quiet fellow, not bad looking, with an air of seriousness about him. For a cornhusker from the boondocks, he seemed to know a lot about big-city life.

"Where do the women hang out?" I asked, more out of curiosity than purpose. There must be a Venetian equivalent to Paris' La Place Pigalle, perhaps called Piazza Porco or La Strada Amore.

"All over. Hookers walk the streets day and night. Even on St. Mark's Square."

"You're kidding."

"That's what I heard," my new buddy said again, this time smugly.

"You mean to say the signorinas with painted faces, all decked out in high heels, short skirts, and skimpy sweaters, traipse around next to churches and historic sites?" I could not believe holy St. Mark obliges, or "puts out," the city's sinful women.

"Not always. Many prosts in Venice wear ordinary clothes."

"You heard that too?" I asked sarcastically.

"Yeah . . . and I'm ready to find out if it's true. Want to come?"

The Nebraskan evidently had Venetian romance, not culture, on his mind. It was not a stone sculpture of some Greek goddess in St. Mark's or St. Elsewhere that he wanted to gaze at. His wish was to dish Thereal Spaghetti. The farm boy who used to shuck now preferred to fuck, trade Midwestern corn for Italian porn, and perhaps put his hands on different ears.

"Okay," I said. "I'll tag along. I want to see St. Mark's at night anyway."

As we left the hotel, I picked up a city map and a tourist's booklet at the front desk, but the boy bulging out of his pants did not. We walked in the direction from which we came two hours before, backtracking our way through the twisted streets and scaling short bridges. It was dark outside but under street lamps I could read the map and we did not get lost. I was not tripping over myself as he was to connect with a signorina della strada, but I did not rule it out either.

St. Mark's Square was a sight to see at night. It was huge. On three sides—the north, south, and west—there were two long and one short stretches of continuously arcadeed buildings with three tall tiers. Each tier had electric lighting emanating from every chamber, spaced close together, that flooded the square with dim rays like candlelight. People were walking around, standing and talking, and sitting at the tables of eating and drinking establishments on the ground level. My touring companion and I stood in the vast open space and looked around. There was just enough light to see what was going on nearby but not at a distance. To me it felt as if I were on some dark, sparsely inhabited planet with only the moon above to help me see.

The horny husker's eyesight was better than mine. "There are two broads over there." He pointed to a spot on the far side from where we were standing. "Let's go up to them."

"I'd rather stay here for a while. You go if you want."

He was too hot and bothered for me to get involved with. Besides, I never liked prowling with someone I hardly knew. And I was not as daring as he, not willing to march up and start shooting a line to strange women, whether they were prostituti or not.

This time *he* shrugged his shoulders. Without saying anything, he walked off. That was the last I saw of him until the next morning.

It was no sweat being by myself in a new city or foreign country. That was me at Fort Ord, and likewise in Nuremberg, before and after I went with Karin. Unlike most American soldiers, I did not need a buddy or two by my side wherever I went on or off post. I found a stone ledge near one of the arcades of a building that did not house a ristorante. I was content to just sit and enjoy the exotic surroundings. Leafing through the tourist booklet, I read tidbits of history about sights the tour guide might show us the next morning.

About a half hour passed. Suddenly, there was a tap on my shoulder from behind and I heard a woman's voice. "Signore . . . scusi."

I turned around and saw a young woman standing over me. She was dressed in a way that did not draw attention to her. Out of courtesy I stood up and brushed off the seat of my trousers.

"Parla italiano?"

I understood the few words of Italian. "No," I said, shaking my head. "Inglese. I speak English."

"Americano?"

"Yes," I agreed and nodded. "Si."

I was not against talking to a strange Italian girl, whatever her purpose for coming up to me, and I took a good look at her. Immediately I was struck by her resemblance to Karin. Short, modestly dressed, not big on top, not plump, okay figure, sweet face, she had the same mouth and smile but darker hair and eyes. She too seemed to be in her early or mid-twenties.

"You turista?"

"Yes," I said again, but added "soldato." German, French, Italian, the word for soldier is about the same.

"Ah," she replied, smiled, and said something in Italian very fast. I only understood one word, Italia. I presumed she asked me if I was stationed in Italy, as there are American troops here.

"No Italia . . . Germania."

"Ah," she repeated. "You come far."

"Si . . . yes."

"Venezia? You like?" Her smile widened.

Was this girl doing some kind of survey, or what? "Yes. It's nice. I like."

I was glad she spoke some English but I nevertheless used simple words. I looked directly at the young woman making idle conversation whose face and body touched my sensibilities via memory of another. She peered at me too, examining *my* face and body, and seemed a little nervous. At last she spoke and I no longer wondered for what purpose she said scusi.

"I geeva you good time?" came out in a heavy but cute accent. "You want?"

I looked around and there was no one within earshot but I felt a bit uncomfortable myself with this brazen and crass proposition. Interestingly, she employed practically the same words as the street girl in Paris. I did not have to think hard or long before asking *her* a question. "Quanto?" I said in my equally simple Italian.

"Cinquemila lire," the little sexpot replied, pronouncing the *C* like a *Ch*. "Fiva tousand." Unlike the Paris pickup, she did not hold up any fingers.

At 625 lire to a dollar, she priced her professional services at eight dollars, not a bad price for impersonal love with not a bad-looking

425

girl. Soon I could be holding up my fingers, I thought, to explore her, inside and out.

"Okay," I agreed and nodded for emphasis.

I could have bargained to pay four thousand, to put the Italian job on equal footing with the French connection I made months earlier, but I did no such thing. With a Karinesque girl, there could be no haggling over money.

"Bene," she added.

I knew she was saying okay or good and I took her hand. She recognized the name of my pensione on the tourist booklet and we left St. Mark's. I did not need the map any longer. She showed me a shorter route over the confusing complex of winding streets alongside thin canals and stair-stepping bridges. Venice at night, in the Castello district at least, was scary. A paisano with a naif could have jumped out from behind any house, slit my throat, grabbed my wallet, and dumped me in the water. At least he would not be the pimp of the girl I was attracted to.

The pensione in Venice was different from the Pension in Nuremberg. No one at the desk gave me a funny look when I walked past it with the girl or tried to stop me from bringing her upstairs. The hotel staff knew we were not one of the married couples on the tour, that I was no groom for the room. Love Italian style was more translucent than what went on between the sexes in public in Germany. Up in my room, the first thing I did was to bolt the night latch on the door. The second thing I did was to go up to the signorina and run my hands over and under her modest, but inviting, breasts. I was the one now holding up fingers.

"Cinquemila lire," she said with the smile I admired, extending one palm upwards.

She did not pull my paws off her. This too reminded me of the first time I saw Karin.

Without hesitation, I reached into my wallet and gave her the five thousand. The big bills looked like play money, and to me it *was* money to play with. She put them in her purse and moved to a chair, undressed except for her panties, and draped her clothes over it. I sat down on my bed, stripped, and threw my clothes on the other bed. There was a sink in the room and she went up to it.

"Vieni . . . vieni," she said, motioning me to come to her.

I went to her not knowing what she wanted. Looking at the naked girl, and in much anticipation of getting into her, I started to extend and fatten. She took a facecloth hanging on the towel rack, wet it, and ran a piece of soap over it. Holding me with one hand she washed me with the other, over my head and down and around my shaft, then rinsed me off and patted me dry with one of the small towels. Being scented as well as clean I thought she might squat down on one knee, lean forward, and harden me the French way, but the Italian girl did not have the mind, or mouth, for giving me a good time that way.

She now took *my* hand, led me to my bed, threw back the covers, and got in still tugging at me. The third thing I did was to pull down her panties.

The signorina had attributes I favored—delicate hands and a sensual touch, soft skin and hard nipples, a tight pouch and rubbery legs. With her heavy breathing and hot breath against my neck, feet crossed near my shoulders, I moved with the rhythm she set. I imagined we were adrift in a gondola alone, the tide pushing me deeper into her canal, currents of love coming my way with every wave. When my ammunition was spent, my rifle came down, and I withdrew from my defensive position. The Venetian girl, as she initially proposed, did give me a good time, but not as good as the Parisian.

There was no toilet bowl in my room, only one down the hall that guests had to share. At the sink, the giver of good times washed her body inside and outside, everywhere I touched her it seemed, spilling some water on the floor as a result. I wiped the puddle up and wiped myself too, then got dressed as I sneaked a peek at her dressing.

"Piazza San Marco," I said, "I go with you." I motioned my intention with my hand.

"Si . . . bene . . . grazie." She put on a happy face, as though it was unusual for a customer to offer to escort her back to their meeting place.

But it was *I* who should have said thanks. I wanted to be with the girl who captured my imagination a while longer, to hold her hand and walk the streets as I did so often with Karin. For just eight dollars she took me in and pumped new life into me, exactly what I needed after the autumn of my discontent. When I arrived in Venice, I put my mind at ease about the transfer to a new post and all things military, hours later an intimate encounter comforted the rest of my emotions. Both times I witnessed a rebirth of sorts in this ancient city. The second would last longer than the six months I had left in the Army.

We left the hotel quietly. Making our way back to St. Mark's, there was little we said or could say to each other. We clasped hands the whole time. In a darkened arcade on the Piazza, the girl I fell for did not pull away when I kissed her on the lips before we parted.

"Arrivederci . . . grazie," I let out, in what little Italian I knew, and turned to leave.

When I looked back for a moment, she smiled and waved to me. I heard her say something that sounded like chow. If that meant what I thought it meant, then she expressed affection toward me with her mouth after all. Our love scene did not take place on a balcony in Verona, and I was not the girl's Romeo, but the parting was still such sweet sorrow.

Walking back to the pensione alone—traversing sidewalks that end suddenly, streets that flow into brick walls, and steps that descend into canals—I tried not to get lost in the Venice I found my way in.

The next morning the guide knocked on everyone's door at seven and told us we had to be downstairs for breakfast in half an hour and be ready to leave for a morning tour of the city at eight thirty. My roommate said little, in the room or while we ate, about his escapade after he left me in the Piazza, save that he did score with one of the women he walked up to. He must have gone to her place and I was glad for that but I said nothing about my bringing a girl back to our room and bolting the door. Now that he satisfied his carnal desires, he had a hasty interest in Venice's cultural heritage. I saw him stop by the desk and pick up a tourist's booklet before we headed for St. Mark's. The romp around Venice on December twenty-fourth, great as that might be for others on the tour, I knew would be anti-climactic for me. The high point of my one-day stay in Waterworld occurred the night before, on a squeaky bed in a poorly furnished room of a cheap hotel overlooking a dirty and smelly canal.

Our touring master escorted his sightseeing bunch to St. Mark's but a woman was waiting for us there and took over for the day. She was a tall and attractive Italian in her mid- to late thirties. Her blond hair connoted she probably was from the North. The local lady dressed well, spoke English well, and was well-endowed. Several soldiers kept looking at her chest whenever she was not looking at them. One thing was certain that morning. As to landmarks around the Piazza, and detailed histories of the city, what the German knew I would not give two shits. She, however, knew that stuff like the front of her two tits.

The salacious signora piloted us first to the Basilica di San Marco, the cathedral of the city's patriarch, and explained that it is commonly known as the Church of Gold because of its opulent design, gilded mosaics, and impressive domes. The holy and showy structure sits at the east or unconnected side of the Piazza, adjacent to the Campanile, the medieval hundred-meter high Bell Tower that collapsed in 1902 and was rebuilt. We were taken inside the Basilica where the Catholics on the tour lit candles, and then by elevator to the top of the Tower. The aerial view of the city was awe-inspiring, especially looking down at the throngs of people in the Piazza and flocks of pigeons. I hoped my body would not fall to the ground from the spot where Galileo demonstrated his famous telescope. The next stop was the Doge's Palace behind the Campanile, where Venice's rulers were housed for more than six centuries, until the Napoleonic occupation of the city.

I was fascinated most by setting foot in the arcaded triple-tiered buildings forming the attached three other sides to the Square, what at night looked so beautiful. At the north end was the Clock Tower, with an archway beneath it leading to the Merceria, the main shopping street connecting the financial district and the Rialto Bridge, and the Procuratie Vecchie, the offices and apartments of the ancient procurators who administered different functions of the city.

The west end, the short side, opposite the Basilica, is the Napoleonic Wing, fashioned to the Emperor's own design, now an impressive civic and archaeological museum with paintings, sculptures, maps, coins, armor, etc. The south leg, the Procuratie Nuove, contained the newer offices for the procurators that afforded them more space. The ground levels of both Procuratie buildings house Venice's historic and expensive caffèes, where legend has it morsels of the best literary works were scratched on tablecloths and napkins.

For an overpriced cup of coffee or tea, today's nobody could be sipping with yesterday's somebody, sitting at a table or on a chair that not many years of yore had been graced by notables such as Henry James, Thomas Mann, Marcel Proust, and Ernest Hemingway.

At twelve we were back at the pensione for lunch. We were instructed to pack and check out by one, leave our baggage in the room behind the front desk, and be ready for the afternoon tour. The lady Nature had not forgotten sat at a table with our guide and bus driver, talking in German. The two men were now redundant and did not accompany us on the rounds of Venetian culture learning. One could not guide through a city with a long and complicated history, the other could not drive where there were no roads or motor vehicles.

"Where are we going this afternoon?" I asked the temp worker before I went to my table. I stood over her but tried to look into her face and not any lower.

"We will take the vaporetto," she said looking up to me, "and go to two islands."

And two we went to. First we took the No. 41 to Isola di San Michele, nicknamed Island of the Dead. This little isle in the Lagoon was only five minutes away, northeast of St. Mark's and Castello, and is Venice's most illustrious graveyard, the final resting place of Ezra Pound, Igor Stravinsky, and other well-known figures. Napoléon decreed the dead can no longer be buried on Venice's main islands so this former prison site became a digging hole for departed loved ones.

I called it Cemetery Row because of its series of huge square-shaped gardens with cypress trees, stone monuments, iron gates, modern terraces, and marble-topped crypts. Elderly people left flowers on graves. The name D'Agostino was on one of the headstones, not uncommon in Italy, but the Luigi who reposed here could have been my friend Richie's uncle on his father's side. We strolled through the island but it did not have the aura of death. Indeed, the silence of the tombs and the paucity of visitors were a welcome respite from the deafening sounds made by hordes of tour-ists in other parts of the city.

Next we did another bit of island hopping, but the vaporetto took longer this time. As we sailed away from San Michele, the guide told us more mortifying tales. On the waterfront of an isle south of the main islands there is the imposing Church of the Most Holy Redeemer, or Il Redentore, erected in the late 1500s to pay homage to the more than one-quarter residents of the city who perished in the bubonic plague. We did not have time to go there since we were headed the other way, to the Lido di Venezia, the famous island fronting the Venetian Lagoon and the Adriatic Sea. Soon we would be on dry land renowned for death as well as life.

The guide-for-the-day said we would be stopping on the north end of the Lido, home of the Venice Film Festival, a casino, and two luxury hotels. Looking out from the vaporetto, I could see the island was a sandbar about six or seven miles long. We docked at the terminal near Santa Maria Elisabetta, the wide main street that leads from the Lagoon to the Sea, with small hotels, shops, and restaurants that catered to tourists. We were the marks of the day, it seemed, as our Lady of Solicit marched her troupe the half mile from coast to coast.

I assumed she had deals going with shopkeepers and restaurant owners for bringing them our business. I told the Kickback Queen I was on familiar territory, that Lido Island was not much different from Coney Island in its length and width and stretch of sandy beach on the Adriatic side.

The tour of Lido focused on its hotels and history, especially the Grand Hôtel des Bains, a stately white structure that served as the setting for Thomas Mann's classic novella, *Death in Venice.* I stood near the hotel's private beach, the spot on the sand made famous by the author's highly artistic account of spiritual and physical death, a German man's demise from cholera in a city known for plagues, contracted because of his obsession for an unattainable love. When I heard that, I hoped I would not meet my end like the Mann in Mann's story, catch something going around St. Mark's or from the girl in the Piazza. Perhaps I should have insisted that the signorina wash me again *after* our intimate contact.

On the vaporetto back to our pensione, I asked the buxom blond if she could take us to the Jewish Ghetto. I read it is in the Cannaregio district, not too far west and north of where we were headed. It was the first ghetto in history, the word itself being derived from Italian.

She said we would not have time.  If I offered her my tip, I'm sure she would have been happy to shaft me on a private tour.

She looked at me and probably pegged me because of my question.  So I looked at her and tried to peg her.  Whose side was she on during the war?  Who in Italy in the early '40s did she let see and feel those big boobs?  For food or favors, she could have given herself to German soldiers occupying her country.  Italian partisans would have been after her too, to keep them company in their mountainous hideouts, assist with guerilla operations, employ as bait in luring Nazis into compromising situations, or have as a courier of secret information.

At the pensione, the German guide and bus driver were waiting for us.  They just finished their cup of cappuccino and assortment of Italian pastries, which no doubt were given gratis.  It was not quite four.  We collected our things and hurried to St. Mark's Basin to ride the vaporetto one last time.  At Piazalle Roma we boarded our parked tour bus.  The trip south to Roma would take more than five hours, plus the time out for a rest stop and dinner.

# CHAPTER 49: ROMAN HOLIDAY

On the bus to Rome I looked around to the other members of the tour, mainly Catholics but some Protestants. I could not help thinking my reasons for taking this trip on the Christmas holiday were not the same as theirs. Ostensibly they wanted to see the Pope and Vatican City or just visit one of the most holy places in Christendom.

After seeing Paris, I hankered to put my feet down in another major European capital and snap plenty of pictures to show the folks back home. It occurred to me too that when I get to college next year I will have something other than Coney Island to talk about in a history class or write about on an English paper. Being in Rome for Christmas was not a priority for me, of course, but a tour to that city sponsored by a branch of the Army was only available at that time.

Ironically, tagging along on this pilgrimage for Christians broadened my horizons about Judaism and enhanced my Jewish identity.

My religious awakening of sorts began on the road south. I was sitting by a window and the soldier from Pinder Barracks was next to me. We were alone near the rear of the bus. We both pushed the button on the side of our armrest, leaned back as far as we could, and tried to get some rest. It was getting dark outside and we expected to reach our destination sometime after 11 p.m. Those who were so inclined could attend midnight mass at St. Peter's, to welcome in the holy day that marked the birth of Jesus. My roommate in Venice and I were relaxed in our seats.

"How long have you been at Pinder?" I asked him casually, just to make conversation.

"Almost five months."

"My ex-girlfriend lives in Zirndorf. Last summer I used to go there two or three times a week." He knew I was stationed at Merrell as I had mentioned it several times.

"That's a hell of a long way to travel," he noted correctly.

"I didn't mind. Sometimes I took her to Merrell for a movie. She didn't want to go to your barracks."

"I can understand that. Must have been a nice German girl."

"Yes she was. I was the first G.I. she went out with."

"Well, you probably won't be the last," he added cynically, "now that she's broken in."

His comment about Karin bothered me but I ignored it. After a pause, I changed the subject. "I met a guy from your barracks one night on the bus going back to Merrell. He was in Artillery, like you. He showed me his finger with the missing first joint. Said it was cut off in a Howitzer because of a soldier's negligence. I never got his name. Do you know him?"

"No . . . but I heard about him. He was transferred before I came to Pinder."

"The guy was very bitter. Blamed someone on his crew."

My touring buddy turned toward me and spoke in a lower voice without emotion.

"Yeah. He attacked the jig who cut his finger off. Jumped on him in the mess hall and punched with his bad hand. Called him a black motherfucker in front of everyone. The Army was going to court martial the poor bastard but gave him a transfer instead. I guess they felt sorry for him."

"I felt sorry for him too. All he wanted was an apology."

"Yeah," he said again coldly. But you know the jigs. They don't give a shit for nobody. Whites especially."

I disregarded that comment too. What could I possibly say to make the rural racist relinquish his views? Why should I start an argument with someone I hardly know on a trip I took to enjoy myself? So, I changed the subject once more. I put a lighter touch on what was turning out to be a strained communication, only to have my efforts backfire.

"How was that girl you picked up last night?"

I said nothing about the girl who picked *me* up. Based on his obvious proclivity for hookers, I thought he might give me a blow-by-blow description of his escapade. Instead, he gave me a body blow I did not see coming.

"She was all right," he started to say in a matter-of-fact manner. "Wanted six thousand lire?"

"Did you pay her that?" I was curious to know if he shelled out a thousand more than I did for a Venetian signorina.

"Hell no," he fired back. "I was able to Jew her down to five."

It felt as if I was hit with a sledge hammer. I had never heard that expression before, to *Jew* someone down. At first I thought I heard it wrong. It sounded like *chew* her down, and that made sense to me, to bargain or chew someone down for a lower price. But I soon realized that was not what he said, that his substitution of a similar-sounding word transformed an otherwise innocuous statement into an ethnic slur and I deeply resented it. He uttered it unemotionally but I certainly did not take it that way. This time I decided not to ignore something he said in bad taste. I questioned him calmly, giving him an opportunity to recant.

"Excuse me?"

"I Jewd her down to five."

He sounded like Karin pronouncing Jude in English. No doubt this was his normal way of talking. The young American's choice of words played into the stereotype about Jews and money, but yet he as a Christian was guilty of doing the same thing. He could be a stand-in for Hitler on the speaker's platform at Soldiers' Field, blaming the Gelt-grubbing Jews for profiting from the first world war. I thought he knew I was Jewish from my name, but evidently he did not or could care less. I wanted to wring the farm boy's neck like a chicken or shove a pitchfork in him. If he called me a mocky, I could not have felt worse. At least that label had some truth to it. I was still calm in tone.

"You shouldn't say something like that."

"Like what?" he said in complete surprise.

"That you tried to *Jew* someone down." I emphasized it for him.

He lifted his head and looked at me with a blank expression on his face, bewildered as to what I was talking about. "What's wrong with that?"

"It's offensive . . . especially to someone who's Jewish."

His head moved slightly and he squinted. "You're Jewish?"

I just looked at him. It was not necessary to nod or say yes.

"But you're going to Rome for Christmas."

"So what?" I said indignantly. "Can't I go to Rome just to see the city?"

He did not answer me. He had no answer. He turned his head away and sat back in his seat. Like the uncaring black buddy in his battery, he did not apologize either. It was not a piece of my finger this artless artilleryman cut off, it was a piece of my heart.

Hours later we checked into our pensione. I did not have to ask the German guide or the Italian clerk to change my room.  On this leg of the tour, I was assigned to a triple.  My two new mates threw their bags on the bed and hurried off to attend midnight mass without inviting me to worship with them.  The Pinder prick must have warned his Christian comrades that an infidel was in their midst.  During the four-night stay in Rome, I made sparse conversation in or out of the hotel with my chance roomers.  With the tourist booklet and city map handed to me by the desk clerk with a smile, I saw the sites by myself or with the group.

In our two-star booking the accommodations were not fancy but we had the good fortune to be in a convenient location, the city center.  Many of the not-to-be-missed sites— St. Peter's Square, the Coliseum, Roman Forum, Pantheon, Trevi Fountain—were within walking distance from the hotel if one possessed a good pair of shoes or sneakers.  And Rome was not Venice.  There was ground transporttation and I could get around Caesar's town without hailing a gondola or taxiing in a vaporetto.

For three days, after breakfast, the guide took us with our bus to some major tourist attraction and left us there.  We were to go around by ourselves, report back to that spot for a ride back to the hotel for lunch, or remain behind.  At 1400 hours we were bused to yet another location and then brought back again for dinner.  Evenings we were on our own completely.

Vatican City, naturally, was our first stop on Friday, December twenty-fifth.  It was a beautiful morning.  The sun was shining, the temperature was warm, not a cloud was in the sky, church bells were ringing throughout the city.  We came to the Vatican about ten.  At that hour, there were not too many people milling about St. Peter's Square and I could walk around and take pictures fairly easily.  I got a good shot of the Egyptian obelisk in the center of the piazza and snapped sections of the colonnades and pilasters with the life-size saints atop the cornice in the massive elliptical area.

Here the Pope would be giving the traditional Christmas Day message to the world at noon.  At the strike of twelve the Bishop of Rome will step out onto the balcony of St. Peter's Basilica at one end of the piazza and bless those standing below him in the walled enclave in many different languages and broadcast live over the radio and television.

I did not need a tour guide that day. There were many tourist groups floating around in the piazza, some of which were led by an English-speaking guide. It was no trouble for me to slip into one or another. In my American-style clothing, and with my Kodak camera hanging from my neck, I fit right in. Despite my young age, not one of the older adults perceived me as an interloper and ordered me to stop following them.

I walked with one group into the Basilica, the burial site of its namesake, whose dome dominates the skyline of Rome. Inside the largest church in Christianity I felt dwarfed by the height of its barrel-vaulted nave. Surrounding the central dome were various chapels, the one for the Pietà being the most memorable for me. Michelangelo's sculpture was in the first chapel on the right as you enter the Basilica, of Mary holding Jesus across her lap after he was taken down from the cross. The highly-polished marble statue of a young and beautiful woman, not the older mother of a 33-year-old son, was meant to evoke pity in the heart of anyone viewing the masterpiece.

From the Basilica I followed the crowd to the nearby Apostolic Palace, the Pope's official residence, famous for its Sistine Chapel decorated with frescoes by the greatest Renaissance artists. Within these hallowed walls, Michelangelo, Raphael, and Botticelli profusely sweated and wiped gobs of paint from their face as they ran horsetail brushes over wet plaster. Michelangelo suffered the most perhaps. The sculptor did not like to paint, but he toiled four years to finish the Sistine Ceiling just to please Pope Julius II's mania for grandeur. The artist stood on scaffolds he designed, supported by brackets built out from holes in the wall near the top of the windows, and looked up all the time in order to paint the magnificent biblical scenes. I almost broke *my* neck looking up at God, the Creation, Adam and Eve, Noah, the Great Flood, and other depictions from Genesis.

The Sistine Chapel was also the site of the Papal conclave, where the College of Cardinals is sequestered to elect a new pontiff. No prelate comes out until white smoke appears from the chimney installed in the roof. It was here fourteen months earlier that Angelo Roncalli was elected after eleven ballots cast over four days. When the tenth ballot failed, the Cardinals must have looked up to the Ceiling and asked for divine guidance. The portly new pope, calling himself John XXIII, appeared on the balcony of the Basilica in a white cassock that obviously was too tight for his frame. No one, not even Roncalli himself, who had a return train ticket to Venice tucked in his pocket, or the Vatican tailor who had prepared several different sizes, expected the election of this 77-year-old compromise candidate before the ballots were burned.

Papa John was known to the world for more than his personal warmth and good humor. He was known for his kindness toward the Jews. During the war, as Nuncio to Pius XII, he helped save thousands of Jewish refugees—from Romania, Bulgaria, Slovakia, Hungary, as well as his own Italy—from deportation and certain death. Roncalli often acted on his own and not as the representative of his Pope, who some accused of anti-Semitism, or the Holy See. Soon after his surprise election, the successor to Pius XII initiated an ecclesiastical policy of Jewish-Christian reconciliation.

Before noon, I scurried back to St. Peter's Square. Swiss guards in their bright blue, red, orange, and yellow Medieval uniforms that looked more like costumes were all about, tall young men speaking different languages in answer to people's questions. A few happily posed for me and I turned my camera sideways to fit them in head-to-toe.

I found a spot among the now thousands of tourists and pilgrims cramming the piazza, to see and possibly get a picture of the head of the Catholic Church with great sympathy for Jews. But I was too far away from the Basilica and too far below its balcony. I heard his voice through the loudspeakers but only saw the top of his head with the white skullcap that looked like an oversized yarmulke. This time I was sure the former Patriarch of Venice was donning a new, and much larger, tailor-made cassock.

After lunch, we were dropped off near the Coliseum. Nothing has symbolized Imperial Rome more for almost two millennia than this circular amphitheater started around 70 A.D., right after the destruction of Jerusalem. I got my first glimpse of today's Coliseum, with the missing levels on part of its façade, from a Hollywood movie, when it was used as background for a smiling Audrey Hepburn driving a motor scooter through Rome on holiday with Gregory Peck. In *Demetrius and the Gladiators*, I saw this ancient arena as it actually was, with its fight-to-the-death contests between men or man and beast, entertainment for the masses with at times a thumbs-up or thumbs-down finale.

I walked inside the crumbling building just far enough to see there was no ground level where blood was shed, only the walls of under-ground cells that housed the doomed slaves and hungry animals. It was hard to believe this marvel of Roman architecture and engineer-ing is still standing at all after the damage over the centuries by earthquakes and stone-robbers. Rome's Coliseum, of course, was the model for Nuremberg's Congress Hall. We will have to wait another nineteen hundred years to learn if the Nazis built their showplace as well as the Romans.

That afternoon I had time to walk west and behold the Arch of Titus. It commemorates the military victories of Titus, the com-mander of Judaea, a troublesome Roman province in the Land of Is-rael. It was he who put down the local rebellion, sacked Jerusalem, leveled the venerable Temple, and caused the Diaspora of the Jews. I went up close to the Arch, to see its detailed carvings of the sack-ing and looting of sacred objects from the Temple. A seven-point menorah is clearly depicted which, ironically, served as a model for the menorah used on the emblem for the new State of Israel in 1948.

As a basic structure minus offensive carvings and inscriptions, this Arch looked very familiar to me. It obviously inspired L'Arc de Triomphe in Paris for the conquests of Napoléon, but also a monu-ment closer to home. I saw the Soldier's and Sailor's Arch in Brook-lyn at Grand Army Plaza every time my elementary school class went on a field trip to Prospect Park or the Botanical Gardens.

After dinner, I walked around Rome taking pictures at night of different statues and fountains. The men in the sculptures often were completely naked but their central body part was nothing like what I was told hung on the Schwarzer in my barracks whose snack-bar Schatzie I went nuts over. I mounted my camera on a tripod and set the lens opening at $f2$, the widest. I placed the shutter in the $B$ mode and attached a remote release to it. I held the shutter open for sev-eral minutes to have as much light as possible around the stationary objects reach the film. There was a beautiful large fountain outside the Railway Station, with angelic figures in various poses all around it, and I took shots of each one in the same manner.

I went inside the terminal. The Stazione Termini was an impressive modern building, started under Il Duce, who promised to make Italy's trains run on time, but completed after the war. It was nothing like the Hauptbahnhof in Nuremberg. The Termini, with its imposing portico and huge vaulted entrance hall, made travelers feel as though they were stepping into a cathedral. I enjoyed just wandering about, peeping into shop windows and restaurants, passing time as if I were waiting for my train to pull out.

A Montgomery Clift in *Indiscretion of an American Wife* I could have been, haphazardly moving through Rome's main station, but I was not looking for Jennifer Jones or anyone else's signora to take out to the yard and into an empty railroad car for a little love before she was to board her train and go back to her husband. If art imitated life, Hollywood would have scripted a handsome Monty sneaking off to the terminal hide-away with a *man* and not a woman.

It was late when I returned to my hotel that Christmas Day. My two roommates were fast asleep. For all I knew, the choir boys who rushed off to mass at St. Peter's the night before could have picked up two signorine a few hours earlier, partied with them in the room, and kissed them arrivederci before I turned the key.


"How do I get to Trastevere?" I asked the desk clerk, hoping my Italian pronunciation was correct.

I held the tourist booklet he gave me the day before and had read about that district. On the map I saw it was near the west bank of the Tiber, across the river from where we were, south of Vatican City.

It was the day after Christmas, Kislev 25 on the Hebrew Calendar, the first day of Chanukah, the Holiday of Lights. After breakfast I stayed behind in the pensione when the rest of the tour group took off to another historical site. On this day my most important Jewish experience in Rome occurred.

The clerk looked at me for a moment. He knew my name. "Ah, Ebraico Ghetto."

Ebraico, I repeated to myself. What the hell is Ebraico in Italian? Then it came to me, it must mean Hebraic. I guess that is how Italians say Jewish. "Yes," I told him, nodding as well. I want to go to the Jewish Ghetto."

"You cana walk or you can taka da bus."

440

"I'll probably walk."

"I showa you." The courteous young Italian man took my map and redlined the route along the small curved streets from the hotel to a road or bridge that spanned the Tiber. "Justa go ova Ponte Garibaldi and you are ina Trastevere."

"Grazie," I said, taking back the marked street map to guide me for my adventure of the day.

"Scusa," he called to me as I was halfway to the door. "Ebraico Ghetto isa now ona da other side ova da river."

The desk clerk advised me correctly. The tourist booklet explained it all. Rome's Jewish community, dating back two hundred years before Christ, originally settled in the Trastevere district on the west bank of the Tiber. Many Jews left their homeland to escape the turmoil and foreign occupations. They gravitated to Rome because of its growing importance and prosperity. In Israel, Jews were persecuted under Roman domination but in Rome they were tolerated, by its rulers especially. Julius Caesar was their friend and he too lived in this district considered the heart of Rome.

It is said that Cleopatra spent many a night here and one can only wonder what Caesar's wife, who was above reproach, did about that. After the destruction of Jerusalem, greater numbers of Jews were dispersed in the Roman Empire. Jews, like the early Christians, were persecuted but when Christianity became the official religion, Christians persecuted the Jews. For many centuries, Jews in the capital of Christendom enjoyed a safe haven in contrast to their brethren in other European cities.

Jewish life was now on the other side of the river, as the clerk said. It began as a result of the Spanish Inquisition. After 1492, Jews expelled from Spain and Portugal flooded into Rome. In 1555, the anti-Semitic Paul IV issued a papal bull forcing Jews to move to the east bank of the Tiber, the Sant'Angelo district. But no saint or angel protected them here. A wall was erected, restrictions were imposed, Jews had to wear markers on their clothing and pay special taxes.

The Jewish Ghetto lasted three centuries, its walls only torn down in 1848. Two decades later, with the unification of Italy, Jews finally enjoyed the full rights of citizenship. The respite from persecution was not destined to last long, however. In 1943 the Nazis stormed into and occupied Italy, rounded up all the Jews in Rome, re-established the Ghetto, and railroaded a sizable part of its population to Auschwitz.

I spent the first day of Chanukah on both banks of the Tiber River. It was nice walking around Trastevere, a quaint and artistic quarter with the look of antiquity and charm of medieval life, old houses along narrow twisted streets with shops and bars and restaurants on the ground floor. But there was very little that was Ebraico four hundred years after the district's several thousand Jews were forced out that I could see. All the streets seem to lead to the Piazza di Santa Maria and the monumental St. Mary's Church with its Romanesque exterior but Baroque interior.

On the east bank, the Jewish presence was unmistakable. The Great Synagogue, or Tempio Maggiore, the largest in the city, looms over the former Ghetto. The half-century-old tall building, with its square-shaped dome, the only such dome in Rome, was a conscious choice of a people bent on a visual expression of their freedom. Inside the Temple were commemorative objects honoring Rome's Jewish victims of the Nazis and, on this day, a large menorah with one candlestick lit. A make-shift museum was in two rooms adjacent to the synagogue, housing Judaica collections and documents on the Nazi occupation of Rome.

This modern Jewish Quarter, I discovered gladly, had kosher restaurants. I took my lunch in one of them, a welcome relief from the traife I had to eat along with Christians on the tour. Before I hoofed it back to the hotel late in the afternoon, I saw, forged into the wall of a courtyard, the one remaining piece of the Ghetto Wall.

After dinner that night I walked around a bit, but unlike the Saturday I spent in Paris, I was not approached by, and did not keep company with, a young woman of La strada.

Rome wasn't built in a day, and can't be seen in a day, but on December twenty-seventh, my last full day in Rome, I feasted my eyes on important sites I missed the previous two days. After breakfast, I went with the tour to the Catacombs of St. Domitilla, one of the many catacomb locations on the outskirts of the city, the underground burial places begun in the second century. Graves were dug out of the walls of soft volcanic rock under the city, in the tunnels and passageways, and laid out vertically with one or more bodies. I was surprised to learn that Jews as well as Christians were buried here, either in separate catacombs or mixed together. Both religious groups frowned upon the pagan practice of cremation, Jews because of the biblical injunction against desecration of the body and Christians because of an expectation of resurrection with the Second Coming.

In life the believers and non-believers in the Son and Holy Ghost could not accept or work with one another, in death they both were willing to share eternal peace side-by-side. We were guided through dark and narrow curved passageways, partially lighted by wall fixtures at wide intervals. The catacombs reminded me of a dungeon in a Frankenstein or Dracula movie.

Before lunch, we were taken to the famous Spanish Steps, the longest and widest outdoor stairway in Europe. In the Piazza di Spagna at the base, to the right as one begins the climb, a house was pointed out to us as that where John Keats lived and died in. I walked up all 138 steps, looking to the right and left to find what the poet might have seen 138 years earlier, a thing of beauty that is a joy forever. Our plump middle-age guide huffed and puffed most of the way, and was glad to see our bus waiting for us at the top.

I saw no one sitting on the steps eating pizza or pasta, a practice forbidden by Roman law, and no one tried to drive a Fiat or Ferrari down the 200-year-old steep incline. Back at our hotel, when food was served, it was apparent the Spanish ascent stepped up the appetites of the American and German climbers.

After lunch we were bussed to the Roman Forum—the marketplace, business district, and civic center of the ancient city. It was an open rectangle surrounded by the ruins of government buildings, the site of elections and public speeches and commercial affairs. Statues of Rome's great men were all around. I asked one of my roommates to snap a picture of me standing on a big rock next to some decaying columns. On the steps of the Forum, I pretended I was Marlon Brando playing Marc Antony, Julie's friend and Cleo's lover.

"Friends, Romans, countrymen, lend me your ears," I shouted.

On my own I went to the Panthéon, one of the best preserved ancient buildings in Rome, a temple, as its name implies, to all the gods. If the circular structure, with its portico and rotunda and massive dome, looks familiar to international tourists, it is. Its design and architecture was obviously the inspiration for the U.S. Capitol and Jefferson Memorial in D.C., Jefferson's home Monticello and his Rotunda at the University of Virginia, California State Capitol in Sacramento, Reading Room of the British Museum in London, Temple Beth-El in Detroit, and many churches and libraries around the world, not to mention the Panthéon in Paris.

My final stop in the afternoon was the Trevi Fountain, the biggest and most famous fontana in Rome. It was at the junction of three roads, the tre vie. Construction was based on the Roman custom of placing a beautiful fountain at the endpoint of an aqueduct that carried fresh water into the city. The statues of men, women, sea gods, and horses form the backdrop for Trevi's theme of the taming of the waters.

My first impression on seeing the fountain was disappointment. It was not as colorful or as beautiful as that portrayed in the movie *Three Coins in the Fountain*. Like everyone else, I stood near the railing, made a wish, and threw a coin over my shoulder and into the water. There were thousands of coins in many different sizes and colors at the bottom of the fountain.

Unlike in the Hollywood fantasy, I did not wish for romance and marriage as the three young American women working in Rome did. Two scrappy-looking Italian boys were using a pole to fetch out some coins but were unsuccessful. Although it is illegal to swim in the fountain people strip and jump in occasionally. The day a dead Mussolini was hung upside down and the day Rome was liberated from the Nazis were probably such an occasion.

I came back to the Trevi after dinner, to see the fountain at night. It was a beautiful sight with everything lit up. This time I was not disappointed. Tossing three small coins, I made wishes for 1960—success on the College Boards, a pleasant transfer to Munich, and an honorable discharge. I did not repeat the wish for romance without marriage thought hours earlier. As I was leaving, Italian workmen were scooping up the catch of the day from the bottom of the fontana.

On Monday the twenty-eighth we left Rome right after breakfast. Almost five hours later we stopped in Padua for lunch. It was a pleasure driving through this oldest and picturesque city in Northern

Italy, just west of Venice. I was taken with its many bridges, arcaded streets, and large communal piazze. Shakespeare too must have felt something for Padua, for he set *The Taming of the Shrew* here. Another bus ride for six and a half hours and we were back in Nuremberg.

Three days of Chanukah in 5720 were, for the most part, *my* Roman holiday.

## CHAPTER 50: JANUARY PASSAGES

A surprise was waiting for me on Tuesday morning, the twenty-ninth of December. I came into the Area Office a little early, before the two Bs usually got there, to get caught up with the work after being away for six days. Someone was sitting at my desk. He stood up as soon as he saw me.

The man I never met before was a Spec 4, the same rank as I was, but looked three or four years older. He was inches shorter and had a weird appearance, something like a weasel—head wide on top, long nose, small eyes, and protruding lower lip. The name tag on his fatigue jacket read Burns. His dirty blond hair was combed with a part on one side and he had a short pompadour in front, typical of a civilian but unusual for a soldier. The most distinguishing feature was his bad skin—yellow and crusty with pimples, pockmarks, and blackheads.

He extended his hand to me. "I'm Peter," he said nervously.

I shook his hand but did not offer my name, first or last. My last name was staring him in the face and I presumed Bentley or Barry had mentioned my first to him. I offered no greeting and waited for him to talk again.

"I was transferred from Vilseck. I came yesterday. They put me in the new part of the barracks everyone will be moving to on the eighteenth."

Burnsy had some sort of tic, another characteristic that set him apart from his new teammates. His hands shook slightly and his head twitched every few seconds. Speech was slow and deliberate. The unappealing soldier was taking over my job and the two Bs wasted no time weaseling him in. I resented that and put the intruder on the defensive.

"Why are you sitting at my desk?"

"Sergeant Bentley told me to sit here." His head twitched more as if his collar was too tight. His face reddened. "He said you're going to Munich on the eighteenth."

"That's true, but where will *I* sit for the next three weeks?"

The newcomer shrugged. "I don't know."

If this is the kind of clerk Bentley and Barry preferred sitting in front of them, they can have him. "Am I supposed to work here too until I leave?" I looked around the relatively small space the 176th had in the odd-shaped room. For a fourth desk there was no room.

"I don't know," my replacement repeated.

Just then the two Bs came in and smiled when they saw me. "Glad you made it back, Strahber," Bentley said in his usual manner. "How was Rome?"

"Fine."

"Did you get to see the Pope?" Barry threw in sarcastically, as if to say "what is a Jew doing in Rome on Christmas?"

"Yes I did, sir, as a matter of fact. But just the top of his head."

"Strahber," Bentley began, looking away from me and moving behind his desk, "Ah see you met Burns. Let me explain the situation here."

With that introduction, my immediate boss tried to assuage my feelings. The sergeant told me they had to bring the new man in now, to learn the workings of the Area Office, because during my remaining time here it will be the New Year's holiday and I was scheduled to be away many days. He pointed out, as if I needed reminding, that he approved a two-day pass for me on the fifth and sixth to take the college test, and five days of non-accrued leave for a religious retreat from the tenth to the fourteenth. Burns had to be broken in before I left for Munich.

I felt humiliated at the way the job of office clerk, the one I carved out from scratch and touched up for seven months, and my desk were taken away from me but I neither said anything to that effect nor showed the two Bs that I minded. Bentley told me I did not have to return to work in the shop, and that was of some consolation to me. Barry, as usual, just stared out the window, oblivious to what was going on behind his back. Bentley said I could hang around the Area Office for the intermittent days I had left, pull up a chair and squeeze in, and show Burnsy the filing system and work products I created. He even hinted I could take long coffee breaks in the snack bar mornings and afternoons when things were slow.

That was exactly what I did. Twice a day I slipped quietly out of the office that now seated *three* Bs, walked across the compound about a hundred feet to the snack bar, and took some R & R before my time would be up in Nuremberg. A serendipitous side effect of my daily rest and relaxation periods, I soon realized, would be opportunities for frequent furtive glances at my dream lover wiping tables or stacking glasses. But such small pleasures before I was to bid farewell to Merrell Barracks were not to be. Perhaps too it was unrealistic to hope the girl in the snack bar would recognize her ardent admirer, eagerly swing over to me, and whisper in my ear that she is no longer a handy white mare for her private black buck. I kept looking for her day after day but to no avail. The blotched blond beauty may not be working for Americans any longer, I concluded. Or she could have been knocked down to permanent night duty to coincide with the dark life she was leading.

With a wink from Sergeant Bentley, an important passage that January was the status change from necessary office clerk to surplus team member.

The thirty-first of December was a Thursday, normally a day in which bed check is at midnight. However, the curfew was extended two hours as on a Saturday, to give the troops extra time to drink and be merry ringing in the New Year. To insure a state of readiness in case of an alert, the higher-ups in the 2nd Cavalry arranged for deuce-and-a-half trucks to be parked before 0200 hours near the main entrance of the Hauptbahnhof. Merrell troopers would be coming back to the barracks one way or the other, drunk or sober. The rumor swirling about that any day now the whistle would be blown did not dissuade the lower-downs from marching into town for their once-a-year special night for hell-raising.

I had no plans for New Year's Eve. There was no steady Schatzie in my life to celebrate with. I could not very well knock on Karin's door, after more than three months of disappearance and silence, and say let's go somewhere. Traipsing into the Flying Dutchman round about eleven to snatch Elsa and whisk her out of there so I can shoot off at the stroke of twelve was also out of the question. This night would be the busiest of the year for her. G.I.s would be getting into hand-to-hand combat just to take the homely hussy home. I would not consider trying my luck again with magnetic Marianne on an important occasion such as this after so many rejections on ordinary nights. Steve was with Ursula and I could not be a third wheel and intrude on their first New Year's together. I was not that friendly with my roommate or any of the other team members in the shop to

448

be heading into town with them for a good time. And socializing with the new man who took over my job was anathema to me.

That evening I knew I had to go it alone. This New Year held significance for me beyond the fact that it was my third and last in the Army. It was the turn of a new decade, the 1960s, and the start of a six-month countdown to honorable discharge and civilian life. I left Merrell before nine, hopped on the Strassenbahn, and got off at the Hauptbahnhof. I walked around Nuremberg for a while, first the Old Town area and then near parts of the Wall. In the waning hours of 1959, it was not cold and the skies were clear. It would be a night to remember and for me an historic date. I made mental notes of the people I observed and the street activities going on, to reflect upon in years to come.

By ten-thirty I was ready for some excitement and company. I decided to go to a Gasthaus I had heard about but never patronized, the Mautkeller, a popular place with both Germans and Americans. It was on Königstrasse, up the street from Luitpoldstrasse, going toward the Old City.

The Mautkeller was in a large rectangular-shaped building with a steeply-pitched roof. There were arches in front and shops on the ground level. As its name implied, the restaurant and bar was in the cellar. Down the outside stairs I went and through the double doors. The Gasthaus had a low vaulted ceiling and thick pillars every five or ten feet. Along the outer walls and between pillars were square tables with chairs and some benches. In the aisle in the middle, tables were pushed together to accommodate parties of a dozen or more. Candled chandeliers and glass-enclosed electric bulbs on pillar walls provided lighting. This time of night on New Year's Eve the basement establishment was extremely crowded, every table taken, with people spinning around on the dance floor. A brass band played polkas, loud enough to be heard at the end of the street and on the five floors above.

I went to a table for four with two empty seats. Two Fräuleins were sitting there and talking. Half-empty glasses of beer were in front of them.

"Bitte . . . hier sitzen?" I said when I caught their attention. It was not perfect German but I liked speaking other languages, even in pieces, whenever I could.

"Ja," one of them answered, and extended her hand out to one of the empty chairs.

"Danke." I sat down and looked at the two young women, but was mindful not to stare at them. I knew it was appropriate in Germany for strangers to be tabled together if there were no empty tables. A cute waitress in a black jacket, short skirt, and white apron came over and I ordered a beer.

"Sind Sie Amerikaner?" the same one asked me.

My hair style and clothing must have given me away. I nodded. "Ja. Yes." My experiences in Italy days earlier conditioned me to respond in two languages simultaneously.

"Soldat?"

"Ja. Yes," I answered again, nodding.

"I speak English," the other cut in. "My friend very little."

"My German very little too," I said with a bit of a smile, keeping my English simple too. I wanted to show some affinity with the two female strangers I was sitting next to on this momentous evening.

The Fräulein who spoke English was sitting opposite me and I could look straight at her. She was prettier than the other one. With short, curly blond hair, a regular bust size, and appealing facial features, she was not too far off from my ideal. She appeared to be the height I liked and had the thin frame I favored. This German girl was not as perfect as the one in the snack bar or as sexy as Marianne, though she had an attractiveness that caught my fancy. The other one turned her head now and then to glance at me. I could see her through the corner of my eye but did not care to focus directly on her.

I sat quietly so as not to disturb either Fräulein. My table companions chatted away but I caught little of what they said. I sneaked a peek at the pretty one every time I sipped my beer.

"Where you are in Nürnberg?" she asked me after a while.

"I'm stationed at Merrell Barracks . . . the old SS Kaserne."

"Ja, ja," she interjected the way Germans do. "I know it."

The other one said something to her in German and then the one I liked looked back at me.

"How long you here?"

"Almost ten months."

"Oh . . . long time. When you go home?"

"In six months." I answered the question exactly as put to me, honestly I thought, but omitted the fact that I would soon be on my way to Munich. I was following my mother's advice, not giving out more information than I had to.

I fantasized about how nice it would be to get into the girl facing me, if not this night then some other time before the eighteenth of the coming month. She would be a welcome relief from Elsa and a better lay than Karin. If this eye-catching Fräulein knew I would be leaving in less than three weeks, she probably would not want to date me, much less pull down her pants.

I came full circle in twelve months, doing the very thing I did at Fort Ord the past December, not telling a girl I liked and wanted to ball that I had orders to ship out soon.

The girls' beers were down to an inch in the glass. "Would you two like another beer?" I was being generous to both of them, and hopeful for one, on this last New Year's in the Army.

"Danke," they seemed to say at the same time, and smiled at me. I signaled the cute waitress and ordered two beers. Mine was still good.

I chatted with the one who spoke English and looked mainly at her, only occasionally turning my head to the other out of courtesy. To get into one I knew I had to be nice to both. I spoke about my recent trip to Rome and the different sights that excited me. She translated to her friend some of what I said. Venice and my earlier jaunt to Paris were mentioned too but minus the young French and Italian women I took back to my hotel.

Suddenly from behind I felt a hand rest on my left shoulder. I turned around. It was Isaacson, one of the new guys in my company, my roommate's buddy from Fort Gordon. His eyes were glassy and he looked a little tipsy.

"What's up, Dave," he said like Bugs Bunny, swaying some.

"Nothin' much, Ike. You here with Dick and D.O.?"

"No. They both had dates. I'm on my own tonight."

Ike and I were in the same boat that evening and I sympathized with him. I looked back at the two Fräuleins and the empty seat next to us, and then at Ike again.

"Would you like to join us?" I was sure the girls would not mind.

My barracks buddy put on a happy face. "Sure. Why not?" He

removed his glasses, put them in his shirt pocket, and sat down.

I introduced him awkwardly. "This is my friend from the Kaserne," was all I said since I did not know the girls' names. They nodded and smiled at Ike. He ordered a beer for himself.

Now I was part of a foursome. I hoped I had not made a mistake, that Ike would not be his usual self and horse around like Harpo or Chico in front of the girls and embarrass me, or worse, hurt my chances of making a play for the one I was attracted to. Racing through my mind were thoughts of how to palm this joker off on the one I was not enamored with. Ike was unaware of my romantic interest in one over the other and I could not very well clue him in without drawing the girls' attention to my favoritism and their likely ire. So I held back saying or doing anything.

Ike seemed to be in a good mood and started talking up a storm with the German girls without knowing if either spoke English. It soon became apparent to him that he could only communicate with one. I hoped that in his pursuit Ike would not unwittingly spoil it for me.

Just before midnight a waiter, dressed in a funny-looking tuxedo with top hat and bow tie, a piglet under one arm, walked around from table to table. He held the smelly Schwein out for all to touch. Everyone did so but I held my hand back. In synagogue, when the Torah is carried around in the congregation, I, like everyone else, touch it with my fingers, the holy book, or the end of my talis. But to hug a hog, and a German one at that, in similar fashion, was not for me.

"You should touch it," the Fräulein I favored advised me. "It is tradition in Germany. It bring good luck for new year."

"I'll be lucky enough in nineteen sixty without touching pigs," I replied confidently.

I hoped I did not give myself away to these young postwar Germans. Their mothers, fathers, and grandparents might have pegged me like a Nazi.

The waiter with the little piggy that did not go to market stood in the center of the restaurant, gazed at his wristwatch, and spoke to his two-language audience in Deutsch only. Then the countdown began.

"Zehn," he shouted with his free hand above his head. "Neun . . .

acht . . . sieben . . . sechs . . . fünf . . . vier . . . drei . . . zwei . . . eins. Alles Gute zum Neuen Jahr."

Everyone around us clapped or held up a glass, cheered, and expressed happiness. Men leaned over their tables and kissed the women. Ike and I followed suit but I kissed the one I liked first, and on the lips instead of the cheek. The three at my table were too absorbed in the celebration of their passing into the New Year and new decade to react to or make anything of my lone act of resistance to a German custom, my not being piggish a few minutes earlier as it were. We all ordered another round of beer. Ike and I split the tab in the Marks we pulled out.

"Danke," the girls again said in unison.

About twelve forty-five the girls got up from the table. Their beers were almost gone. "We go home now," the pretty one said.

"Can we walk you girls home?" Ike proffered, still in good spirits. I noticed he was sitting on the edge of his chair.

The Fräuleins we hardly knew said a few words to each other. "Yes . . . if you want," the one I wanted to zero in on answered.

"We want," I said simply.

For the purpose I had in mind, it was better not to show any emotion or eagerness. Buying the Fräuleins beers must have done the trick, made them feel safe enough with two American strangers to agree to being escorted home.

We all left the Mautkeller together. Ike and I just followed alongside the girls as they led us through several winding streets. I took mental notice of where we were going, like a boy scout with a compass on a camping trip, using the tall, round brownstone Tower by the Hauptbahnhof as a guidepost. Finally, we arrived at the gated entrance of an old building. The girls turned around and faced us. The one who did not speak much English extended her hand, in the common German gesture of saying goodbye.

"Dankeschön," she said, while the other stood silent.

It was not clear whether the two girls lived together or if one was just going to the other's apartment. What *was* clear was that Ike and I were getting the gate, literally and figuratively, a kiss off, just as I was beginning to think something personal and private might develop.

Ike spoke for both of us. "Aren't you going to invite us up? It's a new year. We should celebrate."

"No. Not tonight," the blond I was interested in interjected. "Maybe we see you again at Mautkeller."

See you again. That was a Fräulein's way of saying auf Wiedersehen, of nixing any further involvement. The girl in the snack bar said the same words to me the first time I came on to her. It was bullshit and we knew it, but Ike took the brush personally. His smile all but vanished, he stepped forward as if ready to argue with the girls. Now he was going to play Groucho.

I grabbed his arm. "Ike . . . let's go. It's getting late. We have to be back for bed check soon anyway."

Ike was a bit drunk but not so tight that he would start something with a German national that could get us in trouble. My usually boisterous buddy, known for joking and poking, listened to me and backed away from any confrontation. Though I was very much attracted to one of the girls, I took the rebuff in stride. I was leaving Nuremberg in two and a half weeks. There was not much time for hanging out in the Mautkeller, or any other Gasthaus above or below ground. I could hope to see her again, but not to make a connection resulting in an invitation to come up to her place. I was positive these girls were good-time Charlizes, not hookers. I would have to keep it in my pants until I got to Munich.

We walked away from the Fräuleins without waving goodbye. Ike put his glasses on, we headed toward the Hauptbahnhof, and arrived before one thirty. We hopped in the back of one of the deuce-and-a-halves parked in front of the station. Places on the benches along the sides were mostly taken so we sat near the cab. Our co-travelers that night were all white. The 2nd Cav must have dispatched separate but equal trucks to park outside Mother Tucker's and other cotton clubs on the dark side of town to capture its crapulous colored cavalrymen and tow them back to Master Merrell.

The driver said we would be leaving shortly. He started the motor and kept it running. The tailgate of the vehicle was still down. Just then a G.I. in civies began to climb in but could not make it. One leg kept falling off whenever he lifted it onto the tailgate. This happened several times and we were prevented from leaving because of his clumsiness.

To my utter surprise, Ike, from his sitting position, started yelling

454

at the hapless trooper. "Get the fuck in or out." His ill-tempered words probably flowed from his displeasure at not being invited up to a female's apartment more than his impatience with the unnecessary delay.

The failed truck-climber looked at Ike. "You want the shit kicked out of you, buddy?"

Ike stood up and faced the clumsy and/or drunk trooper who still had both feet on the ground. It was dark where we were sitting and it was difficult to gauge how big this guy was. "Come on, motherfucker," he shot back, motioning with his hand. My electronics teammate, five nine and medium built, not the pugnacious type, was wiring for a confrontation after all.

The white soldier jumped up on the truck without difficulty this time. He scaled the tailgate like a commando on a night raid hopping over a short fence. No doubt he did not appreciate Ike's choice of language directed at him, an obnoxious appellation mouthed so often in his barracks corner by members of the darker race. Now we saw how tall this guy was, well over six feet, and more than average weight for his size. Ike handed his glasses to me, held up his left arm with clenched fist, and moved forward for the first punch. But the big and heavy guy had a hell of a reach and clipped my reckless buddy, landing one squarely on his chin. Ike went down and was flat on his back.

That was not the end of the round for Joe Palooka, though. With no referee to restrain him, the tough trooper with eggshell sensibilities first kicked his laid out offender a couple of times, then threw himself on top, punching him again and again in the head. Ike started to bleed from his nose and around the mouth. Had I not been holding my buddy's breakable glasses, I might have stepped in and tried to prevent the madman from the 2nd Cav, who towered over me too, from committing second-degree murder. But *his* buddies beat me to it. Three guys grabbed the cavalryman by the arms and chest, wrenched him off poor bloody Ike, and saved their buddy from spending twenty years in Leavenworth. The four from the 2nd Cav hobbled off the truck and into another waiting transport.

On the way to Merrell, Ike held his head in his hands and complained of the pain. I gave him my handkerchief to wipe some of the blood off. Back on post, the first latrine we came to Ike ran into. From the plopping sounds I heard, he evidently did get the shit kicked out of him. We went to see the medic on duty, who stitched the cut above Ike's eye, and I put him to bed. The next day my beaten buddy felt better, I returned his glasses, and we spoke no more about events that occurred before we got into the deuce-and-a-half or after.

It was an interesting New Year's Eve, a memorable passage into a new decade and my last calendar year in the Army. I met another blond, blue-eyed Fräulein with a fine face and figure but one I could not get near or take pleasure with. I refused to touch a pig for good luck like everyone else because of the animal's anti-Jewish association. And I witnessed combat and bloodshed between two U.S. soldiers in a Germany no longer at war.

William O. Darby Kaserne was located in the southeastern quarter of Fürth, the headquarters of the Army command in the Nuremberg area. During the previous ten months, I had been to Darby a number of times for its Main PX, often on a Saturday with Karin, to purchase goods not always available at my post's smaller exchange. I left Merrell on January fifth, a day earlier than the date I was scheduled to take the College Boards, in order to avoid being ensnared in simulated military combat operations the next morning if an alert were called. The special pass that Sergeant Bentley arranged for me would not be worth the paper it was printed on if the Army needed me to go to the field and participate in Cold War maneuvers near the East German or Czech border. I did not wish to risk missing the college-entrance examination after studying for it so hard for more than three months, and having to sign up and pay again for the one given in April.

At the Hauptbahnhof I changed to the 21. The end of that tram line was just a short distance from Darby. I reached Fürth in the afternoon, a city that had a large Jewish population before the war, originally comprised of those who fled the mass killings in Nuremberg centuries earlier. I headed straight to the Transient Barracks building, reported to the NCOIC, and was assigned a bunk and locker in a large room on the ground floor. Every Army post, in Germany and the States, had sleeping accommodations free-of-charge for soldiers on pass or leave from other installations. I got myself squared away and went to chow at the mess hall. In the evening, before lights out, I reviewed the study materials I brought with me. This was my last chance to prepare myself for the big day.

The College Boards were given in the Education Center on post. It was a three-hour, two-part test with a short break in between. I awoke early the next morning, January sixth, showered and shaved, and ate a good breakfast. It could be a lucky day for me, I thought, as this was the first anniversary of my leaving Fort Ord to begin the journey to West Germany.

I arrived at the Center before the 0900 starting time. The test was given in a room with desks like those found in any American high school. Yellow No. 2 pencils were in the long grooves on the top of the wooden desk. Most of the seats were occupied by baby-faced teenagers, sons and daughters of military families in their junior or senior year, but I was not the only male about twenty or older in the room. There were soldiers too.

The proctor, in civilian clothes, was a man of about thirty-five, not unlike teachers I knew at Lincoln High School in South Brooklyn. He passed out the Verbal part of the SAT first and warned us not to open it until he gives the signal.

I thought I did fairly well on this half with its reading comprehensions, sentence completions, analogies, word definitions, and antonyms. Ninety minutes later we were given the Mathematics part. I was sure I did better here, as I was confident with my answers to the the multiple-choice questions, quantitative reasoning, problem solving, simultaneous equations, and data sufficiency.

For some reason, we were not supposed to know how we did. "Your grades," the proctor told us, "will be sent directly to the college or colleges you applied to. It is up to the school, whether you are accepted or rejected, to divulge that information."

On the two streetcar rides back to Merrell that day, I felt both relieved and contented. I took my first step on the road to higher education, an important beginning to the new life I sought. I made the passage from high school graduate to college candidate.

# CHAPTER 51: BAVARIAN RETREATS

". . . it's too good for them," Rabbi Jacob Stark from Temple Emanuel on Fifth Avenue and East 65th Street in Manhattan told the audience of Jewish-American servicemen gathered at the General Walker Hotel in Berchtesgaden.

Hotel workers standing to the side around the large dining room—waiters, busboys, bellhops, chamber maids—heard the guest speaker's words but did not react or show any emotion. Either these lower-level Germans did not understand English or they were inured, fifteen years after the end of the war, to slights voiced against their country and countrymen for alleged and proven crimes against humanity committed by Hitler and the Nazis.

It was late Sunday afternoon, the tenth of January, the opening event of a five-day religious retreat, a Torah Convocation. I was in a general session, attended by all who convened in this Bavarian hotel—Army and Air Force Jewish chaplains, officers, and enlisted men.

The rabbi was flown in from New York two days earlier. He was a distinguished-looking middle-age man in a dark-blue suit that offset his graying hair. Standing on the stage in front of a microphone, he projected his voice loud and clear. He waved his arm as he spoke and pointed his finger toward the large picture windows along the outer wall that exposed the resplendent snow-covered mountains beyond.

The General Walker, before and during the war, had been Der Platterhof, a grand hotel in the Obersalzberg, a mountainous area above the town of Berchtesgaden in southern Germany near the Austrian border. With its opulent accommodations, the multi-story building high in the Alps was a favorite, not to mention fitting, resort facility for the high SS and Nazi officials who flocked here. The Platterhof Hotel offered German perpetrators of war and mass killing luxury as well as breathtaking views of Bavaria's countryside and Alpine scenery. Long a target of the Royal Air Force, it was heavily damaged in bombing raids the last month of the war. The crumbling structure stood empty for years until, in 1952, the U.S. Army rebuilt the hotel as an Armed Forces Recreation Center. Original fixtures and furnishings utilized in the reconstruction could be seen in the lobby. Renamed for Army General Walton Walker, recently killed in action in Korea, the appropriated German property now in American hands was restored to its former status as one of Europe's most impressive hotels.

"See how beautiful it is out there," Rabbi Stark said moments earlier, pointing to the blinding white landscape. The leader of the largest congregation in New York brought his arm down, hesitated a moment, and wiped his forehead. "This is where Hitler built *his* retreat, a home on the next mountain called the Berghof. Twenty years ago, he and his band of Nazi criminals met here in Berchtesgaden. Many stayed at this very hotel. They drank the finest wine, ate the best food, enjoyed the magnificent natural surroundings, and mapped out their plans for global conquest and the destruction of the Jewish people. But the German bastards did *not* destroy us. Today it is *they* who are dead or hiding out in South America and it is *we* who survived and are here in this hotel to enjoy ourselves, learn more about Judaism, and reflect on the lives of Jews in Israel and around the world."

The keynote speaker stepped back and lifted his arm toward the window again. "All of this beauty around us . . . it's too good for them," he stressed.

These were harsh words, I thought, perhaps too harsh for an American, Jew or Gentile, to be uttering in public, especially in the presence of Germans. The hotel workers around the room, waiting to serve dinner shortly, stood there like dummies, without facial expression or bodily movement. Whether they understood all or some of what this foreign Jew was saying in a different language, I could not tell.

At the close of his speech, the rabbi from my hometown invited those in the audience who wished him to contact relatives or friends in the States to write down all the names and telephone numbers and give them to him. He walked around, shook hands numerous times, and I waited my turn. In his jacket pocket I saw him place little slips of paper. Scribbled on one slip was "David Streiber," "parents Mr. and Mrs. Streiber in Brooklyn," and "ESplanade 3-6645." I hoped this American-born member of the rabbinate, whom I met for the first time that day and spoke to for thirty seconds, who counsels Reform Jews on the rich Upper East Side, would have nice things to say about me to my moderately Orthodox mother and father in poor Coney Island, in English and/or Yiddish.

After our dinner, this first day of the Bavarian retreat was over. The next morning, following breakfast, small group sessions on different Judaic topics were to begin.

The rabbi was right. Berchtesgaden was the *Nazi's* Bavarian retreat and Hitler spent a great deal of time here. I was staying at a hotel a stone's throw from the Berghof, where two decades earlier human beasts amid boundless beauty concocted great evil to rain on the world.

The Nazi's nexus to Berchtesgaden began in mid-1923. Hitler came here to visit his friend and mentor living at the Platterhof Hotel, and held meetings at local guesthouses with supporters of his plan to take over the Weimar government. Later that year, the famous Beer Hall Putsch in Munich failed. Hitler was arrested, convicted of treason, and sent to Landsberg prison. In 1925, after his release, the Austrian-born traitor rented a small cottage on the Obersalzberg plateau two miles east of Berchtesgaden and 1200 feet higher in altitude. There the future leader of Germany completed the second part of his political manifesto *Mein Kampf*, started while incarcerated.

Hitler rented a small chalet in 1928, a mountain retreat named Haus Wachenfeld, and five years later purchased it with funds received from the sale of his book. In 1935, as Chancellor, the chalet was expanded greatly, completely refurbished, and bestowed with a fancier calling. Top Nazi leaders, notably Field Marshal Hermann Göring and Party Secretary Martin Bormann, built homes of their own overlooking the Führer's Berghof.

National Socialist officials twisted eminent domain like a swastika. Privately-owned houses and mountain farms on the Obersalzberg were bought out or taken over by the government and leveled, to make way for construction of a barracks for the SS guards, administration buildings, a greenhouse to cater to the Führer's penchant for fresh vegetables, housing for servants and workers, and a hotel for visiting dignitaries. The owner of one coveted property, a quaint inn, refused to sell but changed his mind after spending three weeks in the Dachau concentration camp.

"This place is mine," Hitler was quoted as saying in the November 1938 issue of *Homes & Gardens*, an English magazine, in reference to the Berghof. "I built it with money that I earned."

The former artist, who sold numerous paintings and postcards in Vienna after the first war, was not lying. Hitler was his own decorator, designer, furnisher, and architect of the remodeled chalet. The author of the *H&G* article, enamored by what he saw in the Berghof and perhaps intoxicated by the mountain air, turned in a very favorable review of Adolf Hitler's Bavarian home.

The German people likewise were smitten with the Berghof, which became a tourist attraction. Crowds of onlookers collected at the end of the driveway every day. The deutsches Volk had so much love for their Führer's home they gave him another in April 1939 on the occasion of his 50th birthday, a gift paid for with public funds this time. A Teehaus, dubbed the Eagle's Nest by a French diplomat, was erected one mile above the Berghof, with a winding path connecting the two houses. Hiking to and from his Teahouse, under the August moon, Hitler may have reached the fateful decision to invade Poland on Septem-ber first. The gushy words the English reporter eternalized in print about Hitler and the Berghof were likely regretted less than a year later when Germany and Great Britain were at war.

For propaganda purposes, photographs galore were snapped and published of Hitler in the company of dignitaries, domestic and foreign, inside and on the steps of the Berghof. Joseph Goebbels, Albert Speer, Heinrich Himmler, Benito Mussolini, Duke and Duchess of Windsor, David Lloyd George, and Neville Chamberlain all paid tribute to the Chancellor of Germany on his home turf. A German shepherd, Hitler's beloved Blondi, pawed his way into pictures too.

A cute little girl from the crowd was chosen to come inside this hallowed ground closed to the public and have a dish of strawberries. The photogenic Mädele, to the man who was said to love children, was a favorite visitor and patted on the head often. Boorish Bormann discovered the girl had a Jewish grandmother and tried to banish her, but Hitler allowed her to continue visiting his inner sanctum. Perhaps the rumor about old Adolph was true, that he too had a Jew perched on one of the branches of his family tree.

Not surprisingly, in April 1945, the Berghof and other aerial sites on the Nazi-occupied Obersalzberg were in the cross-hairs of Allied bombers. Days before Germany's surrender, the Bavarian head-quarters was substantially destroyed. Looting first by local residents and then by American troops finished off what airplanes missed. Much of the Berghof was in ruins, as were most structures in the complex. One in particular escaped damage. The Eagle's Nest was too small for the big birds in the sky to spot and hit. In 1953—but for Hitler's birthday gift, the Platterhof, and a few intact buildings—what remained on the Obersalzberg was dynamited and bulldozed.

At the now General Walker, there were guided tours for the public. The underground tunnel that led from the hotel to the Berg-hof and the adjoining bunkers, air raid shelters, and emergency exits in the former Nazi compound became the new tourist attraction.

I left Nuremberg early the morning of January tenth. I took the train to Munich and there I had to switch, and change trains again in Freilassing. Altogether the trip was about seven hours. By mid-afternoon I arrived at the Bahnhof in Berchtesgaden. The small train station was a typical Third Reich building, neoclassical in architec-tural style, opened in 1938 to accommodate the increasing flow of distinguished guests coming in by rail to flatter or appease what many said was Europe's most powerful leader. Unbeknownst to me at the time I first breezed into the station was that it once had a separate reception area for Hitler to greet his callers.

I grabbed a taxi to the General Walker, registered, and paid the nominal charge for bed and board. The Chief of Chaplains Office in Washington sponsored much of the cost of the religious retreat. I was assigned to a room with two other servicemen. They were com-pany clerks, draftees, stationed in Heidelberg and Mannheim. Both were a few years older than I and had been to college, but only one graduated, holding a B.A. in history. These strangers from Newark and Boston seemed friendly enough and we talked a while before going to the general session. On the way there, I bumped into Rabbi Washer and his wife and a few soldiers I saw at Shabbat and Yom Kippur services in the Palace of Justice.

Everyone was dressed in civilian clothes. Military rank could not hinder the social interaction expected of fellow Jews convoked to study Torah. I picked up a program listing of lectures, small group discussions, and recreational activities planned from Sunday through Wednesday. Later that night in the room, on this fourth day after I took the initial step toward my college career, I had many questions for my senior G.I. peers.

All meals at the General Walker were strictly kosher. Before the Convocation began, the kitchen was kashered by an Orthodox chaplain and divided into Milk and Meat sections. He supervised all food preparation and cleanup each day. He continually checked to see if the Milchig dishes, bowls, silverware, pots, and pans were kept separate in drawers and cabinets from those reserved for Fleishig repasts. When busboys carried the dirty dishes and utensils back to the kitchen, the rabbi would make sure they were washed in different sinks and placed on separate racks to dry.

We were the only guests at the hotel so the question of serving non-kosher food to others staying there never arose. At breakfast no ham or bacon or sausage was served with the cooked eggs. There was a pitcher of milk on the table to pour over the little Kellogg's and General Mills boxes in front of us. Morning meat-lovers thus could not expect even kosher corned beef or Hebrew National salami to complement their omelets or over-easies. It is stated in the Torah that animals that chew their cud and have cloven hoofs, and fish with scales and fins, are only to be eaten. Kashruth, biblical dietary laws, ruled the Jewish servicemen's short stay at the General Walker.

"Milk shall never meet meat on the table or in the sink, so sayeth the Lord and so observeth the Children of Israel," someone sitting at my table commented facetiously.

For the first time in two and a half years I thoroughly enjoyed the food at an Army facility. It was a welcome relief from the pork and traif served in the mess hall. More important than my gastronomical pleasure, however, was that I began to understand, after talking to a chubby Air Force rabbi, that the ultimate purpose and rationale for Jews to observe Kashruth was not for the presumed health benefits of eating kosher food but for conformity to God's Will as told to Moses and written in Leviticus, the third book of the Torah.

There were lectures in the mornings, attended by most of the hundred and fifty people on the retreat. Different rabbis spoke for various periods of time, and then invited questions from the audience. Two topics seemed to dominate the agenda, those most important to Jews in mid-twentieth century America: the war and Israel. There was much discussion about Hitler's final solution, the six million lost at the bloody hands of the Nazis, the atrocities committed in the concentration camps, the Warsaw uprising, the liberation of the camps, the skin-and-bone survivors, the DPs after the war, the emigration to the United States and Israel.

"The creation of the State of Israel twelve years ago," one of the rabbis said when he had the floor, "was nothing short of a miracle, the fulfillment of the Jewish dream of returning to the Promised Land, held for almost two thousand years." I thought he was looking at me when he continued. "Many American Jews, young people like yourselves, are making Aliyah too, not just those liberated from the camps."

"What about the conflict with the Arabs?" someone in the audience asked, in an apparent reference to the 1948 and 1956 wars. "Doesn't that hinder more Jews from America and from persecuted countries from immigrating to Israel?"

"Don't worry about that," Rabbi Washer stood up from behind and answered firmly without hesitation. "Arabs in different countries will always be fighting among themselves more than with Jews."

The talks about Israel were extremely exciting to me. A new country, a homeland for Jews from all over the world, collective farms, irrigation of the desert, industrial development, growth of cities and universities, and a new generation of young Sabras, Jews who were born in Israel, a word I had not heard before. We were told that if we made Aliyah, we would receive credit for our American military service, would only have to serve in the Israeli reserve forces, one month active duty a year. And we would have dual citizenship.

"And don't worry about the food," a third chaplain informed the young soldiers and airmen before him tongue in cheek. "In the Israeli Army, it's all kosher."

Afternoons we were free to roam around the hotel, sit and talk with new people we met, go sightseeing in town, and partake of the winter sports Berchtesgaden is famous for. On Monday I went skiing for the first time. With no prior lessons or coach to guide me, I was not very good at it. I watched other people as they raced downhill, and I tried to take that course, but soon realized how dangerous it was. I *walked* with my skis more than I slid with them and soon took them off.

On Tuesday I had better luck with ice skating. I had roller skated for years, with metal skates in the streets and with wooden wheels in the Rollerdrome, an indoor rink near Ebbets Field that I used to go to with friends in high school. Although I had never tried ice skating before, I was able to do it fairly well. I tightened the laces around my ankles sufficiently so the single-metal bar under my feet would not wobble. I kept up with others on the ice obviously more experienced than I, even a rosy-cheeked eight- or nine-year old-girl. As on roller skates, I could move at a fast pace and, when I wanted to stop, twisted one ankle to slow down and turn in a small circle. I did not fall once on the ice or lose my balance.

Wednesday afternoon, my last free period at the George Walker, as I did in the evenings after dinner, I sat around the lobby with other young men and talked or went to one of the small group discussions. This called attention to my attitudes about Judaism, impelled me to think of issues I had set aside after my Bar Mitzvah.

Until age thirteen I was somewhat observant, due largely to my mother's influence. I went to synagogue on Saturdays, with my grandfather at times, never mixed milk and meat, never ate ham or pork, and stayed away from non-kosher beef. From thirteen to fifteen, every morning other than Shabbat, I zipped open my tefilan bag, pulled out the phylacteries, strapped them around my head and left arm, and recited the prayers from the little book given to me on my Bar Mitzvah day by the rabbi. I never claimed to be Orthodox but I had an awareness of Jewish laws and customs and tried to follow them.

Other than a Nathan's frankfurter occasionally, I tried to keep kosher. But then, on my fifteenth birthday, I suddenly stopped with the tefilan and thereafter went less and less to shul, with Zeyde or by myself. At seventeen in the Army, away from home for the first time, I still avoided pork chops and baked ham at the mess hall, but off post I began eating traif beef on a regular basis. And, in a final repudiation of my heritage according to some, I started going with Gentile girls.

Notwithstanding my deviation with food and females, the Army actually brought me back to Judaism, helped me gain a renewed sense of myself as different from the Christian troopers around me. My being sent to Germany and living in a post-Nazi society further heightened an awareness of what fellow Jews went through between fifteen and twenty-five years earlier.

Now, sitting side-by-side with my brethren, listening to talks about Jews in the United States and Israel, I came full circle. I had a religious experience that awakened my Yiddishkeit, a word I learned from that chubby chaplain, and paved the way for a new commitment. It was on this retreat that I decided to sign up for the tour to Israel in March around the Purim holiday that was organized annually by one of the Jewish chaplains.

In Berchtesgaden my eyes were opened not just to the beautiful snow-covered mountains. I observed up close for the first time a different kind of Jewish boy, young men from suburban, middle-class, American backgrounds who had been to college. These were the kind of Jews I aspired to be like, not the majority of those I knew back in Coney Island. But yet some seemed snobbish to me, like the kids from classy Sea Gate I initially encountered in Junior High.

At the hotel, I did not meet anyone of my sort, a Jewish boy from an immigrant working-class family who grew up in a decaying city neighborhood and who did not attend college. I was sure there were some in the Army or Air Force in Europe, but evidently they did not sign up for this particular retreat. I was the anomaly I could see.

Thursday morning, the fourteenth, I waved goodbye to Berchtesgaden. On this leg of the trip I was taken to the Bahnhof, along with others, in the hotel's Volkswagen bus. I had a few minutes to spare before I was to board the train to Freilassing. I looked around the station, trying to figure out where the Hitler reception area might have been. Fifteen years after Der Führer last set foot here, it was not apparent where the tea-drinker took his cup and küchen. There was no plaque over any doorway to commemorate the unholy site. The only separate area that might have been reserved for Hitler and his guests was now a men's washroom and toilet.

I arrived back at Merrell in time for chow, one of my last dinners at that barracks. On the eighteenth, I would say auf Wiedersehen again, this time to the city I liked very much and to the Army post I spent the longest time on.

# EPILOGUE: ON THE ROAD

*Four days after I returned to Nuremberg from attendance at the religious retreat, I climbed aboard an Army truck that would take me to Munich for an internal transfer with the 176th Signal Company. I was no longer in Berchtesgaden but it could be said that this was* my *Bavarian retreat, a forced relocation handed down by my superiors for reasons not shared with me.*

*On the road to Munich, I was in limbo between two major cities in southern Germany. Like Jack Kerouac traveling around America, stopping in various cities and making love to different women, I had a seasoned young life in Nuremberg from affairs with two Fräuleins and from intimate encounters on travels to France and Italy. But unlike Jack who wrote about his road trips as they unfurled, my experiences locked in my memory and sensibilities were destined to remain unpenned for decades to come.*

*In Nuremberg I learned about the older people I came into contact with. They were part of a beat generation different from the one Kerouac first described in his peripatetic notebooks, people battered or defeated by war, postwar privation, a struggling German economy, and Nazi persecution. I saw Germans at the barracks doing menial and dirty work, I met my girlfriend's mother and uncle who endured twelve years of Hitler's doomed Third Reich, and I got to know German Jews at services that fled Germany and then returned after the war and prayed for a country free of anti-Semitism.*

*Like the Canadian-born New York beatnik writing about the women he knew across the States while on the road, the American-born Nuremberg soldier thought about the women he knew across Europe while on the autobahn.*

*The two Fräuleins I had affairs with, Elsa the bargirl and Karin the nice German girl, satisfied my youthful carnal lust. The two I craved but was not intimate with, the beautiful color-blind girl in the snack bar and Marianne, Elsa's well-stacked friend, both stirred my emotions and I could only imagine what lovemaking would be like. No imagination was necessary, however, with the mademoiselle in Paris and the signorina in Venice who taught me about love French and Italian style.*

*Of the Nuremberg Four, Marianne weighed the most on my mind.*

*Contacts with Elsa fizzled out and the affair with Karin ended badly when she mouthed a hurtful remark about Hitler and the Jews. The girl in the snack bar was unattainable to me, even if I were not being transferred, since she did not wish to come back to the white side of the color line and into a waiting G.I.'s fold. Marianne nixed all of my attempts to couple with her, but I kept my rifle pointed on the sexy bargirl and her bulls-eye just the same.*

*The horny young soldier being whisked from one Bavarian post to another believed he would never see any of the four Fräuleins again. In Munich, a 180-kilometer road trip away, the opportunity to be in their company, especially Marianne's, and shoot at their targets, was out of range.*

*Or so he thought that eighteenth of January.*

## ABOUT THE AUTHOR

**Raymond M. Weinstein** was born in Brooklyn, New York in 1939. After graduating from Abraham Lincoln High School in 1957, he enlisted in the U.S. Army. He completed the radar repair course at Fort Monmouth, New Jersey, was assigned to Ford Ord, California, and in January 1959 was transferred to Germany. Following his discharge in June 1960, the author enrolled in Baruch College of the City University of New York, where he received a B.B.A. in business statistics in 1963. He also earned an M.A. in sociology in 1966 and a Ph.D. in sociology in 1968 from the University of California at Los Angeles. He taught sociology at Wilkes University in Wilkes-Barre, Pennsylvania, John Jay College of Criminal Justice, CUNY, and the University of South Carolina at Aiken, where he retired as Distinguished Professor Emeritus of Sociology in 2012.

During his teaching career, the author published more than four dozen academic works—mainly articles in professional journals but also chapters in books and entries for encyclopedias. His writings covered various topics such as mental illness, psychiatric patients, illicit drug use, social service organizations, total institutions, urban communities, Coney Island, Disneyland, amusement parks, and Elvis Presley.

This is the author's second novel. It draws heavily on his experiences as an American soldier, most especially his ten-month tour of duty in Nuremberg, Germany.

The author currently divides his time between residences in Georgia and New York.

**The Author**
**March 1959**
**East Block, Merrell Barracks**

**The Author**
**July 2010**
**East Block, Federal Agency for Migration and Refugees**
**Formerly Merrell Barracks**

# ACKNOWLEDGEMENTS

In this work of fiction about American soldiers in postwar Germany, social and historical data covering the Nazi era as well as the period from 1945-1960 are included.  The author wishes to thank very much Gerhard Jochem and Susanne Rieger, historical researchers in Nuremberg and Munich, for their cooperation and assistance over several years that greatly aided him in writing accurately about their country in those times.  Help with important details was also received from others in Nuremberg, notably Eckart Dietzfelbinger in the Documentation Center at the former Nazi Party Rally Grounds and freelance writer Peter Heigl.  The author is also indebted to Stefanie Mühlfelder at the Tourist Information Office in Zirndorf for bits and pieces of data about that city.

Thanks are extended to Karl L. Stenger, Associate Professor of German at the University of South Carolina at Aiken, for the correct usage and spelling of German words and terms utilized throughout the book.  The author also wishes to acknowledge the following professors and colleagues in the English and Foreign Languages Departments at USC-A, in alphabetical order, for giving him the benefit of their expertise from time to time: Timothy Ashton, J. Donald Blount, William N. Claxon, Stephen L. Gardner, Andrew Geyer, Stanley F. (Shimke) Levine, Tom Mack, Layech Malfoudy, Daniel J. Miller, Lynne Austin Rhodes, and Katie K. Smith.

For particular historical material on Nazi Germany and the United States, the author thanks Valdis O. Lumans and James O. Farmer, Jr., his colleagues in the USC-A History Department.  For facts about the military of decades past, the assistance of Delores E. Oplinger at the U.S. Army Signal Corps Museum at Fort Gordon in Augusta, Georgia, and Michael Plumley at the Fort Hamilton Post Library in Brooklyn, New York, is greatly appreciated.

The author's primary task of drawing a true picture of what it was like to be an American soldier in Germany in 1959-1960 could not have been accomplished without the exchange of telephone calls and e-mails with his former Army buddies and civilian friends in Nuremberg at that time, who selflessly shared their recollections of events, people, and military matters of fifty years earlier.  Heartfelt gratitude goes out to Michael H. Friedman, Billy B. Capers, Arlene Gottlieb Dryer, Herbert R. Jacobson, and Joel Prives. The memories of Richard A. Gray, Ivor W. Jeffreys, and Thomas Spahr, who were stationed a few years later than the author at his Nuremberg barracks, likewise proved valuable.

Honorable mention should also be given to long-time friends of the author—John B. Manbeck, William H. Marsh, Alexandra Moravec Ocampo, Sheldon Salsberg, Allan H. Sklar, Mary S. Smith-McCarty, and Donna K. West—who over the years assisted him in sorting out his thoughts for this book.

Last but not least, the author's two sons, Rodney J. Weinstein and Marshall S. Weinstein, are singled out for special thanks. They helped their father immensely with the technical/computer elements of book-publishing, listened patiently to his ideas on character and plot, commented intelligently on thematic parts of the novel, and brought into focus the younger generation's point of view on topics and events that took place long before their time.

Made in the USA
Las Vegas, NV
26 March 2024